ETON VOICES

INTERVIEWS BY
DANNY
DANZIGER

VIKING

VIKING

Published by the Penguin Group
27 Wrights Lane, London w8 5tz, England
Viking Penguin Inc., 40 West 23rd Street, New York, New York 10010, USA
Penguin Books Australia Ltd, Ringwood, Victoria, Australia
Penguin Books Canada Ltd, 2801 John Street, Markham, Ontario, Canada l3r 1b4
Penguin Books (NZ) Ltd, 182-190 Wairau Road, Auckland 10, New Zealand

Penguin Books Ltd, Registered Offices: Harmondsworth, Middlesex, England

First published 1988

Made and printed in Great Britain by
Richard Clay Ltd, Bungay, Suffolk
Filmset in 12/14pt Garamond

British Library Cataloguing in Publication Data

Eton.
1. Eton College
I. Danziger, Danny
373.422'96   LF795.E84

ISBN 0-670-81630-2

To Iona, Nic, Lucinda and Richard

CONTENTS

ACKNOWLEDGEMENTS   11
INTRODUCTION   13

THE RT REV. SIMON BARRINGTON-WARD   21
DAVID BENEDICTUS   28
MICHAEL BENTIN   37
ANTHONY BLOND   43
LORD BROCKET   50
THE RT REV. SIMON BURROWS   57
ANDREW CALLENDER   61
LORD CHARTERIS   67
NICHOLAS COLERIDGE   72
TAM DALYELL, MP   80
THE HON. WILLIAM DOUGLAS-HOME   86
MARK FIENNES   90
GENERAL SIR DAVID FRASER   98
THE EARL OF GOWRIE   108
JOHN GRAHAM   115
LORD HAILSHAM   123
NICKY HASLAM   127
MARK HEATHCOAT AMORY   132
LORD HOME OF THE HIRSEL   138
ADRIAN HOUSE   142
HUGH HUDSON   147
THE RT HON. DOUGLAS HURD   152
SIR MARTIN JACOMB   156
BRIAN JOHNSTON   160

Robin Lane Fox   168
Martin Llewellyn   172
The Earl of Longford   179
Humphrey Lyttelton   185
Patrick Macnee   192
Derek Malcolm   197
The Hon. Nicholas Monson   207
John Moorhead   214
Mary Nicholson   219
Lord Oaksey   225
Dr John Paine   232
The Hon. Jonathan Porritt   239
Jonathan Riley-Smith   249
Benedict Taylor   254
David Thomas   259
Sir Ranulph Twistleton-Wykeham-Fiennes   268
Hugo Vickers   273
The Hon. William Waldegrave   280

Eton Slang   286

Index   289

ACKNOWLEDGEMENTS

My special gratitude and thanks for all their help and hard work: Sally van Hasbroeck and Alison Vallance.

Thank you to: Dr Christopher Tyerman, Toby Eady, Peter Lawrence, Iona Cairns, Hugo Vickers, Nic Barlow.

For photographs I am grateful to Peter Lawrence and the Eton Photographic Library for nos. 2–11, 15, 18, 20, 23–5 (top); Nic Barlow for nos. 1, 12–14, 16–17, 19, 21–2, 25 (bottom), 27–8; Julian Calder for no. 26.

My thanks also to: Lucy Adams, Janet Ashton, Gig Barlow, Ann Barr, Craig Brown, Julian Calder, Lucinda Chambers, Martin Charteris, Tom Decker, Rupert de Klee, Josh Dixey, John Levis, Marcia McCabe, Anthony Powell, Amanda Ramsbottom, Gay Rendell, David Thomas, Richard Wintour.

Finally, my deepest appreciation to everyone I interviewed.

D.D.

INTRODUCTION

———

EVEN now, and for more than five centuries, Eton has simply been the most famous school in the world. Enhanced by the success of its old boys, it is a self-fulfilling, self-perpetuating success story in a country where the well-connected, the rich and the upper class still have the greatest chance of going to the top. And, as is still the case after more than five centuries, the well-educated, the rich and the upper class continue to go to Eton.

There's a sense of England about Eton, an ancient and honourable institution, looking to the future, dynamic and eager to accommodate social change if you're generous, rooted in the past, elitist and anachronistic if you're not. At the same time there is something very un-English about Eton — at least in the sort of stereotyped way the rest of the world looks at England — in that it leaves its boys with an unshakeable confidence in their own ability, combined with the conviction that anything in life is achievable. While these qualities may seem unpleasantly arrogant and mark Etonians as different, even from the products of other public schools that have neither the initiative nor the resources to indulge and fulfil every boy's expectations, the success rate of Etonians in their traditional fields is an inescapable fact of life: Etonians have great expectations — and Etonians are rarely disappointed.

Of course, Etonians for the most part come from self-confident backgrounds. One is reminded of the purpose-bred Alphas of Aldous Huxley's *Brave New World* — and Huxley himself was an Etonian. To claim that the success of those Etonians who now find themselves in positions of power and prestige in the Cabinet, in the City or in the arts is genetically predetermined sounds absurd. But then again, there are plenty of public schools, full of intelligent boys from good backgrounds who don't succeed in such a consistent way.

The point about Eton is that it is not an anachronism, coasting along on the coat-tails of a glorious and privileged past. It is a school which turns out boys who have now, as they had then, a hold on contemporary life in a way no other institution has managed.

You cannot walk around two towns in tail-coats without coming to some decisions as to your importance in relation to the untailcoated population. More than five centuries of Old Etonian Prime Ministers, countless statesmen, great writers, and much of the aristocracy, further encourage the Etonian to feel apart. Their legendary self-confidence, 'effortless superiority', percolates through the atmosphere, even for those who loathed and rejected the school.

It shows in their attitude to life – Derek Malcolm, the film critic: 'One thing Eton gives you is a complete serenity of social graces. You're never worried about what you're dressed in, or how you look, or what impression you're giving, in the way so many poor unfortunate people are, because you're always taught at a place like Eton that you are the top. I mean, there's no higher you can go socially, so nobody's really going to come it over you.'

David Thomas, twenty-seven-year-old features editor of the *Mail on Sunday*: 'I've applied for jobs which I really have no right applying for, and it wasn't because I was a particularly cocky little bastard, it was just because it never ever occurred to me that I shouldn't apply for them – your horizons have never been limited.'

Brian Johnston: 'One gained tremendous confidence at Eton . . . You felt that you had perhaps the best education possible, and that one was sharing in something which was perhaps exceptional.'

The interesting thing is that at the same time that boys have been given this sense that they can go out in the world and achieve anything they like, they are told, 'You have to work for it'; that's part of the ethic – you are taught to work. Lord Oaksey:

'I think now there is a very considerable push to make Etonians realize that if anything they owe something for being here, for being so lucky. *Noblesse oblige* almost, but it's not that. It's just that if you are lucky enough to have thousands and thousands of pounds spent on your education, then you bloody well ought to do something about it.'

Etonians arouse an expectation of extremes – far richer, far fatter, far nicer, far nastier – in a way that applies to no other school, perhaps simply because no other school is as well known, or perhaps as a result of the heightened expectations that surround wealth, power, class.

It seems that no one forgets you are an Etonian. Heathcoat Amory: 'Eton is such a symbol, isn't it? I have a tendency to say "when I was at school" rather than "when I was at Eton", just because I don't want a reaction. It's slightly annoying to be put into a pigeon-hole . . . the other person is thinking of characteristics they believe you're going to have, and I'd rather they didn't think they knew what I was like.'

Film director, Hugh Hudson: 'The label is always put on you . . . "Old Etonian", all the time. People are somehow more interested in that than who you really are. It is put on you when something goes wrong: "Old Etonian fails", because you are not expected to fail. "Old Etonian caught with his pants down in Hyde Park". You can't avoid it, it is part of you, it's like having blue eyes. It's not really a question, it's an insinuation: "Of course *you* were at Eton", as though that says everything.'

David Thomas: 'My first day at the *Mail on Sunday*, they asked me to do a piece about Eton: "Oh, *you* went to Eton, didn't you?" I have no idea what school anybody else in my office went to, but they all know I went to Eton.'

Anyway, Etonians themselves don't forget their Eton days. Explorer Sir Ranulph Twistleton-Wykeham-Fiennes: '. . . so there we were, out in the Arctic wastes, nearer to having done both Poles than any previous humans . . . you're in a tent, and you've got over the last problem of the day, and the conversation might go back to some funny fellow like Toady Mays . . . one might remember some character or other and reminisce about them'. Nicholas Coleridge, editor of *Harper's & Queen*: '. . . We were once in a taxi near Taroudant in Morocco, four hours out in the desert . . . and were becoming extremely bored. So we filled the time by giving ourselves one hour each to write down as many boys as we could remember in the school that were contemporaries.' Lord Home: 'When you come across an Etonian, well, you have somewhere to start your conversation, of course, even if he is years younger; you can ask how the school is and if this, that and the other is the same as it was, that sort of thing.'

Inevitably there's a clubbishness about having been to a school like Eton. There's nothing sinister about that, it's just exasperating for those left outside. John Moorhead: 'My present wife's father and brothers all went to Eton. And there was absolutely no doubt that, although we were totally different people, this was a shorthand pass to getting on and understanding each other. We talked the same language . . . there was a definite bond. One feels that with other schools it wouldn't signify so much. It's not that I and my wife's father sit back and say, "Do you remember the times . . .", it's not that at all . . . It may well have been that in the first efforts of conversation running dry, I managed to insert Eton into the conversation – thus waving a flag that we would all be able to salute.'

Nicholas Coleridge: 'I am bound to say that if I meet somebody that I have never met before, say if I am travelling abroad, or through work or something, and it emerges that they were there, I feel an interest in them that is multiplied by at least ten. There are certain people who weren't there, and I do admit that in some strange way I think, "Now, why weren't they?" And I know in some awful way that it counts against them slightly.'

Anthony Blond: 'Anyone who is honest must allow that Eton was a very powerful influence. And still is, I mean, I have people saying, "Oh, he went to your old school . . ." and I think, "What on earth, forty years ago!" But it does still matter, it matters like hell – *now*!'

Brian Johnston talks about Eton as 'the best trades union in Great Britain'.

Lord Charteris: 'I remember, when I came here as Provost, being told by the boys that if you were interviewed and somebody asked where you went to school, you would say, "Eton, I'm afraid." I think that's bad. They should say "Eton". Leave it at that – and then say "thank God" under their breath . . . I've never found it anything but a huge advantage in my life. But everybody's got to be equal now, haven't they? You know, elitism is under suspicion. I hope we're getting over that.'

Lord Longford: 'Well, it was the only place. I didn't really take anywhere else very seriously. And for Etonians there is no other school, I mean it's like the Catholic Church in its more triumphalist moments, I don't mean like it is today. It is not a question of some other schools – there are no other schools.'

The trouble with an exclusive club is that it awakens prejudice amongst the outsiders. But these implications have been recognized. Oaksey: 'I think and hope that Eton will be able to adjust to whatever change comes, and still be good for the country. I think that the enormous difference in wealth and class at the moment is regrettable and sad, because it creates so much bitterness and jealousy.' Jonathan Porritt takes the point further. '. . . I believe passionately in finding ways of healing divides in society, building better relationships. And part of that passion and commitment to a more healing society is the knowledge that you cannot bring that about if you go on segregating people between public school and state school in the way we do at the moment.'

If one is to gauge whether Eton offers value for money, one can look at the teaching, which – like everything at Eton – is geared to the individual, the brightest and the dimmest. At one level Eton's job is a humanizing one. Birley, the headmaster, used to say that there would be an Establishment school somewhere; his job was to take a lot of people, many of whom were not very clever, and who were going to be in positions of power because of wealth and how the world works, and to show them something of English culture . . . and that was an anaesthetic experience which very many of them in their banks later on would never have repeated.

But there is unlimited potential for the bright boys. Robin Lane Fox: 'Aged sixteen and a bit, I had entered a form where we were reading the whole of Homer's *Iliad* for starters, and Plato's *Republic*, and a detailed translation of Juvenal's Satires, and we aimed to read all of them in the original. We read Boswell's *Life of Johnson* for English, as well as composing Greek and Latin hexameters, elegiacs, everything . . . In any literary education that I had at Oxford, or have ever known anywhere else, I have never had that impression of range, width and concentrated close company with authors who it was presumed would actually change you in some way if you attended to what they were saying.'

I have no personal ties with Eton, in fact as my parents are American and I went to Harrow, you could say I was the perfect outsider. Of course, when I went to Harrow I was told about the rivalry that was supposed to have flamed and burned for centuries – not just at school but forever after – but I felt it was half-hearted, listless almost, as if Harrow had long ago surrendered any thoughts of gaining superiority on the sports field or anywhere else. Part of the reason for this unequal struggle is that Etonians have this finely tuned sense of superiority which implies victory, even before the battle: athletic, moral, individual. I was fascinated by this attitude. Was it mere gamesmanship or a royal flush? In later life it has become clear to me that the Etonians were holding all the cards, the proof of which is to be seen in the various fields in which they've succeeded. This is a phenomenon which simply doesn't exist with other schools; Harrovians, for instance, neither incandescent nor slow, pitch their lives at a level of decent mediocrity.

Now, nearly twenty years on from my own Harrow schooldays, it may seem remarkably obsessive to delve into the Etonian psyche, but it is not with a view to finding out why we lost or seemed to lose against Eton on the playing fields, but to find out more about the Etonian ethos, this self-confidence, 'effortless superiority', which is still coming up trumps.

All in all, I think it's a healthy attitude: unspeakably irritating for those who can't claim kinship, but I believe it would be extremely positive and beneficial if such an attitude of self-confidence and optimism were instilled in children of all backgrounds. Why should optimism and self-confidence be the preserve of the wealthy or well-connected?

There are forty-two Etonians in the book, and, like a magic lantern, back and forth over the decades and the seasons, the memories and evocations of Eton veer between the idyllic and the beastly. Physically, it was no bed of roses; there has always been a deliberate regime of appalling brutality and harsh conditions – no heating, terrible food, and the constant application of physical punishment. You could, for instance, at any time in your school career be eight-tanned, or Pop-tanned, beaten by the Library, birched by the lower master or flogged by the headmaster – those stories, even now, are recounted with an air of palpable terror. There is a backdrop throughout of adolescent eroticism, expressed (and sometimes fulfilled) in homosexual liaisons, sometimes amorous, sometimes lustful, sometimes innocent.

And in their country homes and smart town-houses, with their corduroy trousers and patched tweed jackets, I talked to them, amused and amusing, indulgent, witty, the same insouciance and crushing self-confidence, articulate and clever. There is an eerie sameness about them.

Of course, they aren't all likeable. Some will make your flesh creep. But whether they are twenty-two or eighty-two, whether they are from the highest families in the land or of more modest means, Eton, with the determination and physical potential to encourage every boy in his own interests and ambitions, has stamped them with the same mark, with its attitude that anything is possible, unlimited horizons, belief in the self.

One final, prosaic, but very important point about Etonians and why they are such a potent force in the national consciousness. There are so many of them. With twelve hundred boys at the school, it means that at any one time there are between fourteen and sixteen thousand of them around. Their fathers and their fathers' fathers went to Eton; their sons will go to Eton. It is an incestuous dance to the music of time, played out over dozens of generations as they meet and re-meet and intermarry.

Simon Barrington-Ward makes a telling point as he talks about his becoming a bishop: '. . . it still seems to me rather incredible that somebody like Douglas [Hurd, the Home Secretary] is a Cabinet Minister or that Tony Lloyd is a judge, or that I am a bishop, for that matter . . . There is an incongruous sense that we are all play-acting and that we will go back and find that we are just starting again . . . I'll tell you a moment when I felt it. It was when I was paying homage to the Queen on becoming a bishop, and Douglas stood by her side, holding the oath that you have to read. He read something, and I then repeated it, while the Queen looked on, and that did give me an extraordinary feeling. It was almost as if everything was part of the school, or the school part of everything.'

THE RT REV.
SIMON BARRINGTON-WARD

My father would have liked my brother and me to have gone to Westminster; he was an 'old Westminster', he had been Captain of the School and he was very keen on it. But it had been evacuated because of the war, and he'd heard very good things of what was happening at Eton at that time and felt that it would be a marvellous education for us. He was editor of *The Times*, and he stretched himself to send us both there; I'm sure it was quite an effort.

My housemaster was a man called C. R. M. Routh. He had been a bright young man of great promise, with a flame of red hair, who'd gone to Eton as a student teacher and then just stayed there. And in some ways I think he felt that a little bit; there was a tinge of melancholy in some of his comments, and he had a sort of humility which was quite touching. And yet he was a very warm and entertaining man and cared for us very well. I got a lot from him.

There were one or two bigger boys who dominated the lower boys, who were fairly tough, I suppose, and not very interested in any of the things I was interested in. They used to come to my room and tease me for having French Impressionists on the walls instead of hunting prints, and I was regarded as a little bit odd in that way.

I can remember it all pretty clearly. I remember the coal fires, and work in the evenings – there were only two boys allowed in a room, so as to really get down to your work. I remember washing up and falling on a huge pile of plates, breaking my tooth, and one boy dancing around me shouting, 'You're marked for life!' I can even remember who it was. I can remember the atmosphere of the passages, the boys' football that we used to play up in the top passages, which I rather hated, but took part in out of some sort of sense of duty. And I remember the thrill of first getting to know one or two boys, a little bit older than myself, who were more intelligent and thoughtful, and discovering that we could be allies and that we had a lot of things in common.

I was pretty idle, my attention wandered, and in most of the forms in which I took part at that time, people were rather critical – even my housemaster, in his kindly letters, said, 'This boy will never be a scholar', and so on. But my classical tutor, a man called Claude Taylor – C. H. Taylor – encouraged me, and he said, 'You really can write; this is good stuff.' I think his encouragement meant a lot. I began to get interested in the Drawing Schools and enjoyed Wilfrid Blunt's encouragement and friendship, and there were a number of boys in other houses whom I began to get to know. They shared certain common interests, all of which were to develop increasingly, in writing, drawing, art, books, that sort of thing. And Eton was a tolerant place in which that could happen. In a more narrow kind of school, at that time particularly, when public schools were on the whole pretty hearty and rigid, I think I was very lucky that everyone – from my housemaster to my classical tutor to the art people – were able to give me encouragement.

But the single most important influence, and the most powerful thing that I would go back to as one of the great experiences of my life, was that I went into Kappa Select, a term invented by George Lyttelton, one of the great schoolmasters of any school at any time, I would say, and I was up in that cathedral-like classroom of his for four precious halves, just before the School Certificate time. It was there that I really discovered myself.

I must tell you about this; it is much the most important thing I can say about that period. Shortly before I went to Eton, George Lyttelton, Humphrey's father, created this new concept of Kappa Select. He was beginning to see that there were people for whom the classics didn't speak, and that they must be given a sense of identity and affirmed as intelligent people, not rejects. Hence his title 'Select'. Kappa, of course, simply meant non-

Greek and was generally regarded as a term of opprobrium. And when I gave up Greek I was attacked for doing so – 'No son of a gentleman ever gives up Greek' – and my father, who used to read the classics in the underground, was very upset and worried that I was giving it up. But I didn't get on with it. And to create this contradiction in terms was to make something very original and fresh. Unlike other classrooms, when you first came into the room and took your place at the desk, there was a hush in this place, rather like in a cathedral. And sitting there, rather like a sort of cloud on Mount Sinai, was George Lyttelton, brooding and writing – he was always writing, he had beautiful writing – on a sloping desk. It fascinated me from the start.

Part of the programme meant dividing us up into three groups called 'Freeman', 'Hardy' and 'Poor Old Willis'. And this was a way of getting us to compete on different things like Latin grammar and getting different responses in the form. He'd read us something, like 'Season of mists and mellow fruitfulness . . .', and he'd absolutely have us gripped. I mean, in those days we had early school before breakfast and we always wanted to get back quickly. I can remember at least one morning when we sat totally entranced while he read. It was *Samson Agonistes*: 'Occasion drew me early to the city . . .', and he had his hands on the desk, but when it came to the line, 'He heaved and heaved the massive pillars down', he actually pulled the desk right off the plinth! Instead of giggling, as we would anywhere else, we were absolutely rapt. He had an incredible dramatic power. And he had marvellous stories and anecdotes, things like '. . . which reminds me, of course, of the learned pig of Brighton . . .'. I don't remember now what the learned pig of Brighton did, but he had endless things like that, and he entranced us. Jeremy Thorpe, I remember, was another person in that division who was equally fascinated by him. Lyttelton was leaving at that time, and we gave him in that final half a farewell present, which I think Jeremy chose (he was rather sophisticated), and he bought this dinner set; when we presented him with that, as a sort of final reward, he lit a whole mass of candles, turned out the lights, and read us a tremendous ghost story.

Suddenly everything changed for me, and from having been this rather idle, ineffective figure, a little bit bullied, there was a transition from uncertainty to certainty, and conviction and enthusiasm about my own capacity. George Lyttelton conjured up a lot that I go back to now in terms of his general philosophy. For some reason he made us write at the top of every essay, 'The price of liberty is eternal vigilance', an idea which rather caught my fancy, actually – a kind of idealism, in the strict philosophical sense.

And then my housemaster sent me to the second great man who taught me at school, who was quite different in style. That was G. B. Smith, and I transferred to being a history specialist and realized that I'd entered into a new world.

Smith and Lyttelton. They were twin luminaries. I needed them at precisely the stages I had them: Lyttelton created a human being out of a sort of cipher; Smith then really stimulated the intellectual development.

G. B. Smith . . . well, we used to call him our 'little Socrates'. He taught in a totally different way, by asking questions, very dry and sceptical. Whereas George Lyttelton was a great performer, rich and inspiring, G. B. Smith constantly shattered one's assumptions and ideas and always took the opposite view. And he stimulated one tremendously. If you got on his wavelength and wrote entertainingly or interestingly, as he thought, he was delighted with it and he encouraged you. He encouraged me tremendously and stimulated me greatly. He put us on to a lot of books, things like G. Lowes Dickinson's extraordinary book, *A Modern Symposium*, which has an account of all sorts of different people stating their points of view, a Quaker, a Conservative, a Communist, and so on. And he read this with us and made us take the different points of view of the various people. He was always encouraging one to take up a different viewpoint or stance, and to explore it. At that time I joined the Debating Society, which he encouraged me to do; I joined an archaeological society and I got into the Essay Society which was a special group that met in Claude Elliott's study. A whole new world opened out through all these things, and I began to link up with one or two people in College, like Timothy Raison and Douglas Hurd, when Douglas and I were both going in for the Rosebery Prize, which was the great history prize. Douglas, who was brilliant, had moved from classics across into history, and was just about to bag the Rosebery. He'd already got the Newcastle, so it would have been quite unfair if he'd got the Rosebery as well. In fact he didn't: I did.

It was a great triumph that day when I got the Rosebery Prize. It probably depended on the examiners' sympathies, actually; it just happened that my style and approach appealed more. I'm sure his represented a much more solid achievement than mine!

My father had been very worried about my non-achievement up to the School Certificate period. I was conscious of being a bit of a failure in his eyes at that time, because I wasn't achieving. He talked to me sometimes about taking me away from the school. I suppose he felt that he was putting an immense amount into this stretch, and I seemed to be wasting the opportunity. Fortunately he did live to see my history specialism, and he was very pleased with that. His last words, when I spoke to him on the telephone – our last conversation ever before he went off to Africa where he died quite young – fifty-eight – were, 'Do try and have a go at the Rosebery.' And I thought he must be joking. He never lived to see me make it.

I can remember the piano playing downstairs, someone practising Chopin. And I remember my housemaster coming out and calling me. He was very good, actually. He just very gently told me about it, and then said that there would be much for me to do now. I remember him saying that I would be able to be a great support to my mother if I could respond to this in the right way. And he would pray that I would be able to do this, because he felt that this would be the best way in which I could serve my father's memory now. I was quite touched and moved by that, and I think how he talked to me at that moment helped me quite a lot.

But it was devastating. I was absolutely broken by it, and it really did shadow things a great deal right at the end of my time at Eton, actually. I think that I was reeling. My father was very much the 'norm' of my life and, curiously enough, his philosophy and the Lytteltonian philosophy overlapped. My father was something of an idealist, and I realized that the whole atmosphere I got through George Lyttelton sort of resonated – the idea of goodness, beauty and truth being built into things, all that, which is the religious bit if you like on a broad scale; I'd imbibed a lot of it from my father and was now beginning to get to know him as a friend, and I felt the double verification of that at Eton, and back from him, as it were.

I think that I was consciously working for my father after he died. And the extraordinary thing that happened was that the announcement of the Rosebery Prize came out on the same day as the memorial service to my father in St Paul's Cathedral, and was printed in the same colum in *The Times*. I remember walking up the aisle with my mother in St Paul's, and various people leaning out and saying 'Well done', and so on. It was a feeling of tremendous joy that somehow this had come together. Even now it overwhelms me to think of it.

I haven't mentioned the war, but of course there were air raids, and we went down to a shelter regularly. The victory days there are vivid memories for me. On V-E night we had a terrific bonfire and celebrations on Queen's Eyot, but I remember I was rather horrified by them all rather chasing one boy, Bobby Miles, who afterwards became ordained, strangely enough. He was someone who was not popular in his house or something. I remember them chasing him and shouting, 'Miles to the river', and so on. It was completely out of hand.

I'll never forget the 'Miles to the river' thing, I met him afterwards and I asked him about it, and he said that it was quite terrifying. Why these sudden emotions burst out from this crowd, or what was underlying them, I don't know. I didn't have anything to do with that, nor did anyone from my house.

I suppose the religious side of things was not very stimulating, really. The College Chapel was just a conventional framework. We all enjoyed roaring the psalms and the hymns, and we accepted it as part of the landscape. I got more from my housemaster and his Confirmation preparation than from anyone in a dog-collar.

One of the things about being ordained and being involved with the Church is that you have got to identify with everybody. In some ways having been at Eton could be a rather cutting-off thing. When I came to Coventry as a bishop, there was something about 'Well, we shall see how this Old Etonian will do . . .' in the Coventry *Evening Telegraph*. And at a time when they were desperately needing someone to stand alongside this battered city and struggle for the unemployed, I felt that in a way I had to live Eton down, and persuade people that I was for real as it were, and not just a part of the Establishment. Not that I would disguise my background – I couldn't, I owe it too much.

I think I would say that it still seems to me rather incredible that somebody like Douglas is a Cabinet Minister, or that Tony Lloyd is a judge, or that I am a bishop, for that matter; these aspects of it seem rather improbable, somehow. It is almost dream-like. There is an incongruous sense that we are all play-acting and that we will go back and find that we are just starting again. I do have that strange feeling of: Will we wake up and find that we are all still there? Perhaps that's my unease about being so much part of the Establishment.

It worries me in a way. I wonder if it is what the Labour people are always complaining of, the indication of the limitedness of our society and the constrictions. I have got an unease about it. Great things have shattered, impinged and broken in on me since then, and things have changed. And yet some of those particular little bits of *déjà vu* are in some ways entertaining, and in some ways disturbing.

I'll tell you a moment when I felt it. It was when I was paying homage to the Queen on becoming a bishop, and Douglas stood by her side, holding the oath that you have to read. He read something, and I then repeated it, while the Queen looked on, and that did give me an extraordinary feeling. It was almost as if everything was part of the school, or the school had become part of everything. I think I did dream once or twice after that.

DAVID BENEDICTUS

MY parents, who are still alive, are Anglo-liberal Jews: the family came over towards the end of the nineteenth century, and like other liberal Jews they tended to be very anglicized and wanted to become more so. The English influence was more of a spur than the Jewish one, and with that in mind the English private education was something to be desired. My dad was an accountant and worked at Lillywhites, the family firm.

I went to prep school in Broadstairs. In 1946–7, the wicked winter, the coldest winter of all on the island of Thanet, there was three feet of snow and it was bitterly cold, and from there I took Common Entrance. I had an extraordinary distinction in that I was the only boy in the history of the Common Entrance to get 100 per cent on all three maths papers; I got 100 per cent in algebra, arithmetic and geometry. As a result of which I got into Eton. But actually it was very strange, because I wasn't a mathematician or any good at maths. When I got to Eton the cramming which had taken place at the prep school turned into proper teaching of mathematics, which is more speculative in that there are no correct answers, it's much more a matter of drawing conclusions, and I came bottom of the form. They put me in the one below, and I came bottom of that. They then wrote to the headmaster of my prep school and said obviously I had been cheating; there was no way in which a boy who had achieved those results could be as dumb as I appeared to be. I sat the scholarship a year after I had come to Eton and didn't get it, and the effect of that was to create considerable waves between the prep school and the Etonian authorities.

I went to Eton very much in fear and trembling, because I remember an old boy from the prep school coming back for

Sports Day – he was at Eton already – who said that the only way I was going to survive at Eton was by not saying anything for the first year, which would have been extremely good advice if I could have taken it. I think it is fair to say I was desperately unhappy. I used to make myself ill rather than go back to school. I think if I had been in College I would have been far better off because, although College was quite tough, at least intellectual pretensions were respected there, more than they were in my house.

The fact is, depending on which house you were in, it was extremely important to keep a low profile until you felt more at home. The house I had been put down for was RJNP, Mr Parr's. He was very red in the face, hence Purple Parr. That was in Mullion's, which was the most modern and the ugliest house in Eton. Parr was a very interesting man, I appreciate now, but perhaps unsuited temperamentally for that job. He died shortly after I left from high blood pressure, which he always had. He had strange characteristics. I mean I look back on it and realize that I'm probably older now than he was then, so it gives you a different insight. But he was an extreme snob. He liked to have boys from upper-class families in his house, he played royal tennis, he was very keen on bridge, and while I was there he married, having been a widower, a youngish, very attractive Catholic widow, to everybody's amazement.

He was basically very shy with boys, and I think that the main problem was that he was very distanced from them and therefore didn't know a great deal about what was happening around him. It was difficult to get close to him, although he did have a weakness for me, I think, because he saw me as unusual.

Being Jewish was a problem and I don't know how much he appreciated that it was a problem. The house was a very hearty house. It was important to be good at sport – more important than being good at work – but I wasn't very good at either. I found it extremely difficult to get used to the concept of working on my own. The whole principle of education at that time at Eton was that the actual hours in school were not long, but you did have to do a lot on your own, and I wasn't used to doing that. I needed more supervision, I was very immature, and the result was that I didn't understand what I was supposed to do. I used to get my work given back to me with a tear in the top called a 'rip', which meant that you had to have it signed by your housemaster and by your tutor. And I didn't know what this tear meant; I just thought it was carelessness. So for the first few weeks I never did anything about it, and when it was found out that I had been 'concealing' them by not having them signed, being, it was thought, deliberately obstinate and difficult, I was in great trouble.

I was always wearing the wrong clothes, getting lost and going to the wrong place and being told off for this and that. I think I was perceived as being a natural victim of the system. On my first day at Eton I was wearing my house shoes instead of my outdoor shoes and I couldn't find my way back to my house, and I was told off. This was a constant theme running through my early years at Eton; I was always in the wrong place at the wrong time and doing the wrong thing. One's defence against this was to create an interior fantasy world, which I quickly did through keeping diaries, and through writing a bit later on.

As the years passed I learned how to cope with the system a little better. Although I didn't ever entirely distinguish myself in class, I always did very well in exams, so that in the Grand July, which was the equivalent of A-levels, I got a distinction. In fact I was more than averagely bright, hopelessly disorganized, but good at exam technique, and I always rose to the exam situation. Eventually, as most writers have done, I found one teacher who was sympathetic, a man called Claude Taylor, something of an eccentric character. Looking back on it, he seems gay to me now; I don't know if he was. He played the oboe in local Gilbert and Sullivan productions and he taught English, and for three halves I was up to him and I wrote three essays for him. And each time my essay was sent up for good, which was the highest praise you could get, and when you had three of them you got a prize. The prize was a book token and I chose the short stories of Maupassant. Claude Taylor was the only one who really appreciated that I had some kind of sensitivity as a critic, or as a literary spirit. But I then moved out of his class into Prescot's, and under his more austere influence my work was useless again. So there was just that sort of Prague Spring when I was appreciated by Claude Taylor and I worked particularly hard and well.

I was never afraid of working hard. For my classical tutor, a man called Raef Payne, I remember translating the Juvenal *Satires* into heroic couplets – translating them not into literal English but into a sort of Etonian equivalent, finding the same satirical targets, whatever they were. I was joint editor of a magazine called *Parade* which came out on the fourth of June and therefore I had a market for my short stories, which got published, although they weren't very good except for one called 'Telegrams', which my housemaster actually told me he thought was extremely good. I was very gratified to get some praise from him at last.

Shortly after that he made me Captain of the House and that posed unusual problems. I was captain of a house which was still an athletic house, and I had two, and later three, members of Pop in the Library under me; but I wasn't a member of Pop myself, so I had authority over them in the house but they had authority over me outside the house. Obviously it would have been nice for me to have been elected to Pop and it would have been a feather in the cap for the house to have as many members of Pop as it could, but I was blackballed. In fact it never occurred to me that I would be elected, because I'd never seen myself as a popular boy.

Another thing was that I had an enormous carbuncle on my face, and it was very difficult to have a natural air of authority with this great thing, which I had removed by an operation in my last term when it was getting out of all proportion. So a very spotty face, a lack of natural authority, and members of Pop in the house under me led to all sorts of problems, and it did get extremely difficult.

We were aware of things going on in the outside world. It was a time when we were about to preside over the break-up of the Empire; you were extremely proud of the red bits on the map, and we were just about becoming educated to the fact that this couldn't last, and shouldn't last perhaps. But that was a difficult lesson to learn, and most of the boys were extremely and disgracefully conservative. Joan Lestor brought an African prince to a public hall in Eton; it was a brave thing to do – it was a run-up to an election and there were no votes in Eton boys. We barracked so loudly when we saw a black man on the platform that he was never given a fair hearing. That was shameful and I was very strongly aware that we had behaved disgracefully. I wanted no part of that.

As you might expect, I was good at chess. And one year I won the Chess Cup. Oddly enough, chess these days carries considerable prestige; in those days chess was regarded as a sort of inky-fingered substitute for real sport and there was no great prestige in being good at it. On the day of the Winchester cricket match (alternate years at Winchester and Eton), we had a chess match. While the real heroes were striding up in white flannels on to the cricket green, we were locked in a library somewhere playing chess. It always seemed that that was an interesting parallel of how I failed to slot in, and it's a situation which has recurred throughout my life in other establishments.

The Jewish thing was the area in which I was most vulnerable. One boy saw in his diary that the day I was going away for was the Day of Atonement – I would tend not to say why I was taking the day off. And they found it was called Yom Kippur, and that was a very funny name and a very good subject for a great deal of raucous humour. I didn't have to go to Chapel, but the desire to conform meant that you wanted to be different in as few ways as possible. So I would go to Chapel, but I would have to monitor the prayers very carefully. For example, they still used the collect which was the prayer for the conversion of the Jews. I couldn't say 'Amen' to that, but I would say the Lord's Prayer; it seemed perfectly appropriate until you came to the benediction afterwards, 'In the name of the Father and the Son and the Holy Ghost', and I would then fall silent.

I remember somebody was looking up 'Jewish' in the *Oxford Pocket Dictionary* (I think this arose perhaps from a discussion about it), and they found that it said something like, '. . . of the Jewish faith . . . mean . . . a usurer . . . a dishonest money-dealer';

and then when they looked up 'Christian' it said, '. . . of the Christian faith . . . noble . . . upright', and so on. And after all, there was no arguing with the *Oxford Pocket Dictionary*!

I mean, you could be very popular being Jewish – it wasn't that they were anti-semitic, it was that boys at Eton at that time looked for vulnerable spots and once they'd found them they applied the dentist's drill to them. In my case it was being Jewish; in the case of Hope, who was in my house, he was Catholic, and I remember being party to appalling teasing of Hope because of this. Yet it wasn't because he was Catholic, it was because he was Hope. Boys are very good at sussing out the area of greatest vulnerability.

You can be hugely successful at a school like Eton and it leaves you nowhere to go. Ingleby-Mackenzie was President of Pop and captain of everything when I was first at Eton, and the great height of my first year's ambition was to be fagged to Ingleby-Mackenzie. I once actually went round with a note for him, and *there* was the great man himself – you know how little boys idolize bigger ones. Years later I went into my father's shop, into Lillywhites, to buy some shoes, and there was Ingleby-Mackenzie measuring my foot, kneeling at my feet, and I thought how the mighty fall, what an extraordinary turn around. Ingleby-Mackenzie tried to play cricket for Middlesex;* goodness knows where he is now, or what he's doing. That's a well-known syndrome, the heights you can reach in a school like that, which you can never come close to again.

I didn't have many friends and certainly very few whom I see now: there weren't many in my house who were compatible. Timothy Pitt-Miller, who was a year or two older, was very tall and something of an aesthete. He was fairly paternalistic towards me, but I remember a tremendous sense of betrayal when, on a day when the weather was bad and you couldn't play sport, we all had to go for a run to Arches and back, which was about a five-mile run. I had flat feet, so I was very bad at running, and soon fell behind the others. Timothy Pitt-Miller, who normally I

*In fact he later became a very successful cricketer, and played for Hampshire.

perceived as a sensitive soul, grabbed me by the scruff of the neck and ran me along so that my legs had to run, which was extremely uncomfortable; I felt a great sense of betrayal, because he had been one of the people I had been able to talk to. Of my contemporaries, there was Rupert Lycett-Green, who was an extremely good-looking boy and a very glamorous figure. Rupert was always very fashionable and he was also very sexy; he was a very physical presence around, so he enjoyed the flattery of the bigger boys. And for most of the boys in my year I think Rupert was the flame around which the moths fluttered. Charles Michell was a close friend, probably my closest, but I think I chose him as a friend because he was one I could bully, whereas the others were ones whom I hoped wouldn't bully me. I know I treated him very badly, and I would take huge advantage of him because he was happy to accept that from me in order to gain a friend.

I think what happened was that at Eton I was so concerned with social survival, becoming popular, overcoming these (as I perceived them) disadvantages, that the whole of my personality became geared up to becoming socially acceptable, and in future life the whole of my career became concerned with proving myself in different areas. I mean, you can't argue with having a book published. You get a book published, and that's it – whatever you say it's good to get a book published. Similarly, to direct plays on television. In all the different areas into which I moved, it became far too important for me to see my name in print, as a result of the social inadequacies at school. So I think my personality was partly formed by the extraordinary pressures to conform to the Etonian system which existed then. But in a more sympathetic school, or a less tight-knit school – Bedales or Dartington or somewhere like that – it seems to me, with other Claude Taylors around, I could have become a much more relaxed sort of person and a much less ambitious one.

Talking about Eton, it all comes back with great vividness. That's partly to do with middle age, when memories of your earlier years become more vivid. But I don't think it figures much in my life at all; I have no interest or concern in spending any time there. It never occurred to me that my son should go

there, and when I get the Old Etonian Association brown en-
velopes, asking for this or that, I don't even read what's happened
at the school. I have no real interest in it now. By writing the
book, *The Fourth of June*, the chapter was closed. It was almost
deliberate that when I wrote the book about Eton I thought,
'This will justify it, and that's an end of it.' So many years have
passed and I'm no longer perceived as the Old Etonian who
wrote the book; that's long since passed now, and most of the
people I meet are too young to have been around anyway when
that book came out, and they don't know about the furore it
caused.

It's something good coming out of something bad, a butterfly
from a chrysalis. Whether I was or not, I *thought* I was particularly
unhappy until maybe the last year. I dreaded going back to
school, and I thought, 'One day I'll show them', that sort of
thing. And then one day I did show them, and not only did the
book come out but it was sold out within a few days. It was a
huge subject of conversation in those areas to which I've never
been admitted, the country houses and so on. It was a double
revenge really, a revenge on the Etonian system, but also a
revenge on English society which had not admitted me. I can't
blame them for not admitting me, I wasn't very admissible.

I've never wanted to trade on being an Etonian, and once the
book was out of the way it was really no longer relevant. I'm
grateful that Eton has given me considerable fluency and articu-
lacy. I'm aware of that, and a certain ability maybe to waltz
through social situations, but I'm also an extremely shy person,
and that is a result of it too.

I have recurring sporting dreams about Eton still. It doesn't
matter what sport it is, football, cricket, rugby, rowing: I'm
about to play for the school, and the equipment is never right, I
don't get the pads on in time or the football has collapsed. The
last one was golf; it's the first time I've had the dream about golf,
and I was playing, only all the clubs were twisted . . .

I read somewhere the other day that the greatest pleasure of
middle age was watching your friends fail; well, you could slightly
alter that and say one of the great pleasures of middle age is

watching your contemporaries going to pieces. And certainly Etonians physically do go to pieces quite fast because they tend to be prey to the pleasures of the flesh quite a lot, I think. I'm fit without having to worry about it, I eat a lot but I don't put on a lot of weight.

It's a matter for pride that I would like to meet again the people I was at Eton with and take them on in a sort of Krypton Factor way, because I think I'd be all right now, although I wasn't then.

MICHAEL BENTIN

MY father was one of seven sons who were sent all around the world by his South American family to be educated in different countries in different disciplines. His discipline was to be a mining engineer, because that was the family business, which at the turn of the century was in its infancy. And his guardian here was Mrs Hope-Jones. She was a dear lady; she was very much his adopted mother, and he adored her. Her son, Bill Hope-Jones, was his best friend. They were the same age, and when they were thirteen, Uncle Bill said to Dad, 'I'm going to become a schoolteacher,' and Dad said, 'Fine, when I get married, and I have sons, I will send them to your school.' And thus it turned out. Bill was a tug at Eton, and he then went on to Cambridge, not only as a scholar, but a great athlete. He was a Blue, he was a Maths Tripos, and God knows what, President of the Mathematical Society and everything – wonderful man!

So we went to Eton, my brother and I. If he'd been a beak at Pudsey Grammar, we'd have gone there too. The object of the exercise was to be with Bill Hope-Jones, who had an enormous effect on both my brother's life and my own. He was a remarkable man, great man, truly a great man. Not all that well treated by Eton, I felt, because after all those years he was the Mr Chips of Eton, he retired with some idiotic pension, and went on to become a maths beak at Cranleigh. And when he died at eighty-three, at his funeral there were four dukes, two earls, innumerable knights baronet, and an Anglo-Peruvian clown.

My family made it absolutely clear to me that we were just a very ordinary family and it would be a struggle to put us through. But they felt it would be a good thing – not to go to Eton, but to be with Uncle Bill, which we agreed with because we adored him! We'd known him since we were babies, and I knew his family terribly well because we grew up together, so it was a wonderful opportunity as far as we were concerned.

It was my first time away from home and I was thirteen. One is nervous, obviously. But that was for twenty-four hours, and there I was in the bosom of my tutor's family. I was very privileged to be able to know my tutor's family, and so I didn't feel I was that far away from home. You soon met up with kids of your own inclinations who were interested in the same things, whether it was biology, or nature studies, or science – which I was potty on. Whatever you were good at, they liked you for: if you made them laugh or you played fives well, or you were a bright student, you got on with people, purely because they were interested in you and you were interested in them. I know there were boys who were miserable at Eton. My old friend Patrick MacNee, whom I've known, dear God, long enough, wasn't terribly happy at Eton.

I never heard a hint of anti-semitism or racism. A lot of my mates came from Siam, or Africa, or the Middle East, and there were a lot of incredibly bright Jewish families who sent their sons there, so you had this marvellous bright cross-section of every ethnic background, religious feeling, what have you. No matter what you were, you went to Chapel. Holding a raffle on the hymn numbers was enormous fun every morning, and we all enjoyed the singing. There were a lot of activities there, you know, the Music Society, the Historical Society, the Scientific Society. It was a very busy life. I've heard hair-raising stories, not least from Patrick Macnee, about sexual deviations and Christ knows what going on. I never saw it! I don't know whether it just went over my head because I was with a very happy normal family, the Hope-Joneses, but I didn't suffer from any of that.

I was very privileged; anybody who was at Hope-Jones will say the same thing. We were terribly privileged to be with that man, and it's a measure of him that he showed me no favouritism. He was just as bloody marvellous to all the other boys in the house.

He was a total eccentric. Once a year he used to bathe naked at Bognor, and he was always hauled up before the beak, an old friend of his, who would say, 'Oh God, William, not again.' 'Nothing wrong with the human body,' he would respond. 'Undraped it is one of the most beautiful pieces of mechanism in the world, as I have said before.' 'Oh God, one pound fine, I'*ll* pay it', because he knew m'tutor never had any money.

He was one of the healthiest-minded men I have met. Basically he was a Quaker. He had a lovely deep, resonant voice, he was a truly great oarsman, and runner, and once a year he used to play fives with the boys without gloves, which would tear his hands – a total eccentric. I don't know anybody who was up to him who didn't love him, I mean really love him as a person. So I'm in an incredibly privileged position; I can't give you the average boy's impression of Eton because it was made endurable for me, and sometimes very happy, entirely by my tutor.

There was a man called H. K. Marsden, huge man, about six foot four, called Bloody Bill, who seemed to have a perpetual itch in his lower half, he was always scratching himself inside his pockets – sheer nerves and terror of the boys. I remember the first division I was up to him. He went round the classroom, 'Name . . . name.' And I went 'chchchchc . . .', the usual thing, and the boy next to me said, 'Bonkers, sir', 'Bonkin', said someone else, 'Benskin', 'Foreskin', and somebody said finally 'Bentin', and he said, 'Odd name, odd boy. But while he is in my division, nobody's going to laugh at that stammer,' which was a marvellous thing to say.

I never saw anything unfair, but it depended to a certain extent on how good the boys were in your house, and if you had a just House Captain. I was very lucky, I had Inchcape, and he was very fair-minded. There was a rather bossy, not particularly nice member of the Library, for whom I became a fag in my first half, and he demanded some unbelievable output, like thirty-six sausages and eggs and Christ knows what for tea, and you had to produce all that over one fire. And because I couldn't speak too well, I wrote a letter to Inchcape saying I didn't think this was fair, and he immediately had me up and said, 'Absolutely right, the hell with this bloke'; I won't give his name because he's a very distinguished Member of Parliament now, although he's still a prick − but there it is.

There were aspects of Eton which I didn't like. I thought the living conditions were too Spartan, and quite a number of boys I knew had rather more delicate health than I had and really did suffer from the cold. There was that attitude of the cold bath which I've never agreed with in a climate where I've seen the ravages of rheumatism and bronchitis.

I remember gathering around a radio set to hear Edward VIII abdicate. We were all in our dressing-gowns, clutching mugs of hot cocoa, because it must have been all of ten o'clock at night and a great privilege to huddle around this small radio which the Library had − and how moving it was. We'd been the Guard of Honour at his father's funeral, which was also very emotional, and I saw all those crowned heads of Europe who didn't exist within five, six years. The OTC and the boys themselves at Eton provide the Guard of Honour for the monarch, which was a tradition, because we'd been founded by a king. My first impression was how small the coffin was. Then there were the four princes, two of whom had been to Eton, marching in their various service uniforms, czar helmets on (the dress uniform of the RAF, which nobody knows really), and they all had their greatcoats buttoned up and swords reversed and all this lark. And the guardsmen in their long coats, marching slowly. No horses, and the sailors pulling the gun carriage, which is traditional. And the awful feeling of gloom which lay over Windsor for almost a year; the psychic feeling was dreadfully low.

I have absolutely no sentimental attachment to Eton now, I never go back for reunions or anything like that. I wear the OE tie because my tutor asked me to wear it. He said you might just run into another Etonian and he might be in need of help, and that's really why you do it, to recognize each other. I wear that purely for my tutor, it's as if you had someone in your family who left you something like a watch that you would wear. But I had enormous fondness for this splendid man who was my father's closest friend, who was such fun to be with. I think everybody loved Bill. He was a marvellous man.

If you go to a school and it is part of your life for three or four years, and you have that peculiarly personal attachment to your tutor, and this terrific affection for his family, for the rest of your life you're going to owe them something. I owe Bill Hope-Jones, I don't owe Eton anything. I owe Bill Hope-Jones.

Anyway, how can you have a sentimental attachment to a school where you are probably one of eight survivors of all the boys you knew? Your mind automatically blanks off because you think to yourself, 'Oh Jesus, how I wish they were around', because they were very, very nice blokes. So many of my year were killed. I think of my lot, who left around 1938, we had about seventy to eighty per cent dead, never mind gravely injured or missing. I lost good friends like Henry Maudsley who was killed on the Sorpe, and every two or three months you would hear of another friend gone. The chaps I knew were very positive people with fine minds and extraordinarily outgoing personalities who could have done so much for the world, and they were just massacred, totally massacred. I suddenly see in my mind this boy or that boy and think, 'Gee, wouldn't it have been marvellous if they had survived, what good they would have done in the world; they would have been great doctors and great engineers and great scientists.' I feel very sad when I think of Eton.

If Bill had had his way, none of those boys would have died because he was showing us the evil of the Nazis way back in the early thirties; if they'd listened to people like Bill, Hitler would never have risen to power.

Sometimes when they're introducing you they'll say, 'Old Etonian, Michael Bentin . . .', and I think, 'What the hell did you say that for?' I remember Frank Bough, whom I like very much, had me in on a programme about Eton, and then proceeded to slam it, '. . . effete Etonians, exclusive club . . .' and all that, and I said, 'Have you ever been there?' and he said, 'No', and I said, 'Why are you tearing it down? Why don't you look at the bronze plaques of all the poor bastards that were killed in the First

World War and the Second World War? They certainly weren't sitting on their arse somewhere.'

It sure as hell isn't a Mafia like the Oxford Mafia, which is very much in existence, specially in the media. In fact it's a bit nauseating when you get some creep who comes up and says, 'You were at Oxford, weren't you?', and you say, 'No', and interest in you just disappears.

Bill cured my stammer. He found a man called Harry Burgess who was gigantic, with a great big booming voice, who'd been one of my tutor's pupils. And he taught the four of us who stammered badly. I had a complete 'chchchch' block, so I had to write everything down, everything. They were very good about it at Eton, I must say, and they accepted the written words. And Burgess would say, 'You will learn to speak with a swing and a pause, and then a swing and a run.' And the first thing I learnt to say was 'n'May I have n'fishcake?' – 'n' is the only thing a stammerer can say. I practised this for about a month and then I walked into Roland's the sock shop, with 'n'May I have n'fish-cake?' and there was a stunned silence, as if a gunfighter had just walked into the saloon in a Western town.

But this dear old girl behind the counter, she turned to me and said, 'Yes, dear, would you like cod or salmon?' And I was lost then because I hadn't rehearsed that. I lived off bloody fishcakes for about six months. And then I learnt to say 'n'Bangers and n'mash, please.' The great choruses every time I came in: 'n'May he have n'fishcakes?', 'n'May he have n'bangers and n'mash?' But it was a very good-natured school; I don't really remember any boy that I thoroughly and absolutely disliked, because there was always some saving grace. That was my tutor again, you see.

ANTHONY BLOND

M Y father was at Manchester Grammar School, but in the war he went rather up-market socially. His commanding officer was a man called Ackroyd, who said, as the shells thundered over, 'If you get married, Blond, your boys should go to a good school, and they must go to my school, Eton.' So I went to Eton and to the appropriate preparatory school. Years later I met a professor who said to me, 'You're all right, Anthony, you are *haut bourgeois*', but God, it worried me at Eton not having a country house, and not having grouse sent at the appropriate times and that sort of thing. It really did.

In the war Eton was very bad because the intelligent younger masters all went away, and we were left with some old fools and the occasional wonderful crank. There was a man called Baron Marochetti who had an enormous Hispano-Suiza, who would take boys up to London for the night. He didn't last long. This was just before petrol rationing, 1940. I was very fortunate because there were two refugees; one was a man called Jean Boniy, who was probably the greatest expert on English churches, although French: he could date a church to within three years. He taught me French. We only spoke French, and I was very good at it. Then I had a German who taught me German, so I had, by chance, almost by mistake, two excellent tutors. But the rest of the people were appalling.

The whole place was stuck in pre-war attitudes. I mean, the way we were taught history was mad. History stopped in 1914. It would have been considered journalism to talk about the General Strike. I never knew there had been a General Strike.

There was a man called G. A. D. Tait and he used to make us shout poetry, 'Row-me-over-to-Sirmione', or whatever it was.

He murdered, massacred, Shelley, I could feel Shelley scream in his grave. They weren't all stupid. There was a wonderful librarian. I didn't know him very well, but he once shyly pushed over a copy of *Horizon*, 'You might like this, Blond,' he said. He was a very quiet old man. Cattley, he was called, Mr Cattley. And God, he hit a nerve, because I didn't know what life was like. I was brought up in this Manchester middle-class way. Even before the war we had dreadful food because everybody had such bad cooks, and here I was, reading about peaches and Vichy water – God, I didn't realize the sensuality of life until I read Cyril Connolly in *Horizon*. How this very perceptive old librarian turned me on.

I did terribly, terribly well, to begin with. The first half I was terribly popular, everybody loved me. And then I committed a series of dreadful errors, mostly on the games field, and nobody spoke to me for four years. That simple.

I was rather good at tennis and that was considered not a good game to be good at. I remember I won a prize, five bob, best player in the house. But tennis was then considered to be socially degrading, I think it's something to do with the fact that it is an individual and not a team game. Now that's all completely changed, which is interesting psychologically. At public school the emphasis is moving from the team spirit, and it's not how hard you try, it's whether you win or lose. It's become very competitive. Anyway, I win this tennis competition, it doesn't do me any good, and I hit this boy very hard in the eye.

But the 'baby four' incident was much worse, because although we were a very good dry-bob house, we weren't very good on the river, and suddenly we had this amazingly good baby four and I, being the littlest, became the cox. I was perfectly good in practices, but I completely lost my head in the final competition and misdirected them so they hit the bank, and I lost them the cup, you see. Dreadful. And that was bitter for them and they took it out on me. So I became a very unpopular boy, having been a very popular boy.

I was furious, but I decided OK, have it your way. I went into a sulk – I sulked for four years really, though it was quite good in a way because I don't think I would have read so much. And the other unpopular boy in my house was Swinnerton-Dyer, who is now the head of the University Grants Commission. Sir Peter Swinnerton-Dyer. We didn't like each other very much but we were forced to mess together. We were both disliked quite a lot. He with much better reason than me because he was very good at running, and he was very brilliant at chess and played bridge for England – all individual games, you see, so there was everything to dislike about Swinnerton-Dyer because he was sort of flawless in a way.

After a while, it didn't matter so much. When one reaches a certain age you get privileges. I was in the Library and things like that. What is so funny about the Library at Eton is that it implies it's to do with books, though of course I never heard of anybody borrowing books from the Library. It would have been considered insolent and presumptuous to actually borrow a book from the Library. It would have been like going behind the altar to drink the wine, that wasn't what it was for.

What is remarkable about Eton (and it's why Etonians are such good politicians) is that you are trained in every nuance of social and political climbing, and a young Etonian understands very quickly the art of how to influence people, and how to be helped by people, and that is why they are brilliant politicians, diplomats, ambassadors, employers, generals. There is a certain way in which even a young Etonian would expect doors to be opened for him, literally and metaphorically. A sort of assumption of superiority, I think. They are taught to be very cool, even when they are very, very small, and not to respect any authority except their own. The first thing you're told is not to be too impressed by the beaks. You acknowledged them by capping in the street outside, but in a way one sensed that defer-ence was from the master, not from the boy. So you are the equal of anybody in the land as a thirteen-year-old; it is dinned into you, and of course boys take to that. The schoolmaster is an usher, he's like a butler in a country house, and he's got to be respectful. For instance my housemaster, a man called Nixon, was terrified of his boys. And I remember when I was a fag of a boy called Reeves (a beautiful young man, a marvellous shot, and like many of that generation killed at Caen – almost three out of five of them were killed at Caen), my tutor said, 'Go and get Reeves immediately'; he was in a terrible rage. So I ran upstairs: 'Reeves, Reeves m'tutor wants you', and Reeves said, 'The little man can wait.' And only at Eton would you get that.

Ours was a very pi house. Nothing much happened in our house, reflecting the personality of the housemaster. We'd often ask of him, 'Is he a common little man or a little common man?' We despised him, I'm afraid. But some houses were quite *louche*, and famous for it, definitely. And obviously some housemasters were actually homosexuals and this infected the boys a bit.

The masters were slightly scared of the boys. I was once apologized to by a master. I remember what it was . . . it was about the difference between an egoist and an egotist, and he got it wrong, and I said, 'You're wrong.' He shouted at me, and then the next day he apologized. He had looked it up. I was always very wordy.

They didn't have many expectations of me. They didn't regard me as being at all interesting. I wasn't regarded as being particularly clever or scholarly, despite what I said about words. I got an exhibition to New College, and they were quite pleased about that, but I didn't signify at all. I was regarded as an odd one really. At Oxford they had a lot of expectation of me, but not at Eton.

Anybody who is honest must allow that Eton was a very powerful influence. And still is. I mean, I have people saying, 'Oh, he went to your old school . . .' and I think, 'What on earth, forty years ago!' But it does still matter, it matters like hell – *now*! I mean it certainly matters in people's view of me. I'm absolutely certain that the only reason my in-laws conceived that I might be a tolerable person was that I went to Eton. I wouldn't say it was the only way in which one could get across the threshold, but certainly up the aisle.

It is a terribly powerful influence still, Eton. Look at the bloody Cabinet, for Christ's sake. Dripping with them, isn't it? Jews and Etonians, she seems to like. And sometimes they are both.

I had one traumatic episode. There's a place called Queen's Eyot and we used to row up there, and you could get beer, for which you had to sign a chit saying who you were and your house. And I put on it 'Benito Mussolini' as a joke. And the woman who served said, 'What house, are you in Mussolini?' So I thought, I don't believe it! So I put GWN, which were the initials of my housemaster. This became a serious scandal, it was a fraud, and for a time I denied my own signature. I don't think I've ever told a lie since, it was so terrifying, and I was what they call 'eight-tanned' for my crime – beaten by the head of the eight, which is the worst beating you can have. And I had a moment of spurious popularity because of being beaten. It taught me a great deal about all sorts of things – one: how punishment glorifies victims; two: don't lie; three: don't get caught, and so on.

The house was run on terror, run on fear, definitely. Everybody was constantly in fear; fear of failing, fear of being sent down, fear of being beaten, fear, fear, fear. That's why they are so tough.

We were terribly tough and nasty. I do remember when Peter Swinnerton-Dyer was beaten once. I had the room next to the Library, which was a mistake, in fact. It was a very nice room, but it was too good for somebody my age, and I had to move out of it. I never heard anybody make such a scream. He screamed and screamed, like a pig, and that terrified me. Very few people were glorious in their youth. I mean Swinnerton-Dyer, howling like a pig, he really did scream, I've never heard such a scream, and there is nobody grander than Sir Peter Swinnerton-Dyer. That turned me against corporal punishment, erotic as it may be; for me, its only charm is sexual, not anything else.

There were some very beautiful boys there. I had the most beautiful fag, I had the school dreamboat. He was absolutely lovely, and a bit naughty-looking too. And people used to ask me to fag him round which meant to send him on a spurious mission so they could have a go at him.

In fact the man who beat me when I was eight-tanned was the man who I was fagged round to, so it was a complete sexual circle. When I was a little boy, much smaller, he had fancied me, and had me sent round and tried to seduce me. It was the first time I ever saw anybody naked – he was naked when I went into his room, and I just bolted. And that was the man who beat me. So there's quite a good erotic circle. I remember, of course, who he was, and I know what he does now, but I've never seen him since.

I was convinced a lot more went on than I knew. I was a terrible little prig and had no sex of any kind, any kind whatsoever, only in my own mind, but I'm sure there was a great deal. The headmaster once remarked, 'My boys are often amorous, seldom erotic.' I think that was a rather sweet thing to say. But I think it's absolutely the other way round. There was a lot of hard lust and the expression thereof. And certainly this boy, my fag – he was called Long, if that interests you – was so pretty that when he played in the small house match there was a crowd to watch him, and I think it had to be stopped. He was absolutely beautiful. He was a wicked, angelic boy. I remember somebody saying to me, 'I've got a crush on Long', and I said, 'What do you mean by "crush"?' That was the first time I heard the expression.

When I was young I had one on older boys. I particularly remember the most beautiful boy was Ian Gilmour, lovely looking. And when I was older, of course, I had crushes on younger boys, but I never expressed them in any way, although I think I could have done. I was terrified of sex; I remained so until way after Oxford. I was a very late developer sexually.

But all that was very much a temporary phase. For instance, the most famous bugger I knew went on to be one at Oxford, became a terrific heterosexual and went to Africa and made scandals because of the number of black ladies he had.

I was very unsophisticated. I think a lot of them knew who was who, but I wasn't aware of it. One was a bit aware of who was a lord. It exercised a lot of other people – I mean, a lot of the boys were overt snobs. Somebody like Jeremy Thorpe, for instance, was very interesting. Jeremy completely planned his career from the day he arrived at Eton. He was going to be in Pop, and he made all the right moves. Jeremy worked everything out in his life and just made one hideous mistake, didn't he?

I wasn't very interested in money at all, and as I had a rather good allowance (I think I had three pounds a term) that made me rich, and that was the sort of money I could deal with. I wasn't aware that I was living with millionaires' sons. There wasn't much you could buy. There was no way in which a very rich boy could show he was rich. Colman, as in mustard, who was a friend of mine, must have been enormously rich, but there was no sign that he was.

I remember exactly the last day. I said to my tutor, 'I don't see the point in leaving formally.' I didn't sign any leaving photographs, I just was impatient to go; and I suppose I wanted to wound him really, because he misunderstood me quite seriously. I needed this love of a father figure and was very affectionate towards him, and I didn't get anything back. My parents split up during the war. They didn't come down much. In fact my mother used to come to Windsor to look at the antique shops – she was always buying antiques and selling them – and once or twice she forgot to go on to Eton. She just got trapped in the High Street in an antique shop and took the train back to London. And my tutor said, 'Well, I can't stop you can I . . .', and I said, 'No.'

I bought a motorbike, twenty-five pounds, from a boy called Holder. It was in very bad condition and it could only go in one gear. I couldn't stop and turn around, so I drove into College Field where they played the wall game, and they had just spread some lime on the top. I couldn't stop it or anything, so I just did a great huge circle. I remember the groundsman running after me, shouting, 'What do you think you're doing, you bugger!' I just drove steadily on to London, and went to lunch with my father at the Caprice – during which time he had the motorbike removed, and I never saw it again.

LORD BROCKET

I CAN remember my first day of school very clearly. Rather
bewildered, rather overawed, like anyone when they first go to
Eton. I mean most people, when you talk of school, are used to a
main building, and possibly some other buildings. The first thing
you realize is that you've actually enrolled in a town just like a
university, and the size intimidates you. Then you have all these
very senior boys that to your mind look like men, you know,
that are shaving happily, and you suddenly think, 'Oh Christ,
I've landed in the grown-up world all of a sudden.' And of
course you were top of the tree in your last school, and you then
get plunged in at the very bottom again; it pulls you up by the
bootstraps and just reminds you, Hey, kid, you're not that
special.

Apart from its size, it's also the history of the place. It is so
old. OK, some of the houses were only built in 1700 to 1800,
and there are one or two new ones which are simply ghastly, but
the older bits were built more than five centuries ago. There are
plenty of buildings that age, not just one or two; the whole
School Yard was built about that time. You walk through School
Yard to Chapel, which I used to do every day because I was in
the choir, and one feels intimidated and impressed at the same
time, and a slight attitude of reverence towards what it represents
– as I do when I go in the House of Lords now, which is nothing
like as old, but it too represents an establishment that has been
there for a long time. I think that's the real reminder that you are
getting an education that is distinctly different, because when
you walk through that School Yard it's the ultimate reminder
that if anything is the Establishment, it is this edifice, this actual
real establishment, the building that has been there since 1420,

that despite being bombed still survives and is doing now what it was doing in those days.

When you're at Eton, you are very much aware, unless you are very callous, of the fantastic cost of it. I was particularly aware because after my father died my mother was trying to educate three boys, all at public school, and she had very little means other than a chicken farm. She did have 75,000 chickens, but she started it herself and it was the chickens which totally paid for our education and didn't leave much over after that.

I had two little businesses going which actually made quite a lot of money for me. I love doing cabinet work, and I used to make discothèque units out of mahogany and teak, buy the raw equipment up in London, valve amplifiers they were then, and build big speakers which were all the rage in those days. It was very easy to sell them, and every free moment I had I buried myself in the School of Mechanics.

I also had a little business making racing bikes. There was an Italian boot-cleaner who worked in the boot-hole in the house, and he had a brother in Milan where they used to make *dérailleur* gears and the best bearings in the world. I would pay him to smuggle these bits in from Italy, and I got the frames and put these bikes together.

I think I was looking for some other occupation because I didn't enjoy the school that much. I didn't have that many friends in the house; I thought they were all smart-arses, they thought the world of themselves, and I didn't particularly want to associate with a lot of them. So I was quite happy sitting in the School of Mechanics just knocking things up. Some of the boys were extremely nasty; I can think of one or two who delighted in making other people squirm – they were incredibly childish really, that's what it came down to. If they looked at the way they behaved now, hopefully they would realize that they were being really very silly.

There were some odd people in the house, although you never really thought of them though as particularly different, you were all peas heaped in the same pot. There were lots of Nigerian princes and one or two kings. There was one black chap who was Nigerian, with very Nigerian features, you know, big lips and a rather large head and very large frame. He was an excellent boxer because he was so damned big. He'd just poke someone with his little finger and they'd fall over. Onyeama was his name. He used to get terribly bullied and wrote a book about Eton* shortly afterwards, not talking very kindly about it. He was very susceptible, because he wasn't bright enough, sharp enough, didn't have the wit to come back and make these people look small and idiotic. There was another one called Akintola, who had much finer, more Ethiopian-type features, I forget which country he was from. Much better-read, had a much sharper wit, and wasn't bullied, and they were both there at the same time. It was the old schoolboy thing of taking advantage of people's weaknesses. This other fellow was quite a bright spark. The sad thing was that he was found murdered along with his two sisters in the palace about two terms after he left school. He and his family and his whole palace guard were carved up into lots of little pieces in a sort of coup.

The type of housemaster and boys is absolutely crucial. We had a housemaster known as Wetty Lawrence, and this may be over-reaction – I mean, if I lived those years again I would probably change my mind and say I was being very harsh, but I didn't like the man, I found him incredibly wet. When I thought he should have reacted in certain circumstances, whether it was discipline or anything else, he did nothing. When he talked he went 'er' between every word, I'll never forget that, as if every word, every sentence, was an embarrassment. He was embarrassed to have to tell you that you'd done badly in your exam results: 'Could you possibly – er, try and, er, correct this next term?' And he was a hopeless conversationalist. If you wanted to talk to him about an interesting political thing that happened, he would just say, 'Oh yes . . .', or 'Pity, isn't it?' or something. End of conversation.

I remember one afternoon he summoned me in and asked me to sit down. He got very embarrassed and was stuttering a bit,

Nigger at Eton by Dilibe Onyeama.

and eventually he sort of blurted it out. 'I'm afraid, er, your, er, grandfather has passed away and you're now called Lord Brocket, not Nall-Cain any more, er, is that all right?' End of interview.

But the house was incredibly successful sportwise, in fact the term I arrived, I think fifty per cent of Pop was in that house and some incredible percentage of all the sporting caps of the whole school. I doubt it has ever been repeated since. So Lawrence in a way is a little bit of a legend and people remember his house for that.

I'm not at all sure how relevant Eton is to today's world. I felt that I was such a microscopic proportion of the whole population of this country. For one thing I looked entirely different from the rest of the country; there we were, walking around the streets in tail-coats, we were working on lathes in the School of Mechanics wearing tails. If you think about it, it's utterly ridiculous, the whole thing, and of course walking down the High Street there would be cars passing, you know, with yobs leaning out the window going 'Wa-a-a-a', roaring with laughter.

A lot of people from my background would heartily disagree with me for saying this, but in an ideal world there would be just state education available for people. It would be marvellous if we could all make use of it, and damn it, we're all paying tax for it, I'm paying and so are you, and I probably will never make use of it. But the state system isn't up to scratch, and it's hardly surprising because nearly all the government ministers and shadow ministers in the Labour Party have their sons and daughters, and where do they send them? – private schools. Even the left-wingers who preach the state system have their kids in private schools.

If I found a socking good grammar school that was co-ed, I'm damned sure my son would do better in life if he went to one of those than to Eton. Someone could argue that, being the son of a peer and a future peer, he doesn't bloody well need the Eton education; which again I can't say anything against, because it probably is true.

But having said that the state system is far less than perfect, the fact is that trades are hardly touched upon at Eton. It is no good going into the outside world having probably the best education that money can buy, thinking that you're rather superior, and not having a grasp of what society and industry is about – what is really involved in making products, factory-floor problems . . . So it's hardly surprising that the vast majority of Old Etonians make a beeline for the City and go into stock-broking firms and things because they can wear a suit, they can look respectable, have their lunch at Corning and Barrow, with their gin and tonics, their port at five o'clock when they finish; it's a continuation of the boys' club, which I think does this country a power of no good at all.

In the early part of this century, being, for want of a better word, part of the upper echelon, the upper class, one regarded the workforce in a certain light in that you wanted to see how good they were for your purposes. Nowadays the position is to a large extent reversed, and the workforce look at you as a product of the upper class and put you to the test to see whether you come up to scratch. I think a lot of people leave Eton forgetting that they're on test.

I think an awful lot of people who leave Eton carry the rubber stamp in their pocket, and they're only too ready to pull it out and bang it on the blotter and say, 'There you are, I'm an Old Etonian, don't you know.' And if they get into trouble, or they're running into an identity crisis, they'll remind themselves or other people that they are, after all, Old Etonians, which of course makes a world of difference. I never mention that I'm an Old Etonian, unless I'm asked. But then of course some people could argue, 'Well, Brocket, you don't bloody well have to, you've got a title and a big house', and I can't argue with that one, because in a way that's a rubber stamp as well. But it's a rubber stamp that I've tried to get away from. I usually introduce myself without the title, just Charles Brocket, so unless they ask . . . but then one can't fib. Maybe I'm over-sensitive about this. I always have been, I think. For example, I always try to camouflage my upper-class accent.

But looking back at Eton, I would not be able to say whether they did a good job or not. In fact, being truthful, I'm not sure what sort of job they actually did. I was a bit of a spectator at Eton; it helped me with mechanics and certainly I enjoyed my sport. There aren't many schools where you can actually hibernate and work into the late hours of the night, with fantastic facilities, running a business and making money. I give them credit for that, and the facilities were there to do it. But damn it, at Harrow or Winchester or Radley you can enjoy your sport just as much, and on the academic side would probably have done better. But I was extremely glad to leave, and I felt a great weight off my shoulders. The thing that rather unnerved me was that I had no idea what I was going to do. I hadn't a bloody clue. One assumes that at the end of the production line you get churned out in a certain shape and you say, 'Eureka, I'm going to make nuts and bolts,' or 'I'm going to sit behind a VDU and buy and sell shares.' And I think if I had been exposed to more trades and had training in industry I would have had a better idea of what I wanted to do.

There's a recurring nightmare I have. At the beginning of each term, there's a little blue book you get which is about three by four inches, a school diary. I forget what it's called now.* It's Eton blue, the cover, and in it you write which tutors you're seeing each day, and you have little squares to fill in what lessons you're doing: geography from nine to nine-thirty, ten to ten-thirty history, and so on. Of course they're all in different parts of the school – they're miles apart, some of these places – and if you haven't worked out the formula correctly and put in the right things at the right time, you could end up going to the wrong classroom, or not knowing where to go at all. And my nightmare is that at the beginning of each term I would not fill this diary in correctly, and I would end up going to the wrong places . . . it isn't fear of being punished – it's more fear of just looking a complete arsehole, opening a door in front of a class of fifty or something, who are probably far more senior than you, all discussing politics, and you've come for your history lesson

*Eton College Fixtures

and you look completely ridiculous. You know, I've had this nightmare of not knowing where to go for years! It's quite extraordinary; that's the only nightmare, or any dream, I ever have.

THE RT REV. SIMON BURROWS

BECAUSE my father was a clergyman too, I imagine money was a fairly major consideration if one was to go to a public school. And everyone said that I had to try and get a scholarship, and Eton was one of the very few schools where a scholarship really meant that. I think my father paid ninety pounds a year for me at Eton.

Walter Hamilton was master in College, and Walter Hamilton was God, and he remains God to this day. Walter was an extremely reserved man, and had a splendidly lugubrious approach. I suppose I learned the meaning of the word 'integrity' from Walter Hamilton, he was that absolutely through and through. I've never met anyone else like him; he was totally genuine. A man of phenomenal learning, very, very deeply caring.

He used to come around every single night, and it would be agony to try to think of something to say to Walter, and it was agony for him trying to think of something to say to you! And because he so obviously found it difficult to communicate, in a funny sort of way we all got much closer to him.

A very important character who is still alive, age ninety-two or three, was the Matron of the College, Miss Iredale-Smith. She ruled the College with a rod of iron. I mean, she was the person you really had to make quite sure that you behaved yourself with. The problems of staff, getting food, and looking after boys, at that stage of the war must have been appalling. Every now and then there was a very, very peculiar form of meat which appeared at Sunday lunch, and it was painfully obvious that it was horse. When she was tackled with this, she would always say, 'Nonsense, dear, nonsense! Venison, from the Royal Forest.' And you always got the impression she'd been out in Windsor

Great Park potting one or two deer. I'm absolutely certain it was horse.

In those days, Collegers entered half-way up the school. I mean, not to put too fine a point on it, some of the Oppidans were not immediately very bright – and some of them were quite unbelievably thick! And Collegers tended to stay together for a simple, practical and prudent reason: you were in form with a whole lot of moronic fifteen- and sixteen-year-olds, who were actually physically considerably bigger than one was oneself. I mean, if we had been of appropriate height, we would have looked down on them; we felt we were superior to the Oppidans. And you can say that's impossibly arrogant, but that was the way we looked at it.

I can remember playing fives with some other Collegers and actually being turfed out by much older boys who were Oppidans and being told, 'Our parents paid for us to come here, clear off, you tugs.' But that was a one-off incident.

I still bridle at the use of the word 'tug'. Many Oppidans do not realize that Collegers object to it. No Colleger would ever use that word about himself. And I suspect that's rather the way we often use remarks which are resented as racist in some form or other in our contemporary society.

The war was very much the backcloth to everything, and many of the things that happened at Eton could only have happened because it was wartime.

The most obvious thing was that so many of the very able scientists went off to the war, and we really had some quite extraordinarily bad teachers in these fields. There was a dear man, an able man called Monsieur Le Desire, who tried to teach French, but it was constant uproar and chaos. And I can re-member a wretched science teacher having a frog put down his neck by a boy whose name, I think, was Wilmot-Smith.

It was a much more religious world in those days. I think we were all reasonably God-fearing, and I think I was fairly normally religious. I certainly said my prayers.

The incredible thing to me, looking back, is that in the five years I was there I did not speak to a single clergyman about religion – and there were quite a few around. I think it's marvellous how that's changed now, and the modern Eton is much, much better. But one of the things that fascinates me is that a quite disproportionately large number of men of my generation were ordained, and I think it was the sheer inadequacy of some of the clergy then that made a lot of the boys feel, 'Well, I think I could do it a bit better.'

At my Confirmation, I can remember we went up before the bishop two by two, like a sort of Noah's Ark. I knelt down in front of the bishop's chair, and next to me was a chap called Christopher Shilden (I don't know what's happened to him, I think he was an atheist), and the bishop laid his hands on both of us. I remember thinking that was pretty odd at the time. I can also remember my first Communion. No one had ever told me anything about unleavened bread. I thought I was going to receive bread and I received this sort of circular bit of paper. I can remember feeling desperately disappointed, and saying to myself, 'Oh, I thought it was real; it's only a symbol.' And I remember putting it in my pocket – you obviously didn't eat a bit of paper – and then looking at the next guy and seeing him eating it! And I took the Host out of my pocket and put it in my mouth, and that was my first Communion.

One has a large number of definitive moments in one's life, but I suppose I'd been there about three or four years when one Sunday evening we were singing the Magnificat at the top of our voices, and I suddenly burst out laughing: the sheer incongruity of it! The mighty making a take-over bid for the humble and meek! That certainly influenced me a very great deal.

Some bishop or other came to preach, and after the service he said to the headmaster, Claude Elliott, 'I'd like to see the Ordination candidates', which absolutely threw Claude because a headmaster then was a very, very remote figure, not like they are now, and he wouldn't have had the faintest clue who the Ordination candidates were. And he didn't want to offend the bishop, so he rang up Walter Hamilton and asked: 'Have you got any Ordination candidates?' And Walter, sensing the headmaster's extreme discomfiture and anxiety, said to him, 'I've got two sons of clergymen. Would they do?' So I and another boy, Michael Moffatt, went along and were made party to this deception. And we hadn't a clue what sort of questions Ordination candidates were meant to ask of bishops – it was extremely alarming. As my hand was on the knob to be ushered into the episcopal presence, Claude said to me (he obviously had a slight feeling of guilt), 'You do realize, Burrows, you needn't commit yourself . . .'

I never cease to be astonished when some character comes on the box and begins pontificating about politics or economics or something, and one's been at school with that guy, you know exactly what he's like, even if one hasn't seen him for about forty years. I mean, it is fundamentally absurd to see them being in the position of 'an authority', 'an expert'– because those you have been at school with aren't 'experts', they are other little boys.

Well, I think they regard it as an absolute hoot that I'm a bishop – and I agree with them! I do think it very important that bishops shouldn't take themselves too seriously.

There's a certain sort of lay person who may be impressed that I'm an Old Etonian, which depresses me. After all, if people meet me they don't meet 'an Etonian'. Hell's bells! That isn't the first question one asks. Or certainly not in the Church.

I think being a Colleger makes you an Etonian with a difference. Yes, I suppose I'm prouder of being a Colleger than of being an Etonian.

ANDREW CALLENDER

IT is quite daunting when you go there. New boys' tea is the most diabolical occasion of all time. The wee small thirteen-year-olds were put in another room away from their parents and had to sit around this table and eat cakes. And you looked at these people who for the next five years were going to be your contemporaries, and actually the opinions you had in those first five minutes did carry through. The guy who stuffed himself with cakes turned out to be a pig! And another guy who was trying to be very trendy did turn out to be very trendy, and a bit pseudo. The beginning of Eton is a shock to the system. For me just as much, because there was a lot of: 'Oh, you're David Callender's son, are you?', and a lot of people looking at me as though I was something abnormal, which got me terrifically upset.

My father was not a popular master. He was one of the staunch old disciplinarian types of housemaster. No one really knew my father; he didn't have a nickname and I don't think he had a definable charisma at Eton, which a lot of masters have. He was a very good teacher, everyone admits it, but apart from that, no one had very much else to say. My mother went and shouted at some boy in my year, a friend of mine who threw his sausage all over the place or something like that; my mother flew at him in front of everybody, and of course everyone was looking at me, thinking, 'My God, you've got a dragon of a mother!' That was traumatic.

How they could deal with my parents being at the school became very much an indication for me who my friends were — how they could deal with my father blowing up in the street, or putting them on the bill or on tardy book. If they could deal with that, they were better friends. I was Head Boy too eventually, and I think you have to accept that at a school like Eton you don't get very many friends if you're in a position of authority, if you're doing your job reasonably well. I still ended up with quite a few. I mean, you just find out who your real friends are. I think I was making better friends and losing all the periphery, and I think at the end of it I came out with five much closer friends than they might otherwise have been.

The house turned out to be one of the best houses in Eton as far as stability goes, and not having too much of the gay element. There were two houses that were very gay and did do fearful atrocities with younger boys. But as far as my house went it was brilliant. It was built around a courtyard, and that made it a much more cohesive unit. Raef Payne was a very good housemaster, although he had his problems, put it that way. I don't think he was as good for the younger boys as he was for the older ones. Once you were older he was very sympathetic, very knowing, but never got in your way too much. Very good on discipline, in the sense that he never made a big issue of sixteen-, seventeen-year-olds getting drunk on a Saturday night, or whatever.

Our house was renowned for its Debate elections, for their severity and for how novel the ideas we thought up each time the Library elected Debate. You had an election very late at night and, for those who were elected, various things could happen to you. You could be thrown into a cold bath and covered in a sort of shit and shaving-cream mixture brewed in the Library for a very long time, or you might have your legs shaved. The year above me strung people up on laundry rails, naked, wheeled them around the house, and left them there tied. It was quite dangerous. A boy in my father's house nearly died when he was thrown into a boiling hot bath and was pulled out two seconds, they reckon, before he was going to die. If an unpopular person got elected into the Library, of course you took out all your anger and your hatred on the person, and it was shaving pubes and things like that, which is fairly dangerous, you know, an inexperienced eighteen-year-old with his razor out – you didn't twitch. Another thing was that you had to read porn mags to see who could get an erection or whatever. It had a very sexual slant to it.

That, by the way, is a very feared part of Eton life. If you were waiting to get into Library, people would sit up all night and not be able to sleep a wink. Most people go along with it, because although they hate it – I mean, who wants their pubes shaved? – in a way it is a privilege. You didn't want them to be too lenient with you. You wanted them to make a sort of show of the whole thing, and in a way you had to perform back. We were very conscious of this; you had to prove that you were man enough to take it, and eventually to give as good as you got.

At that stage, going through puberty or whatever, there are no women about, you're sexually very, very active, and certainly there are a lot of carnal desires. We had two very pretty young boys, and all the senior boys used to have them as their fags, get them into the Library as much as possible. 'God, you're attractive,' they'd say, 'what a pert little arse you've got', or whatever. There's a strong element of looking at other males with a vague interest, without defining or even knowing what it would actually come down to. I think some people probably did sleep with other boys in my house, but it was always kept under wraps. I didn't. I have a strong revulsion to other men in a sexual sense – it's not actually that I hate gays, some of them are terrific people. I suppose one turned to the old porn mag, which is one way of getting round it. There used to be a whole trade in them, you just passed them on. One person in my house used to sell them as a business. He used to go round with his little black briefcase to other houses, you know, 'Twenty porn mags, yours for . . .' whatever.

I don't think Eton would work with women, but I think that people who come out of that school . . . well, their attitudes to women are just so warped. I mean, no women up to the age of eighteen – it's a long, long time. We just didn't really know how this other creature ticked. It's very unnatural.

I think Eton does make you expect to succeed, whether in academics or sport, or in music, or whatever. There was a terrific drive to get you to pass everything and to get you to pass it very well. Even amongst the boys. We used to all get together, without any master, and sit down in a room and work straight through for five hours, because we all wanted to get 'A's at A-level. It was very important. No one turned around and said, 'You're a swot.' You can't go wrong at Eton if you achieve. The whole school is geared to achieving, and if you look at the people who get into Pop, all of them have achieved something very, very big. Very few people get in on just the 'nice bloke' ticket.

But success at Eton doesn't equal success in life. I reacted against the pressure; you don't want to feel so pressurized ever again. It's not so important achieving, achieving, achieving. And in a way there are a lot of easy options open to Etonians: going into the City or just moving into Daddy's firm, which a lot of people do, getting a job, getting a flat, living a fairly social life, there's no real drive any more. I think I've got my drive back again, but for about three years after Eton I really didn't give a damn what happened to me. It wasn't very important that I succeeded. I never wanted to succeed at Oxford. Looking at most of my friends, it's exactly the same, they didn't do anything at Oxford. A lot of them really don't care what kind of job they get either.

The nearer you are to Eton, the more it is a series of incidents, a series of achievements, a series of high points and low points, but you don't actually begin to think about the whole and what it's doing to you until you've left, until you've got out of the system. I'm not sure still how I look back at Eton. I mean, in ten years' time I'll have some idea how important it was. I'm sure my views will change – they've changed in the last year. At one stage I was very anti my upbringing because I felt I achieved too much too early and that hadn't been good for me, I was living on a sort of bubble which eventually had to burst. Well, I should never have been on that bubble. You have to keep it in perspective. I mean, I try to forget that I was Head Boy. I never let on to people what I did there. You can't prove to people that you're a nice person or that you're going to succeed by what you did four years ago. I wonder about my CV – there's nothing on Oxford and lots on Eton . . . so did this guy give up four years ago? It might have been true. I achieved so much there and in comparison so little at Oxford. I wasn't President of the Union, or whatever, I didn't have a big post like that. Now I think it would be easy for people to say, 'What happened to this guy? Is he still living on the past?' I'm not, but I'm still wondering what I'm going to do. I still haven't come across something that really fires me up; nothing has really attracted me so far. But I do have a tremendous desire to succeed.

At Oxford you are an Etonian. Socially everyone knows you're an Etonian. You see a lot of Etonians. We really do stick together and, as I'm finding out, you do make your lasting friends at Eton. My friendships with two of them have been going on now for nine years, as long as they could have done at my age.

Eton is still far too much in my life, I mean we still talk about Eton a terrific amount. I had a guy asking me two years ago why he didn't get into Pop. He sat me down and said, 'Come on, Andrew, I really want to know', and I said, 'Does it matter to you?' and he said, 'Yes, it does matter to me.' I think it's quite incredible that someone should be wondering about getting into a prefectorial body two years after he's left, when it has no bearing on your life any more. But that, I suppose, is some of the power of it.

I'm lucky, people think I am the most untypical Etonian they've ever met. But even so, when I'm introduced to people it does come up, and you get an instant reaction. Most times there's a very wary, 'Oh, I see', a sort of 'that changes things' idea. No one ever gives a reason why that changes everything, but people have a preconceived idea of what Eton is, and what the people are like there.

I never talk about Eton unless I'm with Etonians. It's just something I would always stay clear of. I think it's a very controversial subject sometimes . . . you don't know how people are going to react. I never talk about it, there's no point. You have to look ahead, you have to try and put all those glories in the past. People sometimes say I'm over-modest about the whole thing, but I want to succeed again. I think in a way the glory of what it meant then, and how you were looked up to, you will never, ever repeat. I think I'm going to have to be damn successful to do that. It's going to be a very different type of achievement as well. Perhaps you can't make a comparison between the two, because you really were a god in Pop – you were looked up to with total awe, which will never happen again. You will never have the same adulation, twelve hundred people looking at us in awe, thinking, 'My God, look at those gods up there!'

Walking down the street at Eton, you just felt as though you could do anything. You had total control over people. People used to look at you as you came down the street. The costume set you apart immediately and made you aloof, and you just shut yourself off from everybody. These were lesser mortals. You wore chequered trousers, a waistcoat of your choice – whatever colour, whatever design – braided tail-coat, stick-ups, a handkerchief if you wanted, a flower if you wanted, you looked very different from everyone else. It really did set you apart.

The people that didn't achieve at Eton are very interested in seeing how the people that did have got on. I mean, they're not actively hoping you fail, but they're quite interested in what actually happens. When something happens and they hear about it, there might be a sort of, 'Oh really? Oh, he didn't make it? How the mighty have fallen', or whatever. My year, we still keep up with what everyone's doing. It's amazing how many people you bump into in London, and it's immediately, 'What's he doing?' 'Oh, he's gone in to the army. Oh dear! That doesn't sound very good.' The Head Boy who took over after me, I still inquire about him. He's something very solid in the City, and I always go, 'Oh my God, how boring.'

I see the next year as the most crucial one. In a year's time, when I leave Oxford, I'll be sitting somewhere in the world, hopefully in a very good job with very good prospects, doing something I really want to do. And what happens in the next five years is going to show to myself and to everybody else that what happened at Eton wasn't just a flash in the pan – that this, the present, is more important to me. Because Eton was unreal. This is real.

LORD CHARTERIS (Provost)

―――――

It was assumed that I would go to Eton, provided I could pass Common Entrance examination, which in my case was by no means a foregone conclusion. And I did in fact get a pass, called Lower Fourth in those days, which was not very distinguished.

But I was very keen to come, I mean I looked forward to it and it was marvellous arriving there. I remember a sudden feeling of freedom. The feeling of suddenly owning things. I remember the excitement of seeing my japanned can in which one's hot water was brought round, and having an armchair of your own to sit in, and all that sort of thing. Wonderful expansion for a boy!

It was a very, very nice house. At Eton I think everybody lived a little bit under the fear of being flogged or beaten, which is quite different now, but on the whole the house that I was in, Lambart's, was an extremely nice house always. It had a tremendous atmosphere about it.

But I've got to say straight away that my life was somewhat spoilt during the early time of my life at Eton because I was made to share a room with my brother, which was a monstrous thing to do – just because he's your brother doesn't mean you're going to get on with him; and in fact we didn't get on, we fought like tigers. There are scars to this day from what we did to each other. It was very disruptive in the early stages, and it took up a lot of energy. We wouldn't argue about anything specific, we just used to fight, God knows what about. I mean, you don't fight about anything really, you fight about the fact that you're jealous of each other.

That's what happened in those days. It was the custom that brothers shared rooms, in order to squeeze another boy into the

house and get another fee, you see, and of course it's very difficult
to break away from custom, particularly at Eton where the
customs have gone on for five or six hundred years, whatever it
is. It doesn't happen now; everybody at Eton has a room to
themselves.

We are great friends now, but it took quite a time to get
through all that.

I was very untidy, very ill-pulled-together. I'd been a very
slow reader, so I was not good academically. I was very keen and
cooperative, though – nice boy I was, not distinguished at all
during my time at Eton, but honourable. I was very gregarious.
I had my friends, I got on with people, I was popular. My dear
brother wasn't particularly, but I was and I had no problem there
at all.

My father was killed in the First War, and I never knew him. My
mother married again, and I had a very nice stepfather whom I was
very fond of. He went to Eton and he raved about it, he loved it.
He won races there and had three of those little shields on his
watch chain. I think his misfortune was that never in after life did
he succeed in the way he succeeded at Eton, and therefore died, I
think, a disappointed man. But this is a well-known syndrome.

I adored Eton really. And I think the beauty of the place has a
tremendous effect on one, you know, not only the buildings, but
the river, the smell of mown grass and all that sort of thing. Very
evocative. I mean, it's not the sort of thing that you analyse and
talk about, but it has a lasting effect on you.

I think Eton did me pretty well really, but I'm supposed to
have artistic talent, and that wasn't discovered at Eton. I don't
know why it was missed out. I didn't discover until I was thirty-
five that I could sculpt. I remember there was a very intelligent
master called George Snow, and one half he said, 'Every member
of the division has got to produce a work of art: doesn't matter
what it is, it can be a model, it can be a poem, it can be an essay,
or a painting.' And I decided to make a working model of a
Hebridean handloom for tweed – and I won the first prize with
it. But that was that. Finished. I think they ought to have found
out that I had a little talent.

Anyway, Eton didn't bring that out. I suspect it's better at doing it now than it was then, because there are many more facilities. We now have a theatre in which you can act: I would certainly have acted if there'd been a theatre. Also, I was in a rather lag division, I was what they called a 'Kappa boy' and I wasn't considered bright enough to do Greek, which was a huge disappointment. I adored the sounds of Greek language, even at that age, and I longed to learn Greek, but I wasn't allowed to.

Well, I would have liked to have been in Pop but I wasn't. I would have liked to have played cricket for Eton but I was never any good – I never got any cricket colour at all. It was a bit of a disappointment, but it wasn't corrosive in any way.

You could have literally knocked me over with a feather, I think it was in 1975 and I was working for the Queen at Buckingham Palace as her Private Secretary, when Peter Carrington, who was a Fellow of Eton, said could he come and have five minutes. We sat at my round table in the office at Buckingham Palace, and he said, 'The Fellows would like you to succeed Harold Caccia as Provost.' 'You must be mad,' I said – I mean, I thought he was absolutely crazy to suggest it. 'Do you realize that I never went to university, I've got absolutely no academic qualifications at all?' And he said, 'I've checked that's all right.' So there it was, and I took a long time to make up my mind about it, I wasn't at all certain that I wanted to come back. And also I'm not certain at that stage I was so madly sure of the virtues of private education as opposed to the maintained sector, and there's no good coming here unless you're prepared to give your heart's blood for private education. But after a month or two I decided I would, and here I am.

I came back without knowing very much about it. And what fascinated me was to consider which was the more remarkable, the differences or the similarities over fifty years. So much was similar – the look of things, it smelt the same, it sounded the same, the clock was the same, the same noise of people going into Chapel at the last minute and all that sort of thing. One thing that's exactly the same about Etonians is that they still have that ability to put their elders at their ease; it's the ethos of the place, the famous Eton self-confidence, they understand how to talk, they're articulate.

So I started by thinking that the similarities were the more remarkable. Then I came to the conclusion that was not so. I think the changes are much more profound, and I think that they're almost wholly for the good, all of them. I think it's a far, far better place than it was, perhaps than it's ever been. It's a much more civilized place, the education is much more liberal and, of course, the facilities are wonderful.

And also people don't go about in the fear of being flogged within an inch of their lives – it's all finished, that sort of thing. I'm all for it being less frightening. And the relationship between senior and junior boys seems to be very easy, and there's not the same antagonism between the Collegers and the Oppidans as there used to be.

Of course we're not co-educational in any way, but the campus is crawling with pretty wives and children and all that sort of thing. So Eros has slipped into the corners to a very considerable extent, and I think this is wholly good.

I think that arrogance is always the danger for Etonians, but I don't think the present boys are arrogant as a whole. You get some arrogant ones, of course you do. But the great thing is that I don't think any Eton boy imagines the world owes him a living any more. I really don't. They are very conscious of the need to qualify and go on after life here.

I remember, when I came here as Provost, being told by the boys that if you were interviewed and somebody asked where you went to school, you would say, 'Eton, I'm afraid.' I think that's bad. They should say, 'Eton.' Leave it at that – and then say 'thank God' under their breath. I always said, 'Eton, thank God', and I was always extremely proud of being here. I've never found it anything but a huge advantage in my life. But everybody's got to be equal now, haven't they? You know, elitism is under suspicion. I hope we're getting over that.

Of course there are faults left. I mean nothing is perfect, and anybody who thinks Eton's perfect wants his head looking at. We can improve it all the time.

If anybody had said to any of my contemporaries when I was at Eton, 'That boy there is going to be the Provost one day,' they would have roared with laughter. My tutors would have considered it totally and completely absurd – that I can promise you. Well, they're all used to it now, of course, and they're courteous enough not to roar with laughter when they see me here!

I mean, to be possibly arrogant, I now think that when I was asked to come back here as Provost they were not crazy, oddly. I think I do have certain qualities which are useful here: I know the outside world, I like people, and for thirty years I had served intimately a head of state,* so I know something of honourable and ancient institutions.

*Her Majesty the Queen.

NICHOLAS COLERIDGE

———

MY father was there, and endless relations. There is a room called the Upper Chamber which has names carved on the wall; and one of the first things that I can remember about Eton was being taken down to visit it, and seeing the huge number of terribly misshapen carvings of the name Coleridge standing out from the others. So I suppose that, for a very long period of my life, public school meant Eton, and I don't think it ever crossed my mind that I might go anywhere else.

However, although when I went to my preparatory school, aged eight, I was really rather bright, by the time I was thirteen I was ridiculously stupid, and when I came to sit the Common Entrance exam all the predictions that I would fail it miserably proved to be absolutely so. There was a period when it wasn't clear whether I was going to Eton at all.

In the meanwhile, I had gone to see Milton Abbey with my parents on an extremely wet and windy day. I can't remember where Milton Abbey is, except that it is in one of the most distant counties of Britain – probably somewhere like Somerset, I should think – and we drove about eleven miles from the nearest village until one reached this very forbidding school, which I realized, even aged thirteen and even before we got there, was a place that I didn't want to go to. The school had very, very large dormitories of fifty or sixty boys, with no curtains, which I thought was a very poor sign, and I was told that boys entertained themselves by bicycling the eleven miles to the nearest village on Saturday afternoons. And as we left, my mother said cheerily, 'What a very nice school Milton Abbey is', thinking that it would be the only place that would take me in. I said that I thought it was preposterously isolated and that I was absolutely determined to have another crack at Eton.

Luckily I scraped in, and arrived as a very unsophisticated person. My prep school had a very elderly headmaster and had been run on very, very traditional lines, and I think I was quite surprised by how much more sophisticated my contemporaries seemed to be. Craig Brown, the writer, became a very great friend. He arrived the same term and was in the same house, and he was much more informed and more worldly, and much less in awe of the place, than I was; it took me about a year to catch up. I would say that I was probably very dull in my first year at Eton, and found the work very difficult. But I was one of those people who, as I was able to drop those subjects that I was bad at, was suddenly discovered to be really quite clever.

What I like about Eton is the fact that it is so urban. When I think of it now, one of the first images that comes into my mind is the great proximity of W. H. Smith's in Windsor, where I spent a very long time browsing among the magazine and news-paper racks. And I liked the fact that there were record shops and ABC and Kardomah ice-cream bars, and the fact that one could go shopping.

My housemaster was Giles St Aubyn, a very great but ex-tremely eccentric Eton housemaster, and it was my incredible good luck to be in his house because I have no doubt, looking back on it, that almost everything that I found particularly jolly about Eton might not have been as jolly had I been in a different house.

I arrived in 1970, so the sixties were still the prevailing in-fluence at the top of the house. The boys who were seventeen or eighteen wore black T-shirts, had photographs of themselves taken at the Isle of Wight pop festival, and had their rooms covered with tinfoil and Indian fabric. I remember being rather impressed by that.

In fact I arrived at exactly the moment when Eton was in the midst of change, and I very much liked that. The sound of jazz and Grateful Dead and Pink Floyd and things resounded everywhere, and the school wasn't particularly traditional at that time. I was ridiculously impressed by those rather trendy people at the top of the house; they had very well-cut hair, and wore jeans of a sort that I wouldn't have even known where to get, because I was still shopped for by my mother in the Harrods boys' department. All I can remember in my first year was thinking what an amazing, cool place it was.

All sorts of things at Eton were changing. The necessity to go every day to Chapel was ending at that point. There were a great deal fewer restrictions about clothes. The *Chronicle*, which used to be written largely in Greek on yellow pages, went tabloid, and had photographs and became facetious and topical. Fagging was on the out. Beating had ended, pretty well – certainly it never came into my life at all.

Of the people that I met in my first five halves there, several have remained my greatest friends to this day. The friendships I made at Eton provide the entire infrastructure for my life now. In fact it is probably true to say that of the ten men friends that I have, certainly eight are Etonians met during that very short period, and I have not the slightest doubt that it will remain so until I die. Eton made a much more profound impact on me than Cambridge, which I would say really made none, and all my attitudes and real friends were made at Eton.

Craig Brown and I set up something called the Contemporary Arts Society which was where we invited tremendously trendy people to come down and speak, and hardly a week went by when Elton John wasn't arriving in his gold Rolls-Royce, or Angie Bowie was somewhere around, or Brian Ferry or whoever. So by the time I left Eton I was an appalling sort of media hanger-on figure, a groupie, using Eton for all it was worth, because a great fact of the world is that almost nobody can resist an invitation to come and speak at Eton, if it is written in a polite way, with its closeness to London and everything else about it.

We put on a play about the marriage of Captain Mark Phillips and Princess Anne, which was extensively written up in the *Sun* newspaper under the heading, 'Eton Boys in a Royal Howler', and we became rather obsessed, actually, with doing controversial plays and quietly tipping off the papers. It seemed to be so ridiculously easy to have something that was only a very small thing suddenly become half of page five of the *Sun*. The *Sun* is a paper that always has room for an Eton story, written to that formula they have: 'Chaps at Britain's grandest public school (fees seventeen thousand five hundred pounds a year) . . .' We were often tipping them off that Elton John was visiting Eton or something, and then two or three of their men would be lurking around, and we were always hoping to be photographed with him.

It was a terrific advantage to have gone to Eton, from the point of view of being a journalist. I have no doubt at all that one of the reasons a lot of Etonians who were my contemporaries have become journalists is because the *Eton Chronicle* was so terribly good. I don't think there is another public school that has a fortnightly, extremely well-presented school magazine which has a whole network of editors and deputy editors and features editors and things, and that was published, I imagine, at a terrific loss to Eton – for which all credit to them, and I hope they keep it going for ever.

One of the most surreal things about Eton is the fact that you only have to go three miles in any direction to be in some of the most troubled parts of the country. I was there during a period when people from Slough were often roving around on motorcycles with a view to mugging boys in the street. There was rather a shy boy in my year called Philip Daubeny, and I remember an extraordinary story which showed him in a very brave light. He was ringing his parents from a telephone box on the Corner of Common Lane when suddenly a gang of fifteen Hell's Angels surrounded the telephone kiosk, and started revving their bikes and removing lengths of bicycle chain. Because his mother wasn't feeling terribly well at home, he didn't tell her this as he didn't want to worry her, and as soon as he came out he was appallingly attacked.

I can't remember being at all academic; it just wasn't terribly important. I remember it as being something that punctuated the things I wanted to do, which were the *Eton Chronicle* and the Contemporary Arts, and acting, and the Debating Society, which became a great focus of my life. In my last year I won the Jeremy Thorpe Cup for debating, though if you tell someone that you won the Jeremy Thorpe Cup at Eton, they look at you rather suspiciously.

I specialized in English, theology and ancient history. I chose theology because it sounded a rather pleasant minority subject. Only four or five boys do it. I had been told by somebody that at A-level the only other people who do theology are girls who are taught by nuns at convent schools, and therefore the standard is tremendously low; so anything that would get you a 'C' grade in any other subject immediately became an 'A'.

I used to spend afternoons in Tap, eating endless avocado pears and prawns, and 'long eggs', as they were called, which were scrambled eggs on a bap. I would drink two pints of Tavern, which was the particular type of beer they had, and gossip and chat, and eat this food. Mrs Moulton ran Tap, and you would say, 'Can I have two pints of Tavern, Mrs Moulton, and one of your long eggs?' She would say, 'Down on the National Debt, Coleridge?' which would be your account, and then at the end of the half you would say, 'How much is the damage on the National Debt, Mrs Moulton?', and she would reply, 'Not too bad, Coleridge, not too bad!' She would then write it carefully on a piece of paper which was passed highly discreetly across the counter.

I was very lucky to be in Giles St Aubyn's house because it is remembered by our contemporaries as being the house where the most number of people who were nice and quite go-ahead and to some extent interesting were; it was rather a cultured house, actually. Perhaps the fact that Giles wrote numerous books gave it a sort of added colour, compared with various other houses whose housemasters were interested really only in whether their under-fourteen rowing team could catch the boat in front. I don't think I would have been a great asset to a house like that, and therefore I might not have been so happy.

I think it would be unfair to say that he wasn't pleased when his house did well in games, but by and large Giles St Aubyn's house wasn't a good games-playing house, and there was no particular suggestion that it should be. I can't remember really, after the age of fifteen, feeling any compunction, moral or statutory, to play any sort of sport of any kind at all.

I have seen him several times since, and he is a very subtle and infinitely interesting man. There are far too many Eton masters who don't have a life beyond the school. It is rather like the new kind of Thatcherite Tory in that there are too many efficient and bureaucratic and rather dull men teaching there now. But Giles St Aubyn came from that tradition of the man of independent means who was academic and an author, and during the holidays he would be in London and go to his club and have friends who were nothing to do with that world of Eton.

Giles was in some ways quite an awkward man. He found it very difficult to make conversation at lunch, and so he would try and think of stock subjects, rather like a talking point of the day, to occupy it. He would ask poser questions, like: 'Were I marooned on a desert island for six weeks, which boy in the house would be most useful to have there too?', in this rather stilted way of talking. He was tremendously rich, and made a great point of being terribly rich. Sometimes, again to fill time, he would jangle coins in his pocket, and would say, 'I have a quantity of money in my pocket. If any boy can guess what it is to the nearest half pence, they can have it. But before you guess, you must bear two things in mind. One, I am very well dressed, so I would not have very much change in my pocket. On the other hand, it is well known that I am immensely rich, so for all you know I could have many, many thousands of pounds, without it causing me the slightest of problems.'

He was pretty well the last (although Nigel Jaques, I think, to some extent continues that role) of those slightly eccentric – in Giles's case, really quite eccentric – Eton housemasters.

Subsequently, having talked to boys at other schools that weren't Eton, I realize that we were extremely well informed and urbane. I can remember listening to speeches and talks by almost everybody in the Cabinet who would have come during the time that I was there. We read the newspapers pretty carefully, and we listened to the wireless, and there was a constant to-ing and fro-ing of people coming down. When I went to Trinity at

Cambridge, the first person I met was someone who was a school friend who had already been at Cambridge for a year; when I asked what Cambridge was like, he said, 'Oh, it is so dull, it is so provincial after Eton. It is full of people being excited about having their first cheque books.' And although that was obviously a grossly snobbish remark to make, it had a sort of truth in that although Eton was like all public schools, to some extent insular and inward-looking and archaic, the boys there were pretty sophisticated.

In fact, in the *Eton Chronicle* we wrote endlessly on the subject of how cut off Eton was from the real world. But having said that, I can't seriously pretend that it terribly worried me. There was too much happening that interested me.

By the time I was seventeen, the things I wanted to do had already leapt ahead of school in a kind of way, and my heroes were very much the editors and feature editors of the magazines that I admired. Those were the people that I really wanted to be in with. I can remember terribly distinctly being in W. H. Smith's in Windsor and looking at magazines in the rack, and looking at the mastheads, the lists of people who worked for them; their names held a tremendous lustre, completely out of proportion to their real worth.

I am bound to say that if I meet somebody that I have never met before, say if I am travelling abroad, or through work or something, and it emerges that they were there, I feel an interest in them that is multiplied by at least ten. There are certain people who weren't there, and I do admit that in some strange way I think, 'Now, why weren't they?' And I know in some awful way that it counts against them slightly. If we are being completely candid, I do accept that I prefer the company of Etonians to the company of people from other public schools.

I have got a great friend called Napier Miles, who is probably one of my greatest chums, and we often reminisce in quirky ways about it late at night, about strange, surreal incidents. I know that Craig Brown always accuses us both of being to some extent obsessed by it, though we are not really.

We were once in a taxi near Taroudant in Morocco, and the

driver drove, at our instructions, out into the sand because we wanted to see what real desert looked like. And after we had driven four hours out, the taxi turned round and we came back and were becoming extremely bored. So we filled the time by giving ourselves one hour each to write down as many boys as we could remember in the school that were contemporaries. You scored one point if we both got their name, two points if only one of us got the name, and three points if it was one of those particularly piquant, almost forgotten boys — you know how in any school there are one or two people that you can hardly remember were there at all, but suddenly, when their name is mentioned, they come back to you with a terrible clarity. That, I suppose, is a sign of a terrible kind of obsession, though it isn't one that strikes very often, because it is not very often that I take long taxi rides in Morocco!

TAM DALYELL, MP

I WAS put down at the age of eleven, and got one of those chance places that became available in a house that was run by R. T. Assheton. And it was very much a cancellation, because I hadn't been put down from birth. R. T. Assheton was a scientist, a charming man of whom I have the happiest memories but, alas, only of a year, because after my first year he suddenly became afflicted with cancer and died. It was a fast and visible deterioration, and it was something of a shock, because one has a very close relationship with one's housemaster for the first two or three years.

And I fagged for a man called Paul Graham-Watson, who left Eton, went into the Scots Guards, and after cursory training – the normal officer training, I suppose – was sent to Malaya and was killed in the Malayan jungle. And that was terribly upsetting, much more in fact than R. T. Assheton's death, because he was near sixty. When nineteen-year-olds whom one has known are killed in action, it does give one a certain attitude to war in general and, I suspect, to colonial adventures in particular.

I'd better explain to you: the first Dalyell that we know about in detail was a man called Thomas Dalyell, who was a butter merchant. And in 1599 he married Janet Bruce, the daughter of the Master of the Rolls, Lord Kinloss. In 1603 James VI of Scotland became James I of England, and took with him various people who would be useful to him, including his Master of the Rolls. He in turn took various people who were useful to him, including his son-in-law, Thomas Dalyell, who in nine years in London, between 1603 and 1612, made enough money – don't press me as to how – to move back to Scotland, buy a parcel of land and build most of the house at Binns where I now live and have lived all my life. He was one of the so-called 'Hungry Scots'. . . people who did well out of the fact that a Scot became King of England.

But I think that I ought to finish this question. Thomas Dalyell had a son, and his name was Tam. He appears in the novels of Sir Walter Scott as 'a bloody Muscovite', but actually he was an extremely interesting, sophisticated character. The first we definitely know about him is that he was taken prisoner at the Battle of Worcester and was sent to Dudley Castle, and then to the Tower of London, from which he was one of the few people ever to have escaped. Then he was given letters of recommendation to the Russian Czar, Alexis Michaelavitch, the father of Peter the Great, and he served at Twer, first against the Turks and then the Tartars, and was rewarded by the Czar with various presents which we actually have on show at the Binns. He came back to Scotland in 1666, and because everybody of sufficient seniority had gone over to Cromwell, he was made Commander-in-Chief. His relationship with the King was a close one and we have the portrait of Charles II by Kneller that was given him as a present. He lived at the Binns and beautified it, and in 1679, when the Covenanting problems had become acute, he founded a regiment called the Scots Greys. So Tam Dalyell is a celebrated figure in Scottish history.

My house was taken over by Tom Brocklebank after R. T. Assheton's death. Now Tom Brocklebank was an extremely difficult man. He could be very cutting and sarcastic, and he was moody, sometimes malicious. He had been on Everest expeditions, and he was an international rower. He was an appreciator of the arts. He was my great friend after I left. He was difficult as a housemaster. This may have been a very good thing, and I agree with Michael McNair-Wilson, who is a Tory MP and who was also in my house, that probably the difficulty of having Tom Brocklebank rather hardened us long-term and helped us in coping with difficult people.

Having said that, he took a real interest, and, give him credit, because I and a number of my friends were interested in art, what did he do? Ring up his friend Anthony Blunt and get us shown around the Courtauld by Anthony Blunt himself. A marvellous experience. So I take a rather different view from the rest of my colleagues on Blunt. I think he was bloody well asked to tip off Burgess and McLean by Guy Liddell and Dick Brooman-White because MI5 wanted a quiet life. So there we are. In retrospect, Brocklebank was a very good housemaster.

In 1945 Eton was a very serious, rather sombre place. Remember what had happened – all these beaks had been away at the war and were gradually coming back. Those who had been there during the war were mostly rather elderly, often doing it well beyond retirement. And my impression on arrival was that we were expected to work hard.

I did German, and that was part of the beginning of a good relationship with Robert Birley, because the German specialists used to take his German guests round Eton. I had been asked to take some of them round, and he asked me, 'How did you get on with them?' I said that I was a bit shocked because I had asked the lady which was the most beautiful city in Germany ('*die schönste Stadt . . .*'). Her answer was 'Prague'! I thought that this was rather a strange answer, and he said, 'Well, that teaches you something', and from that moment I got on well with Birley. Elinor Birley, in her letter to me, said that Birley had a continuing interest throughout his life in what he called the 'Eton Rebels' and I remained a friend of Birley until he died.

Tom Brocklebank, like Birley, was very much for exposing us to points of view other than those associated with the upper class. He used to send us in the evenings to meetings of the local Labour candidate, Fenner Brockway. I remember a lot of people coming to the school. I remember, for instance, the first Labour MP who I happened to hear at the Political Society explain how he was an ambitious politician and wasn't ashamed of it, and his name then was Len Callaghan! I know Jim very well now, and he was my Prime Minister. I remember Arthur Deakin, the boss of the Transport and General Workers Union, coming to Eton, and Ian Mikardo and Geoffrey Byng of the Labour left. And as an Old Etonian Labour MP I am invited and I like to go.

I am often dubbed the Old Etonian Labour MP, I think sort

of for curiosity value. It is in all the files. But I have never hidden my Eton background from anybody. I have never tried to sweep anything under the carpet. Take it or leave it.

Macmillan was very kind to me on one particular occasion, and they said to me Macmillan *would* bloody well do that – one left-wing Etonian looking after another left-wing Etonian. Until then I wouldn't have admitted it, but I did slightly see the point.

I have only once been chided with being an Etonian, and it was a very interesting occasion. And the chiders were two people who were extremely well disposed towards me. One was James Callaghan and the other was Ray Gunter. The occasion was a Parliamentary Labour Party meeting, and I was at that time Chairman of the Parliamentary Labour Party Education Committee. I got up and said that rather than keeping the school-leaving age at sixteen, wouldn't it be more sensible to have the leaving date after fifteen, but at the end of the school year, so that everybody completed their school year. Jim Callaghan took me aside and said, 'Look. You had better realize that you've had the best. People like me who left school at fourteen always realize it, and don't you go round saying that we are going to renege on anything under sixteen.' Now it was done in a friendly way, but it was a rebuke for an Etonian making any suggestion, albeit an Etonian who cared about state education.

What is said about a number of my contemporaries is that Etonians are quietly arrogant. And sometimes my own colleagues, who are my friends, say of me: 'You are so bloody sure that you are right.' Now whether this is self-confidence or whether it is arrogance I don't know. But I couldn't have pursued Mrs Thatcher on a whole number of issues unless one had had a sort of calmness and confidence that what one was saying was correct.

Curiously enough, in the Tory Party the edgy Etonian relationships are between people who want a senior ministerial appointment, or a less junior ministerial appointment. They are not in competition with me personally. They may in general terms be in competition with the Labour Party, and some of them may not like my politics very much because I am so personal to Mrs

Thatcher, believing that many of the tragedies of this country, the miners' strike, the Falklands War, lay at her door rather than at the door of the Conservative Party. So they are a bit careful of their public relations with me, because they don't want to be seen to be in cahoots with me against their own Prime Minister, whom I loathe! But private relations are very good.

There are one's contemporaries from Eton, people with whom one has worked and been friendly for forty years. I can think of one friend of mine, a man who was in my house, who is afflicted by illness, which he has fought bravely, gutfully and courageously. When I see him sitting there looking old on the Tory back benches I have a great admiration for his spunk and his courage in fighting illness, but because he was a contemporary, and because I knew him very well, it does certainly bring home one's sense of mortality.

I wasn't enamoured with what I saw when I had been down on a number of occasions to talk to the Political Society. I thought that it had become much more of an upper-class place. I just got the impression that the Eton of 1945–50 was one thing, and that the modern Eton is another. You see, Eton is fine if you want to produce pro-consuls. If you want to produce leaders of British industry, I am not so sure. I am dismayed at the number of talented Etonians who just gravitate towards the City. I have no doubt that the queues of Etonians going into the City to make money for themselves would have shocked many of the people who taught me. I am absolutely confident in saying that Robert Birley would have been quite appalled. I know what certain beaks who greatly influenced me would have expected. And I think of René Peyrefitte, I think of Oliver Hunkin, of Captain Chamier, the teacher of mathematics, I think of that brutal man but a very good teacher of biology, Gaddum; I think of my own tutor Brocklebank, of A. J. Marsden, Bush Forrest, Peter Hazell, Peter Lawrence, and many others who taught me. They wouldn't have cared very much about outward success. But what they wouldn't like is for people on whom they had taken trouble to waste their lives. The atmosphere was: 'You have been very lucky, you've had a privileged education, we hope that you do something with it.' Now this is rather different from becoming *quelqu'un*. This is one of the things that I must tell you about Eton beaks in 1945–50. My impression is that they worked extremely hard on behalf of their boys, and they would expect those boys over a life-span to do something for their country.

THE HON. WILLIAM DOUGLAS-HOME

THE train was full of Scotsmen from Berwick-on-Tweed that morning when you came down. My papa in his bowler hat took me down and handed me over to the housemaster.

I thought it was rather small when I got there, a lot of little trees lying about and all the houses very close together.

The first year I was with a lovely old thing called Wells, a Greek scholar, a very famous man who caught every salmon of weights from four pounds up to seventy, and he used to fish in Norway a lot. But he never caught a forty-nine-pound salmon, and he used to put everything back that wasn't forty-nine pounds. He was longing to catch one. He didn't talk much to the small boys; if a boy went in to see him when he was doing his *Times* crossword or something, he always used to say, 'Refused. Eating a bun', because he was always eating a bun. And the story goes that he was walking down Bond Street one day, and a lady of the night said, 'Evening, dearie' or something, and Mr Wells said, 'Refused. Eating a bun', and walked on. Whether that's true, I don't know.

Mr Wells retired. Then I was handed over to a man called Howson. He was a perfectly charming man. A rather quiet fellow, but very, very nice. Very shy and very nervous. He had this splendid dame called Miss Owen who looked after you when you had a stomach-ache or something. She was a lovely girl. Splendid thing that, at a highly moral public school, a bachelor and a spinster are allowed to live in exactly the same house together! It is rather amazing, isn't it?

The food wasn't too good. If you didn't like the food, Miss

Owen used to say, 'There's always ham', and you could go and have a bit of ham. I stood for Parliament in Windsor during the war, and I got a telegram from North Africa from a man called Heneage who was in my house. It arrived at the polling station and it said, 'If you don't win today, don't forget there's always ham!' Cheered me up quite a lot!

Charles Mott-Radclyffe, Sir Charles . . . have you met him? He was the one I stood against and he beat me. He was in my house too. Very nice, dear old thing, he still lives in Essex or somewhere.

I shared for a while with my brother. I had this bronchial cough at night and he used to put a rather heavy suitcase on my chest to stop me coughing. It worked wonders – I haven't had it since. That was Henry, the one who wrote books about birds. He was only there a year, then he went to Oxford.

I then messed with a man called Peter Beresford-Peirse, who died a very distinguished clergyman. My brother Henry used to say he ought to be a bishop because he had the most marvellous calves to his legs.

And then the next year I messed with a young man called Tennyson, who was the poet's grandson. He was killed in the war – he crashed in an airplane rather like the Duke of Kent did up in the north of Scotland. But he started me writing, because he used to be an editor of the school magazine, *The Burning Bush*, and he said, 'Will you write a story in it?' I'd never written anything, but I gave it a try. I think it was about a grouse or some such bird.

I was a very cheerful sort of boy, not too good at cricket and a friend of Johnston* and all that lot. Johnston says he was very good at cricket. Did he tell you? Do you think he was? He was the second-eleven wicket-keeper, and his argument was that the first-eleven wicket-keeper stayed till he was thirty-one, with a wife and seven children – which he didn't at all, he left at the normal time. But he just wasn't as good as him. Johnston was very cheerful, the eight-foot nose, always making jokes in school, and the masters saying, 'Johnston, if you make another joke like

*Brian Johnston.

that you'll be asked to leave the room.' Very popular lad; we all liked him.

I had to beat somebody once, and there was a boy called Gore-Booth in my house who longed to be in the Library, and wanted to see somebody beaten. And I had to beat somebody the evening Gore-Booth got into the Library. I swung the cane for the first blow, and it hit the door by mistake and a splinter came off and went into Gore-Booth's eye. He was taken off to the dame and he never saw any of the beating at all. Teach him a lesson, won't it!

Alington preached these marvellous sermons on Sunday evenings. Instead of going to the dame, boys who got flu on Sunday morning didn't tell her until after the evening service; they wanted to listen to it. He really was good. He looked most distinguished in the candlelight, and then he blew the candles out rather elegantly at the end.

Mrs Alington was the best girl in the world. She looked like the Duchess in *Alice in Wonderland*. My friend Jo Grimond, who was in my house, was President of the Political Society and he asked Mr Gandhi down to give a talk. Gandhi had that girlfriend of his, Miss Slade, with him. They came back to the headmaster's house where they were staying, and Mr Gandhi went to bed because he said he was tired after his talk. And when Mrs Alington went to bed half an hour later, there on the mat outside Gandhi's door was Miss Slade lying under a blanket with a pillow. Mrs Alington said, 'Go to your room, Miss Slade.' And Miss Slade said, 'But I've slept outside the dear Mahatma's door for the last seven years, every night', to which Mrs Alington replied, 'Not while I'm President of the Women's Institute you don't', and made her get up and put her into her bedroom and locked the door. Splendid idea, isn't it?

I did write a play in the last year. It was about a housemaster being murdered in his pupil room. I wanted to play the lead, but Dr Alington put his foot down and said it was subversive. And suddenly I had this great brainwave. I'd met Master Giles Alington, who was his son, in the street, and I asked him, 'Will you play the leading part in my play, Giles?' and he said 'Yes' –

and the ban was lifted then, so it was all right. I played a minor role.

The housemaster wrote to my papa and said, 'I was very impressed by William's play and so was his history tutor, and we think that he should try and carry on in that line', or something like that.

I get it from dramatic critics who don't like me because they think I've got a feudal background. I might have been more successful if I hadn't been to Eton. Mr Tynan used to start his reviews, 'The Honourable William tells us in Act I . . .', he did really, in the *Observer*. I wrote a play about the war, and Tynan put, 'Not many of the officers in the regiment described in this play could have been at Eton because they're much more broadminded than one could expect from such an author as this.' I mean, it's going too far, isn't it?

MARK FIENNES

I SUPPOSE I had parents who wanted to conform to the system, so I had the misfortune to be sent away to boarding school, which is something I always swore I'd never do to my own children. But I was sent away, the good old British system, being hoofed out of the nursery at seven or eight and sent hundreds of miles away to boarding school and a completely hostile pack situation. My mother was a superb home-maker, and it was warm and it was cosy and one was loved and all the rest of it, so boarding school could only be said to be a thoroughly cathartic experience, a real shock to the system.

Obviously one had been broken in by prep school but Eton was a much bigger pond, and I had the misfortune of being educated during the war years, which was when anybody who was any good had gone away to fight and most of the people who were left were old or has-beens. And I had the great misfortune of arriving three weeks late in my first half at Eton, due to measles contracted during the Christmas holidays, so I was unable to kick off at the beginning of the term with the other new boys in the house. So that didn't help matters. The other thing was that the spring of '47 coincided with an extremely severe winter, weeks and weeks of frost and snow which suddenly melted in March, and the Thames flooded, and Eton was flooded, and literally there was water washing around the doors and people were punting up and down the street, and the whole of the Thames Valley was awash. Everybody was sent home early, but not Mark Fiennes, who was sick in bed with the flu and had to remain behind. So it wasn't at all a good start.

I arrived as the lowest form of life, I mean that's all part of the English educational system – or maybe it's part of life – that one moment you're up, then you're knocked down, then you climb laboriously like an ant to the top of the package again – and then you're blown off again. Eton was a definite down for me, and I was not happy really the whole time I was there. But one learnt to grin and bear it and put on the façade of enjoying its camaraderie and so on.

Lots of my father's family had been to Eton and when I arrived the name of Fiennes was plastered all over the games boards, being *victor ludorum* in squash, rackets, fives, the field, cricket – you name it, they'd won it. I was not a good athlete, so it was pretty hard to live up to. I hadn't much brain either, so I fell into that wodge of mediocrities whom nobody encouraged very much anyway, and the only times that one ever did get near the top of a marks system in one form or other, you were always told you could do better. And I didn't like team games, I disliked ball games *en principe*, and so I rowed uselessly up and down the river for four years with never any great distinction – although I did enjoy Saturdays, rowing up to Cliveden, right up the Thames as far as one could go and back again, because it was getting away from the mob, I suppose.

Everybody wanted to put the clock back, the whole thing was: 'We must get back to Eton as it was before the war.' With rationing and all that, top-hat manufacturers stopped manufacturing top hats, so they became a relic, but people went on having them as a sort of nice antique gesture – so there you had in a nutshell the essence of the thing: 'Must put it back to how it was before the war'; heavy accent on classics, flogging through *De Bello Gallico* and the *Aeneid* was still the thing.

But I think that the thing I disliked about Eton most of all, and still dislike to this day, is that it symbolizes, it epitomizes, the English hierarchical system, and God, how the English love hierarchy. Although they say they don't, although they may bitch and whinge behind the scenes (and probably rip their overlords off as hard as they can), they love the forelock-touching and the kowtowing. You can see it with their adulation of royalty; because there is no God in England any more, royalty are the dynasty, they are the people that symbolize the system, right the way down through the Right Honourable This and the Lady That and the Lord This. 'Everybody loves a lord,' they say: look at the country houses, how everybody comes to see them now. And Eton was the cradle of that, with privileges and Pop. You arrived as a lower boy, you were the lowest form of life; the senior boys over you could beat you physically, legally could swipe you; when you fagged, the older boys could scream at the top of their voices through the house, 'B-o-o-o-y', and you would run like scared rabbits to do their bidding. And what was he? A seventeen-year-old, spotty-faced, downy-lipped, self-important little popinjay, and that, I think, is the start of the problem.

And my God, you can see them still! If you walk down the High Street of Eton and look in through the photographer's window, you can see Pop ranged on the Chapel steps, their curly locks and their fancy waistcoats and sponge bag trousers, those proud, sneering, arrogant, Ascendancy faces, now, there, today, with the same names as were there in my day, lolling on the steps, lounging back in Victorian attitudes, superiority and supremacy. And who are they? They are nothing, most of them, they would be nothing if it wasn't for Daddy's money. Possibly they *are* brilliant if they are scholars and they have done very well, but they symbolize the hierarchy at the school.

I know it's all changed now and all changed for the better, but by God it needed to change for the better.

In my day the headmaster started off being somebody called Claude Elliott, and then he became Provost, and Robert Birley, otherwise known as Red Robert, then became the Headmaster. He was tall, Olympian, a very pale figure who could only be described as shuffling or waddling down the Long Walk with his gown and mortarboard, and you had to raise your hand to cap the beak – more signs of obeisance, kowtowing to authority. I never spoke to the headmaster until the day I left, when we were all presented with a standard leaving present, a book of Thomas Gray's poems. And of course he had to spell my name in Latin, and of course he spelt it wrong.

I think that everything is much more democratic now. For anyone who has a genuine beef or complaint or wants to talk about problems, the headmaster's study is open for him, I gather. But it certainly wasn't in my day, because if you felt ill or worried you had to cover it up, you didn't talk about it. And that brings me to my other great criticism of Eton. Although my house was excellently run by the housemaster, m'tutor, and Mrs m'tutor, and m'dame was a charming lady, she was totally, totally un-qualified to be a dame. If somebody was sickening with measles, mumps or whooping cough, she could only just recognize it, and off you would go to the sick-bay. Of course I suppose malinger-ing is endemic in every schoolboy; in those days we used to have early school, which meant winter and summer alike being on parade at half-past seven in the morning, and people used to say they felt ill to get out of going to school. But I did not feel well a lot of the time I was there. We lived in very unsanitary conditions, the house was ancient and like a rabbit warren, no heating at all except tiny little coal-fire grates in every room and lumps of coal. One lump the size of the grate would be brought up every day from the coal-scuttle, otherwise there was no central heating or anything in the house. And when I complained about not feeling well, I was told, 'Nonsense, nonsense, you're skiving.' Then in the end I was noticed by a master in one of the classes to be looking unwell, and he reported it to m'tutor, who reported it the dame, who said, 'You'd better go along and see the doctor.' And so I went down to the doctor, and it turned out I had a serious kidney infection. I had to go and see a specialist in London who wrote a report to my parents, beginning with words I was never allowed to forget: 'I find a somewhat, weedy youth . . .' So I was always known as 'the weedy youth' after that. But it meant that I was made Grade 4 for National Service and I could never join the army, too much of a risk. Although subsequently I went out to Australia and worked in the bush for four years and got better, and I can now get an unloaded life insurance premium, there was a time, because of the kidney infection, because of the unsanitary and rough conditions of Eton, because of the in-adequate medical observation or caring, that my life was put in jeopardy, and my mother was told that I wouldn't live be-yond the age of twenty-three or twenty-four. But even then, the condition was mis-diagnosed: although it was a serious kidney complaint, it was *not* a nephritis, which is a fatal complaint.

I remember, when I was at Eton, my mother sending down her tailor, who made very good men's suits. He came down with his wife at a weekend to measure me up for a jacket. He had been in a German prisoner-of-war camp, so he'd had a very tough war and hadn't enjoyed it at all. And he and his wife were absolutely appalled by the inside of the house. How could the sons of the rich and privileged be sent to live in conditions like this, which were sub anything in their imagination! The corridors went up and down around little corners, the loos stank of urine out into the corridor, the rooms were cold and poky, and the whole thing was dark, just like a rabbit warren; he couldn't understand it at all.

My parents used to come down for the Fourth of June and St Andrew's Day and that sort of thing. They were always late, they were always, always late to take me out, so the time was much shorter. I think they used to make fun a little bit – I mean, one used to tentatively introduce them to one's friends, to whom they immediately accorded nicknames, and so I suppose one was vaguely embarrassed by them. And my father always had to have a flashier car than anyone else's, or always seemed to. My mother was not a typical Eton mum and I think she made fun of it a bit, so maybe in a strange, paradoxical way one became slightly defensive about the school, even though one didn't like it.

Of course the house as I knew it has all been swept away. The only thing they kept was the façade, and a magnolia tree which came in through my window, which I used to love. But otherwise the whole of the back of the house was completely bulldozed and in its place they built a beautiful modern new house, and that shows you the changing times.

I went down there recently to take some photographs of Eton boys' rooms for a magazine, and an extremely nice young housemaster showed me round. The rooms were all beautifully decorated and amusingly done with posters. And the house was too hot, I had to take my sweater off – it was the middle of winter, and it was too bloody hot! Everything was heated and frightfully comfortable.

I never resented my parents for sending me. I just accepted it dumbly, like sheep going to the slaughter. It was accepted that this was the way you were supposed to behave, and you had to succeed. I remember my father coming and telling me one night, sitting on my bed, that he didn't want a mediocrity for a son, thank you very much, and please would I try and shine at something, which is something you should never say to your children – the world's lousiest psychologist could have told him that. But I never held it against him. I hated going back to school, it was like going back to prison, but I didn't hold it against the parents because it was the system, and you were part of the system, and you had been brainwashed to that belief.

They had a very good system of reports at Eton, very civilized. Instead of those mean little bits of paper that most schools provide, enough for just three lines which tell you nothing about your boy, every master used to send a letter to your housemaster saying how they found you, not academically, but as a person. Your classical tutor, who was a sort of master of studies, was the one who collated all the information and then he wrote a much fuller and more amusing letter. My classical tutor was an extremely amusing and erudite man called David MacIndoe, and he used to write very funny letters; 'I do wish Buxton would stop playing the amiable baboon' sort of thing. Then the housemaster used to write in his perfect, lovely, round writing, always in flowing fountain pen, a letter about you as a person, and your general progress. So this sheaf of letters would arrive addressed to my father, and there was always this awful pantomime every time the report arrived. Breakfast time: spine-chilling, he'd arrive with his walking-stick sort of tapping the furniture, being so heavy and Victorian. I know he enjoyed it, and it was all part of the act. One even had to laugh at one's own discomfiture.

It was a long and bumpy passage after Eton. There are so many Eton sons who had well-worn furrows to step into. There was the family business, or they went into the Brigade of Guards or the Household Cavalry, and they either went on to be soldier boys all their lives or they left to run the family estates when Daddy died, that sort of thing. Lots of Etonians I was there with have since become successful Cabinet Ministers and what have you. I didn't really know what I wanted to do and I suffered really until I was forty about not knowing what to do, because one had been conditioned by the school and also the parental background. My mother was very ambitious for her children and she would tell you the whole time you were marvellous when you weren't and, my God, you had to find out you weren't marvellous, and it's difficult to learn those truths.

One had to become a maverick. But I think lots of Etonians were mavericks; my generation were kicking over the traces for the first time. Sure, you'd had your Humphrey Lytteltons before and your Hugh Daltons – I think Eton has always had a tendency to produce mavericks – but the post-war bit was 'All change here, please'. To be a photographer was to be a man in a grubby mac, or somebody who took the wedding pictures: somebody who was beneath contempt. And it wasn't until Tony Armstrong-Jones *et al.* came along that taking photographs was considered an OK thing to do. The arts were not only frowned on, they were killed off by Eton in the early days, because it was not a school which produced artists. Some writers, yes, of course, because the literary thing was very strong there. But I didn't fall in with the system and I left early, a year earlier than I need have done. I was only asked to be a member of the Library the last three weeks of my last term, because it was *de rigueur*, out of politeness to poor old Fiennes they had to do that, but it wasn't because they thought I was a natural leader.

I did feel very excited by the world when I left. I went to France for three months and learnt to speak French, and then to North America for six months, and I loved that, and became very pro-America and have remained so ever since. Those were much more formative things for me, and the world suddenly opened up. One had been unchained, unleashed from the re-strictive background – which people loved all over the world, 'Oh gee, you went to Eton College, isn't that the place where . . .', and all that. You know. It has a huge cachet.

I remember when I was on a boat taking cattle from Canada to Venezuela, and dropped off at Bridgetown, Barbados. I stepped

1 *above* Since 1980 Dr Eric Anderson has been Eton's Head Master. He controls a teaching staff of some 140 Assistant Masters to look after the education of the seventy King's Scholars, for whom King Henry VI founded the College in 1440, and the 1,200 Oppidans (fee-paying boys).

2 *below* Eton from the air, looking north: College Chapel (centre right) was the nucleus of Henry VI's foundation. Above it the road to Slough passes alongside the playing fields, and below it Barnes Pool Bridge divides College from Town. Lower Chapel and the Science area are in the centre foreground, the Swimming Pool at the top left.

3   *right*   The outbreak of the Second World War was the beginning of the end for the top hat: there was not enough room in the racks outside Chapel and schoolrooms to park both gas masks *and* top hats, so the hats had to go. They came back for a few years in 1946, but the post-war expense of a new top hat finally killed them off.

4   *below*   These Lower Boys (boys in their first two years at Eton) are working in pre-war Lower School. This room has been in continuous use for teaching since 1500 or perhaps earlier. On the window-shutters are carved the names of boys who proceeded from Eton to King's College at Cambridge with the scholarships that Henry VI willed for his twin foundations.

5 *above*   Until the 1960s every boy's room had a fireplace (though there was only enough coal to last for about four hours every other evening). Here a fag is lighting his fagmaster's fire. On the right is the gasmask tin, and there too are the gumboots that stood ready for a hasty retreat to the air-raid shelter if the sirens blew.

6 *below*   A 1939 recruit squad outside New Schools (built in public-school Gothic-style in 1876): they are learning to present arms with their Lee-Enfield rifles before joining the Corps, as they were not allowed into uniform until they had achieved some basic efficiency at square-bashing and rifle drill. The Eton Rifle Volunteers were started in 1860 in the wake of warnings about an invasion by Napoleon III's France.

7 *above*   In March 1947 came the worst Thames flood since 1894, and the High Street succumbed. The boys were sent home for the rest of the half (term) when the drains stopped working.

8 *below*   Snowfall a century ago. This ornate lamp-post, known as the Burning Bush, was set up in the centre of Eton in 1864. To the right is Drury's, a rambling boys' house that stood empty and unwanted for years. It was eventually replaced by School Hall and, alongside it, the School Library.

9   *above*   College Hall, where the King's Scholars have their meals. This was one of the earliest of Henry VI's buildings to be completed, and it was probably in use by 1450, ten years after the Foundation. In the undercroft below Hall, the Museum of Eton Life was opened in 1985.

10   *below*   The School Library is a working reference library for the boys, as opposed to College Library, which is more for bibliophiles and scholars.

11 *above* A scene in Upper School in 1939, a year before a lone German bomber demolished the far end, where Mr F. W. How is invigilating the examination for the Lower Boy English Literature Prize. On the bench in the corner can be seen the ARP equipment – stirrup-pump, buckets, sand and scoop, ready to tackle incendiary bombs. Upper School was built in the late seventeenth century because the growing number of Oppidans was overflowing Lower School.

12 *below* As the maps and blackboard show, this is a classical division-room. Should the boy on the left be asleep?

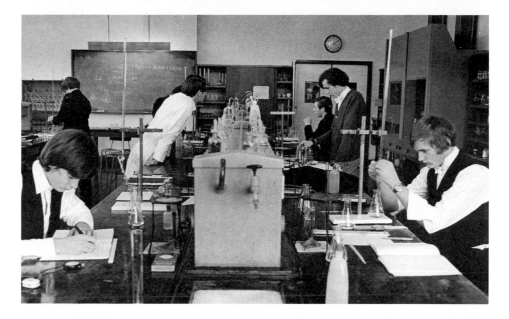

13 *top* Senior boys working for their A-levels in one of the new laboratories that were built with the help of the Industrial Fund for the Advancement of Scientific Education in Schools in 1959. A glance at the blackboard shows that they are studying organic chemistry.

14 *bottom* The Music Schools provide for individual and group tuition, instrumental and vocal, in almost every style. This saxophonist is playing a Jamaican rumba under the eye of Mr P. Ripper, one of the forty visiting music staff who supplement the eight full-time music masters. Among the Oppidans are some twenty Music Scholars, selected for their ability as instrumentalists.

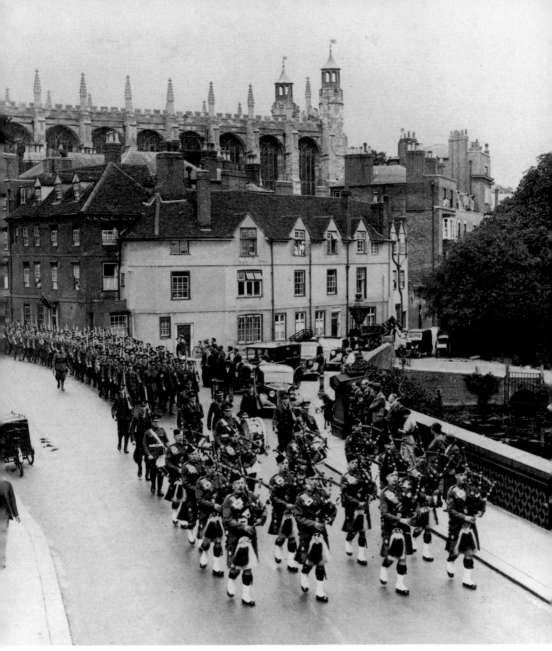

15 The Officers' Training Corps (predecessor of the Combined Cadet Force) marching to Windsor in July 1938 before entraining for camp, in company with other public school OTCs, at Tidworth. They are being played out by the fifes and drums of the Scots Guards, who were on station at Victoria Barracks. Barnes Pool had water in it then: now dry, it is planted with ornamental shrubs and trees.

out into the street off the wharf, and the first person I saw walking down the street was somebody who had been at school with me. And the same thing when I was in Melbourne and Sydney. People would turn up who had been at Eton, and immediately there was a clubbishness about it; even though you'd hated it at the time, you'd still find a little bit of comfort in that club.

I bump into some Old Etonians from time to time, but water flows under the bridge, and they change. I'd like to think I've weathered quite well, but I see some of them, bald and grey and with bloodshot eyes from too much drink and having taken endless stockbroker dinners; occasionally I meet one or two who look like I always remember them, but mostly they're barely recognizable.

I don't want to paint it all black, because that would be grossly unfair. Obviously it has its good points. I just want to de-mythologize it really. And I know it has all changed for the good since my day – it had to, because it couldn't have survived in the form it was. But I'm sure the arrogance is still there, the arrogance of certainty, of money, of position, of privilege. And it gives you a confidence and makes you able to speak the same language. It means you can converse with perfect confidence with people who are running businesses and industries or are in government or places of power. You're able to talk intelligently because you use the same language, the same phrases; it's tribal, you can join that tribe if you want to, you can don the colours of that tribe for the afternoon if you have to perform in those circumstances, in the county with the Lord Lieutenant, or you can go straight down the street to the blokes who are digging the gas main or mending your roof and talk about practicalities because you've done it yourself, and so you can feel perfectly at ease with everybody. The Eton education gives you that confidence because it gives you certainty.

GENERAL SIR DAVID FRASER

―――

M y father had not been at Eton. He was the youngest of a large
Scots family and my grandfather had very old-fashioned ideas
indeed, and one of the ideas was a very strong belief in primo-
geniture; my uncle, Lord Saltoun, went to Eton, but my grandfather's firm view was that younger sons should not go to the
same school. Younger sons were very much meant to keep their
station and were not encouraged to think that anything was
coming to them at all – and indeed it didn't! Anyway, that's why
my father was not an Etonian. I think he resented it, because he
didn't actually like Charterhouse at all and he wasn't very happy
there, and he found later that his friends were very largely
Etonians and he felt rather out of it.

I remember one arrived in the late afternoon, I don't quite
know why, but that was the order. And the first thing which
struck me with surprise was its size. I felt I was in a town –
which in a way it is, it is a small town – and I said, 'Which is
Eton?' 'It's all Eton,' said my mother, who came from an Eton
family. I suppose I was frightfully stupid not to apprehend that
before, but I hadn't, and it surprised me. I suppose I felt, 'I'm a
very small creature in a huge establishment, and I don't know
how I'm going to find my way about; it's all very puzzling and
alarming.' But I was enormously conscious of the visual beauty
of Eton. An awful lot of it is immensely pleasing to the eye, and
some of it is very beautiful, and right until my last day I found an
atmosphere there which enchanted me.

My housemaster was charming. He was a man called Upcott,
J. D. Upcott. He wasn't everybody's cup of tea. Funnily enough
my parents never really saw the point of him very much; I think
he was probably rather shy with parents. But immediately I felt at

home with him and that made an immense difference. I remember that when he came around the house that evening – and he went around the house every evening, to every boy's room, always, even just for a moment – he called me by my Christian name. In those days that was astonishing. I don't think my private school headmaster had ever called me by my Christian name, it was unthinkable. One was Fraser. And on that very first evening I remember he said, 'Well, David, one comes to an enormous place like this and it's strange and alarming – but it's exciting too. and it's a great adventure, probably the biggest adventure in your life so far.' Well, these I suppose rather banal sentences were nevertheless helpful because they put one at one's ease and one felt that one's relationship with this man was essentially a friendly one. And so it remained. Always.

Right from the start I thought that Eton was a magical place. I loved it from the very beginning. The thing I at once felt was that it was an adult place. You had to find your own way about, you weren't bear-led anywhere. And of course that was rather alarming, and one got it wrong, and there weren't many excuses accepted when one did. You would be told that you should have done better, been a bit more grown-up and got it right. And I liked that. I suppose I had rather precocious instincts and interests and the status of adult was one to which I looked forward. I didn't at all cherish childhood. Now Eton suited this because it believed in liberty to an extraordinary degree. It seemed to a very small boy intoxicating – an almost limitless vista of liberty. You were left to sink or swim, which I think is a definition of liberty. There's very little liberty about nowadays, of course, because people aren't allowed to sink. It's considered inhumane. But this was intoxicating stuff, you see, this was magical. You felt, 'I'm my own man!', even though one was a scruffy little boy in an Eton collar.

There was this institution of private business, and once a week, in the evenings generally, one read a book and discussed it, rather as if one was taking English, which of course was not a subject at Eton. Then there were Sunday privates, greatly differing house by house. Upcott very often used to play music to us. Another whole half we tasted wine – he was very fond of claret and he was trying to educate our taste in claret. You got very little!

After I became an upper boy, I went to somebody called Dr Prescot, charming man, H. K. Prescot. He used to laugh at me a good deal and regard me as very intolerant and very firm, in those days, in my rather conservative views. I used to take sides very vigorously in whatever we were discussing and show small patience with opposing points of view. I mean, I wasn't unique, I think it's a feature of youth that when one comes to a view one holds it with some passion while you hold it, although it may be only three-quarters of an hour! And he used to tease me about that a good deal, and then enjoy a somewhat socratic dialogue which eventually showed one how silly one was being.

There were enormously different sorts of people there, among the masters, among the boys, among the influences one was exposed to, and I think that had a certain effect upon one's character. I have the impression that in some schools a certain type is produced. Now it may flower and differ a great deal later in life, but one has the impression that there is a certain rigidity of mould. That absolutely wasn't Eton. It was immensely various, and the boys were immensely various, and there wasn't any effort made to stuff them into a mould.

There was a slightly flippant atmosphere about Eton, an atmosphere of resolute refusal to take anything too seriously. That actually is not my character, but I think that its influence upon my character, which has always been rather serious, was quite good. One was not encouraged to take anything, including oneself, too seriously or too pompously.

I wasn't good at games, or not good enough anyway. I didn't dislike games, in fact I rather enjoyed them, but not being very fleet of foot or having a particularly good eye, I just wasn't really very good at them. I'd been quite a good cricketer at my prep school, but the standard at Eton was extremely high and it was very competitive. But I wasn't bad at work. I wasn't a great scholar, but had I gone back for my last half, which I didn't because of the war and for various reasons, I would have been the junior member of Oppidan sixth form, which is the top ten boys of the school, so I wasn't bad.

I enjoyed the Corps; I was very keen on the army. This was no doubt a reflection of my father's profession: I had seen soldiers moving about and heard drums beating and bands playing from quite an early age. And I had always wanted to be a soldier. So I joined the Corps immediately I was allowed to – in those days it wasn't compulsory but it was the nearest thing to it. The Corps was huge, it was a battalion strong, six hundred strong, and I became a company quartermaster sergeant, which was very distinguished.

One joined up as a recruit, and put on a belt to carry one's bayonet and rifle, and one was drilled in top hat and tail-coat until one was passed out by the Adjutant and became a full member of the Corps, when you got your uniform. I've got black-and-white pictures of the Corps, but the uniform wasn't khaki, it was a sort of milk chocolate/wine colour with pale blue facing, so the badges of rank and piping on the sleeve and round the peak cap were all pale blue. This could have been quite smart, but the smartness was somewhat reduced by the fact that Etonians' uniforms never fitted them at all because nobody was going to buy new Corps clothes for one parade a week. You took what you could get out of the pool that more or less fitted you – and it didn't fit very well. Then, of course, Etonians were not at all good at putting this uniform on in a smart and soldierly way, in fact they almost went out of their way to do the reverse. I didn't like that. I had rather soldierly instincts and I disapproved of the noticeably unmilitary attitudes of my friends and colleagues.

In the summer there was a great ceremonial inspection by some visiting general or member of the royal family. The rest of the year, one was taught subjects like map-reading, or compass work, or weapon training with one's rifle – one did quite a lot of rifle shooting, military-range and open-range shooting with one's .303 Lee-Enfield.

We would go to some not very far distant military training ground like Chobham Common, and one carried out a Field Day which was a matter of high hilarity always. They were quite tiring; one often marched for hours with equipment, and one never really knew what was happening. There was a good deal of mystification. The officers, who were masters, had done courses and so they knew something, but they didn't generally pass it on very much. We would form up, and after a bit one moved over the heather, and then one was told to start crawling, and then run, and all that. Finally you found yourself attacking or being attacked by another school, who were the enemy, and then there was a great sort of schemozzle, and eventually one was disentangled and marched back somewhere where one ate from a paper bag full of a bun and an apple and a bar of chocolate, and then one marched to the station and got in a train and went back to Eton. And that was always a scene of a great deal of lawbreaking. The bolder spirits took the occasion to flout the law, as boys do on such occasions, very enjoyably – lavatory rolls being let out of the window, and smoking of course, and a good deal of drinking too. But when we got to Windsor station, that was very splendid, because we de-trained and sobered up and formed up on the platform, and there was always the Corps of Drums, or Pipes if it was the Scots Guards, of the battalion that was at Victoria Barracks, Windsor, and they played us back. So we marched back in fine style, with drums at our head, and that was rather fun.

My closest Eton friend, with whom I messed from my first or second half there, was a very, very close friend. We shared a great many interests and, believe me, he was the most admirable and charming boy. He was most interesting, very mature. He, unlike me, was good at games and athletic, so he was more distinguished in the schoolboy world, although rather less good at work, so I suppose we balanced each other a little bit. But I think the thing that immediately attracted us to each other was that our tastes and our interests were adult. He was extremely interested in European history and affairs. The political history of our century absorbed him, even when he was fourteen or fifteen. And he watched the current scene, as I did, with enormous concern and a sense of involvement. You couldn't not be aware of politics, because politics was all around you. Boys took very strong positions, because of their parents in many cases – some were members of the Cabinet – and it was quite a political atmosphere really, and quite an informed one. That, together with the fact that we shared a sense of humour: we roared with laughter at exactly the same things in a way that one has hardly laughed since. That of course is a terrific bond too. I suppose we were moving at rather the same pace. You change a lot between thirteen and nineteen, and sometimes people leave other people behind, but we tended to think the same about other people, likes and dislikes – not always, that would be dull, but our likes and dislikes tended to match. And he was immensely good company.

Some of the boys were totally absorbed in the little world we were in. I remember that one boy, who was a great success, was found weeping when he came to leave Eton – sitting in his room, simply weeping, surrounded by all his caps and scarves and these glorious memorabilia. He had lived very much in and for the little world of Eton, in which he was a huge success and would probably never be such a success again in life. I wasn't like that. I had tasted and appreciated the magic of Eton right from the start, but I certainly was very aware of the outside world.

The war, coming closer and closer, was something we were – or some of us were – intensely conscious of.

Munich impinged on our lives enormously. It was September 1938, and immediately after the half began, quite suddenly we were all summoned by our housemaster and told that there was an international crisis. He didn't personally think that it was a very serious one, and he thought it would all blow over. But it had been laid down that any boy whose parents wished him to go home, could go home, and that ordinary school was suspended, and that boys who stayed at Eton would be looked after though there would be no lessons and no work in the ordinary sense. I suppose about two-thirds of the house went home, and the rest stayed because their parents didn't live nearby – or indeed their parents didn't want them to come home, or thought it was all nonsense. My parents were abroad, so I stayed, and we had an instructor who showed us how to lay sandbags, and we sandbagged all sorts of windows and provided air raid sheltering and all that sort of thing. We listened to the news avidly every day, and indeed we were allowed to go to Hendon aerodrome in a bus to see Mr Chamberlain return from Munich. And I went on the bus, which again was an agreeable bit of freedom, with a lot of boys smoking and exulting in this little break from life.

If you ask me what I felt about it, I'll tell you. I and the friend to whom I referred were in a minority. We were both in the Library, and on the whole we were all good friends, but the Library was very sharply divided on this issue, and four of the boys were greatly relieved by Mr Chamberlain's achievements and thought that we had got peace, and that the peace would be a permanent one. My friend and I were absolutely miserable. In fact it's one of the first and perhaps last occasions that I remember, when by myself, sobbing with the pain of what I thought was our country's disgrace. As a matter of fact, in much later life I've come to see that rather differently as it happens, but that doesn't alter the fact that that's how I felt then. I felt shame, because I felt we were running away from reality. I was by then quite convinced that Hitler intended war, or anyway to collect all the fruits of war, and that we were pretending that he didn't. Pretending to ourselves, running away from truth – which is a very shaming thing. You can take anything providing you feel, 'Well, I'm facing up to it and my country's facing up to it.' So that was awful, Munich, perfectly awful.

And the next half, the Germans walked into Czechoslovakia and occupied Prague, by invitation ostensibly, but nobody was fooled by that. Everybody thought Poland was bound to be next. Chamberlain then made a great speech which we heard live on the radio. And of course he was extremely angry because in effect he'd been taken in by Hitler, and he said: 'Let no one think that if it had to come to it we would not intervene with all the resolution at our command . . .', or something like that. There was great cheer, because the whole country had moved from one perception to another and felt a great relief. That summer, '39, my last summer at Eton, it seemed rather quiescent, and then of course it began to hot up in August with Poland, and ultimately on 26th of August there was the Russian–German pact which people seemed to feel gave the Germans the green light *vis-à-vis* Poland.

I think by now war was almost accepted. That was the mood of the country, and although not mentioned, it was somewhat resigned to the fact that this cloud now wasn't going to go away, it was going to burst – when the thunder was coming and the rain was going to fall might be uncertain, but burst it was going to. I think that was the sense of England in the summer of 1939. A great relief when it came, of course.

I wasn't intending to leave. I was going to go back the following half to be captain of my house and in sixth form and that sort of thing. Well, I did leave. I was in the north of Scotland when the invasion of Poland took place. Everything started to seize up; there was no public transport in the Highlands of Scotland, where I happened to be shooting with a friend, because everybody was getting tight, as a matter of fact. Drunk. They thought, quite rightly, 'We're never going to have a world war starting again in our lifetime. We can't live it like an ordinary day; we've got to do something exceptional.' And the exceptional thing they did was to retire to the nearest whisky bottle and stay there for a good twenty-four hours. I rang up my aunt, who was the other side of Scotland – it was always a sort of second home to me because my parents were abroad a lot, they were wonderful to me, my uncle and aunt – and I said, 'Can I come?' and they said, 'Of course, we're expecting you.' I got a lift with a commercial traveller as far as Inverness and then there was a bus running along the north coast of Scotland, and I eventually got home. And the next day was the declaration of war. Third of September. I thought, 'I must get into the army.' I was of military age, you see, I was eighteen and a quarter or something. 'I can't stay a schoolboy when this marvellous war has started.' So I went into Aberdeen and enlisted with the Gordon Highlanders, and they said, 'Well, all right, you swear in', 'attested', as it was called. I had my medical inspection to show that I was fit and healthy, and they gave me one day's pay, and then they said, 'Now you must go home and await further orders.'

I thought that these would be coming any time, and that I would get something from the Grenadiers saying, 'Your country needs you. Come at once.' So I sent a telegram to my tutor at Eton and said, 'Have enlisted and not returning.' Well, they took that rather badly. Very badly, in fact, and I got another telegram by return saying, 'Advise you should return . . .' etc. Then I got a more explicit telegram saying, 'Return at once. Headmaster' – wish I'd kept it, one doesn't keep enough in life. But I ignored these and stayed where I was.

So I left Eton a bit suddenly, you see. Of course it was the most frightful anti-climax, because I was going to be captain of my house if I'd gone back, which was rather a pinnacle of one's little world of the house, and I was looking forward to that, I was going to be in rather a swell. And my friend wrote to me too, and said, 'Do come, we all miss you very much.' But I couldn't. I'd crossed the Rubicon and I couldn't possibly go back. So instead of either the Gordon Highlanders, the Grenadier Guards or anybody else beseeching me to come and save the country and put on a uniform, there was a great silence because it was the phoney war. Unlike 1914, when they had enormous casualties from Ypres onwards, there was none of that at all, you see, absolutely nothing happened. And there were masses of people older than me who were on the Reserves and there wasn't room even for them. I was left very alone, though I had left Eton by then, and so I stayed left, rather ingloriously and no doubt rather foolishly, but never mind.

As a matter of fact, none of my great friends at Eton – and I had a lot of friends – none of them are alive. It so happens we were unlucky, and a particularly large number of my own circle were killed in the war and a number died after it from causes deriving from the war.

I can remember hearing about my friend's death. I'm sorry, I can't bring myself to mention his name. I read it in the paper. March 1943. The casualties were always given in *The Times*. But on the same morning I read it in *The Times*, I had a letter in the very well-known, very idiosyncratic handwriting of my house-master, which said: 'You may get this before you hear of it, but I want you to know that — has been killed.' Nothing else, just that. Very nice. It shows you the sort of person he was, because after all I hadn't been in his house for four years.

Of course, at the time one was saddened: a death like that hit you hard. but one became rather hardened to it – and one always had the chance of being killed oneself, which helped a bit.

I don't really quite know why I can't mention his name. You see, there's nobody I can talk to about him now. It's difficult to put this in a way that doesn't sound spurious or hackneyed. You were asking me about one's friends who were killed or died when they were young and its effect upon one; perhaps everybody finds this when they get older, but I don't feel them at all departed, you know, I feel them very present, and of course unchanged. I don't think I could construct a philosophical or religious theory from what I've just said: a lot of friends that I had, I do feel them very near.

I've had two sons at Eton, which put it back a little bit into one's life in the sense that one visited it and one recalled things that one had probably forgotten. Then you've got the fact that, as you get older, your mind does rather go to earlier rather than middle years, you know. I think Eton is always there. It's in one's life. They were very vivid years. Very vivid years.

I can evoke Eton in all seasons, but perhaps the season that most comes to one's mind is the early part of the winter, just as it's getting dark, just as one was moving back to lock-up, which I think was at six o'clock. And one had, I suppose, played some game or something of that kind, and you'd been down to the sock shop, if you could afford it, and had decided that one had got to get back; and maybe there was some work to do, one was looking forward to tea in one's room, and that sort of thing: a slight drizzle over Barnes Pool. I think that's the hour and the season that one remembers most when Eton is mentioned.

THE EARL OF GOWRIE

M Y father was killed in the war, and I never saw him and he didn't see me, or my brother. So I was brought up by grandparents, and I lived at Windsor. My grandfather was a Governor of Windsor Castle as a sort of retirement job after being Governor-General of Australia.

I don't think I'm what can be called 'main-track Establishment', I mean I'm not a sort of country-house earl, I wasn't shooting at Chatsworth in the holidays. I'm an earl because the person who brought me up was made an earl. He was the middle son of a quite poor aristocratic family, but a well-connected one; he earned his living all his life, and he left two thousand pounds when he died, *in toto*.

I was one of only two boys who arrived that half. And I remember we took it very seriously that we had to learn the names of all the great Olympians who ran the place, like the President of Pop, and the Captain of the Boats, and what the house colours were, and I was frightened that I would be savagely beaten for forgetting these lessons. So I was in a state of terror until I soon found that I had a very agreeable house with benign and agreeable older boys, many of whom have remained close friends of mine, and I never experienced anything in the way of bullying or sadism or anything like that.

It was the Coronation year, and a lot of people were going to the Coronation. The Queen came down, the young Queen, and there were special fireworks, and you felt very much in the mainstream of society. It was a more traditional society then; the culture was still run by the upper classes, and you were at the heart of it. And the people who came down were very distinguished. You saw Prime Ministers and so on knocking around the place. Etonians were tremendously in the swim – I don't know if they still are, I mean people are more defensive now – and I enjoyed that.

I was in Fred Coleridge's house. I didn't have very good relations with him. He was a nervous man. He looked like a rock of solidity, when in fact he was rather sensitive and jumpy. He was a good housemaster to the degree that he let his senior boys – who happened to be good ones – get on and run the house. One had got used to the idea that schools were run by adults, and one suddenly was in a place where the adults were of very little consequence. But he was a bit nervous about me, possibly because of my Castle connections. Also, I was a very literary, intense little boy who'd read an awful lot, and I was very unabashed about letting this be known. I was probably pretty unbearable. Eventually I was teased out of it by my contemporaries, but I think he found it rather rattling.

But as I became quite a well-known and successful boy in terms of school politics and getting a reputation outside the house, he then started to leave me alone, and by the time I was a senior boy he was perfectly agreeable. Funnily enough, I was up to him and didn't find him a bad teacher and had good relations with him in class.

Well, I wasn't very happy at first because I was a bit of a fish out of water, but I found that the great thing about Eton was that it wasn't really like a school, it was like a university. With twelve hundred kids, there was always somebody who was a bit of an odd fish like yourself, and there were one or two close friends who were sort of loners and skewball figures outside my house, and that got me into the habit of always operating a bit outside my house. I found that Eton was a rather more plural place if you were prepared to make your relations outside your house; having sort of arty, intellectual interests, I joined funny societies and gave little talks on Henry Moore and that kind of thing, and found there was a niche for everybody. If you were thought to have those tastes, you were encouraged with them, and so I wasn't in any sense oppressed. I was just isolated for a bit. Eton didn't sit on you – it might tease you, but it was tolerant. And then, I'm afraid (one must just be honest), I became a terrific politician and learned exactly how to play the Eton system. If you played the Eton system, you could have a great time.

Compared with other schools it was much less regimented. There was much more free time. You had to work, but you had a lot of work in your own room. Your own room was a big thing in adolescence. If you were unhappy, and I was miserable a lot at Eton – it wasn't Eton, it was just the processes of being that age – you had somewhere to lick your wounds in private.

I think if you've got to go through that kind of stuff, Eton was not a bad place to do it because it was a lively and absorbing arena to compete in or to grow up in, which rather stopped one from brooding about one's emotional development or whatever. And it was also full of rather witty and ironic people who tended to tease you about it.

It was possible to pursue intellectual interests. I was a big reader. I discovered that if I elected to do rowing I could get all my exercise over in about an hour, and then I had the whole of the long summer afternoons to go to bookshops and browse or read, and so one was wonderfully left alone. Then I had a room down in a sort of basement, rather away from the others; I discovered there was a maids' bathroom nearby, and after lights-out, if I went and lay in the bath, I could read for hours. I've never read as much as I did there, and nearly everything I read I remember.

I had a great friend called Robert Corbett who shared some of my intellectual tastes and who was very well read, and I tended to follow him a bit. I remember sitting next to him once in class and he seemed to be reading much faster than me, and he showed me that it was possible to read by looking at the page, rather as if you were looking at a photograph, and I've been able to do that ever since. It was a great help in business or as a minister when you have to read a lot of paper.

I also spent a lot of my spare time wandering around with a rather aesthetic friend who had a great feel for architecture. It's a wonderful place to loaf in quite an energetic way. And if you wanted to be alone, you could find some funny corner to be alone in.

I messed with the same two people for a very long time. I was a wet and a weed and rather a weepy boy at the beginning of the time, but at eighteen I was rather a cocky, confident young man, and so we went through all that process together, and I got on well with them. I mean, one went through the ordinary adolescent things of crushes and love affairs and excitements of that kind, but these were quite ordinary orthodox friendships which simply have lasted in a very un-neurotic way. It's a good place for friendships; I don't think of myself as a sort of extravagantly Etonian character – though I may be, I don't know – but it is not for nothing that among my four or five closest friends, I suppose about three of them are Etonians whom I've known since I was thirteen.

There were one or two rather remarkable rebel Etonians. I was simply a reader, I wasn't a great cultural inputter. Heathcote-Williams was remarkable, obviously talented and strange, and rebellious and difficult. And he has remained a sort of alternative writer, with a certain kind of Etonian charm which shimmers over the surface of the prose which I like. He painted like Jackson Pollock, when no one had heard of Jackson Pollock – shouldn't think the Tate Gallery knew much about Jackson Pollock at that time. There were a lot of talented painters. I can't remember ever being bored by Eton. It was an entertaining, stimulating place.

Guy Kidston was cool, so much so that he was cool to the point of not being wholly there a lot of the time. And he was relentlessly American, and he even looked like James Dean. He used to sit for hours, silently, and when you asked what he was doing, he would say, 'Playing mental chess.' He was very spaced out, he was in a totally different sphere.

But Etonians at that time were still fairly conservative. Whatever they thought they were, they weren't quite in the vanguard of cultural taste. Probably other schools were more intellectual in that way. I mean, I left in '58, and we wanted to have pigskin cigarette-holders with Benson and Hedges cigarettes. Even those with quite severe intellectual tastes like mine were perfectly orthodox young men who dreamed of having MGs. We weren't exceptionally exciting.

I did have a relationship with Robert Birley, and I was close to him, and liked him enormously. He knew my weaknesses and didn't butter me up, which a lot of the others did by the time I was leaving as quite a successful boy. And I think I always felt one had to sort of perform for Robert really, more than for Eton. He was somebody I had great respect for and wanted to live up to.

I went from Eton to Oxford one afternoon to sit a scholarship exam, and what I found was another institution, only, I thought, a rather grimmer one than Eton. I thought in desperation, 'This just goes on for ever!' And I simply walked out of the exam and roamed the streets for a long time. When I got back to Eton, I pointed out what had happened. My housemaster found this crisis of mine difficult to cope with, and he had the good sense and maturity – and niceness, it has to be said: I didn't get on with him very easily, but I have to say that – to send me off to somebody who could cope with it. And I was very, very strongly influenced by Robert Birley who took a great deal of personal trouble with me. To cut a long story short, Robert Birley, who was an old boy of Balliol, which was the college I'd sat in – or rather not sat in – drove me down there himself, and persuaded me that I would like it, would value the time there and that it would suit me. Now those are the banal facts, and I don't think about it very much now, but that's quite a crisis at that time of life. Walking out of an exam and having the headmaster of your school having to take you back – quite commonplace in a small school where the headmaster might have nannied you through various stages of your career, but in a very, very big school, where you didn't see much of the headmaster, it was remarkable.

I then made great friends with him, and spent quite a lot of time with him privately, and I saw him quite often after I left Eton, indeed after I left Oxford. I very much cherished it when he wrote me a very nice letter when I joined the Government in '79, saying that he was delighted that two favourite pupils of his were working together, because Jim Prior had been a very favourite pupil of his when he was headmaster of Charterhouse.

Looking back at my time, I don't think there was any need to have gone to university. With the Eton liberal arts education, time afterwards was to some degree spent postponing real choices of what you wanted to do. The store of knowledge one got at Eton, particularly if you made use of your spare time and read and so on, was quite enough. And that may give Etonians a certain kind of sophistication, and sometimes, I imagine, a sense of superiority.

Eton gave me some close friends and an ability to deal with male relationships. A lot of professional relationships are still mainly male, so on the whole I am a chap who's not frightened of organizations like Parliament, or the kind of organizations that I've worked in. What I don't think it did give me was much in the way of skills for operating outside those arenas. And of course women were a total mystery, and I think, looking back, it would have been nicer to have had more of one's teen or adolescent years involved with the opposite sex, even if it was only mooning at them hopelessly or just making friends with them in an unromantic situation. I was conscious when I was eighteen that I'd never met any women at all. Even in the holidays I never met women, because I lived in a strange part of the west of Ireland in a sort of very charming and cultivated gay colony in Donegal, in which my grandparents were the only straight couple. And so after Eton I took very strong corrective steps, and I went to work in a girls' school. It wasn't so much that I was brooding about my love life − I had by that time fallen in love and had a girlfriend and so on in the rather chaste way of the day. Nevertheless I simply didn't know the gender, and I lived in that community for a year, where I could go and get some maths coaching and sit my exam, and I had great fun. And indeed later, a lot later, I married one of the pupils; though the marriage didn't last, it was very nice while it did.

When I've been down as an old boy to talk to the Political Society, I must say I've been extremely impressed. It seems to me to be as good a school as it was in my time, except the things that weren't good about it in my time have slightly disappeared. I do think it is a remarkable, well-run institution. I can think of no time probably in its whole history when the Provost and the headmaster were two such compatible and admirable people as now. I think it's in a very, very healthy phase of development. I would have thought unconditionally it's the greatest school in England now.

JOHN GRAHAM

MY father had been a beak at Eton before the war, and decided that's where I should go. He was himself a public school headmaster, of a rather minor public school, Dean Close in Cheltenham. He still knew a lot of the people at Eton; my tutor at Eton, for instance: he and my father had been junior beaks together in the thirties, and my tutor's wife was my godmother.

We were a straight, professional, middle-class Irish Protestant family, and my father had decided that Dublin was too small a pool, too genteel a place, and that we had to move and go to live in England to get the best possible education. I think my dad was a bit of a snob, but he also seriously believed that the education you got at Eton was intellectually very good.

I certainly found it very strange at first, but after three years at prep school I spoke right – I no longer spoke with a strong northern Irish accent – and I was quite a successful schoolboy. I was good at games, good at work, and that was great fun. But I was certainly aware that the social life these Etonians led was extremely different from mine. They talked about things that were meaningless to me, organized shoots and deb dances and cocktail parties and London social life or country social life, and that was a world I didn't belong to, and I didn't reckon I ever would belong to it – and indeed don't and haven't.

It was tremendously strange and new. I do remember we practised dressing, because tying those funny ties was beyond me, although boys from next-door rooms would come and help us. There were an enormous number of places to go to, and there didn't seem any way to find out where these places were, because the classrooms and the libraries and everything else were always such a long way from the house you lived in. And you had to learn all the folklore – who was who, and which house was which – and all that was a bit alarming. The hierarchy is very considerable, and we were immensely in awe of the senior boys, you know, members of Pop in their fancy dress.

I was in Gowan's, a late-Victorian house, in a nice street, with gables and a warren of corridors. There was a very beautiful walled garden. It was a lot prettier than some of the older houses. My contemporaries in the house have done rather better than me. David Sainsbury was my exact contemporary and I messed with him for four years. Sam Vestey was another – a lot of grocers in my house. And there were some interesting eccentrics like Alistair Castlereagh, now Marquess of Londonderry, the jazz musician. But I don't know anyone from my days at Eton, with one exception. The only friend I've got from the four years I spent at Eton was another man in my house, John Moorhead. But then we both became journalists, and we just always kept in touch. It's interesting; you live a very intense life in close proximity with other people, and have deep and very powerful personal relations with them, friendships, love affairs, rivalries, and yet almost nothing remains twenty-five years later, except one very good friend.

What really startles me is to see a lot of my contemporaries at Eton for whom school still dominates their lives. Their close friends were all at school with them, they're godparents to each other's children, they always go down for the Eton–Harrow cricket match and June the Fourth, they go on holiday with each other, they work with each other in their merchant banks or shoot with each other on their pheasant shoots, and of course they wouldn't dream of sending their children to any other school.

I think partly my relative distance from it comes from a feeling I always had of being an outsider. Being Irish. And incidentally, John Moorhead was Australian and he felt an outsider too, although he'd been to English prep school.

After Oxford, I cut off from that whole world. I became a teacher in North America. Then I became a journalist and a foreign correspondent, and it wasn't really until my middle thirties that I found myself living back in England. I spent most of the period between twenty-one and thirty-five abroad, in America and Vietnam and elsewhere.

The real world is so different from school. But school remained in one's mind; one would think about it because it was a powerful place, its traditions and its hierarchies, its quirks and its idiosyncrasies are always there to a certain extent. Whenever I found myself on a story, Beirut, or Belfast, journalists from other papers were always astonished that a journalist should actually have been at Eton and wanted to know what it was like, and I would desperately try to remember. They wanted to know what life was really like in a boarding school. Were the boys very snobbish? Were they very rich? 'Were you all homosexuals?' Typical question. I would say, 'No. Of course we experimented and went to bed with each other; there weren't any girls.'

And in snobbery-oriented societies, in America, for instance, of course they were fascinated. They find the whole concept of Eton just riveting, and would tend to think it was a tremendous privilege having been there. Looking back at it now, we did get quite well taught. There was an extremely varied scholastic educational programme and we were introduced to a much wider range of human thoughts and activities than I know people were at any other school: Eton's rather good in that respect.

I do remember that there were long periods, like a year or two years, when I was emotionally very unstable and wobbled between elation and despair. I suspect that's part of adolescence and whatever chemical changes were taking place, and that would have happened wherever I was. But I do remember that all feelings were very intensified. Either totally elated or suicidal.

But all in all, I had a very good time. I was very clever, and good at work, and I loved to play cricket and the field game and fives and squash and rugger. I was fairly tall and fairly strong and very good at games. Relatively I was less tall at Eton than anywhere else, I do remember; even at six feet, there were an awful lot of boys that tall – I mean, the average height of Etonians must be much higher than in any other school.

I'm sure the influences were enormous, although in the

holidays I never lived an 'Etonian' life. My parents were always saying, 'You must bring some of your friends to stay in the holidays', and I went hot and cold with anxiety about that. I didn't want that. Holidays were quite different. I roamed about the countryside with my brother or the local girls, and played golf and went to the movies. I had nothing at all to do with school during the holidays, and as a result the start of every term was a strange and disorientating period; you had to get out of the holiday-family-at-home mode, and into institutional life. It was so totally different.

My memory is good. I can remember feelings. I can remember what it was like to fall in love with someone and have an affair with them at school, and how desperately jealous one got if there were rivals. I can remember being up before the headmaster and how frightening it was. I can remember vividly the events and meetings and intrigues in my final period which eventually led to my leaving the school. It was a glorious, wonderful hot summer. And I can remember the sheer beauty of the place. I mean, it is very lovely to go out and sit in the fields in the summer and wander up and down the river; the School Yard, Luxmoore's Garden, College Chapel, the libraries. I remember just staring at them and thinking it's very lovely; you're surrounded by beautiful sights, beautiful buildings.

I was expelled for going to bed with another boy, having been caught once before. What I really remember from that is that authority in all its forms – the masters, the headmaster, my parents, the other boy's parents – simply did not understand the meaning of our love affairs with ourselves. We did and they didn't. It was endemic. It did not mean we were homosexuals; we went to bed with each other because there were no girls, and we were at an extremely sexually aware, powerful and moving time of life. And people may talk about sublimating this in playing rugger or in doing well at your lessons or something, but it's not true. There was an awful lot of energy and it had to go somewhere. In the holidays we'd had girls the whole time, and we were never in any doubt at all, but we went to bed with each other as girl-substitutes. The authorities didn't see that at all. It was presented as immensely wicked; we weren't quite told we'd go blind if we masturbated, it was a little more advanced than that, but it wasn't very enlightened. And everyone did it, more or less, very few people didn't. I happened to get caught.

The subsequent events weren't particularly speedy. There were all sorts of discussions, and my parents came down and saw the headmaster, and it was all very embarrassing. I was in fact allowed to stay until the end of the term. But it was quite a shock, suddenly realizing that, at the end of the summer term, that would be it, I wouldn't be going back for my final year. And there was also the problem of where I'd go to school, what would become of me, as it were. Because it was in those days a very big disgrace. This was before the Wolfenden Report, and there was nothing like the tolerance of homosexuality or adolescent homosexual games, which was what we were playing, that there is today.

Only my closest friends knew, and a great many people didn't know until the following September, when I didn't re-emerge at school. And then I lost touch with pretty well all of them, except for two or three who I occasionally wrote to.

My father, being himself a public school headmaster and Chairman of the Western Region of the Headmasters Conference, naturally felt very powerfully a sense of disgrace, and it put an end to my parents' relationship with my housemaster and his wife. They had been best friends, they started their jobs together, my mother and my housemaster's wife were each other's best friends. They never saw each other again, and in many ways I think it was much harder on my parents than it was on me; they felt it very acutely. But they did forgive me. Despite the extremely conventional life my father led as a public school headmaster and a clergyman and the rest of it, he was a very liberal man. He realized that the true intellectual is always a liberal, and he didn't see things in terms of narrow rules and the small print of school regulations. At the same time, I had failed the system, or the system had failed me, and he felt that very keenly, and it made them quite unhappy for a bit. I then had a very successful career at St Paul's and Oxford, and they got over it.

I was suddenly a day boy at St Paul's, forced to make a whole set of new friends, and regarded as a strange and exotic creature because they'd never met an Etonian – and they wanted to know all about it. And dead embarrassing anyway, having to explain why you're not at the school you were at. But I had an absolutely wonderful year at St Paul's after the initial trauma of going there. I looked at these kids and they spoke with London accents, and they weren't posh and they didn't have earls as their parents; they were a different lot entirely. It was a tremendously successful, lovely year, and I have a lot of friends from there. But it was a very different world and even one year later, when I went up to Oxford, I no longer saw most of my Etonian friends, except for John Moorhead and Grey Gowrie, and perhaps one or two others.

For a time – perhaps half a term or a term – I missed the sense of belonging to a unique club. There must have been some underlying feeling of superiority which is simply bred by being at Eton. I missed that and realized it was gone for ever. I had blown that, I had lost it. What I didn't realize at the time was that what I had lost wasn't worth anything in the first place, and in the end I suspect that having to make the adjustment and live a rather humbler, lower-profile life was immensely good for me; it was terrible at the time, but I think it made me a much better person. It's a funny thing to say, but there was a feeling of superiority, you can't get away from it: 'We are Etonians, and they are all inferior to us.' Well, that got knocked out of me, perforce.

Once I got used to it and overcame what I perceived as a social humiliation, unnecessarily, once I had realized that I was just a normal seventeen-year-old boy at school with a whole lot of other seventeen-year-old boys, and there was still cricket, and work, and all the things that schoolboys have to do, then suddenly to be a day boy in London, with the whole city as your campus, was a wonderfully liberating experience. We were treated as adults, we could go to pubs and drink, we could have girlfriends and our own parties.

I was in a scholarship form for classics, and the people in that form with me were just as clever as the Etonians. Less bookish, perhaps, but just as intelligent. It was an exam-oriented school, and we all won scholarships.

Well, if I missed anything at all, I mean it's such a small thing . . . but you spend your first four years at Eton learning the ropes and going through various ordeals, and in your final year you are allowed vastly more freedom and treated much more as an adult; if you're a successful schoolboy, as I was, with friends who all got into Pop and things like that, then your life is that of a demi-god for your last year, and I expect that would have been fun. On the other hand, I had great fun at St Paul's.

It never ceases to astonish me that relatively ordinary contemporaries of mine who happen to have been at Eton are in positions of such prominence, I mean running merchant banks, or in the Cabinet or whatever, because I can remember them as perfectly ordinary, not particularly distinguished or particularly clever teenagers. And you can never escape this if you are an Etonian, because there are so many of them and they are in such positions of influence, power, money, that you're going to be more aware of them than you are aware of Wykehamists or Harrovians or Manchester Grammar School boys or whatever. There just are an awful lot of them — there are seventy in the House of Commons, and they swarm all over the City in the merchant banks and the discount broking houses.

The privilege which attaches to people who come from very monied backgrounds and automatically become partners in merchant banks, or whatever, I think is a bad thing nationally, and Eton, the world of Eton, is a very self-preserving, self-perpetuating world. I've no doubt that most of those people are very talented, I mean people like Lord Gowrie or William Waldegrave or David Howell are talented people, and they've chosen politics and they do well, and it's not because they're Etonians that they're in eminent positions; but there certainly are plenty of people who would not be where they are if they didn't have the whole impetus and system of Eton behind them.

My mid thirties were a changing point in my life, and it might be fair to say that the way I've lived since then has largely depended on unlearning an awful lot of what I'd been taught, or what I'd been conditioned to think. In that respect the expulsion from Eton, the realization that I didn't fit that particular groove, has been quite important in the second half of life. If I'd been braver, or perhaps more independent-minded, I might have been able to use that change much earlier in my life; I might have led a much less conventional life during my twenties and thirties than I actually did. But I didn't, and I don't suppose I got the real benefit of the very dramatic change which took place when I was seventeen until about twenty years later. Now I was going to say, 'I'm completely on terms with it', but I always have been, I think. I realize now that what seemed immensely important then and for some years afterwards wasn't at all: it wasn't a disgrace, it wasn't a tremendous failure, it didn't mean that one's life would be blighted. And when I look at my contemporaries, who proceeded absolutely smoothly through prep school, Eton, City jobs, whatever, they are much more in a mould than I am, and I suspect it would be fairly impossible for them to break that mould. The good side for them is that it gives them a tremendously secure feeling, they know exactly where they stand, who they are, but it's not adventurous; they may be very successful and make a lot of money, but I'm sure it diminishes them, cuts them off from hundreds of experiences which they could have had.

LORD HAILSHAM

——

I REMEMBER reading *Tom Brown's Schooldays*, that was before I went to my private school, that is to say about the First World War period, and I expressed a desire to go to Rugby. 'On the contrary,' my father said, 'you are going to the best school in the world', and I said, 'What is that?' and he said, 'Eton' – and that was the first time I heard the name.

Years later, I went in for an Eton scholarship and, after very many vicissitudes, I came top of the candidates; so I went into College, which neither my grandfather nor my father did.

We looked down on the Oppidans, and the Oppidans looked down on us, and it was a mutual dis-admiration. We were called 'tugs' because we were *togati*, people who wore togas or gowns. The Oppidans tended to say 'dirty tug' because of the time when Collegers were mainly poor boys without sanitary accommodation, and the phrase 'dirty tug' was like 'rosy-fingered dawn' in Homer; it was a sort of Homeric epithet.

And on St Andrew's Day, when the list of the people who were playing the Oppidans went up, there was always written on the top: *Floreat gens togata et ludus noster muralis est perpetuus!** We regarded ourselves as superior to the Oppidans. I was quite good at the wall game, and I played for College against the Oppidans – and on one occasion was bitten on the leg by the present Duke of Montrose.

The standard of scholarship in College was very high; it was high then and it has remained high since. Scholastically, College at Eton (I'm not talking about Oppidans) has probably one of the highest standards of scholarship in the country. Manchester Grammar School was considered to be our equal, but I can't

*'Let the togaed race flourish and may our wall game be for ever!'

think of any others. It was very highly competitive, too, and there was no shame in working hard in College, although amongst the Oppidans you were called a 'sap'.

It was a very full day. Started with early school, seven o'clock in the summer, seven-thirty in the winter, and work went on until after dark by way of preparation, what in other schools would be called 'prep'.

The first fortnight was absolutely like bedlam; it was like a badly run army in that everything went wrong. My election, which was twelve boys, was sent to Lower Chapel because we were new boys, when of course we were supposed to be in Upper Chapel because we were Collegers. Every kind of what in the army one called a cock-up happened in that fortnight and I won't say I was happy that fortnight, I wasn't, I was being messed about.

I don't think I was a boy who formed very close friendships. I'm really rather a private person. I've become gregarious later in life, but I was not very good at games, I mean I was always keen on climbing and walking in the holidays, but I'm not athletic in the sense of ball games, which I've never been good at and always thought rather silly. And I was rather cleverer than my contemporaries, so I suppose I wasn't particularly popular. I didn't excel in some things which were popular to excel in, and I did excel in some things which were not popular to excel in. Like work.

I was never good at artistic things. Words have been my aesthetic expression from the word go. I have never learned music, nor do I really appreciate it as an educated man really should. Art has slightly grown on me as an outside interest.

I think we lived our lives in perfect calm. Like all schoolboys we were noisy and sometimes disorderly, but it wasn't brutal, not at all. I was beaten only once as far as I remember, and I can't remember what it was for. It was a sort of subordinate type of beating called 'siphoning', which was done with a rubber strap or pipe.

My tutor was Whitworth, and at that time Whitworth had a house at the end of Judy's Passage, and to go to his Pupil Room on a December night, in the mist and in the dark (there was no lighting in Judy's Passage), was scarifying and very unpleasant, and cold and wet and damp and everything. Certainly it could be very uncongenial in the Thames Valley on a wet November or December night. But it's not my picture of Eton at all. My picture of Eton is the Fourth of June or St Andrew's Day, you know, with the sun and the river and things like that.

My brother Edward was not at Eton when I went there; he had already gone to Oxford. Indeed he had not only gone to Oxford, he had gone through Oxford. Edward was a tremendous personality. He didn't get the Newcastle at Eton, which I did, but he was Captain of the School for a time, he was in Pop, and he rowed for Christ Church in the Lady's Plate and got Leander and won a double first at Oxford. He was a very great man.

My younger brother did go to Eton and went into College about two years after me. We were as remote from one another as we possibly could have been. He is also a very private person. We've become very close since, although we don't see much of each other as he lives in Switzerland.

My mother was an American, and she was never very good about what Englishmen were like amongst themselves. My poor elder brother was sent to his private school wearing a sailor suit, which would have been an unthinkable thing for an English lady to do. But my mother was under the impression that it was the natural thing for a young gentleman to wear. And poor Edward, because in the way that schoolboys have of exaggerating things, the sailor suit became a purple velvet suit, and he was called 'Clarence' to the end of his days in consequence.

Mother died when I was at Eton. I remember exactly how it was announced to me. By curious and strange coincidence, both my younger brother and I were in the sickrooms, not together, but in adjoining rooms. We had different things wrong with us, I forget what they were. My elder brother came in one day – I think one Sunday – and said, 'I have very bad news for you. Mother died this morning.' I did go home for her funeral; my father was most terribly stricken, and I stayed at home for a week very largely to look after him.

There is a thing at Eton called Long Leave, which is the same as half term at any other school, and I remember in 1924, the year in which my mother died, she took me to *No, No Nanette*. It was the last time we went out together.

I can remember I was really quite ill after she died and I almost had a breakdown, I was excused school and all sorts of things.

I was on fairly intimate terms with Alington, who was the headmaster, although I don't think he liked me. I was very prickly in those days, and he knew me mostly after my mother had died, when I was more prickly still. But I had fairly close relationships with him. I think he was irritated by me and I was slightly irritated by him. I realize now that the fault was wholly on my side. I was too clever – not 'by half', but I was too critical by half, and also after my mother died I was in a disturbed and emotional state, and therefore I was not easy to get on with.

My father always went over my reports with me. They weren't nearly as good, in the sense of being well written, as my sons' reports when they were there; they were rather jejune. I mean, some of the funniest descriptions of my sons were in their school reports. They were terribly funny – some of the comments would make me laugh out loud! I only remember laughing violently on one or two occasions in my life, and certainly that accounted for one occasion.

I think of Eton as the best school in the world. I have great affection for it, and loyalty to it. I sent both my sons to Eton. It was fun having sons and fun having them there. But they were Oppidans and I was a Colleger, and that made a great difference.

I used to dream of Eton, that I was there and playing my part in the school, playing football, playing the wall game or the field game, rowing on the river, attending Absence. I now dream about being at the Bar, which is fifteen years out of date. I still occasionally dream about being in the army, but my dreams seem to have a sort of time lag of about fifteen or twenty years, and it's been a very long time now since I've dreamt about Eton.

NICKY HASLAM

WELL, it was the summer of the Coronation, so that gave my first half a kind of added fillip. There was an extra break in the middle of the half to look forward to, and Long Leave was changed from one weekend to another. And there was a kind of terrific atmosphere, as you can imagine.

My house was How's. He was called Oily How, I can't think why; he was rather dry. Very unassuming, very uninterfering with the boys in his house, giving them their head in a very subtle way. He was a much subtler man than one thought at the time – I mean, I now see that he was a brilliant, brilliant house-master. And unmarried, which I think in those days was really rather a good thing because there was then no rivalry between dames and wives, although it would have been hard to be a rival to my dame, she was the most famous dragon in Eton.

The famous Miss Byron, my God, she was the legendary figure of Eton! Had she been a boy and been able to inherit, she would have been Lord Byron. She was about a hundred then, and the size of a mountain, with hair all over her chin and face, and warts everywhere, and most wildly in love with Sydney Watson who was the music beak, who didn't return this love in any way at all. And she was known to terrify everybody from Robert Birley to boys long after me.

She was terrifying. It was partly the appearance, and no non-sense about anything, and partly this *booming* voice. She was an extraordinarily strong character. My mother once went to see one of my brothers, and on the way into the house, just by the Burning Bush, there'd been quite a bad accident, there was blood, and bodies lying around, and my mother went and asked Miss Byron, 'Do you think I could possibly have some brandy, I don't feel very well.' And Miss Byron came back with the smallest glass you've ever seen with nothing in it at all, and she boomed, 'I *HAVE* WATERED IT DOWN.'

She liked me – she quite liked people who were anything to do with the arts or anything like that. She was extremely artistic herself, and knew a lot about music, and was cultured and used to travel in the summer to wonderful places. She encouraged the painting side of my life and I got away with being terrifically slack at games and things because Miss Byron overruled my tutor and said, 'Let him spend his time at the art schools, it's much better for him.'

She certainly wasn't the nanny type, just there to put Elastoplast on one's heels if one got a blister. She was the last of the great old school of dames.

But boys were meant to get on and look after themselves – you didn't get ill. Frightfully common to get ill. I'd been ill, I'd had polio when I was much younger, so I'd done my illness.

When I moved into my room I realized one could have a bit of fun, and that nobody was against one being different. That's my idea of Eton still, that they love individuality, whereas most schools want you to conform. I just suddenly thought, 'I'm not going to have rosebud cretonne on these curtains, and I'm not going to have flying duck pictures on my walls, and I'm not going to have my ottoman done in *this*, I'm just going to make it all different.' And it was a hoot. I decorated it up to the nines with ostrich-feather plumes and ocelot curtains and things like that. My housemaster used to bring other housemasters around in the evening to see it, and they'd all go out open-mouthed.

I don't think it was outrageous because nobody seemed outraged, that's all I can say. They were amused by it. I think I was considered a complete laugh. The great thing is that it wasn't greeted with disapproval; it wasn't, 'Isn't Haslam terribly showing off', it was, 'What an interesting way of looking at things.'

I've got an American half-sister who used to visit, and she was appalled by Eton. 'It's meant to be the best school in the world,' she would say, and here were these awful little rooms, with horrible beds that folded up into the wall – she just couldn't believe the squalor of it. Well, it seemed quite perfectly all right to us, but to her it seemed awful.

I don't think I thought it was squalid, I thought it was just absolutely what I expected it to be. One knew that school was bound to be squalid and fast-foodish, gulping everything and getting out and rushing off.

I suppose because I didn't especially enjoy games, or didn't really know how to play them, having been ill for so long, I made straight for any kind of artistic or Drawing School life, and through that, quite early on, I was designing school plays and things, encouraged by the famous Wilfrid Blunt, who was the arts tutor then. He was the most gentle, wonderful, cultured man; I'm eternally grateful to him.

Wilfrid Blunt thought I would succeed in whatever field of art I chose. I think he would be cross or sad that I didn't actually become a proper painter – thank God I didn't – but he did say, 'This boy's the genius of his generation' about what I was doing, and I think ever since then I have felt a will to succeed, instilled by that kind of faith that was given one.

I suppose I was quite unusual. The genius of the place is that even if you do stick out they don't make you feel a fool, but I suppose looking back that I was pretty original, I mean I had black leaving photographs, for instance, rather than white, with swansdown bows on them, and signed in gold pen. That was pure Cecil Beatonarama. You see, by this time I'd met people like Cecil; by the time I was sixteen I was going to really, really extraordinary parties in London with Oliver Messel and Beaton and all that world, I mean they used to write to me at school, and come down even.

Cecil used to come down, and people didn't really know who he was then. He's much more famous now. I do remember my father had a great friend called Lowry, who was that painter, and my father and he came to take me out once. Nobody took any notice of them – that whole thing of fame is very recent. Henrietta Tiarks used to come down, Suna Portman and that world. They were much more famous; then people did sort of stand on walls to look at them and of course the great beauty was Clare Ward, Clare Baring, now with Tony Lambton. She's the one that people died to see.

I can tell you the first time I recognized glamour in my life. I remember standing in School Yard, fairly early on now, with little Winston Churchill, and his mother Pam, then married to somebody else, not to Randolph any more, coming to take us out to tea. And she arrived in a beige Rolls-Royce with a beige fur on her lap, and these wonderful clothes, and she brought Winston's half-sister Arabella who was this godlike child. She was four, and of such beauty! And I remember Pam's shoe coming out of the Rolls-Royce and it was a perfect alligator shoe, and I knew then *that* was glamour. That was the first time I'd seen glamour anywhere, then and there.

Again, little Winston, I remember him being flown to New York for the opening of *My Fair Lady* one Long Leave, and thinking, my God, that's the epitome of glamour. Imagine going to New York for Long Leave. And I remember when Jacob Rothschild left, my first half, he gave the Library a television set. I mean nobody had a television. So we had television for the Coronation, and to have one in a school seemed absolutely unbelievable!

When I left I absolutely rebelled against it all. My best friends immediately became David Bailey and Terry Donovan. I lived in the East End. The last thing I wanted to do was be near an Etonian. It took me ten years to buy an OE tie. I fought it completely. I don't know why I bought it, because I'm not a member of the old Etonian Association, and I bet half the boys who went there aren't, therefore they're not technically entitled to wear the tie. But I have got one, and I love it. Among other things, it's the only tie in the whole world you can wear with a black or a blue suit. Very pretty and very subtle.

To be an Etonian in America means something. It doesn't mean very much here any more because there are so many. It means more in America, it's much more fun in America. People love it if you've been to Eton, it sort of seems like the icing on the cake of Englishness, because after all they're the most snobbish people in the world – there's no snob like an American snob.

I think that my age-group weren't given much chance to learn how not to age fast because the badness of the routine at school, the lack of being able to wash one's hair oneself, you know-... until ten years ago the English hadn't any idea how to wash their hair! They just didn't do it, and people got bald by the time they had left school practically. It's getting better now. But I see people I went to school with and I can't believe they're so frightfully old. They're all bald, they look like Harold Macmillan half of them. Unbelievable! I'm sure I do too, but I mean, it's incredible, these old people slouching about. Crumbling to bits, with grandchildren. It's too, too frightening.

MARK HEATHCOAT AMORY

I ALWAYS knew I was going to go there, there was no question. My father wanted me to go very much because all his family went to Eton except him; he went to Radley. He minded about Eton. There was a chip on his shoulder, which was uncharacteristic of him, and so I feel a bit disloyal saying it. His older brother went, and got TB and died, and it was considered to be unhealthy, which is something a lot of people have thought. But I always knew I was going to go to Eton, it was an absolute certainty, and it never crossed my mind to do anything else.

I can remember first going there. I had never seen it before, and it was dank and wet and gloomy; it was quite unnerving. There was a tea with several boys and their parents, and my housemaster, Dr Hitchley Prescot, was spectacularly bad at handling social things like this, so it was the parents who did the work. There was a story about someone coming in to see him, sitting forty minutes with this little old man, and then saying, 'I wonder if Dr Prescot is coming,' and him breaking his silence for the first time and saying, 'I am Dr Prescot.' He was terrified of parents, never spoke to them if possible. The theory was that he knew everything, the boys always used to say, 'It's astonishing how much he knows about the house', but when I got to the top of the house I realized he didn't know that much about it but he was very nice.

And then there was the awful thing of going to have your voice tested, which every Etonian must remember. I remember it as being my first night, taken out through dark, cold streets and what seemed quite a long way, a quarter of a mile or so, and the wind blowing, and when we got there this frightful thing of someone saying to you, 'Sing this note', with someone banging on a piano testing you for the choir, and boy after boy failing to reach that note. There was no possible way I could sing any note at all, and singing was always absolutely bottom of my list of achievements anyway. That was rather an ordeal, in a way.

I would say I was rather unhappy at first. I didn't like it. I made friends, that bit was fine, but I didn't like fagging. I kept a diary, and when I've looked through it what I've found at that stage, slightly to my surprise, is that I was always cold, often hungry, always broke – that was my fault, I had a perfectly decent amount of money but spent it – and always tired. The tiredness was probably to do with growing and so on, but it was quite wearing, and it wasn't much fun being at the bottom of this system.

My best friend was someone called Julian Ormsby-Gore, and he was much worse off than I was. Actually one of my dominating memories of Eton is of him being cold; he was frozen the entire time. He's killed himself now.

He committed suicide long after Eton, but I realized, when he did that, I had underestimated how miserable he was and how insecure. He was so charming at school. He used to always wear pyjamas under his trousers to keep warm, and was endlessly storing coal. For some reason I never had a fire, so I used to give him my coal; and he would leave the light bulbs on in his room, which was illegal and which you were fined for, because he thought they warmed it up. I mean, this was optimistic. So cold was quite a dominating force, certainly in his life, but I think for all of us.

I think like most people I just took the system as it came, and, as a broad generalization, what Eton taught me was what people say the army taught them; how to live in tricky circumstances, how to keep your head down. I also realized very quickly that if you did too well one half you were expected to do well again the next half, so I set about resolutely not doing well.

I'm not sure how much I realized it at the time, but what I think very strongly now is that you know people as you never know them again because of being thrown together. You are locked up from six o'clock onwards and we used to just sit around talking, so you got to know your contemporaries with an unparalleled intimacy. Also you are unguarded at that age. I don't see anybody now whom I knew well then – there is one that I see occasionally, but I always feel that he's sort of on to me, and I suppose I to him, as nobody else. By Oxford, you've put up your defences and you know how to present yourself, and also you don't have this fantastic amount of time together. So I think in a way these were the most intimate friendships ever, but having said that, I drifted apart from all of them and I haven't got a really close friend whom I made at school.

I suppose we all had a slight smugness. In the holidays, people from minor public schools used to come up and say, 'We beat you at shooting', and so on. They would be aware of these things, and there was a rather patronizing way in which we never had the faintest idea whether we had won at shooting or lost at shooting, nor could we have cared less. I realized it was a rather superior position – that they were proud of having beaten Eton at something, and we simply didn't know or care.

Eton is such a symbol, isn't it? I have a tendency to say 'when I was at school' rather than 'when I was at Eton', just because I don't want a reaction. It's slightly annoying to be put into any pigeon-hole, because as you're saying, 'I was at Eton', the other person is thinking of little characteristics they believe you're going to have, and I'd rather they didn't think they knew what I was like.

A friend of mine who was at school with me was going across Australia just after University, and he was bumping along before dawn out on the sheep farm, being frightfully tough along with other twenty-year-olds, when one of them asked him, 'Where were you at school?' And he couldn't face it, because if he said Eton, he thought, it was going to be totally unacceptable. So he lied in some form, and the other boy said, 'Oh really, I thought I remembered you at Eton.'

I remember being told that 1956 was the big year, with Hungary and Suez; I remember my history master saying, 'History is being made.' I think he was talking about Suez, but I have a terrible doubt that he might have been talking about Hungary.

I remember thinking, 'I can't handle both these things, I'll read about Hungary and know about that', so I never understood Suez.

We thought James Dean was wonderful. I remember I had a great plan to break out from Eton to see Jerry Lee Lewis, who was going to come to Slough; unfortunately it was discovered that he had a twelve-year-old wife, and the Lord Chamberlain was so shocked, his whole tour was cancelled. Rock 'n roll was very important, and Elvis Presley loomed large.

Cool was the great thing. Glen Kidston had this gaunt white face and always dressed in black, and he was very cool, and didn't say much. Somehow he was more authentic, you believed him, while other people who attempted it could be easily seen to be posturing. 'There you go' was his phrase, 'There you go, man.' And he liked jazz. Jazz was all part of that, going to a jazz club in London was an exciting event. Nobody hid their enthusiasm for music, because that was the moment it came in. Bill Haley's 'Rock Around the Clock' – I remember that very well, that was tremendously talked about. Around that time, rock 'n roll was really getting going, and there was a wonderful shop in Windsor called T V R which let you play records indefinitely and never buy anything at all.

You were allowed a radio but not a gramophone, and if you did badly at work your radio was taken away; I practically never saw mine. Then the thing was to get another one. Boys used to build them into drawers, and incredible ingenuity was shown in hiding radios in tiny spaces and in having a whole system to turn them off, with bits of string so you could turn it off lying in bed although it was at the other end of the room, that sort of thing.

There was a rather curious convention on the last day of the half, when you were allowed to go home early. People used to get up incredibly early, like five o'clock, and go round in groups and bash up some unpopular person, and that was quite nasty. It was sort of accepted, but it was quite frightening. I used to go and hide somewhere, and although it didn't last very long and it wasn't fantastically severe, it was something out of *Tom Brown's Schooldays*. The rest of the half it depended very much on who was in control. I think that's the thing about Eton, you leave the boys in control, which is an excellent system and does wonders for their maturity, but every now and again it means that you leave somebody who's very nasty in control. There was one person – and I was lucky that I was sufficiently near him in age that I was a little too old to beat – who used to beat lots of people, unjustifiably, I suppose.

Being beaten was absolutely terrifying, the whole ritual of being beaten. It being so slow and inevitable. Sometimes you'd know you were going to be beaten . . . you wouldn't be certain, it was still vague, but you might have been told that you were going to be. There was a terrific amount of ritual. They had to ask the housemaster's permission after Prayers; they would say, 'We wish to beat Amory', and I don't know how much was said then – presumably he asked why, and I think often they would just say, 'He is a terrible impertinent nuisance', nothing more specific. Meanwhile all the boys would have gone back to their rooms. It was very, very serious to be out of your room after Prayers, absolutely out of the question. You went up to your room and you jolly well stayed. To be out of your room or in somebody else's room was very serious, although the Library or the Captain of the House were allowed to wander round, but certainly nobody else; and then you would know that the Library were sitting in the Library and this would mean that someone was going to get beaten, because they wouldn't go there except to beat somebody. And you'd feel fantastically frightened. It makes me feel chills, even now. Some people couldn't hear, but I had the room next to the Library, so I could. And then the youngest member of the Library would go out and he would summon the boy, who would come and stand outside, and then eventually, after a bit of time, would be brought in. And then there was a moment when he would be told what an appalling thing he had done. Usually you'd know, but sometimes it came as an awful shock, something one was completely unaware of, or certainly unaware that anyone knew about. Then a ritual again; they would ask, 'Have you anything to say?', at which stage, if you were extremely bold, you could say, 'I wish to see my tutor.'

You had the right, very legalistic, but that was madness, I don't remember anyone getting off. But then you jolly well saw him and said, 'Look, this is terribly unfair', and he wouldn't agree with you because it would be very detrimental, you can see, to disagree with the Library, it's like supporting your officers. Then you would know you were going to be beaten much harder, so it was a very, very bold thing to do, but some people did it – there was a lot of bravado about being beaten. You were beaten with a house cane. You would then say, 'Good night', and 'Thank you.' You had to say 'Thank you.' And a cousin of mine, an immensely, strong, brave, in this case idiotic, Scot, he just didn't, or wouldn't. And they said, 'You've forgotten something', and he wouldn't say it, so they beat him again, and he wouldn't say it again – and he won – they just didn't dare beat him again. So he had this extremely painful victory.

Beatings loomed large as a worry and a factor. That was all a very big part of life, and none of us pretended that it didn't hurt. Bravado, yes, but no one said, 'I don't care', at least if they did no one believed them for a second. It was known that you jolly well did care.

I could go on talking about Eton for a very long time, and I've always thought if I was going to write a novel I might easily set it at school. People used to write Oxford novels, but I have no interest in writing about Oxford at all; I think Eton is much more interesting. It's the intensity . . . even if you didn't terribly like somebody, you just knew them awfully well, you saw them all the time and talked to them all the time, and you knew everything about them, every weakness, in an appalling way.

It's all very vivid to me. It's not been that important in my life in that I don't think it shaped me, but I remember it as nothing else in my life, and it was actually much more interesting than Oxford – which was much more enjoyable. My memories of it are intense, my relationship with it is not.

LORD HOME OF THE HIRSEL

I GOT to Eton in 1917 in the middle of the war. My mother was in Scotland and my father was away in Gallipoli, and I was taken there by an aunt, a young aunt, quite an adventurous young aunt. That was quite all right, but you were aware the moment she went that you were on your own.

Now and again someone came along and took you to see somebody, but for the first time really in your life, you were left to fend for yourself. Although I would have thought I was reasonably brave, it was alarming, there's no denying.

I was in a house called Whitworth's. A. W. Whitworth was a classical tutor. He had been at Eton himself, and had been quite a scholar, and he taught Latin. He used to come and stay with us in the holidays. He was rather a keen walker over the hills, and a fisherman, and this sort of thing. He was a nice congenial fellow.

It wasn't physically the nicest place one has been in. It overlooked a graveyard which had rats. It would have been condemned by the Ministry of Health, undoubtedly, without question! But it was OK, it was a nice house. There were a nice lot of boys there when one got to know them, but it took a bit of time, of course. I was a lowland Scot, and there weren't all that number of friends that one knew in the school at the time, so there was nobody to sort of particularly pal up with from day one. But one was shifted around in various divisions, and you met people over the next few weeks, and in the games of course.

My second brother, he was in a different house, so I just ran across him, no more than that. And my youngest brother William didn't get there until I was just going. William was quite an eccentric. And he was extremely cheeky. My brother Henry used to complain of him because he was made to share a room with him, which must have been a terrible trial. He constantly bemoaned the fact that he was saddled with this ghastly fellow. My sympathies were with Henry!

At that moment of time, in the middle of the First World War, it was a fairly austere life, with rationing and all that sort of thing. Unlike the next war, there were very few air raids or anything like that, as far as I remember. But because of the rationing, the food was disgusting. There was something called Miss Martin's pudding which I remember to this day. It consisted of cold suet and bacon fat. Can you imagine anything worse? You couldn't get it down at all, it was awful. But that wasn't the school's fault; it was just the situation that had to be coped with.

I started with the classics, for which I have always been grateful. Once you have been taught Latin verses, you can speak and write English, because you have to prune like mad, as hard as you can. So I started with that, and then turned to history with Henry Marten and a man called Headlam, both of whom were very good teachers. Tuppy Headlam was rather an eccentric gentleman. There was a moment when he looked as though he was going to elope with that film star, Anna May Wong. He was an amusing type and conducted his classes in an informal way. He even made Dicey amusing and acceptable reading. Do you know Dicey, who wrote all about constitution and the law? No? Well he did, anyway. You enjoyed being taught by him.

But Henry Marten was the expert; he wrote a lot of books. He was rather a shock-tactic man. He would illustrate his history lessons very dramatically. He also had a tame raven which used to sit behind one's neck, and if you were inattentive, it used to nip your ear!

It wasn't so necessary then to have to get a high degree in order to get into business; you weren't equipping yourself for life in industry, by and large. You could get where you wanted to get without a degree, so I think I took it fairly easily, but enough to get by. I looked upon Eton as a sort of build-up for university.

The headmaster was my father-in-law, Alington, whom I didn't know was going to be my father-in-law then. But he was.

He was an absolutely splendid preacher, with a marvellous presence, a great crop of white hair, and he was a very tall fellow. He really was a most distinguished-looking man, very good-looking fellow too, rather classical features. And in the pulpit at Eton, that was unforgettable.

My mother-in-law was a very remarkable woman too. She was very good. I remember Gandhi came to talk to us when we were there. He was accompanied by a lady of uncertain purpose, a Miss Slade. She said to my mother-in-law, 'Oh, Mrs Alington, I'm afraid you have put me too far away, my bedroom is too far from the Mahatma. I must sleep within reach of him.' And my mother-in-law said, 'No, my dear, not as long as I am President of the Mothers' Union!' She was that sort of woman – and got away with it!

I remember some correspondent asking my mother, when I became Prime Minister, what sort of boy I had been, and she said, 'A very ordinary boy.' I think that is about right! And except for Cyril Connolly, who wrote that thing – something to the effect: 'He will be Prime Minister before he is thirty',* to everyone else, I shouldn't think they had the slightest idea at all.

I was fairly ordinary. Average. I mean I got on perfectly well and whatever work was to be done I did, and I played a lot of games, a lot of cricket.

At the end of the last two years I was in the eleven. The Eton–Harrow match was by far the biggest match that we played. You get the limelight then. I made the top score in one match at Lords, where the rain ruined the second day, so we only had the one day. I was what they would now call a seamer, and I took four wickets or something. There were about three performances that one was satisfied with, where I made runs and took wickets.

I can't remember all of them, but we used to have some funny jokes about Harrow. They don't seem to have the same kind of friendly animosity that we had then. Winchester had notions and rather strict conventions; we didn't have that sort of thing with them at all.

*In *Enemies of Promise*.

The greatest thing I ever did was to take Lady Churchill down to the Harrow song night. After he died she had no one to go with. I thought the songs were marvellous, very good, very tuneful. 'Forty Years On', that's a marvellous tune. A splendid evening.

When you come across an Etonian, well, you have somewhere to start your conversation, of course, even if he is years younger; you can ask how the school is and if this, that and the other is the same as it was, that sort of thing.

I go down to talk to the Political Society at Eton, or occasionally to watch a grandson play cricket or something like that.

I suppose so much of England's history is identified with Eton and Etonians. Of course, I was only half English; my mother was English. Some of my ancestors had their heads rolled down Edinburgh Castle. But even so, I think one did feel, even as a lowland Scot, a sense of England. One felt a part of England. I mean, Eton has a southern English atmosphere about it, doesn't it?

ADRIAN HOUSE

I REMEMBER my father sitting me down about a month before I went there and giving me the first glass of sherry that I was ever given and telling me why he was sending me to Eton. It was not because two uncles had been there, nor was it in the hope that I would acquire a dusting of aristocratic manners and friends, but because he did really believe that it was the best school in England at the time. And I thought, here was a man of wide experience, he'd been a don at Oxford, and was now headmaster of Wellington, and he must know what he was talking about, and I accepted it as such.

I went to a house under a man called Jack Peterson. Peterson was very able, very civilized, and very modest. He had got a soccer blue, he was one of the best fives players in England, he was a classical scholar, he loved good music, and was enormously understanding with the boys. He was also a very philosophical man, possibly a shade too much so; his great dictum was: 'You must take the rough with the smooth', and maybe one emerged from Eton taking too much rough with too much smooth, I don't know. But during the course of our time there his wife died of a cruel, creeping illness, which was a profound tragedy for him, yet he never let it affect adversely his relationship with any of the boys.

As much pot luck as the choice of your housemaster, and as important, was the accident of your contemporaries. Luckily we all got on together. We talked about Eton football and the wall game, prose styles, the techniques of beating, Beethoven versus Brahms, *The Times* crossword, and the relative beauty of younger boys. I never fell for a younger boy, but hero-worshipped one much older, who was probably the most beautiful boy I have ever seen, called Jonathan.

My whole time coincided with the war, which made it, I suppose, different from the Eton of a great many other generations. The houses were very cold, and the food was probably as sparse as it had ever been. But there were great excitements, or what were excitements for teenaged boys, and the anti-aircraft guns used to sound off at night and shower the place with shrapnel. Just before I arrived, an errant bomber had scored random hits on a master's house and Upper School. The raids were preceded by the undulating wail of the sirens. Then came the spooky and distinctive throb of a German plane, soon followed by the pyrotechnics of the Bofors anti-aircraft guns round Windsor Castle and on the Brocas. It was irresistible not to break the rules and look out of the windows, criss-crossed with paper strips against blast, in order to see if the probing searchlights had caught a bomber in their crossed beams. More than once or twice we heard the whistle of falling bombs, no doubt in answer to John Betjeman's poem, 'Come, friendly bombs, and fall on Slough'.

I dare say quite a few boys were windy, and I was quite glad I shared a room with my younger brother, you know, when things were noisy, I was quite glad to have him there to talk to. For some reason the German engines throbbed in a way that the British ones didn't, so that you always knew when it was a German aeroplane. Later on, 1944 I suppose it was, there were the V1s, the doodlebugs, and I remember you were all right if the engines went on and flew over your head, but if you heard the engine cut out, you had instructions wherever you were to lie on the ground and clasp your hands over the back of your neck. Of course this gave rise to a great deal of fun in the classes being taken by some of the lesser disciplinarians among the masters.

Apart from the memory of the noise, my clearest memory during the flying bombs time is of going down to the shelter, and the walk down Common Lane in the moonlight, and the overpowering orange-blossom smell of the philadelphus in the garden round the shelter.

So there was that side which was all rather enjoyable and

exciting and different. And as it was wartime we learnt not only about living, but killing and dying.

I wonder if we were the first generation of Etonians who were given graphic lessons on how to kill? After Dunkirk the army produced a radical new training in section attack and hand-to-hand fighting which was passed through to raw recruits and schoolboys. We were taken out into the playing fields and taught section attacks, and rather improbably our company commander was a man called Geoffrey Agnew, who was a very distinguished connoisseur of painting and, paradoxically, an extremely good corps commander.

Perhaps the most moving experiences at Eton were the evening services of Intercession in College Chapel to pray for any of our families or friends, for the old boys who were fighting, and for the souls of those who had been killed. It made me feel deeply about family, friendship, patriotism, prayer and death. I remember one of the old boys from my tutor's coming back from the front line in France, and describing how my hero Jonathan had been killed, by a burst of machine-gun fire, in front of his eyes.

I had my own personal experience of living and dying. I was playing cricket, and one of my friends who was bowling kept saying, 'Stand closer . . . closer . . . closer . . .' I was fielding short leg, and instead of bowling faster and straighter, he bowled a full toss which was hit with colossal power straight on to my nose, and I was knocked out and carried off the field, straight to hospital. When the nose was mended, I was put in the school sanatorium, but while the surgeon was delighted with what he called the cosmetics, nobody subsequently noticed that the thing was haemorrhaging. I found myself getting weaker and weaker and weaker, and one evening I heard the matron on the telephone in the next room saying, 'You must take him away tonight, because if you don't, I can't be responsible for his life.' And I was aware in some funny way of having the choice of living or dying, just by an act of will. I felt a sense of drifting on the borderline, and then I thought, 'What a terrible waste: I've had this marvellous five years here, and all the love from my parents, and it would be a pity really to just shuffle off and die.' So I thought, 'I'll make a real effort.' And then they carried me back into the hospital and they gave me blood transfusions, and so on.

So one had the experience of the Intercession services, where rows and rows of boys whom I knew had been killed, the experience of one's housemaster's wife dying and seeing how he took it, and then this experience, and it further taught one about dying.

We went to School Yard and heard Winston Churchill broadcast Victory in Europe from a loudspeaker hung on Lupton's Tower. That night gramophone records were spun from windows, fire extinguishers emptied over passengers waiting for the Dorney bus, and the buses were garlanded with the last, slender supplies of transparent and friable wartime lavatory paper. Finally mass hysteria erupted in scenes round a bonfire on Fellows Eyot: most of them were jubilant, but, inexplicably, one poor boy was hounded for a moment like a witch.

My subsequent life has evolved far more from my family roots than from those I put down at Eton. Nevertheless, I cannot deny these facts. When I applied to join my regiment, the colonel happened to be the father of a boy in my house. When I applied to New College, Oxford, its dean, a professor of biblical exegesis, turned out to be an Old Etonian. When I became a publisher, I joined two others of Mr Peterson's boys. My father-in-law went to Eton.

So it has gone on, by accident, not design. Eton keeps on flitting in and out in the most extraordinary way, and I could give you an account of my life which makes it sound as though it was Eton-directed, which it's not; but every day, month, year, it affects the quality: every aspect of life seems to have been deepened or improved by either human beings there or influences which one rightly or wrongly traces back to Eton.

Eton has had little effect on my material life, for I have become neither rich nor well known. But every day, every month, every year, I feel I owe something of the quality that I enjoy in life to influences I can trace back to Eton.

The Eton connection keeps on appearing as if by magic. It is a radio wavelength. Most of the time the transmitters are silent, but the switch is always there, and you never know when the speaker may come to life.

HUGH HUDSON

EVERY male member of my family went there. My great-grand-father, grandfather, father, uncle, stepfather, everybody, every man I came in touch with in my childhood had been there, so it was like a *fait accompli*, wasn't it? It was like a prison sentence. It was evident that I couldn't avoid it; it was there at the end of the tunnel.

The whole concept of boarding school is pretty appalling if you think of it, being sent away at the age of seven from your family, with the train screaming down the platform as your parents recede into the distance. God, it is a pretty shitty thing to do. You get used to it. If you cry it is considered babyish or wet; you aren't meant to cry, are you? Not meant to show emotions.

I wouldn't send my child to boarding school. I would rather be there myself to give him the emotional support and take the responsibility as a father should, rather than off-load the re-sponsibility on to some person you have no idea about. That is the most extraordinary thing that parents would do to a child.

And it was naturally with a sense of foreboding, going there. The amount of people, the blackness – everybody wore black. A sea of tiny black people moving everywhere, like a Lowry paint-ing. Top hats, they wore. Do they still wear those tail-coats? Winter days, all the chimneys belching smoke because every single boy had a fire in his room, that was an extraordinary thing. Very cold all the time, very, very, cold.

That ridiculous test you had to go through where you have to remember the names of all the important people in the school, the colours of all the different teams, the different sports, geographical places, rather like the taxi test, the Knowledge, absolutely ludicrous. If you failed three times you got beaten. Pathetic, really. I am full of disdain and scorn for it.

On the other hand, there was a sort of sneaking, hidden love of the place. Because you go back down there and it is most beautiful.

I was in Herbert's, J. S. Herbert. He was a mathematical genius, or wizard. He was an extremely bad housemaster, he didn't really care, I don't think. He cared more about his figures and drank a lot. But he was a brilliant man. He was involved in the famous Mulberry Harbours that allowed the Allies to land on D-Day. But he was remote. Mathematicians often are. He should never have been a housemaster because his heart wasn't in the education of small boys, bringing small boys from thirteen to maturity. He was bored with the company of children. He should never have had the job. That should have been seen by the headmaster or the governing body of the school, and he should have been fired.

There wasn't any contact, which is terrible really. The house-master is a surrogate father figure, or should be in its ideal form, because you lose your father figure when you leave home. I personally, from a divorced background, who had no dominant father figure, I needed that. And I was an only child. So in a way the school's structure was security, even unhappy and miserable, it was still security. But there was no rapport with Herbert; it was impossible. Nobody could, he was a remote man, which was a tragedy really. I haven't got anything good to say about Herbert.

If you didn't fit in you got beaten. The beating rituals were very weird. They have stopped it now, quite rightly. They put terror among the house. They were always done in the evening when all the doors were shut, and everybody was in their room except the Library. There was a sort of ripple through the house, and you knew when someone was going to be beaten because you could hear them practising in the distance. 'Whoock, whoock'. Then they used to shout the name of the boy that had to come up and it would echo through the whole house. A very weird atmosphere. It would be interesting to re-create it in a film actually. Poor little kids. Or yourself. You were shivering. Up you used to go, you had to answer for yourself, and if you didn't have a good answer you would get beaten. 'Not trying hard enough for the house'. . . I am sure that I was beaten for that, I can't quite remember.

Our house, like most other houses, was orientated around sport. It was very competitive. It's all to bring out the competitive spirit in man, a school like that; you have got to do better than the next man, the house has got to do better than the next house, you have got to win – now.

I wasn't very good at anything there, in fact I was terrible. I didn't care when it came to sports. If I had really concentrated on it I suppose I would have been good at sports because I am quite coordinated, but I didn't really care, I didn't try very hard.

And I wasn't very clever academically, I just got through. I suppose I was unremarkable by Eton standards, so I wasn't of much interest to the authorities, either the boy authorities or the master authorities. I wasn't going to do any good for the school in an academic sense. I wasn't going to be a candidate for Cambridge or Oxford, and I wasn't particularly good at sports. I suppose I was just one of the mass. Some people blossom into great brilliance at school and into university and then peter out. There are different ways of looking at it, aren't there? In retrospect, I was one of those people who developed very late. The last ten years have been my key moment – and hopefully beyond.

The school would think that my success now is a tribute to the school. 'Produced a very successful film director,' they would say. 'Didn't show much promise at eighteen on leaving Herbert's, but these things come through in the end.' It's that attitude, don't you think? *Floreat Etona*, for God's sake, is the school motto.

Well, I think that it was four wasted years, four very important formative years. They were emotionally barren years. Boys between thirteen and eighteen need emotional fulfilment. Maybe that is why some people were drawn on towards a sexual experience. We all had it.

There was a maid. She was a very, very provocative, sexy little creature in a house across the road, I've forgotten the name of the house now. She obviously got an enormous kick from exciting the kids: she used to perform in the window opposite, like Carmen outside the prison wall, performing, undressing, playing with herself, you know, masturbating in front of a window, in front of a number of windows. You thought she was doing it for you, but she was probably doing it for thirty or however many kids were looking out at the time, who were probably masturbating, looking at this woman.

Then I finally got contact with her, I made a date under the Arches! It was a good experience. It wasn't the first sexual experience – as I say, we had all had homosexual experiences – but it was a good experience.

The label is always put on you – 'Old Etonian', all the time. People are somehow more interested in that than who you really are. It is put on you when something goes wrong: 'Old Etonian fails', because you are not expected to fail. 'Old Etonian caught with his pants down in Hyde Park'. You can't avoid it, it is part of you, it's like having blue eyes. It's not really a question, it's an insinuation: 'Of course, *you* were at Eton', as though that says everything. It says fuck all, of course, because each individual in life is different, but it is a handle, a very superficial handle that people put on you. And that is why I have tried to eliminate it from any kind of conversation now because I think it is unimportant, and uninteresting ultimately.

I have a very guilty conscience. The guilt is that I had the privilege, that I was born in such a way that I was given the opportunity while millions of people aren't to go to a place like that. I think it's monstrous really.

I certainly had a great education, the best that money could buy. You can't fault it, any of these top public schools, Winchester, Eton or Harrow, you couldn't fault the education, really. I mean academically.

I had a great education, and therefore I make films which somehow try to assuage that guilt for me personally, point out to people the iniquity of certain things.

You have seen my films, haven't you? *Chariots of Fire* and *Greystoke*. They are all about rebels, people who didn't really like the system. Harold Abrahams was certainly a victim of this system, and Tarzan rejects the system, rejects his own family background.

'Silk-shirt socialist' they would call me, but I'm more anarchist than socialist. But when you come from the background I do, you will always be patronized. People say I'm a hypocrite, 'champagne socialist'. 'Limousine liberal', the Americans say. Because I went to Eton. It's so unfair – why shouldn't you have any kind of view?

I have never been asked by anybody at Eton to come down and talk about my films. They ask other film directors down all the time, because there is obviously a strong interest in people going into films. Everybody wants to go into the film industry, it is the pulse. But it is odd that no one has asked me down to give a lecture or to talk to the boys. There are very few Old Etonian film directors. Why have I not been asked down? It would be interesting to go. I am sure all these questions would come up. Why don't they ask me? Are they worried about me criticizing them, is that what it is?

THE RT HON. DOUGLAS HURD

I WAS at a prep school called Twyford which very much favoured Winchester, but someone said to my father that if I could get a scholarship to Eton it would be a good thing really, because it would be a wider education than Winchester could provide.

He was a farmer then, trying to make a living out of five hundred acres of Wiltshire downland; he was also agricultural correspondent of *The Times*, but that didn't pay very much either, so he was counting the pennies quite hard.

And so when I won a scholarship, there was a fair amount of rejoicing all round.

It was the war, of course, the middle of the war, and the place had been bombed. Upper School was sliced in two, and all the Chapel windows were out, there was blackened glass, and we had to go down to the shelters often.

It was a fearful business. The sound of the siren and getting up out of your sleep and stumbling about, it was a fearful business. The sound of the 'All clear', which meant that you could go back to bed, I still remember that . . . what a blessing! The 'All clear' is an even note, the warning was up and down, so you got to know very well, even through your sleep, the different kinds of noise that the sirens made. There was one night when the siren did not go, but nevertheless we were roused and told to go down to the shelter. We were in a highly mutinous state because this was intolerable – what were the beaks doing? It was the first night of the fire bombs and the King had sent word from Windsor that the boys were to go to the shelters as this might happen, and so we did.

An Eton scholar had to work pretty hard, and I was quite good at that. I mean, not exceptional; there was a chap called

Charles Willink who always came top of our election and passed every exam much higher than anyone, and I settled down into positions of third or fourth in our group of fifty scholars.

There was a strong scriptural element, a lot of New Testament Greek, actually learning by heart the Acts of the Apostles in Greek so that you could recognize every passage, and a lot of composition. They don't do any composition now, but one spent an awful lot of time turning English poetry into Latin, and also turning Shakespeare into Greek iambics. I can still remember a lot of English poetry from having done that. They think they work hard now, but they wouldn't dream of doing that. Actually it was very good for one. You really got a sense of language by having to do that regularly every week. And the Newcastle was a sort of climax of that.

Because I am D. R. Hurd, there was a tendency to call me 'Doctor', which faded, fortunately, after a while. I was a quiet boy, shy and awkward, and gradually coming out of my shell. Well behaved, perhaps to a fault, and so quite liked by the beaks and so on. I don't think that anyone would have thought anything special was around. Nor was it.

There were times when College was very much a separate sect, but we weren't, because in my election there were people who were good at games and got into Pop early and who made College very much a sort of star in the general firmament, so one got carried along with that.

One belonged to endless societies, and I became particularly interested in the Political Society. By 1945 my father was in the Commons, and my grandfather had always been an MP, so I was political. There were several other people there who were political, so we chatted a lot about politics, and very distinguished people used to come down and talk to us.

We even did plays, which the headmaster, Claude Elliott, didn't really approve of. We did a marvellous *Henry the Fourth, Part One*. Now they do plays every day of the week, I suspect, but in those days it was quite unusual.

I played Worcester, who is a bad baron. I was very bad, very wooden. I can't remember any of my lines, but I can remember one of Tim Raison's* lines as the King when he said, 'Worcester, get thee gone; for I see danger/And disobedience in thine eye . . .' Tim reminds me of this occasionally. Raef Payne was, I think, the funniest Falstaff I have ever seen. He was superb. It was a very, very good production.

Our religious instruction was very orthodox. I remember 'For all the Saints' on November the 1st; we made an amazing noise. We sang much louder then than they do now. I am not talking about deep spiritual experiences – I am talking of orthodox schoolboys – but a kind which sticks and makes a difference, and you get the feel of the words into you, and you learn them by heart, and that is a great thing. But I remember Alington in Holy Week. The Chapel was full, even though it was completely voluntary. He was a great actor. He leaned heavily on a stick and hobbled up the aisle. One night he was Pontius Pilate, one night St Peter. They were marvellous sermons; he had a great gift of language. He was up in the pulpit, and the lights were out except for two candles on either side of this great white mane of hair, marvellous lion head. He always ended with a marvellous theatrical sentence or two, and then he blew out the candles: and before the lights went on, you were just left for a moment in darkness. He was a great performer.

Well, I was never an athlete. I used to get by at games, but I was never very good at them. I disliked cricket, and I remember looking through the windows just hoping that it was going to rain. I remember the wall game, which was a peculiar game that Collegers in particular play, which I was quite good at – it was the only game I was any good at, probably because it is a clumsy game! I played wall which is the three people inside, nearest the wall, and you need to be fairly resistant to pain and tough and physically strong, and I was those things. In those days it was much tougher – you had to put on helmets and uniform. Now they don't. It has become rather a soft game now. But I used to enjoy that. The sweat and steam used to rise in masses from the boys. I remember St Andrew's Day which was the classic match of that season, and the high emotions.

*Rt Hon. Timothy Raison.

I stayed with the classics until I won the Newcastle scholarship, and then I switched in my last year to history and ran second for the top scholarship, which is the Rosebery.

The Bishop of Coventry won it. I didn't mind him coming first because I am devoted to Simon, but I did mind what the judge said: he said something about Simon being a true historian, and he thought that I would be a very competent civil servant – and that did rather rankle, I must say!

I got a scholarship to Trinity, Cambridge, when I was sixteen and a half, and there was a beak called Martineau who said, 'Now you have got your place at Cambridge you will have a certain amount of time, and I want you to read Macaulay's *History of England*. You can sit in my garden in the summer and read.' And I thought that this was going to be frightfully boring, because although I had never read Macaulay's *History of England*, I just knew that it went on and on and on. But I did do that, and it proved immensely stimulating. That is the sort of thing you can do at Eton, and I don't think there are many schools where that would happen.

I am embarrassed when I'm introduced as an Old Etonian. I went to speak for another MP the other day, and he made most of his introductions on these grounds which he thought was very laudable, but it didn't go with a swing with the audience.

I dream of Eton. Of particular rooms rather than people. If you lived in College, which is alongside Lupton's Tower, the clock looms very large in your life. I went through a phase when I couldn't sleep, which I think teenagers do, and you could measure the passing hours when you weren't sleeping by the clock which never stopped. I am a Fellow now so I go back quite often, and Eton is not just in the past, but I still dream of it.

SIR MARTIN JACOMB

I CAN remember arriving with a whole lot of boys who seemed to know each other. There were nine new boys; I messed with John Julius Norwich and John Dashwood. They appeared to be older, more sophisticated and generally more men-of-the-world than I – and that was partly because I was slightly younger, I was still twelve.

I can remember it all much more clearly than I can remember more recent things. The school year started in Michaelmas, and I can remember very distinctly the beginning of every Michaelmas term, with the chestnut trees and the conkers falling on the ground, and what it felt like to go back after a summer holiday, and whether one was apprehensive or going to enjoy it. I can remember every foot of the house; I can remember the pictures of film stars pasted on the walls of the Library, people like Jennifer Jones and Lauren Bacall, and Greta Garbo, of course.

Herbert's had been a spectacularly successful house under the preceding housemaster, J. D. Hills, who hadn't retired that long before. It had lost some of its glamour, but it was a respectable house, untainted by the evil which affects some houses at Eton.

Herbert was a marvellous man. You could tell immediately that – although apparently remote – he knew perfectly well what was going on, although in fact he played an incredibly limited part in our lives. He was a very clever man, a mathematician, and he spent a lot of time – I didn't know it then, but I learned it subsequently – working on military projects like the Mulberry Harbour and the floating airstrips, and things like that. His wife came to lunch every day, but you always felt that she slightly resented the fact that he was totally absorbed in the house, and

I always felt there was a tension between her and the dame.

The dame was an important figure in every boy's life, because in those days a lot of the boys were unfit because of the war. I mean, people had chilblains and the usual winter ailments, but they often took a more severe form. And in fact I had pneumonia when I was there. It was an absolutely appalling life in comparison to now; the diet did leave you continually hungry, I mean there was no question about it that rations were fantastically short, and it was really hard to get nourishing food. And double daylight-saving time in the winter meant that not only did you get up in the dark for Early School, but you came back to breakfast and it was still dark. And it was unbelievably cold. The only heating was a coal fire every other day in your room. When you go down to a boy's house now you find the windows wide open with the central heating blazing. It's a big contrast.

It was always a great thorn in my side that I didn't grow tall enough to get out of Eton jackets until long after other boys of my age; I thought that Eton jackets were relatively degrading, you see. And I was immature for my age and therefore a great deal of what was on offer at Eton passed me by. I just felt that everybody else was more at home and more successful. I felt much less privileged than the other boys, who came back with pheasants from their estates and had extra butter sent to them and appeared to be much richer and grander. My father was a wool broker, which is just an ordinary City occupation; he wasn't particularly rich or anything. My mother was Quaker in outlook, and her whole life was dedicated to prison visiting and the Salvation Army and all that kind of stuff.

But life went by smoothly, I mean I took an undistinguished form and I don't think the work was difficult, and I certainly didn't feel unhappy. It was easily the most important thing for me, because, unlike a lot of more privileged boys, my life in the holidays was a great deal duller than life at school, so what happened at school was the important and interesting part of it.

I specialized in a thing called classical general, and I was absolutely mediocre at work, I hasten to admit. I got School Certificate and so forth, but you couldn't possibly find any academic distinction in my career if you look back at the records. I was just totally middle-of-the-road.

But my classical tutor was wonderful. He was a man called Dennis Wilkinson. He well understood mediocre small boys and how to motivate them, he was wonderful company, and I never felt afraid of him. I wasn't mature enough to get the benefit of understanding either classical or English literature – for instance in French I can remember reading Stendhal, *La Chartreuse de Parme*, and *Le Rouge et le Noir* which must have passed largely over my head at the time. But it laid the groundwork, and I turned to it avidly as soon as I became mature enough to do so.

I think you'd find in my housemaster's reports to my parents references to the fact that he felt there was potential which was never, ever realized at Eton. I suppose part of the motivation came when my older brother died when he was very young, and I got an extra boost, in motivation through the desire to justify, in my parents' eyes, that loss, whereas had he lived I think I could have coasted along quite happily – which was basically what I would have much preferred to have done.

You were extremely conscious of the war. Once a week there were Intercession services in College Chapel to remember the fellows who had been killed the previous week, and we frequently spent nights in the shelter against the V2 rocket attacks, and we had gas masks.

I remember V-E night. It was a deeply memorable experience. I can remember that it was a wonderful feeling, because there was no doubt that the war was a deep worry. You knew that everyone around you was frightened by it, and elder brothers were killed, and God knows what, and we all knew that the atomic bomb was in the later stages of being developed – I don't know how the hell we did know: the Los Alamos project was still a closely guarded secret – but somehow or other we knew. So it was a huge relief and there was a sort of outburst of spontaneous joy, and, I think, a holiday. But it developed into a sort of witch-hunt against a boy who symbolized strict authority. He was a perfectly reasonable boy, an absolutely entirely sane, sensible boy, he wasn't a bully or vicious or anything like that, but he just happened to be the personification of strict authority. And it taught me a hell of a lot about crowd psychology. What happened was that a lot of boys chased him and got quite close to physical violence against him – in fact I can't quite remember the end of the story; I can just remember the crowd turning against him as a sort of unanimous mob, and I've never, ever since, doubted the force of crowd psychology and the need to be vigilant against it, because of the evil which comes to the surface, and the wrong which it invariably does. And that left a deep, deep impression on me.

BRIAN JOHNSTON

WELL, my father had been there, and both my brothers and an uncle, so it was rather following in the footsteps, you know, and I was expected to go there. Although my father had died three years before I went, somehow we scraped the thing and I went there. It was much cheaper in those days, but even then it was pretty expensive.

We lived in Herefordshire, a place called Much Marcle, where we had a lovely old house. In those days we would come back for Long Leave, and we used to hunt a bit – I'm terrified now – and they arranged a special early morning meet for Etonians that started at ten instead of eleven, so we could get back in time on the Monday evening. We used to go on the Cheltenham Flyer which took an hour and a quarter, which was sensational.

When I went, my older brother had left, and my second brother and I shared a room. The conditions were simply unbelievable. We were in a place called Coleridge House in Keats Lane. I went first to R. H. De Montmorency. He was a grey-haired man, keen on golf, an amateur champion. His daughter in fact married E. W. Swanton, the great cricket writer and broadcaster, retired now. But the conditions were unbelievable. We had about forty to forty-five boys, and one tin bath which you put in front of the fire. You had one bath a week. I remember the housemaster would come round and say, 'What are you doing, little boy?' I said, 'Having a bath', and he said, 'Lucky dog', and he was quite right. I was really very happy there. But it was unbelievable really, the conditions. There was a KCB, who was Knight Commander of the Bath. About seven people would have a bath each night; the lower boy got in at 7 p.m.: 'Out, 7.10

p.m.,' the KCB would say, then the chap would go round to the next room: 'Right, your time now.'

You were only allowed a fire on three days of the week. We were lucky because as two brothers we could have a fire every day, so with a brother you were all right. But if you were a single chap, the other days either you went and sat in someone else's room, or you just sat in your cold room. It was unbelievable. There wasn't any central heating, or carpets, or anything like that.

In the middle of the night, the night watch came round. She was a woman who used to stoke the fires and take away the ashes. She used to come in between the beds and people would put things to trip her up, and she would swear like anything. She smelt like a trooper! She would get down on her knees, rake the thing out, and set it for the next day. Night watch, she was . . .

De Montmerency had a wife and two daughters, so inevitably the food was not too good, because they didn't have as much money. The great secret in going to Eton is to go to a bachelor's house, because the food was always better – he would have more money to spend on it. I remember once King George V came down and asked for a week's holiday for us, much to the delight of my tutor because it meant he had a clear one hundred pounds profit which it would have cost to feed the house.

So the food was pretty awful, but there was a place called Rowland's which was the tuck shop and you used to have an allowance of one shilling per day. In the break, you could go to your house and have biscuits and milk or something, and you then went down to Rowland's and had eggs and bacon, in addition to the food of the house. It was extraordinary how much people went and ate there in addition. All boys are hungry, and it was always a popular place. But the shilling seemed to last. A shilling a day: we didn't grumble, we thought that was rather good.

I was fairly lucky because I was quite good at games, which played a very big part, undoubtedly. When I was in my private school I wasn't very good at football, but when I arrived as a new boy, I suddenly found – where I got it from, I don't know – that I ran very fast. In the Eton field game, if you can run very fast you don't go in for the hurly-burly of the scrum, you go and play in a place called fly, or corner, behind the scrum, which is much better. When we had our lower-boy matches, I was quite a star at that. The Captain of Games would watch on the sidelines, and at half-time he would come out and give us the most tremendous bollocking: 'Go twice as hard or you'll hear something about this after' – I mean, it was taken terribly seriously.

You had to 'do a time' every day, which meant you had to do some sort of exercise. I went for a run along the river bank. You had to go as far as Easy Bridge; of course you tried to cheat and not run all the way, but if you were found out, you were beaten. There was always the threat of corporal punishment, which is a very debatable thing, but it kept one on one's toes. A lot of the things were very unfair. We once had what is called a G T, which was a general tanning. Some graffiti had appeared in the loo and it was asked who put the graffiti there, and no one owned up. So they said that if no one owned up by the next day there would be a general tanning. And no one owned up, so we were all beaten, which is unbelievable today; but we just thought this is what public school life is like.

I was lucky in that I was good at cricket, so one had a certain sort of status amongst the boys. Also, I have always been a bit of a joker, and I used to make people laugh, and I was moderately well liked. So I felt confident, although I knew that if I did something wrong I would suffer. But I think the effect on some people was disastrous – there is no question that on a delicate or a sensitive boy it was far too tough.

There was the fagging thing. You would be sitting in your study, and you had to be on the alert for a shout of 'B-o-o-o-o-y'. And then everybody had to leave what they were doing and race down, and the last person had to do the thing. It might be, 'Go up to my room and fetch a cardigan, I'm cold', or it might be to take a message round to so-and-so's house.

They have stopped that now, because it meant that you could never do any work. Imagine sitting doing your prep, and suddenly having to throw everything up and run down; it was fantastic.

Old Monty left after I had been there for about six halves, and then a man called Huson came, who had one skin less than everybody else – I think he had seven layers instead of eight. He was always very red in the face. He was a very nice man, mad on cricket, and he helped me tremendously. We had a tremendous friendship; he used to stay in the holidays and I thought he was marvellous. He used to jolly people around and say, 'Look, have you seen this young wicket-keeper?', because he used to coach me and all that.

I hadn't got a father figure and certainly Huson was the first big influence in my life. I didn't want to go to Oxford. I was rather keen then to become a business magnate, I wanted to get into the City quick, but Huson said, 'No, why not enjoy three years now, and cut them off from the other end of your life?' So I went to Oxford and had the most wonderful time there, and never regretted it. He was a big influence on me, undoubtedly, and helped me enormously.

Cricket became absolutely vital . . . it was very much part of one's life. You had house nets three nights a week, and on Tuesdays, Thursdays and Saturdays you had proper games of cricket, so it was a non-stop thing. I absolutely loved it, but it was murder for people who didn't like cricket. They ended up in a thing called Little Club, and of course made a farce of it. You had to go on playing until Absence, and after Absence you didn't have to play if the game wasn't going on, so they always used to make sure it *had* ended. But the other people were very keen. I happened to like the field game, and so that was important in the winter. I also played rugger, which very few people did at Eton, and had a lot of fun there.

So games, I'm afraid, played a very important part. But I wasn't unintelligent, I kept going. Much to everybody's surprise, I won the Brinkman Divinity Prize, which got the biggest laugh I have ever heard in Upper School when the results were read out. I think I had copied out of a book which the examiner didn't know about.

I got my Field, which in those days was *the* accolade really. Your Field was more important, very nearly, than the Eleven. I also got my rugger colours. I was in the twenty-two which was the second eleven at cricket, for two years, and captain for the second year. There was a chap called Burleigh, and he stayed on a bit later than perhaps he should have, so he kept wicket at Lords and I didn't. But I captained the second eleven, and we had the most tremendous fun. We always tried to win, and didn't mind if we lost.

I remember King George came down to the school and shook hands with the captain of the eleven. I was standing within a few yards. 'I hope you beat Harrow this year,' he said in this very deep voice. Queen Mary had a toque on, this funny sort of hat she always used to wear. They often used to come over from Windsor. On Sundays there was no question of playing games like they do now; you had to go to Chapel twice a day, and in the afternoon you could walk up to Windsor, although you weren't allowed down the side-streets, or into Peascod Street because it was evil, naughty, but you could walk into the Castle grounds. And we used to go up there in the evening, especially in the summer, and there would be the King sitting in his window looking over the East Terrace there, all dressed up.

I got into Pop. That was very important. That was one's ambition, like a politician getting into the Cabinet. I suppose it was silly: you rushed off to your tailor the next day to have special braid put around the tail-coat. We were allowed to wear fancy waistcoats and stick-up collars with ties, and you could put sealing wax on the back of your top hat if you wanted to. But I think it gave you a sense of achievement – you felt that you had got somewhere, although a great many people didn't get into Pop who have probably done far, far better than I have ever done in my life after. But it gave you a little kudos and everybody likes a bit of kudos, don't they?

There were marvellous teachers. A man called Tuppy Headlam, we used to go to his house . . . there's a lovely story from the time we were there, when Anna May Wong the film star was all the rage. She used to come down and have dinner with him, and there was always talk of him and Anna May Wong. If ever the telephone rang in the room during school, one of the boys would go to his private side to answer it. It rang one day, and we always tell the story about Martin Gilliat,* although *I* think it was McGillycuddy of the Reeks† who went to answer the telephone, and Headlam was waiting there, obviously expecting that it was going to be her. The chap came back and said, 'Sorry, *Wong* number!' There was absolute uproar.

The housemaster used to come round every night in his dinner jacket, because often they had dinner parties, and just look in and say, 'All right?', or come and sit down and ask what you had done that day. That was a very important thing, and I believe, to my regret, that they don't do it now.

The strength of friendship with the masters was very important. Very often you would go to tea with them. I was very lucky because I often went to supper with Monty James, who was the Provost, and he used to read P. G. Wodehouse; to see this marvellous man reading P. G. Wodehouse, he hardly ever got through a page because he used to laugh so much! And if they came to dinner with your housemaster, they would come round and see you too. They always refereed or umpired in games, so you got to know them in that sense, and you got to know them at Corps. They were splendid. And the masters' wives, they were terribly nice. It was all very close – it was a happy ship, as they say.

The great thing is that I have kept friends from my Eton days. Whenever you meet any of these people, it is extraordinary, you just go on, and even if you haven't seen the chap for a long time, you pick up. It wasn't just people in one's house. My best friend now is probably William Douglas-Home and he was in another house; in fact a lot of my best friends, funnily enough, were in other houses in the end as I grew older. I always call it the best

*Lt.-Col. Sir Martin Gilliat, private secretary to the Queen Mother.
†John Patrick McGillycuddy, The McGillycuddy of the Reeks (d. 1959).

trades union in Great Britain because in my life, where I go round all over the place, there is always some Old Etonian somewhere. It is not quite Masonic, but it is certainly a widespread thing.

Eton is very important to me. I owe it a tremendous debt. The great thing in my life is that I do have a tremendous number of friends and acquaintances. A large number inevitably are Etonians, now fewer than before because they have died off a bit. I went into broadcasting, and I made friends there, and they obviously haven't all been Old Etonians. But my very firm friends – well, certainly my best three friends – are all Old Etonians. We were all there together and we have kept in touch ever since, and it is very important to me. We all say to each other that we look the same as we did then, and we talk quite a bit about it still. We tell stories, some true, some that probably aren't, but they make us laugh.

I sent my first son there, but it wasn't a great success. He did absolutely nothing really, except learn guitar. He was more of a gentle boy, I think, he liked music and stuff, and wasn't very good at games, so he was rather the opposite to me. I didn't send my other sons there, because of the headmaster at that time. You may have heard of Mr Chenevix-Trench. He was a marvellous success at Bradfield, which is a small school, and he brought it right up. Then he came to Eton. He was a little man, physically, and Etonians were used to impressive people like Alington. It sounds stupid, but he thought he could carry on like he had done at Bradfield, and he tried to call people by their Christian names, which is completely fatal at Eton because they rather like to look up to the head beak really.

I would have liked all my sons to have gone. I would have liked them all to have played for Eton at Lords, but none of them was any good at any game at all, but that is just life. Well, you are bound to be disappointed in sons in some ways, but the final thing about the son is whether he is a nice person, and all my sons are nice.

My grandson is left-handed. He's marvellous, hits the ball very well indeed. He's down for Eton, but I shall not be there to see him; he's only four. That would have been nice.

I do have strong memories of my Eton days, and if I have a

recurring one, it is this: one of the joys of Eton in the summer was playing cricket house matches. The dame would bring up tea, and she would spread a big white linen tablecloth, about the size of a bed sheet, on the playing fields, and on it would be the most marvellous egg sandwiches, and strawberries and cream. It always seemed to be fine, too, but it's like only remembering the good things in the war – it must have rained like hell, but I remember the sunshine. As far as Eton summers go, it was always hot.

People say it is boring to do, but I do a lot of after-dinner speaking. Sometimes the chap gets up and reads out my biography and when he says that I went to Eton it often gets a laugh, I don't know why. I'm probably a bit un-Eton-like really, because as far as the public is concerned I'm a joker on the radio, and cricket and all that. I think they probably don't associate me with Eton. Old Fred Trueman pulls my leg about it. But I am not ashamed. If someone asked me if I had been at Eton, I would say yes, and bloody proud of it!

One gained tremendous confidence at Eton . . . that is what you are paying for, I suppose, confidence. It really made you confident. You felt that you had perhaps the best education possible, and that one was sharing in something which was perhaps exceptional. And we knew, I think, that we were very lucky, and in a sense it set one an example, that you should not let them down. It all sounds terribly pompous, but I think that was always in the back of one's mind.

ROBIN LANE FOX

M Y family have been to Eton for years, and it was never thought that I would do anything else. My brothers went to Eton, father, grandfather and great-grandfather – on both sides of the family. We're a very Etonian family. The only mild complication that I raised was by getting a scholarship, which was not a Lane Foxish thing to do. My father hesitated for a moment because he had to pay the bill, but it was never discussed, it was assumed quite naturally, and confirmed by my brothers, one of whom was then at the school, that it would be perfectly out of the question. My mother declared roundly, 'You can't possibly be a tug', so I went into a house as an Oppidan. She was right, of course . . .

MacIndoe himself was an ideal choice for me; I could not possibly have had a better housemaster. He himself was a rather ascetic, spartan figure, very, very, sympathetic. He was strict on punctuality and presentation, but liberal on rather essential things like beating and eccentricity. Scholarly achievement was very close to his heart, and that was good. He wasn't just some sports-playing wally, although he was a superb games-player, really formidably good. He had no point to prove. The MacIndoe family had probably been going to Eton for longer than I had. We got on extremely well, and it was a very, very happy setting, I like to think, around my year. We were all great friends in his house.

I loved sports, but I was appallingly bad at them and I probably over-compensated by working. There was a tension between being technically quick and bright at Greek poems and being a member of a house where the football team was very important. I think that I was respected by people for being quick, but rather as if my academic performance made up for the fact that I probably let through three goals on the soccer pitch. But I wasn't reviled for scholarly activities; no one questioned the worth of what you were doing.

It is rather an academic thing to say, but if you ask me what is my dominant impression of Eton, it is utter amazement at the education that I had, above all through Richard Martineau, who took the top form and was perhaps well suited for it. Martineau – the brilliant amateur. He had effortless command of classical language and literature, and understanding of them without any fuss or barrier between him and them. He was a scholar and a wide-ranging gentleman of letters. Immensely appealing. Aged sixteen and a bit, I had entered a form where we were reading the whole of Homer's *Iliad* for starters, and Plato's *Republic*, and a detailed translation of Juvenal's Satires, and we aimed to read all of them in the original. We read Boswell's *Life of Johnson* for English, as well as composing Greek and Latin hexameters, elegiacs, everything. And it was assumed that we could prepare ourselves for an outside exam involving close knowledge of biblical texts, Greek and Church history, and a whole range of classical literature. It is still utterly astounding to me. We were simply treated as equals in the available kingdom of letters. We had the most enormous respect for what he was passing, without frills, to us: the sense of humour, the encouragement, and the God-like range of his command of literature. The key to it, I think, was that we weren't made to read books and articles about authors, we were made to read the authors as much as possible, and regard it as being a dialogue with people who were not so dissimilar to ourselves – and with the authors he chose, this worked very well. There was very little blundering about, worrying about critical works on Homer; we read Homer instead, and my God, we read it right through. I absolutely loved it. In any literary education that I had at Oxford, or have ever known anywhere else, I have never had that impression of range, width and concentrated close company with authors who it was presumed would actually change you in some way if you attended to what they were saying.

Then we had Van Oss, of whom I was immensely fond. I studied history of art and wrote long essays on landscape gardening and the changes of style in the garden, and he lent me all his eighteenth and nineteenth-century gardening books . . . we studied landscape painting and I was familiar with the whole business of eighteenth-century debates about the picturesque in landscape. That sort of thing you could only do at Eton. I loved all that, it was wonderful. And we weren't the least bit pretentious – I think that Marlburians, for instance, are more pseudo-intellectuals.

Etonians are beyond social-climbing, so they can be rather more honest and direct and frank than people who are desperately worried that they are going to jettison everything. They have things to apologize for rather than to prove; I think that is a very important point about it all. The snobberies are internally generated by the school, not imported from outside. The school generates very strong snobberies but it abolishes worldly ones, and I have never met an Etonian on the make. I sometimes see people from public schools who have patently been told to be on the make – because Dad is spending good money, 'getting the best education that money can buy, my boy'.

Eventually, when I was at Oxford, I was bored out of my mind. I thought the whole thing was very low-key. I had a teacher who was resoundingly dull, the place was incredibly boring, and people seemed drab, playing sort of games of running their own amateur newspaper or a pathetic political society that we had all finished with when we were sixteen – and I hope in a way that we perhaps did it rather better. So I was miserable and I had an unhappy time.

I think if you put any number of boys into the setting of Eton of my time and give them the teaching, it doesn't matter whether they come from a five-thousand acre estate with a pheasant shoot, some of them would gain from it tremendously. I was always impressed when, after forty years of teaching the top form, Martineau retired and went off to Southampton to give lessons there in a grammar school. When asked what it was like – it must have been such a change – he said, 'No, boys are all the same: it is how much of a chance you give them to be different.'

I'm sending my own son there next autumn. Financial crucifixion, but I wouldn't dream of doing anything else, of course. For me there is only one school, one really good school. There are plenty of schools that are obviously good, but there is only one really good school. The thought of something like Bradfield or Wellington . . . well, I wouldn't.

I hope that he has the same chance presented to him to develop the great self-confidence I have. Total, crushing self-confidence R.L.F. would have fairly been viewed as suffering from – and probably does for the rest of his life. I am tall, I am reasonably self-assured, I come from quite a high social background, I don't get flustered if they get at me, and I suppose I project a totally misleading image, still, slightly, of being the man who is bright despite himself. So there you are.

If the pay of really good teachers is put up to what it should be, I wonder how many Etonians will pay the fees that these teachers then should quite rightly demand. I gather that the quality of the housemasters is changing rapidly, and I think that will be a great weakness and undoing and difficulty. It is very difficult to get former Etonians to go back and be housemasters, and I gather that they are now rather narrow-minded men in a broader sense. And if characters, perhaps like me, who have low to bottom Etonian riches could no longer think of sending their children there, it would become then a playground of half-wits, international white trash and freaks.

MARTIN LLEWELLYN

THE whole of my family had always been there, both on my father's and mother's side, and as long as my parents could actually find a way of sending me there, then it was fairly inevitable that I would go. My father's now a bishop, but at that time he was vicar of Tetbury, and to send three sons (I've got two brothers) to Eton off a vicar's salary is almost completely impossible. But it actually turned out that Eton was one of the cheaper places that we could go, because my mother had three Etonian brothers killed in the war, and a war memorial bursary fund supported all three of us. Otherwise we certainly wouldn't have been able to go at all.

Once they made this important decision to send us there, they regulated their lives around it. They really fought and scrimped and saved to send us there, because that's what they considered to be important.

I'd been sent there to do a scholarship by my prep school, which wasn't one of the kind of Eton breeding-ground prep schools, and they had no idea about the standards required for an Eton scholarship. I wrote an essay about the inability of the fishermen in Wells, in Norfolk, to send their whelks to market any longer on account of the Beeching cuts to the railways. Apparently my papers were quoted for years afterwards as probably being the most stupid scholarship exam that had ever been sat, and they made me sit Common Entrance as a result of it.

My house, Coleridge's, was a very tough house indeed. It was one of the new houses, built in the mid-fifties, and a really rotten piece of architecture, looking back at it from my point of view now. And my housemaster, who was my cousin as well, thought that it was his duty to make sure he showed no favouritism at all to his cousins, and as a result we were flogged more than most. He encouraged the boys to run the punishment system, and after about seven weeks of being there I was beaten for the first time for not heating up somebody's potted shrimps to the correct temperature. And beaten incredibly hard, too.

The way it would work was that the Library would run around the house, taking the longest route to your room, running their canes along the upright grooved boarding at the same time, which made a kind of alarming whirring noise. If they started near you, you knew you were all right. But if they started miles away, you sat there and just shat in your pants, or pulled on your *Lederhosen*. And it was always done at the time of night when you'd actually gone to bed, so you'd be lying there in your pyjamas, and the door would burst open and someone would shout, 'Llewellyn, you're wanted in the Library in three minutes.' And it was a very upsetting time indeed. Panic!

The Captain of the House then called you into the room, where the whole of the Library would be assembled, and stood with his cane behind his back. 'Explain why the potted shrimps weren't the right temperature and how this is a question of poor attitude,' he would intone. And after the unsatisfactory response, there was the inevitable phrase: '. . . and, Llewellyn, I'm afraid I have no alternative but to beat you'. They were rather keen on beating. Then you had to bend over a chair, and it was arranged so that the light was behind the cane so you could see it coming. It was a Burmese cane with insulating tape tied around the end into a blob, and it wasn't the cane hitting you, but the end, the blob of insulating tape coming around, that used to actually draw the blood down the side. And I was absolutely amazed – I mean, I'd been beaten a lot in my prep school, but not like that. Chilling! I mean, that's my first burning memory of Eton – sheer pain.

It was completely unjust; there were eight of us new boys, and we all made a resolve that we'd stop beating in the house when we got to the point when we could stop it.

Coleridge was one of the great Eton statesmen and went on to be lower master and Vice-Provost and so on. In his private life and as a cousin, he was a sweet and charming man, and his son is a friend of mine now. But he enjoyed the feudal system and having a lot of people in his house with large estates; he would go and shoot with them in the winter, and fish with them in the summer, and he joined in their lives.

Then, half-way through, he retired and a new young house-master took over, with a complete change of actual physical accommodation. With the change of house there was a total change of character.

Well, it was the old school giving way to the new school, and for me it came at the ideal moment of about fifteen. The Coleridge days were to do with discipline and hierarchy, when I think you probably most needed it, and although you obviously hated it at the time, and it was extremely painful, at least you knew exactly where you were. Anthony Ray wrote books about pottery when he wasn't being a housemaster and was incredibly encouraging to me about my art. He had a much more liberal approach, he believed in the value of art – and contempoary art at that – and was very keen to let you go where you wished to go.

And so the whole feeling changed and it became one of the most left-wing houses at Eton, which was a fairly refreshing transformation. Corporal punishment was abolished, fagging was reduced to tasks which served the public need rather than the private need. No more heating up potted shrimps for people. We were fiendishly democratic.

We didn't beat, as we'd agreed. We'd seen how futile and stupid it had been, and we felt that it would actually be degrading for the people and for us. I mean, I wouldn't claim to have any profound individual political insights which led to this, or that anybody in our year had any either, but the whole fashion for deregulation, 'do it your own way, man', 'let it all hang loose', was right on us at the time – and so we did.

I don't suppose I got too involved in the sixties, but somehow in the cloistered life of Eton these things were there, there were shreds of the sixties world; and although we were wearing tail-coats, we had as long hair as we were allowed to, and flared pinstriped trousers – but wearing Chelsea boots was a beatable offence, so we didn't wear those much. And you were always aware that the oldest and naughtiest Etonians were leaving Eton every night in chauffeur-driven cars and going up to wild parties in swinging London.

I was amazingly stimulated by the cultural environment. I mean, it is an incredible environment, and by the age of fifteen or so I'd discovered the art schools, where a master called Gordon Baldwin, who taught pottery and sculpture, encouraged me to really get that side going. About that age I suppose you begin to read a bit, and Eton's quite close to London, so you could actually get to plays . . . and suddenly the whole thing changed, you weren't just trying to be naughty the whole time and have a kind of 'laddy' good time, but you actually had, I suppose they weren't serious interests, but wider interests.

And within the hierarchical set-up of Eton, where everybody has a kind of place and you're a particular type of person within the community, I became a sculptor, and was expected to be covered in clay and plaster dust when I walked around the streets, and was very much encouraged by some of the boys. The boys are all divided up into cliques, and I think a large proportion of the boys there thought that going to the Drawing Schools was homosexual and long-haired and wet. Anybody who attempted to think more widely was actually thought to be pretending to do so – you were a 'pseud'. 'Pseud' was the great word at the time. But within the Drawing School clique there was terrific encouragement; and I have never got back to the point of enjoying art as much as I did in those Eton days.

I think that Eton sets you up to be a little conceited and arrogant about your own abilities, but that's really because there's such amazing teaching. The tutorial system looks at what your interests are and actually helps you research and understand the implication of being interested in something. It gives you a very broad education which is not based on some outside curriculum, but is actually based on you and your own interests.

So I think it's a bit of a shock, when you come popping out into the real world at the end, to realize that there isn't a kind of niche for you, where a whole lot of people are going to help you the whole time, and I don't suppose it really prepares you particularly well for the outside world in that way.

Well, I'm not quite sure how we were selected, but when I was fourteen, three or four of us went to Biggleswade Secondary Modern on an exchange: we went there for four days, and they came to Eton for four days, so we could get a flavour of each other's worlds. I think it was a misconceived exchange, in that because it was a secondary modern it was entirely filled with people who had failed to get into a grammar school, by definition. And the intellectual capacity of your average Biggleswade Secondary Modern pupil really shocked me. At Eton, with its six-to-one pupil-to-staff ratio and with its Common Entrance selection, you were used to working and sharing your school life with people who knew a whole lot more than these people knew, but at Biggleswade Secondary Modern you'd sit in a class full of people two years older than you, and you could easily keep up. The other extraordinary thing about it, to me, was that not being a boarding school, the actual school and its curriculum and its hierarchy played a much, much smaller part in everybody's lives. School was something you did from home rather than it being a full-time profession, unlike at Eton where you were at school more than you were at home.

It was an exaggerated form of being an Etonian, or an Old Etonian in later life; you were a bit of a curiosity, and everybody would sort of gather around and prod you to see what you were going to sound like, or what you were going to do, or whether you'd suddenly turn out to have pockets full of gold. It was very unreal, and in three or four days you didn't really get to integrate with the system that you were going into. My most powerful memory of it is a photograph, which my mother still has in her photograph album somewhere, of me sitting in a tweed suit at the end of a table in the domestic science laboratory, with a queue of girls offering me treacle tart to taste. And I think that's a fair illustration of how artificial the thing was – that I wasn't in there doing domestic science with them; it was like a visit by a Martian and they put on a performance. So I don't really rate the whole experiment very highly. I don't think it was a very important moment in my education.

I felt very sorry for the guy when he came back to Eton with me. Eton is full of strange, cranky mannerisms and peculiar customs, and it is also a place which has pretty well a single-class society in it, and it was very difficult for him to enjoy himself and to integrate. Being at Eton's like living in a big city. You can be alone very easily, you can be quite isolated, and there's a kind of social life which builds up within it, with very tight little cliques. Unless you're part of it, it's very difficult to break in. And of course I took him round and introduced him to all my friends and to all my interests, but we were very much like tourists in each other's schools rather than people living in each other's countries.

It· was faintly embarrassing really, having seen the pathetic level of provision by state education compared with Eton. I mean, a chemistry lab. at Biggleswade Secondary Modern compared with, you know, an almost research standard chemistry lab. at Eton. There was no comparison. I felt guilty then that I should be enjoying it and that he wasn't. And he felt very homesick, that was another thing; he was really upset to be in a strange world with a whole lot of strange people, and he wasn't used to being away from home. He hated it.

Well, it was part of discovering. Certainly now, as an architect building schools in the state sector, I'm very aware of how lucky I've been with my education, and I hope to try and bring that into other people's education as well.

We talk about the importance of being at Eton at that period of your life, between thirteen and eighteen, but the real worries then were the worries about growing up. You woke up to see whether that spot was still there, or your armpit was smelling, or whether you'd grown as much as the other people on your passage – I mean, everybody is a human animal, they all suffer and enjoy the same kind of things, whether you're a bricklayer, an architect, a convict, a drug addict or an Etonian. Eton is only a very small part of it; the basic human experience is a shared one.

In the evening at Biggleswade, for example, we jumped on to his scooter and went down to the youth club where we could happily share the kind of things that young fifteen- and sixteen-year-old people like to share, like girls and dancing. The experience of being an Etonian, to anybody who's been to Eton, is just part of growing up. When people discover that you're an Old Etonian, they expect you to be far more than you can ever be. Far nastier or far nicer or far richer or fatter. It's an expectation of extremes. It doesn't feel exceptional while you're there, you just feel a little guilty about it when you've left.

I would like to say Eton is no longer a big influence in my life, but I met my wife through her brother who was in the Drawing Schools with me, so my family life has terrific Eton connections. We've been talking about it a lot recently because we now have two sons, both of whom have been put down for Eton. We've debated long and hard whether we will actually send them there, but it seems likely, God willing and various other things being in order, that we will.

THE EARL OF LONGFORD

WELL, it was the only place. I didn't really take anywhere else very seriously. And for Etonians there is no other school, I mean it's like the Catholic Church in its most triumphalist moments, I don't mean like it is today. It is not a question of some other schools – there are no other schools. You just picked it up in the air, straight away. It wasn't a question of somebody sort of addressing you and explaining it was the only school, it was just in the atmosphere.

I was in Wells's house. The cricket connection was very strong in my house. A few days of arriving at Eton in the summer half, 1918, I was fielding long leg to the bowling of G. O. B. Allen, Gubby Allen, who later captained England at cricket, and so I was aware of very high-class cricket from early days. My housemaster had played for the Gentlemen and could have played for England. In my house was a boy called Pelham Warner, Plum Warner. If you know about cricket, you will be aware that at Lords there is now something called the Warner stand, and Warner played for England and captained Middlesex when the war ended. And so cricket was a very big feature, but I wasn't particularly good at cricket.

My housemaster was the top classical master as well as being sporty. He was very athletic, very classical, and, one has to say, very philistine.

There was a story that once Wells went to Glyndebourne, and after the first act of the opera he came out with his fingers in his ears, saying, 'Can't they stop that caterwauling?' That was the attitude to music of my housemaster. But he was an absolutely brilliant classicist. He could put anything into Greek verse. So one got culture through the classics, but not in any other way.

I'll tell you a story which you may think I've made up, but it's true. I became Captain of the House – and you couldn't be very unpopular if you were elected to Captain. I was also quite popular in my division. I wasn't conscious really of any unpopularity, because if you were popular in your own house and in your form, you felt you were quite popular enough. And I always assumed at the end of my last but one summer half that I would be Captain of the Oppidans, and the Captain of the Oppidans and the Captain of the School are both automatically in Pop. I mean, Hailsham might not have got in otherwise, but he got in through being the Captain of the School.

Anyway, I assumed that I was going to be Captain of the Oppidans until a friend of mine broke me the news, almost the last day of the summer half, that someone called Bridges was staying on, which was the most appalling thing. I had assumed for five years, having calculated it (because you could at Eton), that I would be the Captain of the Oppidans, and would not have to bother with being elected to Pop because I would be automatically in. Then there was this awful news. And I said to my friend, 'Oh God, I suppose that means I won't get into Pop.' Then I brightened up a bit and thought that I might get elected anyway. Then he paused for a long time and said, 'I think that I ought to tell you that you are the most unpopular boy in the school.' This was a frightful shock; I thought *he* was, which was the joke, you see – having the news broken to me by the boy that I thought was the most unpopular!

I could have stayed on an extra half after the end of that year as I was still young enough, but my mother rightly didn't believe in obtaining honours in that sort of way, so I never was in Pop, and therefore left with this ringing in my ears: that I was the most unpopular boy in the school.

I never quite knew why – I think that I was regarded as a prig. I suppose I would have to say I was rather a priggish little boy. Well-behaved. Like boy, like man; I suppose I'm priggish now. That was sixty years ago, but you don't alter much, do you?

I was humorous really, as a matter of fact. I mean, I will mention one joke that got a lot of laughs. I went to the Political

Society, and I had somewhat the reputation of being a bit of a wag, and I asked the question to a visiting speaker who was a high politician, 'Has Mr Winston Churchill got any political future?' And this got loud laughter, because it was thought absolutely ridiculous that he could have any political future. That was my joke. So as you see I went in for being funny at Eton. I mean, I don't know why I was so unpopular, but obviously I was not popular outside my own circle because I didn't get into Pop.

When I left Eton I had more success at Oxford. I got a First. At Eton I hadn't really done all that well at work; I didn't really try. I did work at Oxford, and I came away full of self-confidence. That was much more the scene of my juvenile triumphs, and I got into the Bullingdon, which was the smart thing in those days; I really was a more successful figure at Oxford. But the great majority of people who go to Oxford wouldn't ever know that Bullingdon existed, whereas at Eton you could not fail to know that Pop existed. Of course it is often said that people become Socialists if they fail to get into Pop. It is the Etonian jibe, 'Oh yes, he only became a Socialist because he didn't get into Pop.'

In my first volume of memoirs, which came out in 1953, I described my life at Eton, and Evelyn Waugh, who was a great friend of mine (I'm the godfather of Bron), was very scathing about the book, but he did admit that the Eton chapter was all right. He then said no one can write badly about Eton.

It's a romantic place. Whether I was or wasn't popular, I certainly was under the spell of Eton, and I can see why – just take the Yard and the Chapel and all that, and with Windsor Castle sort of brooding over the whole thing, don't you think that is all very romantic? Particularly as compared with Harrow, if I may say so.

Most of the people who got into Pop did history. But we despised history. We who did classics thought the others had opted out of real intellectual life, and science was worse still. And similarly we looked down on people who went into rowing. Dilhorne, who later became Lord Chancellor, was derided because he was too short-sighted to play cricket, and so he went in for rowing. And we used to go and shout at him from the bank, 'In, Buller,* in, in . . .' so he might crash into the bank, 'Out, out . . .' so he might crash into a pleasure steamer, or something. My brother, who did rowing, was derided for being a Sinn Feiner. The narrowness of our outlook was unbelievable.

We thought that Eton was the best school in the world. Our house was the best house in the world. To really count you had to play cricket passably well and do classics. You may say that derived from the personality of a very strong housemaster.

I was captain of the junior cricket team which got into the final, and then we were beaten. I was really rather short-sighted, and I was reluctant to wear glasses. I remember the bright sun, and the shadows lengthening, and the difficulty of sighting the ball, and sure enough we were beaten. Perhaps if I had worn glasses we would have won. At any rate, that rather affected my cricket career.

But the wonderful moment was winning the House Football Cup, and that was in December 1920. It was a very glorious moment. We drew the first day, the captain on the other side had a nervous breakdown, he was so exhausted, so he didn't play on the second day. We won by one rouge. I scored the winning rouge, I think, but my memory may be deceiving me. I wonder if I did score that? I think I did . . . perhaps I have persuaded myself that I did. I led the winning team after six years of dedicated preparation, and as I led in the team I was hissed, on the theory that I was the most unpopular boy in the school. Basil Dufferin, who became Lord Dufferin (I got to know him very well at Oxford, and I was his best man when he got married), he always said that I was hissed as I came off the field. He would tell the story of my being hissed and how he had joined in the hissing. I didn't hear it, I was much too happy anyway.

I think that I was distinctly ready to leave school by that time. I had shot my bolt there, I felt, I really had reached my climax at the end of December, winning the House Cup, and was quite ready to push off.

*Reginald Edward Manningham-Buller, later Viscount Dilhorne.

Intellectually I developed very little at Eton, but I was with very clever people. After my first year I was put in the form with College, therefore I was getting a better education than I really deserved. I went up the school with Collegers, the clever boys. Nearly all the clever and certainly hard-working boys were concentrated in this place, Orwell, Connolly, Macmillan, Hailsham, all the people that one thinks of as the cleverest Etonians were in College. When I went into the top form Alington, the headmaster, was a remarkable teacher, so I sat there under all these stimulating influences.

He would start: 'Well, that's that. Well, is that that? Gentlemen, is that that? Pakenham, is that that?' He liked that sort of verbal argument. There was a lot of religion thrown in too, in the preaching and so on. The same missionary used to come round, every year: 'It's not your money I want, though God knows I need it, but it's *you*, my dear fellows, you.' As it was a rather well-known peroration, people used to take it up and chant with him. 'It is *you*, my dear fellows, you', before he could finish it. I remember Alington would preach a special sermon on Sunday evenings. He would have the candles lit, because it would be dark. He was a very good-looking man, he had a great wave of grey hair which he was very proud of, and he would toss it back with his hand: 'It was on just such an evening as this, when I myself was coming to an end of my time at Shrewsbury' (he had been the headmaster of Shrewsbury) 'and a boy was sitting on a bench on the cricket fields, just as it might be Upper Club here. And a woman of the town came across and sat beside him and said "Coming home, dearie?"' – all of this in the pulpit, mind you – 'and he looked at her and said, "We don't do that sort of thing at Shrewsbury," and the ironical thing was,' said Alington, 'not only did they do a lot of that sort of thing at Shrewsbury, but he had been expelled from Shrewsbury for doing it that very day.' And he blew out the candle. 'Good-night, and don't forget to pray for your headmaster.' That's after sixty-five years I can remember that.

A lot of boys got expelled from Eton for homosexualism. I'm told that simply doesn't happen now. But there was a lot of homosexualism. One boy once made an advance to me, but only once. We used to share a bath after games, you see, and if two people were at all that way inclined, they would be last into the bath, and so when everyone else had gone, they would mess about with each other. But how far that went on one didn't know, but certainly there was a lot of, well, messing about, masturbating and so on. I never masturbated at Eton; it never occurred to me.

I'm bound to say I think Eton does give you this confidence of having been to this school that you think is supreme; and without doubt it produces arrogance, snobbery, and to say the least, elitism.

Now as far as I stand for anything, it is the opposite of elitism. When I became Lord in Waiting, George VI asked me, 'Why did you join *them*?' When I realized that he meant the Socialist Party, I didn't say, 'Because I think all men are equal', that seemed impertinent, so I just said, 'I'm on the side of the underdog.' But really behind that is the conviction that we are all equal in the sight of God. Well, I think Eton stands for something far removed from that.

I would not want to disown Eton, and I am very much moved when I go there, but I have built up my life on separate lines. If I hadn't become a Catholic and, earlier, a Socialist, I think my children would have gone to Eton if we could have afforded it – I mean, I did see it, as Gladstone said, 'the Queen of all the schools of all the world'. But really, I'm not emotionally involved at all. Having become a Socialist and a Catholic since, I have repudiated Eton in that sense.

HUMPHREY LYTTELTON

FOR one thing I was born there, I went to private school at Sunningdale which was eight miles away, my great-uncle Edward was headmaster of Eton, my father was a housemaster, and subsequently two of my sisters married Eton masters; so it did loom large in the early years.

Because I didn't want to leave home, like any normal eight-year-old, I was kind of shanghaied at Sunningdale, literally to the extent that my parents said, 'We're just going to do something-or-other, we'll see you later', and the next thing I saw was the car disappearing down the drive. But I was one of those sort of people who hated places when I went there, and for quite a long time, and then hated it when it came time to leave. I think that was really the same thing with Eton.

I wasn't allowed to set foot in my father's house for the first year in order to make the break with home and all that. I boarded at the next house down the Lane, which meant that going to school for me wasn't a huge upheaval, it was a matter of getting the odd-job man from my father's house to wheel a trunk about four or five hundred yards away.

I was at Butterwick's, and Cyril Butterwick was a friend of my father. Looking back, letters from Cryil Butterwick to my father indicated that they didn't really know what to expect. My father constantly used to refer to me in correspondence, fairly proudly, as an original, which was his way of saying somebody who didn't conform. In some respects I've no doubt I was a disappointment to him, but then in most respects everybody's a disappointment to their parents, and it doesn't bother me in the slightest.

I was gangling and hopelessly untidy. Size twelve feet from the age of about twelve onwards. I wasn't particularly at ease there for four years for the simple reason that everything I did was wrong – you know, things like getting two out of a hundred for maths at trials, which caused terrible rows over the breakfast table with my father. The trial results came in, and my mother and however many of my four sisters who were having breakfast at the time got up and tactfully left the room. My father would be buried behind *The Times*. Suddenly he crumpled the whole paper up in his enormous hands and threw it to one side and weighed into me. It wasn't until I did School Certificate and was physically sick with fear every day for about a week before the results came out, and then got six credits, to my enormous surprise, that I began to enjoy life a bit more. Then I was the blue-eyed boy with my father and with the housemaster, and eventually I became the Captain of the House for two or three terms – you see I can't talk about them as 'halves', even now. I also got into Pop, probably on the strength of just being a genial sort of bloke who played the trumpet. I was popular largely through the trumpet, I mean I was something of a comic turn.

On Sundays after Chapel you had the whole day to yourself, and I quite quickly started leading a little band which eventually developed into a quartet in which I played trumpet. There was a piano in the large room underneath my father's study where we used to play, and I organized what we didn't call jam sessions in those days, but what have since been called jam sessions.

The first group had the guy who used to call himself, and therefore we used to call him, Reg Compton, who's now Sir Robert Compton of whatever stately house it is up in Ripon. Haven't seen him for years, although I saw him on the television the other day. He played guitar, and David Oldham played piano, and Ronnie MacAndrew, who died later in a shooting accident, was on drums. His father was Sir Charles MacAndrew who was a Conservative MP for Largs and Rothesay, and one of the first gigs I ever did was in his constituency.

My memories aren't so much of events that happened, but simply of the smells of late autumn, usually fairly lonely in holiday times when the rest of the school had disappeared . . . I mean, all one's friends were in school time, and it was particularly bad for me at the end of term because I didn't then take a train and go on to a completely new thing. I just walked back to another house and woke up the next morning to an entirely dead place from which all your friends had vanished, as though off the face of the earth. I was left at my father's home with a family consisting entirely of sisters, and not knowing people in the town of Eton, I tended to spend the school holidays almost entirely on my own; I used to bicycle all around the place, and go and listen to the band up at Victoria Barracks in Windsor, go to the movies, twice, three times a day.

During term time, the outside world hardly touched us. I was totally unaware of the Depression and the slump and unemployment and everything else. I think the hunger-marchers came through, some sort of cloth-capped cavalcade walked through, and I remember seeing that. One was more aware of things like George V dying, because you were part of the same village, you went up to Windsor Castle and watched the funeral proccssion.

I think it must have been fairly soon after war was declared, and I was just walking along the street, when it suddenly occurred to me that the likelihood was that I would be dead within the year. I could point to the actual flagstone on which I was standing when I suddenly thought that. And that was the first time that anything going on outside really impinged upon me at all.

I signed on at the very beginning of the war from school and there was roughly a year to go before I was called up. There was a waiting-list, believe it or not, because they didn't have enough equipment, so I went to work at a steel works in Port Talbot. And after a very awkward period when we were regarded as the toffs from London, I was imbued with a kind of romantic socialism which has never left me since. I became aware then of the extent to which I'd been conditioned by the private school and public school thing of never seeing or mixing with anybody outside at all – and it was quite a cultural shock. There were a lot of social reasons: the fact that you did refer quite naturallly, and every day, to the ordinary human beings who lived in Eton and Windsor who weren't of upper-middle-class upbringing as 'oiks';

and you never saw anybody of the opposite sex unless you happened to be in a family which led a sort of racy London existence, and went off to parties. In fact, living an academic existence in Eton, you were totally unprepared for mixing with people other than those that you'd lived with all your life.

And for that reason I consciously divested myself of all that kind of conditioning. That meant making a complete break with the school, and I used to argue a lot with my father – I made a sort of temporary break there as well, and I divested myself of all that and became a sort of *Observer*-reading, Hampstead liberal.

The only sort of comeback I've ever had about having been to Eton is through people who assumed in the early days that I was going to be a certain type of person because I'd been to Eton, and then bent all the evidence to conform to that picture of me: if I didn't speak, it was because I felt myself so far above them – never occurred to them, you know, that I was absolutely paralysed with shyness and a fish-out-of-water feeling. I believe that the world is divided pretty well equally between prefects and snotty-nosed kids and I've always felt myself to be on the snotty-nosed kid side of things . . . anyway, the jazz world is a very, very hard world on people who are pretentious or stuffy.

I never felt one of the Old Etonian mob. If you went into one of the OK, or what in 1945 was one of the OK professions or careers, then the whole set-up tended to give you enormous confidence. And so in that respect I don't thank Eton for having not in fact given me a tremendous amount of confidence for life in general, combined with a certain genetic diffidence which belongs to the male side of the Lyttelton family.

A lot of OEs used to come and watch me perform. I think it was little bit 'Oh let's go and see him', you know, 'How extraordinary!' and all this. The comic-turn thing again. Some of them were friends of mine who'd enjoyed listening to Fats Waller and Benny Goodman with me at school. They all exuded confidence and really took the place over, and I used to rather resent the fact that I was their property. And that type of Old Etonian tended to be extremely rude in the sense that if I was talking to one of the ordinary punters, they would come up and interrupt and sort of take over. In fact the term 'Hoorays' was coined within the jazz club ambience fairly soon after the war, implying the sort of public school teams that used to come down to my club at 100 Oxford Street.

I think if you turn your back on somewhere like Eton, people rather expect you to say, 'Oh, I hated the whole thing', but I didn't. I loved almost everything. I'm that sort of temperament. I loved being in the army. I felt the end-of-term blues when I was invalided away from the Salerno beach-head – because I didn't want to leave. I mean, it's an absolutely idiotic thing to say.

Nevertheless I don't enjoy wallowing in nostalgia. I always like to look forward to what's going to happen next. And therefore I make a point of not dwelling on these memories. It was a beautiful place to live in, there's no doubt about that . . . to be brought up during those years in a place which had not one cricket pitch but ten cricket pitches and huge great playing fields and things like that.

Most of my memories are painful things, you know, playing-fields-in-autumn sort of things. But it was all tied up with other things, because in those days, although I never went through a homosexual phase, all one's very strong friendships were naturally enough with other boys in the school, and they were very close heroic friendship type things, too romantic to last; that's all associated with certain memories that come back and all seem vaguely absurd now when you look back on it – especially when you meet the people concerned. People who were fairly close friends at school – it would be impossible, even with six months in seclusion on a desert island, to get back on those sort of terms.

I don't know why the nostalgia is so terribly painful. The actual moments that I recall hearing a sight or a sound or a smell are now painful; I mean, if I heard a whole male roomful of men's voices singing 'Lord, Thou hast brought us to our journey's end', which is the old hymn that we used to sing on the last day of term, I'd get a lump in the throat just from the memory of what one used to feel, despite the distance between that and all the things that have happened since. And hymn-singing in the Upper Chapel . . . I think it's all changed now, but then it was Upper and Lower Chapel. Upper Chapel – five hundred male voices roaring into the hymns. I used to love that. We used to sing with enormous gusto various hymns that I can't listen to now.

I think it's all to do with forgetting things, as well. I think when you get a little whiff of something from the past that hits you really strongly, either through a bit of music or a smell, or something or other, you realize that it's gone, not in any sort of temporal sense but that it's gone in a memory sense – you can't remember a lot of what happened then and you have this feeling of regret that these chunks have vanished from your life.

The fact is that I suppose eighty per cent of my friends were killed in the war, which is probably why I have in a way made a break with the past.

Eton was where I had a lot of friends. It was a place that I hung on to for a short while, maybe a year or two after I left, and then it became a thing of the past, it became just the place where I was educated, and years go by, not weeks or months, but years go by during which I never give it a single solitary thought.

There are professional Old Etonians for whom these six years in their life were the high spot and everything else was downhill from then on. I've known a lot of people like that, especially people who were sporting heroes and have really been slightly sad characters ever since, because nothing in life after they leave is ever better than their Eton days; they became fairly mediocre members of Lloyd's and this kind of thing, and constantly look back on Eton as being the focal point.

I had an uncle by marriage whose life was blighted by the fact that he was in the Eton XI; he was a hero, played at the Eton and Harrow match, made a big score, literally tremendous, and the rest of his life was just one long, dreadful anti-climax. He declined until eventually he got some mental derangement and all that sort of thing. I suppose subconsciously, or even consciously, he felt that Eton had been the big moment and everything else after that had been a bit of a come-down, which was sad. And there are a lot of Eton masters who hung on and hung on and then eventually were forced to retire and had no life of any sort, a lot of them had no families. All the way through Eton history there have been poor old sad relics hovering around on the perimeter, who used to have a role to play and when it finished life was at an end. Bachelor housemasters and, I think, some of the dames. I know my father had a bit of a horror of that thing happening to him.

Sometimes even people like Michael Bentin who have been a success in very non-public-school-type professions adhere to this professional Etonian thing. Michael Bentin was only there for two years, which was a third of the time I was there, and yet no doubt when you speak to him he will mention the fact that he was at Mr Hope-Jones's house, and he's the only person I know who still remembers – that's an exaggeration, quite a lot of people would remember, but I don't – he was known as Hope-Jiggers for some unknown reason, and Michael Bentin always refers to him as Hope-Jiggers and does various imitations of him and everything else. I'm embarrassed if I meet people who still talk in that lingo. I don't know where to look if somebody says, 'I was up to your father . . .' It all sounds so sort of quaint to me. Bentin and I were on a TV show once and he rather chided me, half jokingly, for not wearing an Old Etonian tie. I said, 'I haven't got one, never had one,' and he said, 'Oh, I've got thirty-two, do you want to borrow one?' And this is the difference, in a way; I think Old Etonians are probably divided almost equally into those who thought, 'That was it, it was nice, but it's over now', and those who regularly go, wouldn't miss a Fourth of June – even though they've probably written to *The Times* about the fact that it's now held not on the fourth of June itself but on the nearest Saturday.

PATRICK MACNEE

My mother was a fairly strange lady and she left my father, who was a little alcoholic racehorse trainer, when I was about eight, and she went off with a woman, a very dominant, strong woman who was the heir to Dewar's Whisky, and she took not only my mother over but myself. And as a result, I don't know how my mother worked on it, because presumably we were pretty indigent, but I was transported to the Great House. I've always thought small and I hated the idea of it; I wanted to go to Radley. But that's what happened.

I never saw my parents at all. I mean they went out of their way not to see me. There never was an occasion where either of them visited me, not once, the whole time that I was there.

I was in Sladden's, which was the worst house of the lot. He was a science master with a great big Adam's apple and extremely little sense of humanity, and was rather looked down on by the other houses, because there was tremendous class-consciousness and the house wasn't one of the privileged houses, it was easy to get into.

There was no feeling of aristocracy about it. The spirit of the house was functional; it was very unemotional and very unartistic. Later, when I was a member of the Drawing School, I met Michael Bentin and Robert Diamond who became a very famous painter. Wonderfully advanced artistic time, compared with my extremely primitive house in which people weren't interested in the arts at all. I was cut off from my house, isolated, when I went into the arts. The boys in the arts side I thought absolutely lovely and exciting, and the boys in my own house completely ordinary and uninteresting, just sort of ciphers really. If you mention the words 'Drawing Schools' in that period, the

16 *right* These boys, in School Dress but wearing
football-boots against the mud instead of the
regulation black shoes, are cheering their house
side in a league tie, with a continuous cry of
'Blenkinsop's' or 'Robinson's', according to the
house in which they board – houses being known
by the name of the current house master,
irrespective of the building in which he is located.
Only the swells in Pop are privileged to roll their
umbrellas.

17 *below* New & Lingwood's have kept a hosier's
shop in the High Street since 1865. In pre-war
years the shop was a social centre where boys met
and gossiped while 'Soloman' lushed (ironed)
their top hats. Copies of the *Sketch*, the *Sporting
and Dramatic News* and the *Tatler* were provided
by the management. Here Mr Hewitt is deciding
what size collar this young gentleman takes.

18 *above* At Eton every boy has his own bed-sittingroom right from the start, and he adorns it according to his taste. A century ago the proud athlete would decorate his wall with the caps he had been awarded and the ribbon-framed printed lists of his various teams. Much of the furniture has remained of standard design for well over a century – for example, the burry or desk and, beside it, the bootbox with a silver challenge cup on it.

19 *below* Today the wallpaper is concealed under a different style of decor. But the burry (provided by the School) remains the same, and the lamp on the right is standing on a bootbox.

20 *above* Meals for the King's Scholars are still prepared in the original kitchen, situated where the Founder planned it, though over the centuries the equipment used there has changed. Today's scene of spotless hygiene in College Kitchen would hardly be recognizable as the place pictured in this photograph, taken in the early 1950s

21 *below* Half of the twenty-five boys' houses have their own catering; boys in the others go out to Bekynton, the central self-service refectory. Here, in The Timbralls, the house master, Mr M. C. Meredith, sits at the head of his family of forty-eight boys, at a table adorned with the sporting trophies that his boys have won. Lunch (Boys' Dinner) is a formal meal, with all the boys assembled punctually for grace.

22 *right* An idyllic summer scene in a garden created from waste land, early in this century, by a retired house master, Mr H. E. Luxmoore. Senior boys are privileged to enjoy it. To the right of the twin turrets of Lupton's Tower may be seen the roof and lantern of College Kitchen.

23 *below* The Cloisters were built in the Founder's lifetime, and until Long Chamber was built the Scholars were accommodated there. College Pump used to provide pure, ice-cold water, which boys returning from games could drink from a silver cup that hung there until it was stolen. (They drank at the pump from their cupped hands until the 1960s, when the well ran dry.) The seventeenth-century steps on the right lead up to College Hall.

24 The Chapel was the Founder's first care: the Foundation Charter was signed in October 1444, and Henry VI
laid the foundation stone for his great new church on Passion Sunday the following year. Forty years later
Provost Wayneflete saw it completed, though its length was only half what the Founder had intended. A
bomb smashed all the stained glass in 1940, and a new east window, by Evie Hone, was installed in 1952,
seven years later a new fan-vaulted roof replaced the old one.

25 The Wall Game's rules are highly complex and understood only by the relatively small circle of boys who play it. The wall along the Slough Road was built in 1717, and the game grew up soon after that. To the uninitiated the Wall Game appears to consist of endless scrums pushing to and fro along the wall in the mud, punctuated by occasional wild kicks, but strategy plays a major part, so that brain can often defeat mere brawn. On the right of the photograph stands the umpire/referee, Mr M. A. Nicholson, now Vice-Provost. Goals are rare, but the game can be won on points (shies, similar to rugger tries). Boys playing directly alongside the wall wear padded sacking jackets and helmets to afford them some protection against the rough brickwork.

26 *above* The Beagles (Eton College Hunt) had existed for decades before being legalized by the Head Master, Dr Balston, in the 1860s: previously the fact that the boys must inevitably have been out of bounds while participating was winked at by authority, just as boys used openly to row on the river for years before 1840, though until that time it was officially forbidden.

27 *right* These young cricketers, probably in their third year, are watching their Upper Sixpenny game on a field inexplicably known as Mesopotamia.

28 The golfer is turning out of School Yard into Fourth Form Passage, which passes alongside Lower School. Above was Long Chamber, now divided into separate rooms, but originally a single dormitory, 57 yards long and 7 wide, where for two and a half centuries the seventy Scholars were accommodated.

late thirties, it meant an enormous amount. It was our total reason for living.

I'm not a highly creative person but I deliberately mixed with people who were. I found them very exciting and slightly beyond my ken. I wonder how I got into the arts: how the hell did I get there? I must have been pulled there, must have walked down a lane from my house to where the Drawing Schools were and looked in on them, and said 'Hello' to somebody. I'm sure it's as simple as that.

There were certain masters there who had that sort of personality which immediately makes you feel inferior, and they seemed to work on it. I think the school masters were dreadful. None of them related on a human level at all. That's why boys went to boys. You had very close relationships with boys, very. Physical and intellectual and emotional. People tried to pretend that it didn't happen and that they went naturally into heterosexuality, which we did, but while we were there it was far more sensual than almost anything else in our lives after. There was no buggery at Eton, it was all based on sensuality, and never entry. So it wasn't homosexuality in that sense, it was a great need for friendship and love. It's the highest time of sexuality in life, and the most dangerous, because it happens with the same sex, which I think is infuriating.

It's also the biggest access to all forms of learning, music, literature, art, and you don't appreciate it, unfortunately. So it was a mixture of extraordinary sophistication at the age of twelve, thirteen, and yet it was far too young to appreciate Maurice Baring and all the writers that one's classical tutor would tell one about. It was the ideal university, Eton. Something that one really should have appreciated from eighteen onwards, not from thirteen onwards.

There was an awful emphasis put on physical beauty, I seem to remember. The freaks you could point out very easily. Freaks were spotty or ugly, freaks were scholars, basically, people who had too many brains, and were looked down on because they didn't pay.

At Summerfields, where I was before, I was rather handsome,

rather beautiful, and very acceptable. I was called Smee, who was one of the pirates in Peter Pan. I had a very easy passage. At Eton I was very spotty, not tremendously attractive, but I think I was attractive in another way. I don't know. I know I was popular, let's put it that way.

I played a lot of Shakespeare and did a lot of theatre. That was a total passion, that kept me alive. I played in *The Happy Hypocrite*, the Ivor Novello/Max Beerbohm play, naturally the part Vivien Leigh played – I was the attractive non-broken voice in the theatre – so I must have been very popular.

I hated sports and I took up beagling, because you never had to take any exercise with that at all. Because hares always go in circles, you could sit in the centre of a hill and watch the hounds going around after the thing, without moving at all. I hated rowing, bad for the back, and loathed football of any kind, you could break your neck – I did as little exercise as I possibly could.

A lot of the people I knew are dead – most of them are dead, in fact. A lot of them were killed in the war almost immediately afterwards. At least fifteen members of my house were killed within two years of the beginning of the war in action of some form or another. I always got the feeling that we were being trained in the OTC for a war, and in fact I left just two months before war was declared.

When I think back on my Eton days, I think about how many Etonians were killed – much more than anything else. We were all trained for that. We went blazing into battle with complete sense of folly and bravery, and very little intelligence, because we were trained to do that. That's why we're all such good officers.

I used to have great fear, an awful lot of fear, at that place. We had to gather twice a day, I've forgotten now what it was called, but gatherings, large gatherings, upset me still. That's why I think that most people from Eton can go easily into big groups, lawyers' groups, stockbrokers' groups; they always seem to converge. And I was completely the opposite. Most actors are like that, aren't they? That's why they act, usually: they come from broken homes and they indulge themselves in acting because the rest of their lives they want to draw away from the mass.

I was sacked, actually, for two reasons: having dirty books and running a book. So it was frustrated sexuality and losing a lot of money at Ascot. Anything that was out of the norm, you see, and didn't relate to being trained for a platoon or a flotilla or something like that, was looked on as subversive.

I went and saw the headmaster, Claude Elliott, and he didn't do anything brutal. I remember him saying to me, 'Well, I hope that you will have more success now, although I have great fears for you because I feel your personality and character do not bode very well.' Then he said, 'I hope in your chosen profession you'll find some success . . .'– as if to indicate that being an actor was something that let you get away with a lot more than you could get away with in normal life.

There was a great privilege in being an Etonian, particularly when you put it alongside the Depression and the Jarrow marches and all that sort of thing. It was a time of real devastation in Great Britain in the so-called working class. We were totally privileged in that respect, I mean we didn't even know about all that. And that's what I find terrifying about schools like that. I didn't find out about the real world until I was in the navy and I found it quite a shock meeting so-called ordinary people.

What the hell, we're just people really, aren't we? I mean, the fact that I was there means absolutely nothing to me whatsoever.

I think one is rather archaic for having been there. Do you notice that there's still a class system in England? When I see all these young royals rushing about, Lady Helen Windsor, et cetera, I find myself mildly nauseated, but then, you see, I'm not conventional in that sense. I'm very Labour in my politics, and I'm not even remotely from the privileged classes – except, I suppose, my great-uncle was an earl, but I mean only just that he happened to be; it's of no interest to me at all.

The one thing I remember is sex, and the other thing I remember is fear . . . and one other thing I remember is this wonderful insight into the arts. As everybody has probably told you, we were a very highly sexual, sensuous community, and we had great affection, so our affections were totally focused on the boys there. The masters were total enemies. Anybody old was an enemy.

I wish that I hadn't gone, because I think it gave one a definite sense of over-privilege. I find it very difficult to fight if things go badly; Eton didn't give you resilience and strength. I feel it's been very detrimental to me, because I haven't fought nearly hard enough in my profession. I have very much taken things for granted and let things slip, I haven't fought very hard for anything. If I'd been to a grammar school I think I'd have worked a lot harder and would have achieved a lot more. I think the great danger of Eton was that when you left you felt you could then live a life of indulgence. What it does, unfortunately, is to give you the illusion that everything's going to be done for you. I think when you leave Eton you really have to go on to financial security, you can't be suddenly on the street. I immediately assumed everything would just happen, and one would still be looked after.

I remember, way back, I did see Elliott driving by. I was with a woman, and I said, 'I hate that man.' But this is years and years ago. I had a deep loathing for the authority figures at Eton. I have no feeling about it at all now. I very occasionally have slight erotic memories of it, that's all.

DEREK MALCOLM

━━━

I HATED all the schools that I went to. I never really fitted in. I was not the type that should have ever been sent to boarding school, I naturally rather dreaded it. I was not a natural winner, and there was nothing I could actually offer such places to get any honours from them.

Well, I was put down for Eton before I was born, so it would really have been rather amusing had I turned out to be a girl. And willy-nilly I was dragged from the age of four onwards through preparatory schools. One preparatory school prepared for another preparatory school, which prepared for another one, which was the crammer for Eton. So all my life was preparation for this great day. I was scared as hell, since I was academically extremely dim and sportingly pretty awful too – a sort of weak, asthmatic, nervous creature, dragged into this place which I knew was my destiny ever since I could learn to speak or comprehend, and I found it exactly as bad as my worst fears.

I was in R. J. N. Parr's. It was going through a terrible transition from a very elderly man, C. J. Rowlatt I think his name was, who had let things slip, and there was a great deal of bullying and viciousness going on. Just to give you a slight and horrific instance of it, I can remember a particularly obnoxious boy who is now a famous solicitor, and he had a regime of terror which involved us actually eating cold cream mixed with shit, human shit. But I balked at that, and I became quite a good defensive player against bullying because I always had a good tongue and could make people laugh at the bullies. I was small, weedy, all the rest of it, no way could I fight them, but they didn't bully me a great deal for fear of jokes that I would make about them, and people saying, 'Did you hear what Derek said about so-and-so?'

So it was a bad, bad house when I arrived there, although Parr sorted it out by the time I left. But my introduction to Eton was not very good. If you were a small, weedy boy at Eton, as I was, you wore bum-freezers for years and years and years, until you were about eighty. Everybody else is wearing tails and there *you* are. I had a kind of inferiority complex about my work, which was unfounded because I was actually quite bright in certain ways, and really could hold my own. So what Eton did, with this appalling atmosphere that I went into, was actually to stunt any capacity I had for learning, or indeed anything that would give me honour in my community. The only honour that I ever got was that I was thought to be a wit, and nobody really crossed me too much for fear of what my tongue might do to them.

But the wife of Parr, who was a civilized sort of lady, would occasionally invite me to dinner, and always used to say, 'There is something about him, I don't know what it is, but he is not the dunce that you think.' Well, just one person saying that is an enormous confidence-booster to someone who is not going to win any exams or sports or anything like that. I remember one master who taught me English and thought I could write very well; he used to give me ten out of ten all the time, and say things like, 'If original, most original.' His encouragement saved me completely. He thought that somehow there was a talent there which nobody had ever got at. That, together with the comment from the housemaster's wife, was about the only encouragement I ever had during the five years I was at the bloody place.

I hate the place in every way. I mean, I hate it politically, I hate it culturally, I hate it socially. There is not an aspect of it that I remember with any kind of affection at all. The war was just about ending, but of course it was rationing time still and the food was fucking awful, there were outside lavatories, and it was a miserable experience being at Eton in those days. I was endlessly cold and endlessly miserable, and endlessly frightened among my peers.

I really try not to remember my past life at all because I was so miserable up to twenty at least, probably thirty.

My father was a hunting squire, deeply conservative and

reactionary, and I didn't have much in common with him, although I got extremely fond of him when he got old and doddery. My mother was extremely beautiful, having affairs with all sorts of people most of my life, or trying to, hating her marriage, and treating me at one moment marvellously, the next moment ignoring me, which was deeply unsettling for a little boy.

I did gradually realize that in fact Eton, although an appalling place in many ways, was the kind of place where you could develop on your own introspectively, and do all sorts of things which in a tighter, smaller public school you probably couldn't. I used to go campaigning for Fenner Brockway in Slough. It must have been a ludicrous sight, this little bugger in bum-freezers knocking on working-class doors, saying, 'I hope you are going to vote for the Labour candidate.' Quite ludicrous. I don't know how I ever dared to do it, but I did, and nobody objected.

Homosexuality was a very prominent thing in my day. Just to show how prominent it was, when I was about fifteen I came back from holiday, and we grouped in a room together, about five or six of us, and I said, 'Well, I don't know, I think women are really quite interesting, and I'm not so sure about little boys . . . perhaps one should forget about all this.' And everyone in the room turned on me and said (I will never forget it), 'You bloody pervert!' They were saying it in a half-mocking tone, but by God I think they meant it.

So it was a homosexual society, a pederastic society. There was hardly anybody who didn't desire the little boys, and there was great competition to get the most attractive fag, in which I sort of joined, because in that kind of atmosphere there's no way you could escape. I must tell you that when I left Eton at eighteen, I was in pretty good terror for about a year that I might be gay, and of course the worse kind of gay, liking little boys. What a disastrous life to go through, desiring little boys. I mean, what can you do? What an awful fate. On the other hand, I think one of the reasons I didn't turn or become gay was because I never actually did anything – maybe if I had, I would have, who knows? I never actually did get into bed with any of these little boys, or tamper with them; I was too frightened really. I remember getting into bed with my best friend, who was my age, and we were fiddling around and I thought, 'I'm not enjoying this at all', and so I just got out of his bed and said, 'Oh, forget it.' That was just mutual masturbation. I was not attracted at all to people of my own age, but I was certainly deeply attracted to small boys. The sexual drive has got to go on to something, but I think most of us never really did anything. We desired, we might have touched, there might have been some mutual masturbation, but it was a phase we were all passing through, because there was nothing else.

In my house, in my circle, nobody dared do a bloody thing, except one fat boy, who was generally despised, who got hold of – by some miracle – the prettiest boy in the house. I think the most erotic moment of my life was when this boy everybody fancied, called B—, was with this dreadful sleazy fat man called S—. I was in the room below S—'s, and I had my window open one summer night, and I heard B— saying, 'Oh S—, don't. Oh S—, S— . . . Oh S—' 'Oh B—, Oh B—. Oh, B—!' 'Oh S—.' I was absolutely going mad with lust because he was such a beautiful boy, but the awful thought of this dreadful creature managing to get hold of the object of everybody's desire – I can't remember anything quite so erotic in my life.

Another moment was eating some apple crumble in the house dining-room – the apple crumble was delicious – and I can remember another beautiful boy, with the most beautiful bum in bum-freezers, going up to ask for a second helping . . . I was eating the crumble, just watching him and thinking what bliss to be eating the crumble and going to bed with him at the same time. And I don't think I will ever forget those two moments, one very brief moment of about half a minute, and the other which seemed to last about an hour. I just wish that any hetero relationship that I've since had measured up to those, and I don't think they do, because at sixteen somehow everything is so fresh and intense. I think everybody remembers their first sexual desires, and mine were definitely, without any question, for small boys.

One of the housemaids I found very attractive. She was a nice bouncy little girl of about eighteen and, very unfortunate for her, a friend of mine had a room which was right above her bedroom; we could see what she was doing through the cracks in the floorboards. And I can remember the most dreadful erotic thrill of watching her masturbate, from the room above. Maybe that saved me from being gay. Jesus, I think that probably cured me.

At the same time I remember, my very last night at Eton, trying to break into the room of my fag. I think we'd all got drunk, I don't know how we got the booze, but we did. And my fag was Lord Vivian – I should imagine he is dreadful now, but he was very pretty at that time, and he rather liked me and I certainly liked him. But he had locked the door. God knows what I would have done had I got in, probably just kissed him or something, I'm not quite sure. I wouldn't have known what the fuck to do.

My problem was that *I* was a pretty boy and therefore loved by all the seniors. But since I was much older than I looked, maybe same as now, I was after the juniors and I wasn't the slightest bit interested in the seniors. I can remember them trying to get into my room, and I thought, 'Fuck me, just my luck, those buggers are after me and I don't want them.' I cannot remember a decent sexual experience at Eton.

I do think there's an awful number of people whose first sexual experience is the pattern of their life. Had I broken into Vivian's room and actually got him – presuming that he had been attracted to me – and something had happened, I believe the pattern of my life might have changed, indeed had I not seen the maid masturbating . . . who knows? Who knows what one's sexual drive is? But one is never so sexually intense as when one is sixteen and can't get at what one wants.

I can't remember ever being so terrified in my life as that time when one is sitting in one's room, knowing that one is going to be beaten. Your fagmaster comes up to you in the morning and says, 'I'm afraid you are going to have to have a beating.' And then you wait for the evening. 'Malcolm, come down to the Library and wait outside.' You have heard this story hundreds of times before, no doubt, but being small and weedy I was terribly frightened of anything like that. Then you were told, 'Down here, and wait outside', and you had to march down the corridor, and they would make you wait for four or five minutes. 'Come in', and you would go in, and you knew that once they were determined on a beating, no excuse in the world, '. . . my mother and father, were both tortured to death yesterday and I lost my nerve . . .', 'I'm sorry, no excuse.' And they were all sitting in wicker chairs with the *Daily Telegraph* in front of them so that they weren't actually looking at the beating. You just saw these *Daily Telegraph*s everywhere, except the person with the cane, and he would say, 'Well, Malcolm, there is no excuse for this. Three times you have failed to light your fagmaster's fire, and this is insufferable. Go outside.' And again you had to wait. It was a real fine piece of torture. 'Come in!' they would eventually shout, and in you would go again. 'Bend down.' They were not allowed to take your trousers off, for fear that they would instantly want to bugger you rather than beat you, I presume. I used to stuff the racing calendar up my arse. I can remember one beating I got, the head of house gave me one stroke and realized there was something in there that was not flesh; and he couldn't decide whether to take my trousers off and be accused of God knows what, or just to beat harder. So he thought, 'I'll just beat all the harder.' And he lined up and hit the light on the backswing, the bulb burst, and it was done in complete darkness. I took it all on my elbows, which is of course far more painful than on the arse, but nevertheless it was a great triumph, the racing calendar and the elbows taking the brunt of the blows.

But the effect on the beater as well as on the beaten! The effect on the beaten was just to cringe, really. Fortunately I didn't enjoy it, but it seemed to me that the beater rather did.

One other occasion that I ought to mention; I was talking in Chapel, in fact I was singing a rude, ribald verse to some psalm, and unfortunately, like an idiot, I thought that there was another verse, and in dead silence I went on for another line or two. I was summoned to the lower master for a birching and that was potentially a terrible thing. That actually drew blood – it was a real torture. I can remember, you have got to kneel on this block, and then you do have to take your trousers and pants off, and they do it on a bare bum. You were summoned and were held by two College servants. I am sure it doesn't happen now – if it does, then that place really should be burnt down – but it did then. There was a tradition that once you were down on the block, if you could wriggle free, and run and get out of the door and touch the Founder's Statue, which was only about one hundred yards away from where you were being beaten, apparently that was it: OK, you've won, and no beating. But unfortunately there were railings round it which I wasn't athletic enough to leap, so I didn't try it.

In fact the lower master was a dear old chap, not at all a vicious person, who could see that I was trembling all over and white as a sheet, absolutely terrified, and he gave me six strokes with the birch on the bare bum, but hardly touching. It did draw blood, because the birch can't do anything else but draw blood, but I can remember leaving and thinking, 'Well, that's better than a beating with the cane . . .' As I left, he said, 'Malcolm', and I turned round, and in front of these two thugs who were College servants of some kind, he said, 'I'm sorry.' You could see in his face that he was deeply ashamed, and I remember thinking, 'My God, what a stupid system this is, how ridiculous it makes us all.' I remember going back into class, and everybody saying, 'Where's the blood, where's the blood, are you all right?' I said, 'Yes, I'm all right, it didn't hurt at all really, very soft.' And I had to take my shirt off and show the blood on the shirt-tail.

Of course the whole religious thing in the end made me an atheist. Going to Chapel eternally, all those boring, cold, horrible Chapels; I hated God, I really hated him and all of His works, and have done ever since. I can't bear to go anywhere near a church.

Although I was pretty well an atheist, I decided that the term before my Confirmation I would really try and kick masturbation. I had a little calendar in my bureau, and I would ring the days on which I masturbated. And the previous term there was a great mass of days, but that term I had only one one week, terrific, and none at all the next week, and only one the week that I was to be confirmed, so I suppose I must have had some residue of religious feeling, or why should I bother? I can remember the day I was confirmed, nothing, nothing, nothing; then five days after I was confirmed, ring, ring, double ring, ring. It was no wonder one masturbated – one had held off for about two months, as long as one could humanly do, and within five days I must have been a complete sexual wreck.

When I left Eton I was in floods of tears – privately, not manifestly– and I can remember wandering around those awful quads in the College, saying, 'I'll never see this place again', and instead of relief there was this terrible nostalgia for it. You see, it's a funny thing, when you're very unhappy, or very happy – it's the same thing – you remember it very intensely, and anything you remember so intensely you regret. And I think anywhere that was familiar was comforting to me, since I was such an insecure child and an insecure young man. Because I had a bad home life and I never had a proper base I could call a home, I was like a prisoner coming out of a long-term prison, and looking back in and thinking, 'I wish I could go back to my cell', because that was my womb.

Yet despite all the horror and all the things that it didn't give me and should have given me, it did give me the feeling that I could walk into anywhere because I went to Eton. I realized, when I left Eton, the enormous advantages that were to be accrued simply by having been there.

One thing Eton gives you is a complete serenity of social graces. You're never worried about what you're dressed in, or how you look, or what impression you're giving, in the way so many poor unfortunate people are, because you're always taught at a place like Eton that you are the top. I mean, there's no higher you can go socially, so nobody's really going to come it over you. You can arrive with your flies open or in jeans, fuck 'em. And that is quite a valuable thing in a funny sort of way, that if you want to pull rank, you can pull the rank, you can pull it on the working classes, and they go, 'O-oh, wonderful', and you can pull it on the middle classes, because that's what they aspire to, and you can pull it on the upper classes, because you're one of them.

All my life I've been defined as an Etonian. You can't get away from the fucking place, however hard you try, and you can't resist telling people, just as a joke. You've no idea the effect it has on so many people. When I came to the *Guardian* I was a sub-editor, and every night I used to stone in the various pages with all the working-class Mancunians. And they loved me, they adored me. Why did they adore me? And this is the pernicious nature of the class system in this country, it's still here, right now, today: they adored me because I was nice and jolly with them, I was little Lord Fauntleroy, and they used to say, 'Isn't it marvellous, he was at Eton and he still talks to us, and he jokes and laughs and he's really quite a nice guy.'

It's very easy if you are socially superior to everybody to be awfully nice to them, to ingratiate yourself; it's awfully easy if the compositors think I'm a frightfully nice chap because I went to Eton and I still say 'Hello.' What a great chap!

People love my pieces about Eton. The *Guardian* loves them. 'Do one of your pieces about Eton, Derek.' It's dead easy to roll off, and accurate too, the awful things that went on and the aura of the thing. People write in by the droves saying, 'Do write more of those pieces.'

I do feel quite pleased with myself, in that I opened the eyes that were closed for me by places like Eton. I've overcome my education, my family, class structure; I overcame all that upper-middle-class crap of the fifties and the educational system which really supported it in those days. Maybe I was unfortunate, maybe I just didn't have very good teachers, and maybe I was unlucky to go into a bad house. Maybe I was unlucky in all sorts of things, maybe it was substantially my fault because I was so timid. I've no idea what it all amounts to, but I think it's damaged me in certain ways which are very, very difficult to get over after the age of eighteen. I mean, the deepest things we know in our psyches about ourselves and which we don't really tell anybody, and which if we did wouldn't really be explainable in words, I think are damaged by such a place. And I'll tell you why I believe that. I had some great friends at Eton who were imaginative, nice, civilized people; when I met them afterwards, I was horrified. I thought, 'I don't believe this.' It wasn't just the effect of going to Eton that was retrograde or damaging, but putting on the Old Etonian tie after you've left Eton is the really pernicious thing. Somehow these normal people have become intolerable to me within five years. But *he's* just a pompous arsehole. I don't believe it! *He's* gone to the City, I can't believe it! The whole thing, it just closes in on you. If you let it close in on you, it does.

All my life, up to about forty anyway, I was much desired by homosexuals, even now sometimes, and all my life I've had relationships with homosexuals, quite deep ones – I mean, nothing to do with sex as far as I'm concerned, but certainly they would have liked to. There was one particular person who was one of my best friends, he's just died aged seventy, who made a homosexual pass at me when he was forty and I was twenty. And I said, 'No, I'm not', and made a fuss about it. He was very contrite and never touched me again, but he fell deeply in love with me and remained in love with me the whole of his life, without anything of a sexual nature passing between us ever again.

It may be that I was once attracted to small boys and therefore know what it's like. And I was in terror of being gay for at least a year after leaving Eton, in terror, because I knew I still desired boys, and couldn't get anywhere near girls. So I was really pleased when I met a girl at Oxford whom I fancied, and who fancied me; but even then I could do nothing, I was so stunted by all this crap. I think the sexuality engendered in public schools in my day was a very, very stunting thing, although I'm perfectly convinced, at least in my circle of friends, all of whom fancied boys, that hardly any of them – except the lucky S—— – ever did anything. If you were to ask me if any of them were gay now, I should say they've probably naturally grown out of it like everybody else, but I would think S— hasn't. God knows about B—.

I think the only thing Eton left me with was that I rather like boyish women now, and I rather like bums – I'm a bum man rather than a tit man. I'm sure that's the only legacy of homosexuality I've got, thank God. Well, I don't say thank God now, it would be quite convenient to be bisexual, but I don't think I am in any way.

THE HON. NICHOLAS MONSON

WELL, I suppose it's not unique at all, but my family have been going to Eton, every male member, since 1745, the time of the Jacobite rebellion, so we have all had our characters shaped by it, my father and my father's father, and so on and so forth. I did actually feel genetically that this was correct, that I was right being here.

My father is a peer of the realm; he inherited the title when I was three years old, Lord Monson. I suppose the particular distinguishing thing about this title is that it is a relatively old one, 1728. We also inherit a baronetcy, again one of the oldest, I think it's the fourth oldest in the country, 1611. We're an old family. We've never played a crucial role in British history but we've always been there on the sidelines, in the shadows. There's always been a Monson around; the Monsons are the Rosencrantz and Guildensterns of British history. For instance, a Monson was a quartermaster at the battle of Agincourt; there was a Monson who was chaplain to Anne of Cleves (the Monsons did very well out of Henry VIII); there was a Monson who commanded the *Victory* at the sack of Cadiz under Drake, and there was a Monson who was Admiral of the North Seas and another who was responsible for the murder of Sir Thomas Overbury – though a Lincolnshire neighbour took the rap for that particular crime. We were offered an earldom by Walpole, which for some curious reason the Monson of his time turned down, saying: 'Monsons have been barons for the last one hundred and fifty years and barons we shall remain.' I really can't see the logic in that. If I had been him I would have gone straight for the earldom.

Eton must be many different things to many different people, and it depends not just on the time you were there but on such things as which house you were in. I, unfortunately, happened to be in a very ugly house, a hideous red-brick creation, which sat as uneasily as a council estate in the middle of Belgravia. It was a modern house, run at the time by a sort of ex-Second World War spymaster called James McConnell who had a fairly fearful reputation, and the house itself I remember being described as 'an animated filing drawer'. There were three floors, and on each floor there was just one long corridor; the architect, to give it what he thought would be character, had put a curve in this corridor. But to my mind it was the worst form of modern architecture – I mean, it was absolutely ghastly. Had we been in one of those large, rambling old houses, with all their different nooks and crannies, I think the whole atmosphere and character of the house would have been different. As a consequence I've always been able instinctively to understand, from my experience within my house, the disturbed behaviour of people who live in tower blocks – which I know sounds very funny coming from an elitist establishment like Eton.

I think you will gather that I didn't actually enjoy my house. The architectural shape of the house bred a form of unpleasantness. The term before I arrived one of the boys committed suicide, and there was another suicide later on in a similar modern house just down the Lane. Now those were the only two suicides, and they happened to have come from modern blocks. You could say that's just chance, that's probability. But my house was not a particularly happy house. I don't think the other modern house was a particularly happy house. As it was, in my house there was a disproportionate amount of, it may sound pompous and priggish, but bad apples, rotten eggs – there were lots of people expelled, lots of people taking drugs or drinking. One boy, I remember, grew marijuana plants with the aid of infra-red lamps in his cupboard, another erected a gin still. There was something of the tower-block psychosis.

I must say that my house was very unrepresentative of the school at large. My contemporaries in other houses seem to have had a very normal life, and I think, with all the facilities that

Eton offered and with its traditions, they must have had a wonderful time.

The important thing about Eton is how it fashions character. By its very constitution, Eton breeds a very early maturity in people. The school is not run by masters, masters only run the academic side of the school. The actual power over a boy's life is held by other boys. The prefects or members of Pop have the highest degree of power, and within the house you have the Library system. A very interesting thing I read by some psychologist, about transactional analysis, is that if you have people behaving to you as if you are a child, it doesn't matter how old you are, you do actually behave in a child-like fashion. At Eton it's the other way round. Everyone treats you as an adult, they have adult expectations of you. Young Etonians always have the appearance of confidence because other people have invested confidence in them. I don't think any boy of twelve or thirteen, once he goes away to school, wants to stay within childhood anyway.

I never knew what I wanted to do in life; even now I'm thirty years old I still don't know what I want to do with my life. But it was at Eton I discovered a great love of good writers, so I had in the back of my mind that it would be rather romantic to be a writer. For a while I did quite well at English, but I was extremely idle and I never really learnt how to construct good essays, so my academic results were always quite bad.

I don't think there was a sort of body of people who sat around saying, 'Well, we've got expectations of Monson here, why isn't he fulfilling them?' But the very nature of a very old and extremely distinguished school with magnificent traditions, and people who have done brilliantly, whose busts you see standing on walls, people who have become Prime Ministers and great generals, creates a form of insidious pressure on you, and you think, yes, I've got to be one of those people, or at least I should try to be one of those people.

As I've grown older I've realized that the chances of me becoming a great writer, or captain of industry, or statesman are extremely remote, but I wouldn't think that if I fail to be a great statesman, or a captain of industry, or a great writer, I would have failed in life.

I think modern life is extremely difficult. Holding a family together is a form of success, holding a job down, making a living in this day and age, is a form of success. The conditions for Etonians are totally different now, and what was true for my grandfather or indeed even my father is no longer true today, because unless the family money is well handled, which in most cases it isn't, there's going to be less money in the family, and the privileged classes are becoming less and less so. They may have titles or whatever, but the money has been and is being re-distributed. So at the end of the day, power is being completely redistributed, and the idea of Eton as a breeding place of elitism is out of the window.

I don't advertise the fact that I went to Eton. I don't make a lot of it. I mean, there are people who go and stick school photographs around their houses. That's not something I particularly want to live with. I don't want to live with memories of Eton; to me it was a time in my life which was inevitable, being the son of my father. I don't look back on it with any particular affection because I didn't much enjoy my time there, but it may have been that I'm the kind of person who just didn't enjoy adolescence, so wherever I was it wouldn't have made any difference.

I don't mean this in any unkind sense, but I think there are a lot of people who use Eton as a status symbol, and they make an awful lot out of it because they don't actually have that much themselves – if you strip them of their Old Etonian identity, they wouldn't be anything at all.

There is no sight more pitiful than that of a person who's been trained for a privileged existence and then let loose in the world, and they've got no money. It's pathetic, it makes them unhappy, and it makes a nonsense of their education which has given them all the expectations and none of the wherewithal. I feel that it is pointless if the family who put a boy through Eton don't at the end of the day give him the wherewithal to lead the life of privilege for which he's been trained. If they haven't got the money, they would be far better off educating the child more cheaply so that he has lower expectations, and with the money that they save go and invest it for him; then at least he's got something when he emerges.

If you are poor and you save all your life to send your child to Eton, I think you're doing the wrong thing. It is not comfortable for a person to be at a school where you are poor amongst a lot of rather rich people. It makes you feel very uncomfortable and it's very unnatural. But afterwards it gets worse. Basically what happens is that you're bred in terms of privilege and education to be a racehorse, and you end up having to toil in some sort of office block somewhere in the City, not earning that much, living in some grotty flat in Clapham. I mean, it's a waste of expensive training. You don't go and take a donkey to Fred Winter, do you?

I know various people who've got no money at all who went to Eton, and they end up in the most terrible jobs. They think they will go into the wine trade because it is gentlemanly, and end up serving behind a counter in Sutton for a huge supermarket chain, or Victoria Wine or something. That is no way to lead an existence. And they feel bitterly disappointed. Whereas another person who never had much expectations would be delighted to have such a job, because he thought he was going to end up in a factory and now he thinks he's rising in life.

If you're set off on this course of Eton you've got to be given everything to help you continue it. If you suddenly have the rug pulled from under your feet and you're having to struggle in the market-place like everybody else, Eton doesn't give you any special advantages. No one is going to hire you because you went to Eton. No one is going to say, 'Gosh, Mr Monson, you went to Eton, that's wonderful, we'll get rid of all the other candidates, you're the man for us'– it doesn't work like that, it hasn't worked like that for years. People say, 'Oh yes, well, it's the old school tie . . .' Old school tie is bollocks, complete and utter rubbish. In fact it works the other way: they say, 'Oh God, we don't want some hoity-toity snob here. Who does he think he is?' I don't know of any case where somebody has actually got a job because he went to Eton. Because you're not representative of the market-place. They want people who are going to fit in, people who will assimilate. Etonians don't assimilate.

Well, I must say I had a lot of second thoughts about sending any son of mine to Eton, but I found it was a reflex that, as soon as Alexander was born, within three weeks, I went and registered him and he's down for Eton. I do feel it was the force of history which made me do that. Mind you, I didn't do this thing of ringing up Eton before you ring up other members of the family to say you've got a son, which a lot of Old Etonians do.

I don't have any private money and I thought perhaps the thirty-pound cheque for the registration fee might bounce. But in ten, eleven years' time, there's not a chance of Alexander going to Eton unless the family provides. I certainly couldn't do so as things presently stand. Hilary and I have a good laugh occasionally when we look at our bank statement and we discuss Alexander going to Eton – I mean, it's just a complete impossibility, it's a laugh, a joke.

And why on earth should I have to gear my activities towards sending Alexander to Eton? I'm not going to sell my house to send Alexander to Eton and live in a council flat, I mean that's taking things to an extreme . . . utterly pointless.

But I hope to be changing all this; within the next five years I'm actually stopping work as a writer because I have a few material ambitions for the family, just one of which happens to be sending Alexander to Eton.

I just don't think it's true that Eton provides some sort of golden pathway to success, but I think that it gives you a certain resilience and toughness. I mean, there's nothing in life that I haven't been able to handle. There was a time when I went through a nightmare stage on a magazine with another OE who's well known for being a bully as an executive, vile and unpleasant. He used to reduce a lot of people to tears in the office, including my wife, on a very regular basis, knowing precisely what he was doing. And he went for me for six months. To me he was a second-rate bully. I had people who worked in that office coming up to me saying, 'I don't know how you can put up with this, he is so foul and unpleasant.' He would try and humiliate me in front of everyone, and it was like water off a duck's back to me, I just despised him – to me he was just a total wanker, he was pathetic. And the reason I could take it, whereas other people couldn't, was because I went to Eton. Now that was my advantage of going to Eton.

I do know of one or two people who sort of wake up screaming in the middle of the night and have nightmares about being back at school. I certainly wouldn't want to re-live my Eton days: if you asked me to re-live them, I would say no. I don't think I could have ever been happy anyway in that house. I know it sounds rather effete to say that architecture does affect your life or happiness; I'm just telling you that, for some extraordinary reason, it does. I think people who choose to live in council tower blocks are lunatics; I feel very, very sorry for them . . . it's a form of living hell. I'd rather live in prison than live in one of those. Farrer House. Ghastly hideous place, it was a nightmare. Talk about the traditions of Eton – there were no traditions there. I mean, I could have been anywhere. I could have been in Nevada.

JOHN MOORHEAD

My father was Australian, he didn't come to England until he
was twenty-five; my mother came from a solid middle-class English family, doctor's daughter, not Eton at all. They were both
journalists. When my parents went down there with a view to
getting me into Eton, they went to see a man called Bobby
Vaughan, a bright but opinionated man. And halfway through
the interview, Bobby Vaughan turned to my father and said,
'Anyhow, I can't imagine what on earth an Australian like you is
sending your son to Eton for.' Typical. I mean, he had a point,
but a typical snobbish, insular, parochial Etonian master.

But there was always a sense that there was an oddity about my
going to Eton. My parents were not particularly political, but in so
far as they were political they would have voted Labour. But my
father believed in the best education, the professional class sort of
attitude, and (although I never talked to him about this), I should
think he was slightly concerned with neutralizing the prevalent
English attitude to Australians. Being an Australian in England,
you were an outsider. The short-cut to not being an outsider was
to send your son to Eton. I don't know whether he would have
admitted that, but he was absolutely right in some ways.

You see, they were tied to no particular tradition, nor to some
progressive ideal; they were footloose. My father was an im-
migrant, as it were, and therefore the field was open. Where he
was right was that when I'd gone through the mill, and survived,
and got out the other end, it left me absolutely unimpressed by
the English class system. And that was worth five pence. It was
worth something. There are more battles to fight in life, as we all
know, but it meant that I was never overawed on a social level in
England, which has been quite useful.

But it was certainly very strange for me. Eton was a completely strange land, and the very first day there were four new boys in the house, other than me, who sat around and talked about this mysterious institution called Pony Club, which they all seemed to know completely backwards, and I had no knowledge of it at all.

I can remember standing next to the notice-board and looking down a list of people, and seeing that it said Moorhead and Simpson and Jones and so on; then it said 'Mr Eliot', and I asked, 'Why is my friend called "Mr Eliot"?' A voice behind me said, 'One day, young man, you will learn that the younger sons of Earls are given the prefix "Mr".' But the curious thing about Eton is that within its walls it was not a snobbish place.

It was an exclusive place. There were some very rich boys in it. I once worked out that when we used to have tea together in the Library, I was having tea with Bell's, Bird's Custard, Bowden's, Raleigh bicycles, Vestey's meat and Sainsbury's groceries.

My house was called Gowan's. It was undistinguished, middle-of-the-road, decent, average . . . not a great deal you could say about it. God, he's alive and well and living in the Lake District – he'd be unpleased by that. But he was a silly character. He was an intelligent man, definitely intelligent, but he was a snob, he was a weak character, he was petulant. He seemed a disappointed character. Many of his contemporaries got headmasterships and things like that, and he never did, but felt he should have done. He was a man of no real substance.

Eton had a bad effect on me, there was no doubt about that. The cliché about never being seen to try was indubitably true. The people who were admired were people who achieved things, but in this laid-back kind of way, so it was not apparent that they were trying. And of course to a large degree it was an illusion, it was the style and not the substance, because a lot of people who carry on that type of thing are in fact secretly working away extremely hard. Until the age of seventeen I worked extremely hard, and that was the only way I could ever achieve anything. But it got to me in the end and I tried to emulate it – I fell for the appearance of it. Up to seventeen I loved Eton. I was totally happy there, as a matter of fact; I was the model schoolboy. My reports were always excellent, I tried hard, worked hard. At seventeen it suddenly completely changed and the reports were terrible, and I frantically tried to get into Pop, which I failed to do. I did nothing, achieved nothing, wasted my time, and I don't think it's totally escaped from my character to this day.

I wish I hadn't fallen hook, line and sinker for that. I wish at the very least I'd had the maturity or the independence to say, 'This isn't for me', which it absolutely wasn't.

I must have been insufferable at that age. I don't know whether my father understood the wind that he reaped. He was very, very worried that I was going to be gay. I think he made his judgement on the friends I brought home from school, because they were effete and not what he remembered from Scotch College, Melbourne. They were just foreign to him. He couldn't make out these sometimes elegant manners and rather mature grown-up characters who would be extremely solicitous about whether you had another drink, and behaved impeccably and had good manners, and who appeared to be without enthusiasm or interest in life. To him, who came out of Australia and worked through Fleet Street, they were a bunch of wimps.

Well, we were all gay, we were all queer, as we called it in those days. Gay Eton! The wonderful hypocrisy about the whole thing, I mean, you were odd if you had not had some homosexual experience when you were there, and yet the rules were that if you did have it, you got thrown out. Certainly it was a main part of one's life. My first and greatest love was a contemporary of mine in my house at Eton; I stayed on a whole extra term, motivated five per cent by the wish to get into Pop, and ninety-five per cent by love. Or adolescent lust.

I had an affair with this boy and loved him with a passion. Wonderful! I did certainly think for a while, at the age of seventeen, 'Goodness me, I must be gay', but I discovered I wasn't, and he certainly wasn't either. It was just established practice; everybody did it all the time and it was absolutely part of your life. I suppose because it was the cardinal sin, that made it more exciting. The hypocrisy of the people who invented a school like that, and then said it's the worst sin! Ridiculous, because of course it was bound to happen.

Looking back, it was all very innocent, but quite promiscuous. A new, pretty boy would arrive in the house, and then people concentrated on him, and to this day one could still define various people in that context. There is a dignified figure on the *Financial Times* who's synonymous in my mind with only one thing – he was the school tart. He wasn't very pretty, it's very odd.

There was a completely open thing about it, and still is. My boyfriend from the last term at Eton lives in the south of England, knows my wife's parents and everything. My wife went over to have a drink there, and I said to her, 'Ask C – how he is, and tell him John sends his particular love.'

I have hardly seen him since, but if I met him at some party, or whatever, we would certainly make a mention of it because it was the salient thing in our lives at that particular time. One doesn't want to make too much of it – it probably had a greater effect on my life simply because I put more into it, because there was no alternative. He went back home to the Pony Club dances. There wasn't any of that in N W 3, and we were always moving. I never met anybody for more than five minutes, so Eton was my life, and therefore not only my social life but my emotional life went into it.

I went to Oxford after that. Now that would be the moment when the Etonian experience could have been diluted. It was not. I went to University College, but by far the greatest number of my friends were at Christ Church, where I spent all my time, and the great majority of those were Etonians. And so it seemed that my life was very much formed and determined by having been to Eton. Eton was the place where I met people, knew them, put them in their context, stayed with them in their houses, and for a while, coming out of Eton, I thought Eton, Etonians, that was the real world.

If I've got one major thing against Eton, and always have had, it is the mixture of arrogance with ignorance, I mean the complete social isolation in which they lived – that you could believe, for instance, that grammar school boys were oiks. It took me years to discover that grammar school boys were the absolute elite of the state system, and this arrogance and sense of superiority is, I think, one of the real inescapable faults. I've always wanted to know how an intelligent apologist for Eton would defend that.

It wasn't until I became a trainee journalist in Cardiff, having gone around the world, that I began to see Eton in perspective, and began to meet other people outside the magic circle. But still, to this day, a lot of my friends are based in my time at Eton.

I've been married before, but my present wife's father and brothers all went to Eton. And there was absolutely no doubt that, although we were totally different people, this was a short-hand pass to getting on and understanding each other. We talked the same language. And that game I can play very easily. Although they're hunting and shooting and fishing sort of people, which I know nothing about, there was a definite bond. One feels that with other schools it wouldn't signify so much. It's not that I and my wife's father sit back and say, 'Do you remember the times . . .', it's not that at all. It's just an understanding. It may well have been that in the first efforts of conversation running dry, I managed to insert it into the conversation – thus waving a flag that we would all be able to salute.

I go to old boys' dinners occasionally. I go to them because I go with a friend of mine. That's not an apology for doing it; it's just that I wouldn't go if I was on my own, and yet there are quite surprising people who do go. It's never as boring as one thinks it is going to be, nor is it as outlandishly absurd. It's actually quite pleasant. I went to one the other day – and there was David Sainsbury, who was a very close friend of mine at school. He'd gone alone. Now what on earth was he doing there? It really is extraordinary, because David Sainsbury's an extremely hard-working and busy man, apart from being the richest man in the land; he's not sentimental about Eton; his world is nothing to do with Eton, his world is full of Liberal/SDP people solemnly and seriously trying to find the third way and all this kind of thing – and yet there he was. I must ask him what he was doing there.

MARY NICHOLSON*

I HATED my girls' school; it was after O-levels, and Dad wanted me to stay on, but I wouldn't. And I had the chance of going to Eton, which offered the best education in the world and cost, I think it was sixty-five pounds a term for me to go there, and I wanted to meet all these boys that my friends had already met, and it seemed crazy to go somewhere like Marlborough or Bryanston, which would have cost a fortune on a teacher's salary. But in retrospect I should have; I would now.

I was fifteen, and I was taller than all of the boys. The first morning there were three new people on what they call the knife-boards in College Chapel, which are pews that face the entire school, and there were two new girls. This poor boy . . . some idiot had put him between the two new girls, and we had to sit there, staring face to face with all these really senior boys; it was just ghastly.

The other girl was called Virginia Sumsion. The headmaster called us in and told us that the school wasn't geared up to taking girls, and they were really rather taking us on sufferance. And the clothes we were to wear, he told us, were to be called sober. There was one instance, it was the late seventies – I had a pair of boots which came just above my calf, and one of the masters complained that Mary Nicholson was wearing thigh-boots – that's how switched on they were about women's clothing.

I lived on the private side in my normal bedroom. But Keats House is right in the middle of Eton, in the middle of all the activity, thousands of boys going past it every day. You couldn't

*Only daughters of masters on the staff can go to Eton (the first girl to go there was in 1971). There are currently no girls at Eton.

go out of a single door without being seen by them, all leaning out of their windows, watching every move you made.

For the first year at least I wasn't supposed to go on the boys' side, and so there wasn't really anywhere that you could go where you could just be friends together.

I had always found life at school really quite easy, socially, friends-wise, until I went there. That was the main problem. It was lonely because there was nobody that you could relax with. Mum and Dad had warned me. They were so wise; they knew what it would be like.

I always got approaches from boys I didn't want them from. Making friends with the nice boys wasn't easy when you were that young. In my first year it tended to be the ones who thought it was cool to be seen with a girl, and so by the second year, when the nice ones were ready to start talking to girls, they thought I was like all these rich boys that I was with. So I didn't get to meet the nicest ones, because they had no reason to want to meet me. There was nothing about me that was obviously attractive, I shouldn't think, particularly because I was surrounded by these people.

All I longed for was to be treated like a part of the furniture. I was desperate for that, longing for that every minute of every day for seven terms. The funny thing is that recently I was going out with this rugby crowd who were having a farewell lunch before they went on tour, and one of them said to me, 'Oh, I suppose you can come along, Mary, because you're one of the boys.' Suddenly after all that time, without realizing it, I had become one of the boys. But that wasn't Eton.

I wanted to be a boy all the time I went to Eton until I suddenly found that it is really great fun being a girl.

I did have some very good friends, like David Thomas, for instance, whom I used to confide in an enormous amount because he was going out with a housemaster's daughter, so he was safe. But he left, and I have just never seen him again. I find it very strange that you can be that close to somebody and then it just fizzles out completely. I thought I had made friendships, but nothing has lasted really. And I remember once, when I was with my two good friends, one of the boys saying that we were a threesome, and the other one said, 'Well, whatever happens, us three will always be great friends', and it didn't happen because they have got girlfriends now, and that kind of thing.

Nowadays if I meet an Etonian, they are the sort of people who say, 'Oh, how wonderful to see you, we must meet up for a drink, I'll give you a call.' They are just so insincere. In fact, I bet Steven McCrum a hundred pounds that he wouldn't give me a call.

The boys in Dad's house in my year were an extraordinary set. There was Hugh Laurie who was House Captain – you might have seen him on the box quite a lot recently, he has been on all sorts of things and is probably going to be extremely famous. He is the funniest person that I have ever met, and the strongest character. There was Nigel Burney, for whom Cambridge University wasn't social enough, so he spent most of his time in London. There was a chap called Henry Holland-Hibbert, who is utterly, totally, completely army, but who has since left the army. There was a chap called Lockland-Campbell who went into the army, and has now become a poet. What happened was that those ones that I have mentioned formed a gang and bullied, mentally bullied, the others, principally a chap called Mark Anderson, who was not a very happy person, a chap called Alistair Prescott who used to do all my physics for me, and me. My nickname there was 'Dribble', because according to Hugh Laurie I dribbled around like a pat of warm butter. Well, no one can believe now that I was wet, and no one would have before. But it was just that they ground you down. It was an odd bunch, you see. Usually the people in Dad's house were OK. If I had been a different year, I think it would have made quite a lot of difference.

The worst thing was lunch, when these boys used to gang up. They would take bets on how many words Alistair Prescott would say over lunch. And I remember one day they played Chinese whispers so loud that I could hear. They were saying, 'Mary is going to have a face-lift this afternoon.' One time they brought in a back-scratcher with a hand on it, which they were trying to drag across my knee. Another time Hugo Guinness said, 'Oh Mary, your clothes are so horrible. I think I had better give you some money to buy some new ones', and wrote me out a cheque which I lost, which was about the best thing that could have happened to it. I remember time and again he would say, 'Your father is only a teacher.' And they used to say things like, 'Oh, Mary, we hate your family, we hate your mother, we hate your father, and your brother is even worse' – things like that. I tend to remember those things rather than the good bits, I suppose. But that's quite nasty, isn't it? To a sixteen-year-old who has got nobody to fight back with.

I used to come out of lunch and just sit in my room unable to do anything. Those sorts of things weren't specific enough to make you cry; they just made you think: 'There's something really wrong here.' Eventually I just refused to go in to lunch with them.

They didn't give you a chance, really. If I had been shy, they would have written me off as being boring. I *was* terribly shy and I was very scared, but I still managed to think of something to say, however trite it was at the time, so you couldn't win really.

I am bitter; don't I sound it? But it is all my own fault for insisting on going there.

I shouldn't think that they are sorry, because what they thought I should do is fight back and lose my temper. They were goading me into reaction, and they did teach me to lose my temper towards the end. I don't think I can ever forgive them, I don't think so.

I kept getting dumped by all these boys. They set out to see if they could get me, and if they discovered that they could, then they'd dump me, because they didn't think that I was good enough for them. There were quite a lot of bad moments, but I think that those were probably the worst. I didn't lead them on, I don't think, certainly not knowingly. By the end I reckoned it up, and I found scores were about equal, which is fair enough, and I dumped as many people as had dumped me.

One trait of Etonians is immense charm. They are capable of really charming the pants off anybody. It starts from when they start at school and an immense emphasis is laid on it. If you are funny at Eton you can get away with virtually anything. Another thing they have got is great wit, and they can turn it on and off at will. Time after time I fell for this. I still would, I'm sure I would – I'm not cured . . . it's very difficult for anybody to see through it.

After Eton I became a despatch-rider, and I went out with a chap who lived in East London. I found my niche at university. When I went to Exeter I had no idea where I was going to end up, with the despatch-rider types or the Etonian types. I ended up in the middle, which ever since then has proved to be just right for me, with people who went to minor, or what Eton would call minor, public schools, whose parents are in industry or something like that.

When some cool dude at Exeter took a fancy to me, and took me to the coffee bar where all the cool people hung out, I couldn't believe that he was proud to be seen with me next to him, which is a terrible thing I think for any young girl to feel. But gradually, over a year or two, I went back to how I was at girls' school, when I had been much more confident. So it hadn't changed me at all, although it has given me that sort of extra uniqueness, I suppose.

If I go to a cocktail party, quite often I get recognized by people, which isn't very nice. How would you like to be eating happily somewhere with some nice friends, and having a nice time, when somebody points at you, saying, 'That's Mary Nicholson. She went to Eton'? I don't like it.

I sometimes cannot believe that I ever went there; it just seems so bizarre, so peculiar, such a long time ago, and to have made so little a difference. When I go home now, which is about twice a week because you can't keep me away from there, I can't believe really that I was a part of it.

These boys in Dad's house, some of them, I would just love to be able to put down, especially Lockland-Campbell. And there is another one called Chris Brooks, who had nothing to do with me at all, but he set up an anti-Mary campaign. It was just so mean. I would love to be able to get back at him.

I should have forgotten and forgiven by now. I still feel I have scores to settle. How awful . . . why can't I just let it go? It was ten years ago.

Eton instils confidence in people, it's famous for it. Well, it destroyed mine for a while. Eton nearly knocked me sideways. If I hadn't been strong I might have survived it better, because the boys were always looking for a weakness in me, they were trying to goad me into reacting, and if they had just seen me as a defensive little girl things would have been a lot easier; they wouldn't have felt threatened.

It was so difficult then, and now I feel in such a strong position because I have got everything that I could want. I am happy as a kite really.

LORD OAKSEY

I WAS at Bill Marsden's, who was known as Bloody Bill and was quite famous as a sort of horror figure to boys outside his house. He was probably a sadist at heart. He used to beat you himself sometimes. He would definitely spend an awful lot of his time trying to discover crimes. You didn't smoke in our house, it just wasn't possible, because the slightest whiff of tobacco and he was on to you like a flash. Beating was just part of life. You were summoned ceremonially to the Library after prayers, and it was extremely painful. I was only ever beaten twice, and it was awful really, particularly as I had the bad luck to be beaten by a sort of Botham figure called Henry Hely-Hutchinson, who was Captain of the Eleven, and who had an eye like a hawk and a wrist like steel. It was extremely painful.

I was a fag to a man called Teddy Hall, who has since become one of my greatest friends. He is a professor at Oxford now, and a very extraordinary professor, because he is a jolly good scientist, extremely rich, and very good at enjoying himself. My first bad experience was being told to polish his Sam Browne – in those days a senior officer in the Corps had a strawberry-coloured uniform, not khaki, and the actual Sam Browne. And this one had on it the patina of age, with layers and layers of polish. I had never seen anything like it, and I had never cleaned anything in my life, so I attacked it with a scrubbing brush and absolutely ruined it. But happily for me there was a senior fag who got beaten for not pointing out to me what I was doing.

People, outsiders, always say, 'We know about Eton – they play the wall game.' In fact only the scholars and a few older boys play the wall game. At that time, the only game that the whole school played was the Field Game.

We had a uniquely successful house in the Field Game. My first half we got into the finals of the house side, but Teddy Hall was the only man who was in the Field in our house, and our opponents, Assheton's, had five members in the Field, so to say that they were favourites was an understatement. I mean, it was regarded as such a foregone conclusion that they had the picture of Marsden's team, with the caption 'Runner-up', taken before the match, because it was quite impossible that we would win. And then when in fact we did win by a single point, the cup had to be cut out from Assheton's photograph and pasted on to ours. Anyway, we won by one rouge after the other people had nearly scored about forty-eight times, and it was the most exciting game of football that I have ever watched. So that was a great thrill, and there was great *esprit de corps* in the house. This sounds ridiculous, to be sort of braggadocio, but until my last half I was never in a losing team at the field game; when we were beaten in the finals of the Lower Boy, luckily I had jaundice and didn't play in that one.

Bill was enormously involved with both the sports and the house. Apart from the fact that he was a slightly perverted sadist, he was a marvellous housemaster. For instance, all the time he was a housemaster we only ever had one person sacked, and he was sacked for the usual Etonian offence, and was involved with about twenty other people from different houses, so Bill couldn't save him. Otherwise people committed the most heinous crimes, and he always used to have them beaten to within an inch of their life, but never allowed them to be sacked, because he took the view – and I think that it is a right and proper view – that you are being paid to teach boys, not to send them away ruined and disgraced. He thought that it would have been a terrible failure for somebody to be sacked from his house. So he was intensely involved and took a tremendous interest in us, although it didn't appear to be at all a friendly interest.

I was still at prep school during the Battle of Britain, which I remember we watched. We used to go out and find crashed aeroplanes and all sorts, but that was over by the time I got to Eton in 1942. I had gone through an extraordinary metamorphosis; during Munich I was absolutely longing for peace, and dreaded the war, because I thought that my mother and three sisters and everybody would be bombed and I would be left all alone. And then when Munich was a success, an apparent success, I was thrilled with that. I can remember, when the war did start, I followed it keenly as if it was the football league tables, and I remember actually thinking, when an advance of about a quarter of a mile was reported from the Maginot Line, 'Oh Lord, what a bore, it's going to be all over in no time at all.'

I don't remember going down to the shelters until the flying bombs. Then, when they came, for quite a long time we went down to the shelters damn nearly every night. It was a good gamble, because if you were in the shelters after 11 p.m. you didn't have Early School, so if you had work to do for Early School, you sat there at 10.50 p.m., hoping and praying that another little flying bomb would come buzzing over. We treated them as a joke. I don't remember feeling any kind of fear that they would land on us, because it didn't seem likely to happen. As a matter of fact it was quite likely to happen.

I suppose the war affected us in that there wasn't very nice food. But actually Bloody Bill was marvellous about that. He used to take us out in the summer on fruit-picking expeditions, he on his famous bicycle, which was the only bicycle that I have ever seen which had two crossbars to make it taller. He looked like a sort of stick caterpillar: huge, long, black legs, encased in black trousers. We would bicycle out to neighbouring farms and pick raspberries and currants, and all sorts of things which were taken back and made into jam by the dame. We reckoned to be better fed than most houses too, which was quite a serious matter. But you didn't notice the rationing much, because unless you had a very long memory you didn't really remember peace time. It was brought home to me in my last summer holidays that we didn't have luxury goods, because by that time my father was presiding over Nuremberg and I spent the summer out in Bavaria, in the American zone, and you had a card at the P X. We suddenly realized what it was like not to be rationed – you had Hershey bars like there was no tomorrow. Unfortunately, on account of being the judge's son, I wasn't able to enter into the black market quite as keenly as I would have liked.

The one very, very vivid memory I have of the war is the end of it, V-E day, which was of course thrilling. Everybody rushed about and misbehaved themselves. I don't remember whether we overturned buses in the street; we certainly stopped them. That night, there was to be a bonfire down on Fellows Eyot, and there was a little, physically little, member of Pop called Brunner – I forget his christian name – who during the morning had been sent out by his housemaster to control the crowds in the High Street. It was an unfortunate choice as he wasn't very popular anyway, and I wasn't there at first, but I gather he didn't do it well and there was a considerable anti-Brunner feeling. The awful thing was, I'm pretty certain that there was an element of anti-semitism in it. The reason why I say that is because, down on Fellows Eyot that night, suddenly there was a chant: 'Let's throw Brunner in the river.' And there was a sort of mob movement to chase this poor unfortunate little fellow. There was a thoroughly unpleasant attempted lynching scene, in which (and this is probably benign censorship) I claim not to have taken a very active part on either side. Fortunately for him he had a lot of large boys on his side, other members of Pop.

And then (and this was definitely anti-semitic) there was a scholar called Vosks, and really the only thing that he had ever done wrong was to look extremely Jewish, and to be a very scholarly scholar. A cry went up from somewhere, 'Let's find Vosks and do him as well.' And there was actually a moment – and I can't be wrong about this, I can't have made it up – when quite a large number of people were roaring around Upper Chamber looking for this unfortunate fellow, who, luckily for him, was tucked up in the loo or something, I mean he certainly didn't appear.

That has always been a horrible memory. We had won the war, which was against the cruellest and most horrible and most anti-semitic government there has ever been, and here the so-called cream of English youth were behaving in a thoroughly fascist and detestable way. It is a very clear memory for me.

I had one really terrifying, idiotic experience. I wasn't particularly keen on racing at that time, and on the day of the Derby
I honestly don't think I even knew it was Derby Day. Suddenly
Bill Marsden appeared with a telegram which had been addressed
slightly wrongly to me – Lawrence had been spelt wrong or
something like that: anyway, sufficiently wrongly, and it didn't
need much for him to open it. It said, 'Have drawn Black Panther
for you', signed 'Seymour'. 'What is this?,' he said. 'What's this?
It's a bet, isn't it – you have been betting!' I said that I didn't
know who or what Black Panther was or who Seymour was. I
really had no idea, I genuinely didn't. 'Look at this . . .' he said (I
think that it was the only time that he had ever opened a paper at
the racing page), 'Black Panther is running in the Derby, ridden
by Sir Gordon Richards – you are betting.' I could say nothing
in my defence, I really didn't know what was going on at all. So
the shadow of the block was hanging over me all day, and finally
I was so miserable and in such a panic that I rang up my mother
like a snivelling little boy, and told her this story. 'Oh,' she said,
'Seymour . . . that must be that idiot Beecham who's Daddy's
marshal.' What had happened was that my father was at judge's
lodgings on circuit, and they had a sweepstake on the Derby;
there weren't quite enough people for the tickets, so he said that
he would get some for the children, and told his marshal that it
would be more fun if they knew about it. So by the grace of
God, in the nick of time, I was able to get my mother to ring up
Bill and exonerate me.

I was terrified by the threat of being beaten by him. He was
quite terrifying really. He was in many ways a horrific old man,
and people used to put down sugar in the corridors so that they
could hear him coming as he crept along the corridors. We put
down a lot of sugar. As I got bigger, and into the Library and his
beloved football teams, he became a friend in a way, but it was
always a slightly prickly type of friendship. I mean, I very much
admired and loved him, and he was a wonderful housemaster,
but on the other hand, I think that if he had been psychoanalysed
they would not have let him anywhere near little boys for years
and years.

I can remember the cold. It was very cold. You had to rely on fires, and we did have jolly good coal fires. Once you got them going, they gave out a lot of heat. And I remember coming home after playing football, and the joy of getting warm again, and having tea. We used to have smashing teas, sort of tea-dinners, eggs and bacon and sausages, and that was great fun when you were doing it for yourself.

I messed with two rather remarkable people, one called Peter Gatacre, who later became Managing Director of Madame Tussaud's, and John Barton, who is a major director of Shakespearean drama. And showing that little boys are like what they later become, they used to have the most incredibly elaborate board-game – it was a bloody nuisance because it took up the whole table – and they used to make their own little pieces, and had huge armies and navies battling against one another. Only they knew the rules. It was incredibly complicated and beautifully done, and it always fascinated me.

Eton allowed you to do your own thing, and it certainly made life a great deal more interesting in that way. I enjoyed Peter Gatacre and John Barton's antics. There was a splendid man called Colin Fyfe-Jamieson, who was once climbing up a rope upside down in the gym when, I regret to say, a contraceptive fell out of his pocket. A master was standing at the bottom. 'What's this, Fyfe-Jamieson?' Colin, upside down on the rope, said, 'Oh, don't you know?', which was rather cool. In a lot of houses he would have been sacked, but he was just beaten. He had the ghastly total of fifteen blows of the cane, fifteen up, and is alleged to have said, as he turned at the door of the Library, 'Thank you, gentlemen.'

When you're with people who were more or less contemporaries of yours at Eton, very likely something comes up which only Etonians would talk about; there is that element of club-ishness about it, even now. For instance I have got a friend called Tony Lloyd who was in the field with me, and we therefore played a lot of football together. He is extremely grand now, he's a Lord Justice in fact. I was sitting in Brooks's Club, of which he is also a member, and I was scribbling away at my *Horse and*

Hound article, when Tony came up behind me and said something like, 'Are you doing your extra work?' And I immediately knew, without looking, who it was.

There are certain in-jokes. For instance, Claude Elliott was supposed to have said in a leaving lecture, 'I don't mind what you do when you leave here, as long as you don't fornicate in your Old Etonian braces.' And 'fornicate in your Old Etonian braces' had always been a password between me and Edward Cazalet.

I think and hope that Eton will be able to adjust to whatever change comes, and still be good for the country. I think that the enormous difference in wealth and class at the moment is regrettable and deplorable and sad, because it creates so much bitterness and jealousy. But there are a lot of people who, just because you are a lord or because you talk with a toffee-nosed voice, think that you must be against them, and they are against you, which is jolly sad. And I admit that Eton is a cause of bitterness and jealousy, but I don't believe that we are going to achieve total equality of opportunity ever. I don't believe that people are educated at Eton to think that they are better than anyone else: I think the reverse is true now. I think now there is a very considerable push to make Etonians realize that if anything they owe something for being there, for being so lucky. *Noblesse oblige* almost, but it's not that. It's just that if you are bloody lucky enough to have thousands and thousands of pounds spent on your education, then you bloody well ought to do something about it. Although, of course, it is arguable whether being a racing correspondent is a very good way of doing something about it.

I'm sure I would always recommend anybody with a son to send him there if they could afford it. I think it's the best, the best place.

DR JOHN PAINE

I REMEMBER my first day. Our housemaster, Archie Nicholson, and his wife were just so awkward and shy, completely unable to put anybody at their ease, and there was this tremendously formal tea-party which was painful beyond belief. There were a lot of people meeting for the first time, all very different socially. There was a general and his son, there was a guy who's quite a socialite now – the Earl of Westmorland's son, Lord Burghersh. Another boy, I don't know what his father was, I think he was a professional of some kind, but he was an only son, came from Surrey, and they were a little sort of inbred unit. Father, mother and son had a special language which they would speak, whole words and sentences that other people couldn't understand. The fifth was a funny little blond boy; I don't remember his parents at all. But I remember thinking, 'What a lot of weirdos', from the beginning. I never really got on with any of them.

My father's a solicitor. He was an incredibly successful boy at Eton, President of Pop, Captain of the Eight, Captain of Rugby, and Captain of the Field, and loved it, perhaps because he was so successful. It was a big thing in his life – you know, 'You should go to Eton because it gives you so much opportunity.'

At Eton you become more independent at fifteen or sixteen, when you specialize and get into the sixth form. Up until then I think I was a very ordinary, boring sort of schoolboy, and I don't really recall those first three years at all. 'Conventional successful schoolboy', that's what my housemaster put in my reports at the beginning. But I changed when I specialized. My modern tutor was a guy called John Ellwick, who's left Eton now actually; he's gone to work in Alton in a handicap home. Ellwick was someone that you could go to and just talk about what your feelings were – mine were always very sort of moaning feelings about the school and authority. He was a very strong Christian but also a very good educationalist. He knew what adolescents went through, and he identified me as an awkward adolescent. He was very good at enabling me to understand myself – which to me is what education is about. The first book he gave me to read was *The Catcher in the Rye*, and it helped me to understand a sort of confused feeling of rebelliousness in myself. It may have been a slightly dangerous book to give me, because it kind of fuelled this feeling of the world on one side and you on the other.

You do have this potential at Eton to have a relationship with a master, and if the master is good, then I think that system is amazing; it doesn't really happen in any other school. As a doctor now, I think that if I was going to identify what his quality was as a master, it was that he listened and he didn't judge: for an adolescent that is a tremendous thing, because the worst thing about authority is that it judges all the time. You question the value of your opinions, because you keep getting put down: 'When you grow up you'll understand better' sort of thing, which may be true – I mean, the kind of ideas I had then were naive and adolescent, but they weren't put down by Ellwick, they were even in some ways fostered.

I was successful at sport, and I suppose that I'd been slightly indoctrinated by my father's record. I distinctly remember, when I got my field colours, the first thing I did, before even going back to have a shower or anything, was to go and ring up my parents and tell them.

In my last year, the last winter, I got into the Library, and the House Captain was David Leary, who was a very nice fellow, quiet and artistic, interested in painting, very much the antithesis to the rowdy sporting type of successful Etonian schoolboy. I was beginning to be rather ashamed of that other aspect, it was too much part of authority really, and I quite identified with this new scale of values and interests which David represented. So we formed a relationship which orientated itself – being the sixties, you know, the days of schoolboy power – around trying to change everything. With him as House Captain and me a member of the Library we had quite a lot of power, because, of the other members of the Library, although two were very antagonistic to our ideas, one was very easily led, so we had a majority. And we found ourselves in a position to change things that we didn't like, things like personal fagging, and we started on that road.

We would have house meetings where we'd get everyone to come to the Library and ask them what they didn't like about the house, and then we would tell them what we thought we were going to change. The greatest opposition to any change came from people in the middle of the house, because they would think, 'We went through this shit, having to personal fag and clean shoes and run baths, so why shouldn't we have fags doing this sort of thing for us?' Also, there was a kind of ingrained feeling that this was the right way, this was the way our fathers had it and we shouldn't change it. You cannot imagine how conservative Eton schoolboys are.

Nicholson was keen on change, too. He felt that a lot of the actual traditions were abused by a handful of privileged layabouts – doing a boy call in the middle of the day, sending people down to buy them a Mars bar whenever they felt like it. He was as revolted by that sort of behaviour as I was. I wasn't too worried about the little boy who had to go and get the Mars bar; what disgusted me was the person doing the boy call.

I wrote a letter to the *Chronicle* full of quotes from Bertrand Russell and liberal educational ideas which are anathema to Etonians. Archie got a lot of flak from that – you know, 'What's going on in your house?' sort of thing. But he defended it, although he had worries as to what was going on. But one or two masters were very interested, particularly Raef Payne, and Dick Haddon in whose flat we used to have our revolutionary groups – he nearly got sacked for that. We would have our meetings there to discuss our ideas, and Haddon would be fostering and helping intellectual and conceptual developments in the kids, while other masters thought of it as being part of this underground movement, and that all their authority would be undermined.

We tried to take it beyond the house to the school. One of the ideas was to get rid of Pop – if you wanted a school body, then it should just be representatives from each house or something like that. We tried to get all the House Captains together to sign a petition to take to the headmaster, and there was quite a lot of support. But people weren't really interested: they had to get on with their A-levels. Although we got quite a few signatures and actually took them to the headmaster, somewhere along the line it was dying a death – even before the dope.

During one of the holidays of my last year, round about 1968, I went to San Francisco to see my sister who was living just off Haight Ashbury, and in with a bad lot. She was living with a black fellow, and there were a lot of drugs around and things. It was quite an eye-opener, a taste of an alternative form of life; and as you can imagine, living in the south-east of England and going to school at Eton, this was all quite disorienting.

I first smoked dope at that time, and that definitely had an effect on my career at Eton. I met with a couple of friends in London before going back to school, we were going to a pop concert of some sort, and before we went we scored some hash. We'd heard about this thing through the older brother of one of them, and we went into Lord Kitchener's Valet, a trendy clothes shop in the King's Road, walked up to someone and asked, 'Have you got a score?' And sure enough he had – he looked the sort of type, with long hair and hippie clothes. He took us back to his pad, sold us a bit of hash, no doubt at an extortionate price, and we smoked a bit of it then and there. I can't remember what happened next, but we took it back to school, and two of us would every now and then go up and smoke it. You go from Haight-Ashbury to the King's Road very quickly.

It totally devastated my A-levels. It did what it does, it caused inertia and apathy. Then I was a bit irresponsible, I was sort of mucking around, and beginning to annoy people, and got a reputation for being someone who didn't take things seriously, and was even banned from entering the Corps, which was an almost unheard-of thing.

I blew it, actually. There was a guy who was President of Pop called Faber, for whom I had a strange kind of antagonism, although I never really knew him, and he had a particular sort of antagonism towards me. And we were having a school fair in the fives courts, selling things for some charity* and in one stall I remember there was an old copy of the Pop rules, with flowers and criss-cross canes across the cover. Nobody would buy it, so I bought it, pinned it up on a tree and set fire to it. This guy Faber walks by just as I'm doing it, and goes straight from there to the headmaster to tell him. And of course all the credibility of our movement lost its momentum and I myself lost a lot of credibility by that gesture. I think I was beginning to get a bit fed up with it all anyway.

I remember that event very clearly. I was summoned to see the headmaster that same evening, and he asked me what it was all about. Chenevix-Trench . . . his career spanned exactly the same time as mine, he came when I came and left when I left. He didn't make it either, poor guy! Whenever we would go to see him, he would say, 'Yes, but I don't have much power, the power's in the hands of the housemasters; it's up to them if they want to change things. Also we have to please the old boys, they have a lot of power . . .', etc., etc., etc.

One of the things that happened as a result of my burning the Pop rules was that I was prevented from getting into Pop. I was supposed to be made Keeper of the Field, and Faber was at that time Keeper of the Field and just leaving. I was the only remaining person who had my field colours, and in order that I shouldn't get into Pop *ex officio*, which was the rule, he then made somebody else Keeper of the Field — and this with the headmaster's approval, who had insisted that I be blackballed from getting into Pop. In a way I suppose it rather pleased me, it was a kind of martydom, but my father was very upset.

I think I had rather liked the idea of getting into Pop and then saying, 'I don't want to be a member of this organization', and tearing off my waistcoat or something dramatic like that.

I wanted to go to the LSE, because that's where everybody

*Eton Action

was tearing off their waistcoats and all that sort of thing – and of course you were supposed to go to Cambridge. I wanted to study sociology, and in those days you couldn't study sociology at Cambridge, for goodness sake, it wasn't even a subject!

I said I would take the Cambridge entrance if I could leave the school, that was the proviso, and went to live in London. And of course that was a disaster. That was when LSD came in, and if dope had stopped one studying, then LSD finished off all mental powers.

So I didn't take the Cambridge entrance. I had to end up finding a university place on my A-levels, which were pretty awful. So I can see now in retrospect that things fizzled out a bit because of the dope. I mean, I should have got better A-levels . . . all the people in my class got 'A's, and 'B's, and I got C, D, E – and I'm sure it was simply that I couldn't really study properly, because every now and then I was going off and smoking a joint and I couldn't concentrate. I'd lost the motivation, I recognize that now, you see.

I can remember the last Fourth of June. My parents came down, and although I wasn't in the Eight any more because I'd given up sports, I was still allowed to captain one of the eights because I was an ex-Eight member. And I remember leaving my family sitting by the river while we had to get changed into that funny gear, a little short coat, starched striped shirt, bright tie, white trousers and a boater; and you row down the Thames and then you stand up with your oar in the air – and people hope you fall in. I remember sneaking off and having a quiet joint in my room, just for a laugh, you know. It was disaster, because you can imagine the difficulty of trying to stand up in a boat when you're stoned, and not just that, but some joker in the crew had decided he was deliberately going to turn the boat over, and I was feeling wobbly enough as it was. This guy was rocking the boat, and my heart was pounding because I didn't know whether I'd be able to swim if I fell in. But I remember the thrill of this big traditional festivity, and doing something illegal, 'Gosh, if only they knew' kind of thing. It's odd behaviour, isn't it?

I think there were three people from my year who eventually

went on to become doctors, and that was very unusual. In fact at one of my interviews at Bart's I was asked, 'Why do you think that so few Old Etonians become doctors?', which I suppose is quite an interesting question. But I resented being called an Old Etonian, so I rather blew the answer.

Being an Old Etonian came up again when I started working in this practice. Sometimes it's mentioned as a joke, sometimes it's mentioned as a curiosity. But the most common comment that I have is, 'You don't look like an Old Etonian.' I don't know what Etonians are supposed to look like or seem like; I'm not sure what they're trying to say; I'm not sure if they know what they're trying to say.

I think if there is a typical Etonian, it's simply the stereotype of the upper-class, or upper-middle-class, privileged Englishman. So few societies would accept the concept that the English find so easy to accept of a privileged class. You know, it's still there, it's quite revolting. Effortless superiority.

I would never send my child to Eton. And yet I don't know why I say that. I mean, it's just a school . . .

THE HON. JONATHAN PORRITT

I REMEMBER the new boys' tea-party where the housemaster meets the parents as they officially hand over their wretched little child to the tender care of the school. We turned up late, for one reason or another, and while my parents were out parking the car, I was met at the housemaster's door by this wonderful Italian person who worked in the house called Michalo. And the first question that I was asked was, 'Indian or Chinese?' I didn't know what he was talking about. I wasn't quite sure whether I was meant to say, 'No, I'm English actually' – the whole occasion was a bit nerve-wracking, and it was a fairly thick Italian accent. Fortunately my mother came to my assistance and realized that I was being offered a choice of two kinds ot tea! And as the tea-party developed, there were these five boys starting that term, not knowing how to break the ice with each other, and each one looking marginally more gawky and unhappy than the next. It was a pretty grim experience, it has to be said. But funnily enough from that tea-party I still retain a very close relationship with two of those people who started in the house that year.

I was in Bob Baird's house. The man was tremendous. A great bear of a man, enormously kind and considerate, and very good with boys. He was extremely sensible about discipline – I suppose some might have called him a bit too liberal in some respects, but I think that he was very good at handling the situations that inevitably crop up. And I got to know him extremely well. I still see him now, he's quite a close friend, in fact he'll be coming along to our wedding in November.

The house we were in – and this isn't terribly long ago, it's only 1963 – was remarkably archaic. It had old lead mullion windows, and in the winter it was just unbelievably cold. You were only allowed so much coal per week, and basically you had to move from room to room according to who had the fire, and huddle around it, because it literally was that cold. That created a tremendous sense of community quite quickly. But I do remember the extraordinary degrees of cold in those days — it's impossible to imagine now.

In the middle of my second year we moved from across the road into one of the more modern houses, it was quite comfortable, but there was a slight problem during the third year when the roof burnt down. We used to have fire drills from time to time, and on one occasion everyone thought it was just another routine fire drill. After we all piled out into the garden in our dressing-gowns, the Head of the House said 'OK, that's it, you can all go back to bed now.' But by this time great gouts of flame were shooting up into the sky! And of course this was huge drama, a real fire — what had caused it? Was it someone smoking up there? Was it an electrical fault? Nobody ever really knew. The whole house was dispersed around different houses, staying with different masters, for the next six months. It was a very disruptive time, but quite interesting.

I went to stay with my classics tutor, John Faulkner, who was an extraordinary man, terribly stiff and unbending in many ways. He's what I imagine the American Puritan founding fathers would have been like. Very strict, very good, a tough teacher, I mean he really put us through it. But staying with him, one got to know his family and saw him in a much more human light, and I suddenly began to penetrate behind the self-defensive barriers that teachers tend to put up. I began to realize that there were ways of developing relationships with teachers that weren't purely based on pupil–teacher ritual relationships; there were degrees of warmth that you could achieve, and I think that from then on I established very close friendships with a lot of teachers.

I suppose that I was an averagely disrespectful boy. I've never held particular respect for authority *per se*, I respect people for what they do and what they are rather than for the fact they have a position. This did not go down terribly well, it must be said, and I did run into trouble fairly often, and was beaten on three occasions, once by the housemaster and twice by the House Captain. And those occasions stick in my mind, I can't deny that. Especially the occasion when I was actually beaten for no less an offence than 'my attitude to life' – which taught me a great deal about power relationships in a microcosm of that sort. I suppose they were right that I had been fairly cheeky and, not exactly disobedient, but I managed to stake a claim to do things my way. So I was seen to be a sort of subversive influence on my colleagues, and the House Captain of that time, who was not a particularly pleasant person, indeed he was rather a malicious character in my opinion, I suppose had just had enough of this after a while. And inasmuch as I hadn't flouted any particular law, the idea was that I'd accumulated sufficient small omissions or sins to warrant a beating just for my attitude to life.

It certainly hurt, there's no doubt about that. It was a genuine old-fashioned beating, and drew blood and everything else. But it hardened me in a certain way, it made me think much more consciously about how to cope with authority and how one shouldn't ever push things so that you end up in that kind of position of vulnerability.

Well, I just have to own up to being an unbelievably lucky person in that I was good at work and enjoyed it enormously. I mean, there was no sense of drudgery having to truck off to lessons or anything. In those days we had Early School, this great ritual of getting up at quarter to seven, hot tea and biscuits, and then shuffling off to early morning school before breakfast. People half awake at their desks, teachers half awake as well! Basically I loved the work, I found it challenging. I found it a great liberation after the prep school I'd been at, I liked the new horizons opening up in the kinds of work we were doing, and I was quite quickly put into the top classes.

I also was lucky enough to be good at games, and at Eton that counted for a lot. Looking back on it, I spent a formidable amount of time playing games of one kind or another, year in, year out. Every single day I would take part in at least one kind of sporting activity, the field game or football, cricket or tennis or athletics, I did boxing and judo and basketball and fives, I mean it just went on and on and on. I basically loved the whole business of playing games. There wasn't anything that I didn't want to take part in, apart from cross-country running which I've always seen to be a particularly stupid way of spending time.

Eton was just so easy; there wasn't anything that was particularly difficult about it, I greatly enjoyed the contacts I had with people there – very close relationships and a very warm atmosphere in the house in general. I enjoyed the games, I enjoyed the work, and I suppose bit by bit things began to go very well, and I got into all the sporting teams at a ridiculously young age, I was playing for the house football team when I was in my third year or something like that. And that helped build a series of relationships with people who were older than me, and gave me an insight into the things that were to come, and put me kind of mentally one step ahead of the stage I was actually at. I got into Debate very early and into the Library very early, and became a House Captain four terms before I left and got into Pop at the same time. By that time I was in all the school teams and was Keeper of Athletics and Deputy Keeper of the Field, and well, you know, it's boring, I'm not holding all those things up as wonderful, tremendous accomplishments. Actually, it didn't make much of an impact on me because I was being rewarded for something that I just loved doing.

But the whole sense of getting so much out of it came through to me. In my last two years there was a determination to use the school as fully as possible, because by that age I'd begun to realize that there were a range of opportunities and privileges there that I wasn't likely to get access to again, and which I wanted to make the most of.

I began to develop an interest in the arts and French literature towards the end of my time there, and I was lucky enough to have two extremely good teachers, I mean really powerful, inspiring teachers. One of them was a French professor who was over on a sabbatical year at Eton, and he was an extraordinary, charismatic man, terribly Gallic, and rather predictably emotional, I suppose. He filled me with a love of Baudelaire and other French poets, which at the impressionable age of seventeen is an interesting experience. And my tutor gave me a wonderful grounding in the arts; he encouraged us to read a lot of books outside our specific A-level courses, took us to the theatre, to concerts, on trips, and opened horizons in the general field of the arts in a way that I don't think is achieved elsewhere.

My relationship with my housemaster was a very warm relationship, I think from the age of sixteen onwards. He came to trust me in the way that I trusted him, and we got to know each other very well. The whole relationship was made more intimate because my younger brother was also in the house and, as is often the way with these things, if there is a relatively successful older brother, then the younger brother has a hell of a time of it. I was extremely sorry for my younger brother, and felt that he really shouldn't have been put in the same house. Anyway, predictably he began to go from bad to worse and was a real tearaway, and came very close to expulsion on several occasions. This drove poor old Bob Baird to despair, because he didn't know how to handle my brother really. When I was House Captain my brother was going through a particularly difficult patch. It put me in a difficult position because I clearly couldn't exercise authority in the same way with him as I might with others. And there were several tricky moments. I'll never forget one time when I was up late and just happened to hear an odd noise in one of the rooms on the ground floor, which were normally locked. I opened the door, and there was my brother kind of poised on the window-sill with a brown paper bag, which, when he saw me, he inadvertently knocked over; it fell on to the ground with a great crash, and Dubonnet spread all over the floor in a great lake, and actually lapped up against my shoes. Situations like that were hard to handle.

A lot was happening in the outside world, and I would have known very little about it. I mean, I look back with horror at the extent to which I was a kind of cloistered innocent in those days. My eyes hardly lifted from the horizons of one exam target, or one cup match, or whatever else it might be. I was very, very narrow-minded in that respect. I was opening up in terms of literature and the arts and a love of all those things, but as regards my interest in the broad world, I was untouched. I was untouched by the whole of that dramatic pop culture of the sixties, it just made no impression on me whatsoever – until my last year at school when we had a rather special change in circumstances in that an American was suddenly imported into the system, and he happened to end up in our house. He was a guy called Ned Cook, a wonderful Southerner from Tennessee, and he just changed everything. He came with all these terribly hip ideas, and he played a guitar, and was a bit of a bad lad – he knew a lot about drinking and all the rest of it – and he was a great revelation really. We by comparison must have seemed like real hillbilly innocents, but he was wise, much more world-exposed than we were, and he certainly made me more aware of what was happening culturally than anything or anyone else, and I had a very close friendship with him indeed.

As far as I was concerned all the terrible stories about homosexuality and so on never really crossed my horizon. Yes, there were sort of crushes, I suppose, between boys of different ages, and there were quite close friendships, and certainly there were incidents of homosexuality that were rumoured to be taking place. It never was part of what I experienced at Eton, I'm happy to say in retrospect. But it wasn't whether it was boys or whether it was girls, it was just the whole notion of sex that didn't actually feature terribly large at that age. There were one or two extremely embarrassing dances where we'd go off with Wycombe Abbey, and a few slightly sordid parties in the holidays when girls suddenly seemed to appear out of nowhere. But it was a sort of irrelevance, frankly, at that age. And I felt almost no frustration about how life was going in those days at all. Nothing seemed to be missing from what was happening.

I've never had any doubts at all that, as far as I was concerned, the five years that I spent at Eton were just completely happy educational experiences. There's not a shadow of a doubt in my mind. I recognize the unbelievable privilege of having been there. I was one of those people who was able to seize hold of every bit of it and make the most of it, and I don't really have a word of criticism to say about those days at all, which is boring, but there we are.

But since that time, obviously I have changed a great deal. It started at Oxford when I began to do this kind of eye-opening which I should have been doing years before, and I began to become much more aware about the world, and much more aware about politics and what was happening. My life moved very rapidly away from a sort of public-school-based set of relationships. I actually started to resent the rather cloying atmosphere of old public schoolies hanging together, and apart from one close friend that I had in the house, really all my relationships with people who'd been at Eton were very quickly ended. Not sort of ended dramatically, but they simply dribbled away. Gradually I began to form a whole set of political and philosophical ideas that left the whole issue of public schools somewhere in the distance, I mean I wasn't attached to any of those ideas that seem to go with being a public school boy. And I suppose that there's been a progressive moving away from that, because when I left Oxford I went into teaching and taught for ten years in a Comprehensive. In fact, just after I'd left Oxford, the headmaster of Eton heard that I was thinking of becoming a teacher and wrote and asked if I would be interested in having a job at Eton. There wasn't any question of an interview or anything; I was just offered a job. But I had to write back to say, no, I wasn't particularly interested. Anyway by that stage I was committed to working in the state system, as that was where politically I felt I ought to be working. And since that time I have worked in the state sector and have loved it.

My job as Director of the Friends of the Earth, and a leading member of the Green Movement, the environment movement in this country, means that most of my colleagues are radicals of one kind or another, and there aren't that many Old Etonians in those kinds of circles. So to a certain extent there's something of a paradox about my privileged education in the kind of jobs that I've done since then. But I don't feel any sense of guilt about it – I mean, there is this terrible syndrome of ex-public school guilt, 'Oh, God, I went to Eton. How awful!' I don't feel any of that.

If people ask me about Eton, I'll tell them how much I enjoyed it and that it was something in my life which I now need to use for other people. I don't like it when people use it to make a clever point, as if to demonstrate, 'Well, he may be Director of Friends of the Earth, but actually he's okay because he went to Eton and Oxford.'

The impact of Eton is quite extraordinary. It's utterly out of proportion to the ability of Eton to educate people better than any other school. And it goes on and on. I do find it most odd. And it's not only in this country; when you go abroad, it's extraordinary how it carries with it this aura of 'Wow, Eton' still. Still! In this meritocratic age, you would have thought that something of that gloss had worn off, but it hasn't.

I am aware of the extent to which my contemporaries are all rooted deep in the Establishment today, and I suppose I have become depressed on occasions by the ways in which people just get locked into this desperate predictability of a career in the City, and mortgages and children and a house in the country; everything that fills me with gloom, frankly. I made a choice early in my life that I did not want to pursue that kind of career, but I wanted to do the kind of work that I felt would fulfil me in a more demanding way, where I could use my skills and talents to serve other people. I don't want to exaggerate that, it's not an overdeveloped social conscience, I just happen to get more out of life if I'm doing that sort of work. Obviously I am very aware of a huge divide between where I am and where my Eton con-temporaries are. I mean the kind of salaries I'm earning now are ridiculous compared with theirs!

By and large, my memories of Eton are just a nice hazy miasma of having had a good time, although I still do have amazingly sharp moments in my memory. I can recall specific occasions in enormous detail, which is odd, because I don't actually have a particularly good memory. I was amazingly impressed by this wintry quality of my first years in the old house. I mean, I loved it because I'm a winter person, I like the cold and I like being out on winter days. But summers at Eton are phenomenally beautiful, with those huge playing fields: it is archetypally romantic. And it does seep into you, however much of a hard-bitten cynic you may be. Something of that sense of England permeates the being of a person at Eton, even if they don't want it to.

There was a strange man called Father Peter who came over from Italy, and I don't know why, but he wanders into my dreams from time to time, even now. I can remember him very well, clearly, as a picture. He wore this brown robe, and a white knotted rope to tie it up with, and sandals. He was a monk, a kind of peripatetic spiritual adviser. He used to go around to different houses talking to the boys. And he was a wonderful man. He was a truly inspired person, he wasn't a heavy, evangelical, you've-got-to-be-a-good-Christian type of person, he just was very good at talking to people, providing them with a sense that there's a spiritual depth to life rather than the superficial stuff that we were mostly into. He had quite an influence on me. I got to know him very well, and it was just when I was getting confirmed, so it was a fairly interesting time in terms of my own spiritual development.

I haven't turned out in the conventional Eton mould. And some might say that it's a pretty funny thing to do with an Eton-type education, to end up in the kind of things that I'm doing. But it's never really seemed to me like that. Eton gave me formidable skills that I've been able to use. I mean, part of my ability to be a teacher was because of the confidence that being at Eton gave. I do an awful lot of public speaking, and that sense of feeling absolutely at ease when I stand up on my two legs and spout, and the ease with which one can meet new people, I am so grateful for that.

I would not send my children to a public school. This is complicated – having had such a wonderful time myself, it seems pretty odd, if not inhuman, to actually deprive any children we might have of the same possibility. And yet I have become convinced, firstly, that it's possible to be equally happy in other schools, and also, that the public school system as we have it at the moment is genuinely causing social divides. I'm not in the school of opinion which would close down public schools, but I do think there isn't any need to encourage public schools through the kind of tax advantage that they have. I personally think that it should remain a personal choice. I am committed to the state education system and dedicated to making that system work, and I think that parents with those feelings really do have an obligation to make those schools work by participating in them. I'm a Green, I'm an ecologist, and because I'm a Green, I believe passionately in finding ways of healing divides in society, building better relationships. And part of that passion and commitment to a more healing society is the knowledge that you cannot bring that about if you go on segregating people between public school and state school in the way we do at the moment.

JONATHAN RILEY-SMITH

—

I REMEMBER my first evening, I thought it fantastically beautiful. For some reason which I didn't understand, except now I imagine it was simply that a boy had stayed on to do the Oxford and Cambridge entrance exam who otherwise might have left, I couldn't move into the house which I was down for, and I was put in another house for one half. That house doesn't exist any longer; it's all been rebuilt. But it stood on the other side of the cemetery from College Chapel, and I remember looking out of my window, and I can see it today – it was September, a lovely sunny evening, and the sun was falling on the walls of the Chapel, there were pigeons flying around between the buttresses, and I just thought how beautiful it was. So that's my first memory of Eton, as being very beautiful.

I was perhaps one of the last generation of people who assumed I was going to Eton and then that I would go to Cambridge, and did. I never thought at all, up to graduating, about what my career was going to be, I just made an assumption that I would go the same way as my father and grandfather. And the difference had already occurred with my brother, who is three years younger than me, and who didn't go to Cambridge.

The house I was down for and I went into after this and for the rest of my time was Oliver Van Oss's. He was a man of great presence, a big fat man, and of great culture. I must say I was not very happy at Eton, I have all sorts of criticisms of it, and I never felt I got on very well with him; but when I left Eton, my father presented me with all my reports, and Van Oss was extraordinarily acute in his judgements of me, and, it turned out, a good deal more sympathetic in the letters he was writing to my parents than I thought he was at the time.

I was not popular, and in those days popularity mattered very much. I think small boys want to be accepted and to be popular. I was very unathletic, I was extremely fat and unfit, and just one of those people who were not very well coordinated. But I wouldn't want to explain this unpopularity simply in terms of not being very good at games: that would be far too crude a picture.

Even then, unconventional people were tolerated at Eton in a way I think it is true to say they weren't elsewhere; nevertheless there were certain conventions, and if you didn't quite fit into them in one way or another, or rebelled against them, this didn't help. Most of the great heroes at school were good at games. When I was a little boy there was a chap who was a very good cricketer, called Ingleby-Mackenzie, and when I was a small boy at Eton he was a great school hero although I was far too small and insignificant to have dealings with him.

But I have never been able to explain to myself the fact that I wasn't very popular. It was more a passive than active unpopularity, it was more that I was ignored and cut out. But there was a streak of anti-semitism at Eton in those days. Now I am not Jewish, but I looked Jewish, and I and another boy in the house, Monassas, who was Jewish, were teased for being Jews and we were called Monassas United. So I can understand in a small way what Jewish people go through.

The funny thing was that when I left Eton and went to Cambridge, I found myself quite popular, and I found myself quite popular with those very people with whom I had not been popular at Eton. The only explanation I can give, which is perhaps not a very good one, is that my kind of personality was one that did not appeal to small boys, but appealed more to people when they were a bit more mature. But I wasn't very popular, and I think that I was rather bloody-minded, and I was certainly very unhappy.

Van Oss was himself cultural. There is a sort of cultural, civilized element which runs throughout Eton history, and Van Oss was definitely part of that. And that was the part of Eton that attracted me, though I would have said on the whole it was rather philistine. I mean, there were boys around the school who were cultured, but I cannot think of a single member of my house at the time whom I would have put into that category.

Robert Birley, who was headmaster then and taught me history in my final year was a genius as a teacher. He always looked tremendously ill, he was gaunt and pale, and when he took us for Early School at seven-thirty in the morning, he looked as if he had hardly slept. He was enormously kind and tolerant of what must have been very often rather silly and pretentious statements by small boys of seventeen or eighteen years old. I remember he asked me to breakfast, and I was jabbering on and saying some damned silly things, but all I remember is the encouragement, Birley listening, encouraging. He had a way of teaching which was rather undemonstrative; there wasn't any fire or anything like that, but in a very gentle way he was always picking out the interesting things intellectually. I think he was a tremendous teacher.

Birley set me an essay on a Byzantine emperor, Leo the Third, who was an iconoclast, a heretic, and I date my interest in East Mediterranean history from that. It excited me enormously. I am an historian now, a medieval historian, and work on East Mediterranean crusades history, and my interest in all that dates from Eton. And there was another history master, Giles St Aubyn, who taught very well, and encouraged me a great deal. I remember that with gratitude. In fact Giles St Aubyn founded a film unit, and I directed the first what you might call feature-length film – it was about twenty-five minutes. He paid for all the equipment out of his own pocket.

There is a category of people who have been going to the school for several generations, and may therefore be said to be from established families, and there are people who are first or second generation, and may be said to be upwardly mobile. It has always interested me, how far the ethos in the school is affected by those who represent families with several generations at Eton. Now these people in general were people whose ambition was limited for the rest of their lives, to sitting on the family farm, going racing, shooting in the winter: they were so comfortable, they didn't need to be ambitious. There is no doubt that there were masters who were quite openly snobbish and favoured aristocratic or upper-class boys, and I think that particular ethos affected Eton then.

I think I would have wanted a community which was less snobbish, less materialistic, more concerned with intellectual excellence. But the point is, Eton in the fifties reflected society in the fifties, and the expectations of that particular stratum in society were very limited and low. What was wrong with Eton was probably what was wrong with the English upper classes, which was the pursuit of the wrong goals and irresponsibility, by which I mean that people enjoyed wealth but felt none of the responsibilities which traditionally have been supposed to go with wealth.

I am the eldest of seven children of whom six are boys, and all the boys except one went to Eton, and now my son is in his final year, and I have nephews there and cousins, and for that reason I have been in touch with Eton more or less continuously since I left. It is very remarkable how the atmosphere of the place has changed, how much softer a place it is now – I mean that in a good sense, it is much more relaxed, much less severe. I went back to Eton to have dinner with the history masters and I asked them then why it had changed. They said it was the introduction of A-levels. When I was at Eton no one did an A-level, and the boys therefore had to be beaten into working, there was literally nothing to work for – they all expected to just go on to Oxford or Cambridge or whatever. I was told that A-levels had created a kind of sword of Damocles over every boy: they all knew that they couldn't live lives of idleness and jolly well had to get on with things.

And McCrum did wonders for the place. One of the criticisms I always used to make was that if you actually tap into that cultural tradition at Eton, it's like wallowing in a warm bath, it's spineless. It's tremendously humane and civilized, but it's got a spine of rubber, and if you compared it with a great school like, say, Haberdashers, there's a kind of toughness and a steel there which I always thought was not at Eton. And certainly, speaking as a Cambridge don, a feature of Eton always seemed to me that it was very good at getting boys into Oxford or Cambridge, and getting them scholarships, but not so many of those boys got Firsts. McCrum added a bit of steel to the place, a bit of intellectual muscle. There's a sharpness about it now which there used not to be. So I think he did a marvellous job.

Since Eton, I have converted to Rome, I became a Catholic. And as my wife is a born Catholic, of course it was an issue whether we should send a Catholic child to Eton, an issue over which we agonized. We had him down for Ampleforth and we looked very closely at Worth. In the end, my wife was still extremely unhappy with it, but we opted for Eton. There are a lot of Catholics at Eton, one hundred and sixty now, that's well over ten per cent of the school, and it was negotiations with Eton over the Catholics that made me realize what an extraordinarily open and responsive place Eton is now. Because actually the condition of Catholics in the last two or three years has very greatly improved: they have even got their own chaplain, and it was only a few years ago that a local parish priest had to come to say Mass for them.

It was quite remarkable the way Eton was prepared to respond. The whole issue of getting a full-time Catholic chaplain – the problem was never the school, the problem was the Catholic community. There was a fear in the Catholic community that if a school like Eton had a full-time Catholic chaplain, then the great battle for Catholic education, and the demands that Catholics send their children to Catholic schools, would be undermined. And I must say the way Eton behaved through all this was, I thought, absolutely admirable.

My attitude to Eton has been transformed, not so much because Toby is there, but because I have been connected with some developments at Eton, I have seen how responsive the school is now to needs and changes in society, and in fact I think Eton has done my son proud, and I'm glad he went there now.

BENEDICT TAYLOR

━━━━━

I was at a school called Feltham Comprehensive, and they had an arrangement for six boys from Feltham to go to Eton for about ten days, and six boys from Eton to come to Feltham. The idea was to see how the other half live. Feltham is an extremely rough school out by Heathrow airport, and most of the kids from there – I'm sure they wouldn't thank me for saying this – went on to either local jobs at the airport, engineering or mechanics, or they went into open prison at Ashford. There was a very high crime rate. Feltham Comprehensive was one of the first big Comprehensives, it was massive. It was very modern, built in the sixties, a classic Grange Hill type of building. It was a real stereotype school, very large number of people, five hundred people or something in each year. None of us there had any idea what a public school was like, and vice versa. A very good experiment is what it was.

There were some dangerous aspects to life at Feltham. Unless you paid your dinner-money as protection when you were in the first year, you used to get hung out of the top window by your ankles, small things like that. There was a fight at least every lunchtime and every afternoon, and the peer pressure you were put under was not books to have read and films to have enjoyed, it was how much beer you could drink, and how many girls you could snog behind the bike sheds, and that sort of thing. It was a completely different culture and system.

I didn't enjoy being at Feltham, I thought it was very stifling. It was the lowest common denominator. For instance, with five hundred people in my year, nobody passed English Literature or a language O-level. The standard was very low. You'd think you were doing all right because you'd look around you and take stock, but there was nothing to ever push you. And it was a very ugly environment as well, which I didn't like.

I had quite a lot of potential at school, but I was incredibly lazy and I found that by bullshitting I could get out of doing almost any work. At that time I always wanted to try and see what else was around in life. I was trying on personalities as fast as I could, and I would put on a personality like an overcoat for a few weeks, see how it fitted, use what was useful for me and discard what wasn't. And one of the big fantasies of my life, which came from reading endless P. G. Wodehouse, was a side of life which you never had a chance to indulge in at a school like Feltham.

We weren't chosen by the school, in fact only six people from our school volunteered; everyone else thought it was a ridiculous idea, 'going to visit a load of poofs in a snobby school'. The boy from Feltham who came into the house with me was a guy called Joe Panou. I remember laughing at him in the uniform. I remember us sitting there and saying, 'God, this is a laugh . . .', but I remember we were both quite keen to make a go of it, to not embarrass ourselves – we didn't want to be treated as the oiks from Feltham. We wanted to be treated as equals, and I think most of the Etonians were at pains to give us a lot of time and space. They were very hospitable, they weren't judging us out of hand, they were letting it ride to see what we had to offer.

But they probably thought we would be as rough as they come, they expected us to be in Dr Martins and Ben Sherman shirts, and they said we were allowed to wear our own clothes if we wanted to, but they did lay on uniforms if we felt like it – you know, 'if it wouldn't be too much trouble for you to wear them'. I think both factions thought of the stereotype and took it to its extreme, and were then rather pleasantly surprised with what they found. They treated us with kid gloves because they thought we could be a potentially very violent influence inside the school, and they even said, 'If you want to smoke cigarettes, you can', although we would have been shot or garrotted for smoking in our school. But we were given that leeway if we wanted it. There was a slight holiday atmosphere about our visit.

If it was the trappings that had attracted me to Eton, wearing the uniform and strutting about and indulging that Brideshead side of one's character, the moment that you got there it was no longer a fantasy, and with that stripped away I could then appreciate it for what it was. It was a good place to learn, and I met some extremely interesting people there who have remained friends to this day. It was a fantastic learning experience in what there is in life.

It was the first time I'd had a conversation that I wanted to have, a conversation that I found stimulating, with a group of people my own age. I had two or three good friends at Feltham whose opinions I respected and enjoyed, but whenever you were in a group of people, it was bikes and birds, and fights and smoking cigarettes, and proving macho things to each other, and this was the first time I'd been somewhere where I had the opportunity to sit down and talk. I can't remember exactly what the conversations were about, but it was about, you know, life and philosophy.

I thought that the uniform made a hell of a lot of difference. Wearing a stiff collar, you'd suddenly be walking with your head right in the air, because you had no choice. And you would be strutting around and feel a million miles taller than everybody else in the street. You'd walk over the bridge to Windsor and the tourists would all be gawping at you. It is an environment in which you feel special, unusual, and dealing with being unusual or the centre of attention gives you confidence. I've been lucky in my life in that being the eldest child in a family gives you that sort of feeling on a smaller scale, and if you spend a proportion of your life as the centre of attention, you react to situations differently later on. You become used to it, and I find a lot of people from a public school environment have a deep-rooted confidence, a way of holding themselves that gives other people the impression of supreme confidence, and it opens a lot of doors. And that atmosphere I noted. You got the feeling that you were groomed for something in that environment.

So it was a place in which the individual could flourish. Although with that goes hand-in-hand the constrictions of that class which most of the people who go to the school came from. One of the great advantages that someone coming from my background has is that you go home in the evening, and you have massive arguments with your family, and you fight, and kick, and scream, and you are given the opportunity to develop emotionally. You only need a couple of tantrums to realize whether it is going to work or not. In an environment like Eton you are treated as a grown-up from the day that you arrive, you are expected to behave in a certain way, and violent displays of emotion are rather frowned upon. Whereas I came from a large family built on love and battles, and I have an incredibly close relationship with my family and I thank God for the security that's given me, and the pleasure we give each other because of the closeness that we have now. But a lot of people from the Eton environment have found it very difficult to get close to their families because in those formative years they weren't smashing down the barriers that are naturally there between parents and children, unless you do a bit of work to break them down.

It was an academic environment, and that was something I had never experienced before, and it was one that worked. At Feltham we couldn't wait to get out of school, because what was most important was getting on to our bicycles and pedalling off and getting into mischief. Whereas in the Eton environment you had to do an enormous amount of prep. We had hardly any homework to do at Feltham, and what we did have we never bothered to do anyway. And Eton, with the study, and books to read . . . it just seemed conducive to learning. It was so attractive as well, you could go for a nice walk and clear your head, whereas at Feltham the aeroplanes were flying overhead, you were on a dual carriageway, and it was an unpleasant atmosphere that you wanted to get away from.

I thought how lucky they all are, it is such an attractive place.

At the end of my time, I thought, 'This is the educational environment in which I'm likely to flourish the most, and I want to continue to go to this school.' Well, my parents certainly couldn't afford it, so I spoke to a friend of our family who offered to lend me two thousand pounds, so long as I paid him back when I'd finished school and started working. But they didn't have any places in the house. Maybe I'd have been just as much of a bum as I turned out to be. I never really worked for the exams when they came up at Feltham, I then went on to a sixth-form college to re-take them and got most of them, but only at O-level, and then thought, 'Fuck it, I'll go off and see what else is around.'

We were teased before we went, but we weren't teased when we got back, because the boys who had come from Eton had got in with the roughest crowd in the school, the nucleus of two or three real hard-nut, gang-leader bully boys, and when I got back, some of the toughest nuts in the school were saying, 'Oh, they were all right, you know, they were terrific, that Eddie Farquharson, smashing bloke he was.' And the ones who excelled at sport made a bit of a mark for themselves as well, because we were quite a sporty school – we had a good gymnastics team, and a good rugby team. People make preconceptions and they can live by them for their whole lives, not given the opportunity.

DAVID THOMAS

————

I VIVIDLY remember my first morning, having woken up for the first time at Eton. Half seven, I suppose. There was a knock on the door, and the boys' maid poked her head around the door and said, 'Good morning, Mr Thomas, it's time to get up.' And I was appalled that I should be called 'Mr Thomas', I mean that a woman of – she seemed immensely old to me then, I suppose she was fifty-five or something – the idea that she should be calling me 'Mr Thomas' struck my good little liberal soul as being incredibly offensive. But the point of it is that no matter how low you may be at Eton, and at thirteen you are dirt on the floor, you are still 'Mr Thomas': in other words, as far as the outside world is concerned, you are still an Etonian.

The other new boys were very socially assured, but thick as two short planks. The only other guy who was intelligent in my year was a boy who was tremendously looked down upon because he smelt, and he wasn't kind of pukka. And there was this guy called Andy Johnson who had gone to Summerfields, which is a very smart Oxford prep school, and whose father and brother had both been to Eton, and he was frightfully well up on all the kind of minutiae of Etonian life, and the words you could use, and the things you could do, and what Pop was, and which people you cap and which people you don't, and all that sort of stuff. Andy achieved the kind of ultimate Twit of the Year status by the time he was twenty, because he had an Old Etonian, a Guards and an MCC tie.

I got there in the early seventies. I was there on the kind of cusp from sixties to late seventies attitudes, by which I mean it was quite clear that one was part of a reaction against *laissez-faire* liberalism. And that showed itself in the sense that we worked bloody hard at school – and you were expected to work. You were worked very hard. The notion is of Etonians as these sort of frightfully laid-back fellows: and they'll tell you, 'We don't really work here.' But at every level of the school they work incredibly hard. For example, the rowing eight is doing computer-guided weight training from the first day of the autumn term, even if they're not going to get on the water for months. And you get ten tests within your first year or two there, and so you're being guided towards the best that you can possibly achieve from a very early age. I mean I was told when I was thirteen years old that I was going to get three A's in my A-levels and you just said, 'Oh, right, OK', and you trotted along and went down the production line, and bang, bang, bang – you got them.

A little nephew of mine goes to a state school where they don't tell you where you are in the class because it's considered bad to be competitive. That is as far removed from the Etonian ethos as you could get. From your first term, when you're a lower boy, you go into the school hall and they read out the results to you, and if you're an academic boy you will be competing very closely and very fiercely with your friends, first for the distinctions and then for the honours which that provides, like Sixth Form Select, which is the kind of First Eleven for being a swot.

My first term I had been put into a Greek division of an awful man called Dippy Simpson, and I was the only person in the division who was a new boy, so I hadn't done what they had done the previous term. And he chose to ignore this fact and treated me like a complete idiot. It was one reason why I didn't get a distinction my first term, and the only time I didn't. I remember dreading Greek lessons more than anything I ever dreaded in my life. The following term, I was up to the head man for Greek and I thought, 'Bloody hell, out of the frying pan into the fire.' I was terrified. But he was incredibly nice to me all term long, for which I've always had a soft spot for him ever since, and he took great efforts to make me catch up. That was McCrum.

There was no intellectual repression. I mean, you get this split thing: Etonians are incredibly articulate, incredibly self-confident about their right to be anywhere; I've applied for jobs which I really have no right applying for, and it wasn't because I was a particularly cocky little bastard, it was just because it never ever occurred to me that I shouldn't apply for them – your horizons have never been limited. That's a very great plus point for the school. The interesting thing is that at the same time that boys have been given this sense that they can go out into the world and achieve anything they like, they are told they have to work for it – that's part of the ethic: you are taught to work.

But at the same time you have all this, so you also have a battening-down of any emotional response. Most Etonians I don't think would necessarily think about that, because of course it's in the nature of such a repression that you don't think about it. The biggest single criticism I have of the school is that I think it can be tremendously emotionally stultifying.

You have to maintain a very cool façade there. You're aware from a very early age who the cool guys are, and of course the cool guys are really cool. It's not like they're just cool in Basingstoke, they're kind of nationally cool. You know that they're going to all the smartest parties in the whole country, and the prettiest girls from the smartest families are liable to be dating them. Now faced with this and faced with the other thing, which is that you can't be seen to be too emotionally involved with any of your friends for the obvious reason that you don't want to appear to be homosexual, there's a very strong pressure to maintain a façade at all costs: whatever you're feeling inside, for fuck's sake don't give it away. I mean this is true of men in general, but it's particularly true of public school. And as Eton is the ultimate public school, so it is ultimately true at Eton.

And so one kind of lost one's emotions. I can think of friends who are incredibly competent and successful, but if you look closely they all seem to have a problem expressing themselves emotionally. I was terribly neurotic, far too articulate for my social capacity to deal with it. I was like a sort of Woody Allen character, one of those Jewish American heroes you read about who is kind of intellectually tremendously advanced but socially tremendously gauche.

My last two years I went out with housemasters' daughters and got a lot of stick for that, a tremendous amount of stick. It was a very deliberate, conscious thing on my part, to try and rediscover whatever it was that one felt one had lost, and if I didn't have a letter from a girl in my pigeon-hole every morning I was really *angst*-ridden and unhappy.

I was gauche and spotty, and I think the only thing that saved me was girls. I really liked them – they seemed like a lot nicer people than the people in my house. And the thing about teenage girls is that if you like them, they're quite prepared to like you too. So I substituted girlfriends for close male friends – I mean, I did have two or three very close friends, who were the other intellectual kids really. But when I wasn't in class, because I didn't really like the people that were in my house I used to go and snog the housemasters' daughters. I'm not saying that as a kind of 'What a stud!' because it wasn't at all like that; it was much more innocent than that.

Also, my relationship with my parents was friendly, but it was not emotional because I'd got used to being apart from them, from about the age of eight or nine, for long, long periods. I think you find that a lot of kids who go away to prep school and public school get used to not being with their parents. Parents are just like nice people whom you see in the holidays, and you don't develop the kind of emotional attachment you'd develop if you were living with them and were kind of bound up with them.

Rock and roll: it really saved my life, and kids at Eton were – and I'm sure still are – very hip, really hip. I mean, we were all real Bowie kids; it was just when he first started. By the time I left, the first punk had hit Eton. There is still that connection between Bohemia and the upper classes, and Eton is a very fashion-conscious place, very aware of all that. And it's quite a camp place, there's a lot of performance going on, and Bowie, with all that kind of make-up and stuff, quite appealed to Etonians, it appealed to their flamboyance and their whole idea of hiding yourself – and all that sort of gender-bending. I mean he was such a hero at school, him and the Stones. The Stones are real public school rockers, aren't they? All public school boys adore the Stones.

I was in Ray's house. He seemed very eccentric and odd to us. It was not a cool house to be in, it wasn't a socially smart house. He had a hard time establishing contact with people, I think. He was intellectual, very pro music, eccentric, and had the most beautiful wife and daughter in the entire world, a fact which used to baffle us all – how could he possibly have got them? Sophie Ray was the great fantasy figure of my adolescent life! I mean, Mrs Ray! – well, that's where Sophie gets her looks. Veronica Ray is beautiful; she had a stroke, which was very sad, in my second or third year there, and was very ill for about a year, then slowly got back together again. Beautiful bones, very translucent pale skin. I felt very sorry for Sophie because she was in an impossible position. I mean, she was quite stunningly beautiful, she really was spectacularly pretty. People used to come down to breakfast really early just so they could see her go in to collect her packed lunch for school. We were all desperately in love with her, and really she was our only contact with female life, I suppose. She and her mother. One just saw Sophie flitting around the place, and pined. But girls had a very hard time at Eton because there were very few of them, and everyone mocked girls who were not fantastically attractive, and if girls were fantastically attractive everybody thought they were slags and tarts and invented terrible stories about what they were up to, which was why Sophie couldn't go to school there.

Young boys at Eton who were physically attractive were almost like pseudo-girls. In fact I often think that those kind of boys must have a very good understanding of what life for a girl is like, in the sense that they were remarked upon visually and physically and what have you. And you could go a long way by being pretty, because you would probably get to fag for smarter people. This was in the last days of fagging. All the boys deeply resented it when fagging was banned, which was McCrum's parting gesture, one quite out of keeping with the times into which he was moving, of course; I mean, had it stayed two years it would have stayed for ever, because in Thatcherite Britain, fagging's perfect. So you had all these pretty boys and they would be sent round from one Library to another for comparative purposes on the most spurious pretexts. And when they installed a house telephone system it got really decadent, because people in the Library would ring up, 'Hi Mark, how are you . . .? I'm just sending around Miss Simpkins with a note – fucking pretty, do take a look.'

A lot of it was the manifestation of either displaced hetero-sexuality or camp, or just a joke of a rather decadent sort. There were always rumours about who was supposed to be going to bed with whom. But the real homosexuals, the people who were actually gay, didn't join in those kind of games, because it was much harder for them to do so. There was one gay person in my house, and I can think of another couple of gay people in my year who have since come out, and they were much more intro-verted. The people who were most flamboyantly homosexual almost certainly were not. I suppose there was a degree to which it was a bit like at girls' schools, where you have 'pashes'. I don't know how much active homosexuality went on, one had heard rumours – I mean, I can tell you that none went on in my life.

A lot of my ambition was formed at Eton. There was the school attitude that you will succeed, but there was my own personal drive and needs above and beyond. You see, there were people who I knew would just do it automatically. They were so self-assured and came from such smart families and had probably got private incomes already, and you felt tremendously neurotic and chippy about them. People underestimate how chippy an Etonian can be. Compared with the rest of the world, how can you conceivably be chippy when you've had that sort of privilege? But one's tremendously aware of that, because you're so close to people who have so much. If I have a drive at all – it's calming down these days – that's where it comes from; it comes from wanting all the things which those people seemed to have auto-matically.

There is this incredible sort of swagger amongst senior

Etonians, all the Pop guys dressed up like peacocks and all the rowers with their colours. And you go to Tap or Rowland's or somewhere, and it's all 'Hi Johnny', 'Hi Bill', kind of hail-fellow-well-met. You're looking at guys of seventeen and eighteen who are just learning what it's about, but they feel tremendously kind of cocky. They can do whatever the fuck they want in that school by the time they've got to that stage, I mean, their last year there is pretty fine, there is no question about that. You feel pretty bloody good, because they really give you the goodies. You will never, ever in your whole life, be in a position of such unchallenged superiority and control as you are if you're a boy in Pop. You're dressed better than everyone else, you've got these flash waistcoats and spongebags, and you walk around the streets and it's like, well, *'He's better'* – you know, that guy there, he's a lot better than the rest of us. I mean I had stick-ups, thank God, because I was in Sixth Form Select, and that sort of saved my life – at least I had stick-ups. But if you could imagine what it would be like to walk down the street every day of your life, and there's some little badge you've got for being a better human being than anybody else – that's what being in Pop is like. And because you're aware that Eton is The School, you're The Elite at The School, so you're kind of super heroes. They have all these great dinners and you get invited to really smart country houses, because all the chaps in Pop would invariably invite all the other chaps to their parties. At least half of them will have really sensible parties, and they'll have sisters who are coming out, so you're really in there, you're right in that whole scene. And it *is* a smart scene because, unlike other teenagers in the country, it's your parties that are appearing in *Tatler* and *Ritz*. That's what I mean: if you're cool, you're cool, like nationally. Of course the rest of the country doesn't give a fuck about the fact that you're in *Tatler*, but you think that's really important, and I suppose in a certain way it is.

Of course, you simply never repeat that in your life; everything else is a bit of a come-down. It's like becoming a pop star or something – if kids are given that degree of public praise, it's very hard to do anything after that and it fucks them up a bit.

I never thought that I was going to make it. I had these metal-framed glasses, because I react quite strongly to light, and they were meant to be slightly tinted. And they came out too tinted, they were almost dark glasses. I remember walking into a French div. and a very nice man named Richard Graham, who had an extraordinary kind of drawly voice, just leaned back on his chair and said, 'Bloody hell! It's Shades Thomas.' The name just stuck, I was Shades. I had a column in the *Chronicle* called 'Shades'. Anyway, I never thought . . . one always hopes . . . I mean, you always lie there on Pop election day, but I didn't seriously think I had the remotest snowball in hell's chance to get into Pop. However, about two years after leaving Eton, I was at a party and bumped into a chap called Willie Nicholson, and it was late in the evening, and we sat down – we were pissed, I suppose, stoned, more likely – and he said, 'David, you probably don't know this, but you were elected into Pop.' And I said '*What?*' and he said, 'You were elected into Pop and you were blackballed on account of those bloody shades of yours!' I was livid! I mean, *I could have been in Pop except for those fucking glasses!* I was absolutely furious. I thought, 'God, I could have gotten into Pop.' I'm sure I would have been a completely different person if I'd gotten into Pop. I'd have probably been even more unbearable. I'd have been much more self-confident. God, if you got into Pop . . .

I'll tell you one thing which I still have problems with now. Although my school fees were to a large extent paid for by the government, because my father's a diplomat, my father still had to scrimp and save a bit. We weren't poor, but my father was getting a Civil Service salary, so he was being paid absolutely fuck-all. It affected me very strongly that my father could never have anything for himself; the money he had went on me or my kid sisters. He never had enough money to give his kids the education he wanted to give them, and to buy himself a stereo or something, and that has had an absolutely fundamental effect on my life. I am obsessive about money for that reason, and I always swore that I would not be in that position.

My first day at the *Mail on Sunday*, they asked me to do a piece about Eton: 'Oh, *you* went to Eton, didn't you?' I have no idea what school anybody else in my office went to, but they all know I went to Eton. Every so often, you get the occasional kind of, 'Oh well, he's the Etonian, he'll know about that', when it's some awful snobby thing.

I get paid pretty well, but in the last fifteen years the ante has been upped so much, school fees and house prices have gone up by so much, that even though I earn as much now as my father did when he retired, it's still not enough to send a kid to school on. I would definitely feel that I had not succeeded in life if I could not afford to send my kids to Eton. But then, just when you're thinking, 'Oh fuck, I'll have to send my kids to a comprehensive', something like *The Times* comes along and says, 'This is the best school in the whole country', and how could I possibly turn around and not give it to *my* kids?

SIR RANULPH TWISTLETON-WYKEHAM-FIENNES

I GREW up in South Africa from about two until ten. Because my father had been killed in the war, my family had a thing called Founder's Kin which entitled me to go to Winchester at a very good rate. As my mother had four children to look after, getting a scholarship into Winchester would have been a good idea to help out with the funds, but I didn't quite make Common Entrance, although I just managed to get into Eton, middle fourth.

Being a baronet anywhere else could have been a slight oddity, but not at Eton. I was a slight oddity because of my lingering South African accent, but any sort of thing like that gets drummed out of you pretty quickly anyway.

I noticed in Wilfrid Blunt's book it says that when he said to me, as a bright young new boy in his art school, 'I can't call you Twistleton-Wykeham-Fiennes', I replied, 'Call me Twinkletoes', which I certainly never said – that's sheer invention. I was called 'Sir Griswold', which lingered on into the regiment, and that came from some strange comic strip which had a knight rushing in saying, 'You have four minutes to get out of the castle, Sir Randolf's coming!' – that was at the time of the first four-minute warning system, and that seemed to catch on.

I arrived very bumptious and very confident and had that rapidly removed, mainly owing to the fact that I was a pretty boy, which completely haunted my whole life. I so hated being called 'a pretty boy', and having the larger boys looking at me, that I told my mother, 'I want to be removed at once.' This was a new experience and a very unpleasant one. But above all I wanted to get out of those bum-freezers which seemed to highlight the 'pretty boy' situation. And so she went to Purple Parr, my housemaster, and Purple Parr explained that five-foot-two was five-foot-two and had been since King Henry the whatever. I told her I'd jump off Windsor Bridge.

On two occasions, once in Judy's Passage and once in the clothes room at Eton, I was attacked physically, and I fought off by putting my fingers in their eyes, which I suppose they didn't expect. But that wasn't the point. I could put up with physical bullying because I could fight back; I was no good at fighting back verbally. It was the verbal teasing all the time – you know, suggestions that one had done this, that and the other – simply because one was pretty.

It completely dampened me down for the next three to four years. My instant reaction was to take up boxing, and to be aggressive and to wear a permanent scowl. And I suppose it coloured my memories of Eton so that I find it difficult to remember the good times, and it was such an unpleasant shock that it made me find it rather difficult to concentrate on lessons. All I did was to box, and I lived for boxing, for being aggressive.

I got a thing called chorea, a type of rheumatic heart fever, at about sixteen, through too much boxing and trying to get my weight down to paper weight, and I went to a specialist in Ireland who said I had to leave school. So I left for a whole summer half and summer holidays, and I suddenly grew six and a half inches and got a lot bigger, and really, when I got back, the tart troubles stopped.

Then I discovered night climbing, and that became an extremely bright spot. Night climbing made my last year at Eton, but then by the last year I was no longer pretty, so that was no longer a worry.

Well, initially we weren't very successful because they had put barbed wire all around the place after some previous generation of climbers. We would go down to the School of Mechanics to get clamps which we used to climb up the dome ridges, and then afterwards we would return them so they weren't missing. There are really only two suitable buildings in Eton, but we did them in various different sorts of ways. We did Lupton's via the front route, the north face, and we put a black flag on the top. And we'd sit there drinking cherry brandy, by way of celebrating.

I only got four pounds a half from my mother, so in order to go to Rowland's, or get any sock, I had to supplement this very meagre income. Jeremy Deedes was the friend and accomplice I did it with. We got three pennies on a pack of Gauloise, and sixpence on a bottle of whisky. And we had it immaculately arranged. I knew the daughter of the owner of the White Hart who let us in the back to change into workmen's overalls and leave our tails, and from there it was straight through a tiny back passage across Peascod Street to the Victoria Wine Company; it was very neat. We once actually walked right past Dick Wheadon, who was the keenest and cleverest beak at catching Etonians in the wrong areas, and that was the ultimate triumph! And then Jeremy would deliver everything to the people in Pop who'd actually ordered it – before Corps camp exercises was usually the best period – and we could make about two pounds a half that way, which was fifty per cent of my income, so it was well worth while.

In 1966, with about five other O Es of my vintage, we decided that we didn't like a book written by David Benedictus, called *The Fourth of June*, so we planned to kidnap him and hoik him up on top of School Hall, with a large sign around him saying: '*Malus Scriptus Benedictus*'. We had sent him an invitation to a charity to get him out at the right time on the right evening, and we had a taxi all laid on with an O E at the wheel. But it all went wrong, and instead, for that Fourth of June, we put a message on the roof, 'Happy Eton – Happy Fourth of June' or something like that.

And the next day, where the boat procession goes by, opposite where the Queen sits if she's there, but she never is, we left a rope under the river. We had frog suits, and then when the time came, we went under water by the island in the middle where all the willows hang down. The point being that thousands of people go to enjoy the evening boat procession to see some fun; very often they never flop into the water, so there's no fun. Anyway, under the water it's amazing, you can actually see the whole outline of the boat and the oars. And you can see when the last one lifts up, so you know when they're at their delicate stage, and it's very easy to put your hook on to the rigger on the left-hand side, and just pull up and down, and they all topple over. We had four boats over that evening. Unfortunately, I was using my wife's water system, and she had put it back wrong; one of the valves burst, and I found a hundred and sixty pounds per square inch trying to force itself into my system. So I had to surface, and with all the floodlights on and everything, one felt like a fly. I swam as hard as I could with this big heavy pack to the far bank and tried to hide it, and then this boat with watermen and masters came along, so I swam across to the far side where the big field is, and took off my flippers – and was chased by about six men in the dark across the field. When we got to the little wooden plank that goes over the muddy pond under the three arches, I dived into the mud and sat there while they all drove over the bridge. Incidentally, I'd seen one of the men who was chasing me in the boat was Dave Callendar, which quite put me off! I don't like to do anything wrong with Dave Callender.

Dave Callender was an excellent teacher, and he taught me how to write. And as my only way of making a living now is writing books, that was entirely through Dave Callender making the language come alive. So of all the beaks, Dave Callender was way and above the best beak for me. I intend to dedicate my next book to him because I think he's a really excellent beak.

I suppose, despite what I said about the earlier years, Eton is a bond. Well, a lot of my friends are Etonians – I mean, the fellow whom I go on most expeditions with was there. Every now and again, you're in a tent, and you've got over the last problem of the day, and the conversation might go back to some funny fellow like Toady Mays, some strange anachronism of a beak. Or one might remember some character or other and reminisce about them.

I remember we were sort of making rhymes up about the noise that ice made – this is on the Arctic Ocean – and Oliver Sheppard was giving it a go, and I said, 'What you're trying to do, unsuccessfully, is get pentameters and hexameters.' And he instantly quoted back at me the three things which G. A. D. Tait had taught both of us separately, which were the methods of remembering hexameters and pentameters. 'Eat a potato' and 'Yesterday's dinner and tea', and then Olly came up with another one which I'd forgotten for twenty years, which was: 'Clearly the rest I behold of the dark-eyed sons of Akayuh'. And so there we were, out in the Arctic wastes, nearer to having done both Poles than any previous humans, and coming out with some Gad Taitism from twenty-five years ago.

I remember the beauty of my prep school, and any time I hear a pheasant bark, or rooks, I can remember the countryside round it. I have no form of romantic clinks like that in my memory of Eton. But even now, if I'm in a quiet street at night, I can remember the thrill of dodging around in the semi-lit streets, behind the houses and up the drainpipes. Even now, I sometimes find myself, when I'm looking at some church, working out which lightning conductor we'd use to get up it, and really my memories of Eton are all to do with its edifices. I've got an edifice complex.

I suppose I might have got through life to the age of eighteen without having had an unpleasant experience, but because I had such an unpleasant experience at Eton, I suppose I ought to be grateful in that it did at least teach you to have some defences, which are very necessary before going out into life. So from that point of view – a rather negative way of looking at it – Eton is responsible for forming me and playing a part in any success I may have had. And if I did have a son, providing he wasn't pretty, I might send him there.

HUGO VICKERS

━━━

I SUPPOSE with any new school your first day must be the worst day in your life, however nice they try to be to you: and things do actually get consistently better thereafter.

There takes place a tea with the housemaster and the dame, and other parents. And then of course the parents go away. That sort of thing is rather grim – I remember it being an ultimate dread moment, and I think nothing quite as bad ever happens to you again as that feeling of being left. I remember sitting in the window looking at the other boys, and you know that you're destined to be thrown together for five years; so you have no choice but to pretend to like them, even if you don't really. They were perfectly all right, as it happens, but, you know, it's rather a nightmare thing.

I don't remember anything particular about the first night except that it was all so confusing. One went rather early to bed, and then you heard the others arriving, a sort of terrible clatter of feet, suitcases and greetings, and things like this. And the next morning, the first thing that would happen is the door would open and in would come a boy's maid with a jug of hot water to pour into the bowl, and this was what you washed in. You did your best, you didn't have to shave in those days, of course, but it meant that you cleaned your teeth and spat into the thing, and therefore you left behind you this rather nasty bowl – I remember that very clearly. Your new clothes are there, there's this strange suit which you're going to put on the next day for the first time, you're going to struggle to tie your tie, and you're going to be very worried about it. I think somebody came in and asked, 'Do you need help with your tie?' Most Etonians never tied their tie properly; they just flicked it over the top and stuck it down behind their collar, which wasn't really quite as it should have been, it should be tied rather like a bow tie and I always scrupulously did that. I was proud to wear my uniform, I enjoyed wearing it actually.

All the older boys seemed like men. The headmaster, Anthony Chenevix-Trench, used to say in one of his sermons, 'Some of us here are men, some are nearly men, and some of us are still merely children.' That was one of his lines; we used to imitate him quite often.

I remember my House Captain, a man called Fremantle – he seemed like a man, but he was only seventeen or eighteen. He's dead now, I'm afraid, I don't know what happened to him. He was a very nice person; he was very fair, but he was incredibly frightening. Extremely good-looking, handsome fellow, and a man who could sing a bass solo in the school concert at the end of the half, so you can imagine the sort of power of the person. He was an extremely impressive character.

So we went through the first day and met these masters, and I thought, 'This is extraordinary, they're all so nice' – until I met the one master, at the end of the day, who suddenly made me think, 'Oh my God, this is not going to be all fun.' Instead of being terribly welcoming and rather gentle and friendly, he walked in and announced in French that from that moment onwards we were only going to speak French and that was it. In fact he was a very good master, and I know him still, but he instilled in one, at the age of twelve, a total horror of schoolmasters.

I had a particular passion for Windsor. Literally on the first Saturday I rushed up to Windsor Castle, bought a ticket and walked around St George's Chapel, which I've loved ever since. I spent a lot of my free time in Windsor Castle, learning about it, later on taking a job showing people around St George's Chapel on Sunday afternoons. And that's led to things which I still do at St George's Chapel today. It would be perfectly fair to say that there was a strong escapist quality in what I was doing, but that was the freedom of the school, you know. If one person wanted to go off and play the piano enthusiastically on Saturday afternoon or Sunday afternoon, fine, there were very good music schools, they could do that. And if a rather strange little chap like me wanted to go and wander around Windsor Castle, that was equally acceptable, and my housemaster was very understanding about it and encouraged it in fact.

It saw me through some difficult times. I think there were some days at school that were absolutely desperate. I hated games, particularly any kind of regimented games. Having to be a wetbob and negotiate in a whiff, a little tiny boat, was utterly grim. The first time I went out I just floated, desperately and miserably, certainly in tears – I remember that very clearly – to the other side of the river, which is terribly dangerous with all these boats, huge Windsoriana tourist boats plying up and down, and had to be rescued: people were shouting at me from the bank, 'Left hand down', 'Just swing it around' . . . absolutely hopeless, total nightmare. I dreaded and hated anything like that. I was never good at the field game, or football or rugger, or anything like that, and alas! in the early years, until about the age of fifteen or sixteen, one did have to take part in a certain amount of all that. But as you grew older you didn't have to do it; you became what was called a 'slack-bob'.

The worst thing was a grim event which took place in October which everybody went on, this long, long, long, exhausting run, a cross-country run, which had some sinister name,* and ended up by us all having to jump some ghastly ditch. And that really was absolutely the worst, because there were members of Pop standing around with Pop canes to sort of tickle you up, as it were, if you were slacking. They never did, actually, but it had that atmosphere to it.

That feeling of fear . . . I think it was quite strong when I arrived, and totally absent when I left. It was the sixties. It was a time of change. Somebody like me could go through Eton without getting into trouble. I don't think I would have been able to do that two years earlier, because I think they would have made one get into trouble. They would have given those instructions,

*The Steeplechase.

like they used to do at Osborne: 'All naval cadets put your hands over your ears so that you can't hear! Right! Take your hands down!' Now if you took your hands down, you could hear, you were listening, so then you were in trouble. If you didn't take your hands down, you hadn't obeyed an order, so you were in trouble again. That sort of atmosphere had gone by the time I was at Eton. If you did something wrong, you got into trouble, but if you didn't do something wrong, they left you alone. I am naturally frightened of people who have authority over me and I am not a rule-breaker, so I was what you might call a 'goody-goody' – odious school expression – and I was allowed to be that, that was all right. I had a peaceful life therefore.

Perhaps I was lucky that my house was a fairly friendly, civilized place. There was a certain amount of ragging and teasing of people, in which I could have easily been a victim. I do remember that when I was about sixteen there was a slightly hostile unit in my house, and I think the nastiest thing that ever happened to me – it doesn't sound nasty, but it was very nasty – was that I had some very nice new window-boxes and somebody painted an unpleasant slogan on them. I can't remember what the slogan was now, I genuinely can't, but it was nasty.

I think when people did do bullying, it could be very nasty indeed. There was one boy in the house who, because he had a slight sallow, yellow complexion, was nicknamed 'Chigger', which was a terrible sort of Eton joke. And he used to get very heated and would pick up his poker and wave it about when they baited him. One person had the extremely unpleasant and ingenious idea of turning the handle around and heating it so that it went red hot, and then turning it back again, waiting until it darkened, then going through the necessary bait; when the wretched boy seized the red hot poker . . . I remember seeing a fading blister, although I didn't see it until well after the incident.

The only time I ever was commended for good effort or anything like that was when I wrote a long biographical essay about Queen Victoria's children. And that was sent up for good. It was the only time I ever got anywhere near anything like a prize – and I see now that it formed the basis of my being a writer, without my even realizing it. But I have always thought of sixteen to twenty-three as being my lowest cycle. I didn't really know what I wanted to do, and I didn't achieve very much, and I always felt that I was letting everybody down.

You had the feeling that you were at the best possible school. You were made aware of that by the continual appearance of tourists, and by the number of times in the summer when you were photographed as you were walking along the street. You pretended you didn't really like it, but in fact it was quite nice, ending up in some photograph album in Minnesota or somewhere. One would say, 'Please don't photograph me, I'm not allowed to be photographed' – you know, standing absolutely rigid so that they could get a good shot.

You were aware of some boys in the school who were famous in some way. For example, Winston Churchill died while I was at the school, and one saw the two brothers Soames taking part in the funeral and walking in the State Procession. One was aware of people who impinged in another world. There were some sons of the Duke of St Albans who ran away and got into the newspaper. Beauclerk, I think they were called. The odd sort of person, like an Ethiopian Crown Prince's son or something like that. And we had a couple of black men, Dilibe Onyeama and a man called Akintola, and one day we had to pray for Akintola because we heard he'd been murdered in Nigeria. In fact it was his father who had been murdered, and a couple of weeks later Akintola sort of sauntered into evening chapel. I don't know whether this is true or not, but I believe that Akintola and Onyeama came from different tribes and absolutely loathed each other.

I think that the confidence of having been to a school which I always thought was the best school is a wonderful feeling to carry through life. I suppose that it is a trump card that you can pull out if you have to, let's put it like that. If somebody says to you, particularly somebody who's getting a bit stroppy or something, 'Where were you at school, then?' if you say 'Eton', it is actually quite a nice answer to give and it usually terminates the conversation. What I'd quite enjoy would be a situation where somebody had assumed that you came from a minor public school, as it were, and you could see them coming to that conclusion, perhaps indeed allowed or encouraged them to come to that conclusion . . . and then you bring it out of your hat when prompted by them. It is a trump card, there's no question about that. But you only play your trump card when you have to, don't you? Otherwise you keep it to yourself.

I don't think that I was what you might call a particularly memorable Etonian. I didn't have a distinguished Eton career; I went through the system rather quietly, achieving little, not getting into trouble, just doing my own thing as much as I was allowed to. I did not have any school distinction, but I was able to wear what they call 'stick-ups', which was the white bow tie with the wing collar, because of being the head steward at St George's Chapel. Now this was perfect for me because it looked as if I had an important position in the school and some authority, but in fact I had no power at all. But it meant that others scampered into doorways when they saw me coming, rather than me having to do so.

I saw my housemaster years after leaving the school, and he said that he was glad that things seemed to be working out. He said, 'We weren't sure, you know, quite whether to let you keep on going up to Windsor the whole time; or if perhaps we should have tried to direct you into something else.' But he decided that it was to be encouraged, and he was pleased to see that it had led somewhere – into writing, I suppose, eventually.

I still go a lot to Windsor, and I used to be involved with the Windsor festival for quite a long time, so I'm quite close to Eton. I occasionally go to a concert at Eton. I know Eton masters. A friend of mine has brothers at Eton, and we recently had long, long reminiscences and talks comparing Eton then and Eton now, and reminiscing about the characters.

If ever I write anything about my own life in any form at all, I think that the chapter about Eton will be tremendous fun, painting portraits of the characters and things like that. I love all the stories, I remember the silly story about a housemaster who caught two boys drinking champagne up a tree. And when it was discovered that the champagne had in fact been warm, the housemaster said, 'My God, you've had your punishment, now get out of here!' Drinking warm champagne! These sort of stories – I've got hundreds of those, and I love that sort of thing, and I love that kind of attitude and the atmosphere of the school.

THE HON. WILLIAM WALDEGRAVE

THE Waldegrave family background is an ancient, back-into-the-mists-of-time-and-beyond, minor English aristocratic family which has always been sort of near the centre of power. I'm also descended from Robert Walpole, but apart from association with bigwigs in the eighteenth century, and some bigwigs in the sixteenth century, we have never been real stars. My father's a Wykehamist, but my mother was a Grenfell and her mother was a Lyttelton, and both Grenfells and in particular Lytteltons have been terrific Eton families, so I don't think they ever considered sending me to Winchester.

I was in the house of a man called A. J. Marsden, which was dominated by rowing. One assumed one was going to row, and cricket was thought a very eccentric activity that nobody seriously undertook. We used to win the Aquatics Cup, and the gap between us and the next house was usually wider than all the points that all the others had scored together. I mean, we regarded it as a defeat if they won anything. We were just far more professional about it. In those days Eton had a very characteristic, old-fashioned style of rowing; the Eton crew at Henley always looked nicer than anybody else, but didn't necessarily win. Marsden wasn't at all interested in that attitude. We used to go out in the dark with Marsden and cut branches off the trees at Lower Hope so that we could get another six inches into the bank and out of the stream on the way up. It introduced one to the concept of total dedication to winning and to an iconoclastic view about the traditional ways of doing things. Marsden had a considerable effect on my character in that he gave one, early on, a very strong dose of the idea that hard competition was the way of the world.

Early in my first year, I suffered, as I think quite a lot of twelve-, thirteen-year-olds do, from insomnia. Marsden's characteristic solution to this was that when I couldn't go to sleep, I should run to Bray, which was quite a long way away, three or four miles, in the middle of the night, and he would come too. That cured the insomnia pretty quick. It was complete lunacy, but it made one rather fond of him.

He was a good housemaster. He was one of those slightly mad geniuses of schoolmasters whom Eton rather attracted, who would probably not have been given jobs by other schools because they were not at all the conventional schoolmaster types. The confidence of the institution is part of all this. They were able to say, 'We will have him because we know the structure is strong enough to support him.'

Marsden's was dominated by the concept that everybody could do something excellently well. Most people could row. But if, inexplicably, they couldn't row, then there was bound to be something you could find that they could do well.

Marsden was not a great intellectual, though he spoke German and knew German literature very well. But he knew his own limitations, and he knew that if he had a boy who was by way of being an intellectual, he had to take special steps because he couldn't do it himself. He had as classical tutor for lower boys the most wonderful, cultured, aesthetic man called Claude Taylor. The contrast between these two was wonderful. And Marsden did that quite deliberately. I remember once, when I was about fourteen, he came most charmingly to the conclusion that I needed extra intellectual stimulus, and he found a wonderful master called Nigel Foxell, who didn't have a very long career at Eton but would have been quite a sort of aesthete at King's or somewhere. I was sent off twice a week to have extra tuition with him, which I remember starting with a thoroughly well-omened beginning because we went into his room, and on the wall was a picture: 'Who's that picture by?' he asked, and the words just came into my mind, from where I don't know. 'It's a Fantin-Latour.' 'Correct,' he said, and so we had a good start. Then he said, 'You will remember in *The Stones of Venice* . . .' so I said, 'Excuse me, I haven't read *The Stones of Venice*.' 'You haven't read *The Stones of Venice*!?' Anyway, I was then introduced to that grand tradition of Ruskin, which amounts to about thirty volumes, and we more or less read our way through the whole thing. And all that I don't think could have happened in many schools. That was the strength of Eton – depending partly on Marsden's personality, but even more on the fact that if he looked around he could find all sorts of people about in those days under Birley's policy of employing and hiring all kinds of amazing irregulars. But really that goes back to the Etonian tradition of saying that exams weren't frightfully important. I think maybe my period of the early sixties was the last where that tradition remained – combined with Birley's confidence in taking on people whom many other schools would have looked at quite askance.

I was very well taught. My philosophy teacher and modern tutor was John Roberts, who was a formidably good Oxford philosopher. Martineau taught me ancient classics in a wonderfully old-fashioned way, the last of the direct line from C. M. Wells, Macnaghten and all those people, but it's still a damned good way of teaching classics. You start from the texts, and there's quite a lot to be said for that. The other person who was important in my life, a distant figure, but not all that distant, was Birley himself, who wasn't really a scholar but was a wonderful enthusiast. He noticed that I was interested in books and he took me round the College Library where there is a Gutenberg Bible, and so one was able to sit down and handle fabulous sixteenth- and seventeenth-century books. It was an extraordinary privilege.

You were surrounded, as you probably never would be again in your life, by an incomparable mixture of things, ranging from that very considerable Egyptian collection in the Macnaghten Library, to Luxmoore's Garden, to the physical beauty of the place (less surrounded by motorways then), and by a hundred and twenty masters amongst whom there were some extraordinary, able people. You should use it all – you shouldn't waste it, any of it: that was the philosophy.

I was very aware of the beauty of the school. I still have an idyll in my mind . . . in the summer, bicycling back along the river – which was something of a privilege in those days – and going to Tap, run by a couple of whom I remember John Roberts saying to me, 'Here's an example of the randomness of career choice. He is one of the ablest people in the community of Eton.' And then you would bicycle up the High Street on a summer evening – I mean, all that *works*, all that magic does work . . . it is fabulously beautiful.

I think that Eton produced then a community which provided enough stimulus and enough things to permit you to fill your life very effectively, and being at the head of it, as I was as President of Pop, was very fulfilling. It does have that very strong communal feel which enables you to think that the things of its own world are very important.

I think it perhaps explains why a lot of Etonians seek worlds which are rather hierarchical, because they are good at that kind of thing. And there are people who don't ever have a stimulus later in life which is equally strong. I know that everybody always writes that Etonians never escape from the image of Eton and the rather imaginary sort of 'culturabiless' and all that stuff that Cyril Connolly invented. But I think that those who haven't escaped from Eton have failed to escape with more style than those who haven't escaped from other schools, and they write good and rather elegant novels about it. The image of the Etonian that I like best is the one that says you can't predict what an Etonian is like: whereas I think you genuinely can spot a Wykehamist, and there are certain kinds of house style that you can spot in other schools. One of Eton's self-images, and self-images are important even if they are not achieved, is that you *shouldn't* be able to spot the Etonian. There was that arrogant thing that Etonians used to say: people whom everybody points to as Etonians actually come from Marlborough!

I think there was a very powerful sense in which a tradition of England – which is in danger of collapse – was strongly represented by the Eton of my day, with the mixture of the Anglican Church and of high English culture. I think Eton did have a shot, under Birley anyway, at representing a kind of tolerant high-culture tradition, which was very powerful, mixed in with the fabric of the buildings, the fabric of the connection between the Church and the school, the music, the literature.

I mean, Eton's job was really a humanizing one. Birley used to say explicitly that there would be an Establishment school somewhere, there would be a top one in a hierarchy somewhere, there might be half a dozen. His job was to take a lot of people, many of whom were not very clever, and who were going to be in positions of power because of wealth and how the world works, and to show them something of English culture. And it didn't work too badly. You were putting in front of a lot of rich and otherwise uncultured people an incomparable mixture of the Book of Common Prayer and wonderful music, and that was an aesthetic experience which very many of them in their banks later on would never have repeated. I have a great deal of regret that Eton tightened the raising of entry standards for that reason, because a lot of people who are still going to be rich and powerful are not now exposed to the beauty of the place and its culture, and are not going to get anywhere else. 'I'm running a comprehensive school here,' he used to say, and he bloody well was, in terms of IQ. The bottom fourth form at Eton when I was there could barely read or write, and yet you had at the other end people who were extraordinarily talented, and it made for a much better community, of course. That is why I always thought then that it was a more attractive community than, say, Winchester, which had a much narrower range of types of people.

I think Eton itself did have a sense that there was so much; it offered you such riches of culture and of alternatives to sport that there was a slight feeling that if you hadn't found anything to interest you, you must be a fool. It was amazingly adult; it was much more adult than my first year at Oxford, where one was living amongst people who had never lived away from home before. In terms of actually having lived, they were about ten years behind.

I suspect that I was at the end of the period when the internal bonds of the community were able to resist a certain amount of dissolution from an outside pull. As head of Pop I was trying to prevent people from growing their hair long, all those pressures were there, and probably it was the last time when – and this is more to do with the English class system, perhaps, than the school itself – you could get people to assent to the maintenance of those bonds against the ordinary teenage culture.

Eton itself has tremendous prestige, much greater prestige in this country than the equivalents which jolly well exist in other countries, because I think people here are still curiously deferential. It is a particularly English thing. It is because we are not really democrats – I mean, people despise democratic institutions in this country. If you look at the institutions that have the greatest public support, they are hereditary institutions. Peers are respected more than members of the House of Commons, the Royal Family is respected more than the peers. The further away you are from the democratic process in this country, the more respect you have.

Well, as long as there isn't such a guerrilla warfare against private schools that people can't actually afford them at all, there will always be one that's the best, one that is extremely difficult to push off its pinnacle because it becomes a self-fulfilling story. The best masters want to go there, it's got more resources, and so I think it will go on in much the same way.

ETON SLANG

ABSENCE Roll-call

BEAK Master

BILL (or to be 'put on bill'). A situation where a boy is destined to meet a master, or the headmaster, for punishment

BOYCALL When a senior boy shouts an elongated 'B-o-o-o-o-y', and every fag must run to meet him, no matter what he is doing. The last boy to reach him runs the errand

BUM-FREEZERS Attire for boys under 5' 4". Not a tailcoat, but a short Eton jacket which ends at the hips

BURNING BUSH Wrought-iron lamp-post outside the Library where boys meet their tutors at break-time

BURRY Desk

CAPPING The action of touching index finger to forehead, or more usually forearm flung in air, to acknowledge a beak or dame passing in the street

CAPTAIN OF THE HOUSE Most senior boy in the house

CAPTAIN OF THE SCHOOL Most senior colleger in the school

COLLEGER Scholar. There are seventy scholars, and they live in their own house and wear gowns (Latin: *togati*, hence the nickname 'tugs'). They are not necessarily, indeed not usually, from an unaffluent background

DAME Matron

DEBATE Self-electing group of prefects, from which members of the Library are chosen

DIVISION Lesson, class or form room

DRY-BOB Boy who plays cricket rather than rows

EIGHT Member of the rowing team

EIGHT-TAN (as in 'to be eight-tanned') To be beaten by a member of the eight

EXTRA WORK   Work done outside school hours

FAG   A new boy who runs errands for a senior boy for his first year, as well as responding to boy calls. Personal fagging no longer exists

FLOGGING   To be beaten by a birch by the headmaster or lower master

HALF   Term

HALF-CHANGE   Casual wear, sports jacket and tie

HEAD MAN   Headmaster

KNIFE-BOARDS   The rows near the altar in Chapel which face the rest of the school. A very conspicuous place to sit

LIBRARY   Power clique within the house, a self-electing body. Their common-room or meeting-place is called a Library – not that any reading is known to go on there

LIBRARY FAG   Fag assigned to the Library

LOCK-UP   When the house is locked up in the evening

LONG LEAVE   Long weekends in the summer and Michaelmas halves

LOWER CHAPEL   For the younger boys

LOWER MASTER   Master in charge of lower boys

MESOPOTAMIA   A playing-field

MESS WITH   Share tea with somebody

MOB SOMEBODY UP   To provoke or tease somebody

M'TUTOR   'My tutor' (also 'm'dame')

OPPIDAN   (Latin: *town*). Full fee-paying boy

POP   The most prestigious self-electing group of boys. Being selected is akin to winning the pools, being in the Cabinet, etc. Members can wear multi-coloured waistcoats

POP-TAN   To be beaten by a member of Pop

PRIVATE BUSINESS, PRIVATE   Informal lessons with boys' tutors in their homes, for extracurricular work.

PROVOST   Titular head of the school, who runs the school with the Fellows. Always an Old Etonian, usually a peer

REARS   Lavatories

RIP   An unsatisfactory piece of work which has literally been ripped

ROWLAND'S   A tea-shop on the High Street

SAYING LESSON   Periods set aside for memorizing poetry or prose

SENT UP FOR GOOD   Work commended for excellence

SIXPENNY   A playing-field

SIXTH FORM   Twenty of the brightest boys, half of them Collegers, half Oppidans

SLACK-BOB   A boy who plays no sports

SOCK   (as in 'to sock somebody').   To treat somebody, generally to food

STICK-UPS   Wing-collars worn as a privilege

STRAWBERRY MESS   Strawberries and ice-cream (also 'banana mess')

TAP   A place in the High Street where senior boys may drink beer and cider

TART   A boy, usually young, considered attractive

TRIALS   Exams

TUG   Colleger

TUTOR   Master assigned to a boy in his first two years

UP TO   (as in 'to be up to someone').   To be taught by

WET-BOB   A boy who chooses to row

INDEX

Agnew, Geoffrey, 144

Akintola, 52, 277

Alington, Cyril Argentine, 88, 126, 139, 154, 183

Alington, Hon. Hester, 88, 141

Allen, G. O. B., 179

Assheton, R. T., 80

Baird, Robert, 239, 243

Baldwin, Gordon, 175

Barrington-Ward, Simon, *Bishop of Coventry*, 21–7, 155

Barton, John, 230

Benedictus, David, *writer, and executive at Channel Four*, 28–36

Bentin, Michael, *actor*, 37–42, 191, 192

Birley, Sir Robert, 82, 84, 92, 112, 251, 282, 284

Blond, Anthony, *publisher*, 43–9

Blunt, Wilfrid, 22, 129

Brocket, Charles Nall-Cain, 3rd Baron, *land owner*, 50–56

Brocklebank, Tom, 81, 82

Brown, Craig, 73, 74, 78

Burgess, Harry, 42

Burrows, Simon, *Bishop Suffragan of Buckingham*, 57–60

Butterwick, Cyril, 185

Byron, Miss, 127–8

Callaghan, James, 82, 83

Callender, Andrew, *recently down from Oxford*, 61–6

Callender, Dave, 271

Carrington, Peter Carrington, 6th Baron, 69

Charteris, Martin Charteris Baron, *Provost of Eton, former Secretary to the Queen*, 67–71

Chenevix-Trench, Anthony, 166, 236, 274

Churchill, Winston, 130

Coleridge, Fred, 109, 172–4

Coleridge, Nicholas, *editor*, Harper's and Queen, 72–9

Compton, Sir Robert, 186

Connolly, Cyril, 140, 183, 283

Cook, Ned, 244

Corbett, Robert, 110

Dalyell, Tam, MP, *Labour politician*, 80–85

Dashwood, John, 156

Daubeny, Philip, 75

De Montmorency, R. H., 161

Deedes, Jeremy, 270

Diamond, Robert, 192

Dilhorne, Reginald Manningham-Buller, 1st Viscount, 181–2

Elliott, Sir Claude, 59–60, 92, 153, 195, 196, 231

Ellwick, John, 232–3

Faulkner, John, 240

Fiennes, Mark, *photographer*, 90–97

Fiennes, Sir Ranulph Twistleton-Wykeham-, *explorer*, 268–72

Foxell, Nigel, 281–2

Fraser, Sir David, *author and retired soldier*, 98–107

Fyfe Jamieson, Colin, 230

Gatacre, Peter, 230

Gowan, Christopher, 215

Gowrie, Alexander Hore-Ruthven, 2nd Earl of, *Chairman, Sotheby's International*, 108–14, 120

Graham, John, *journalist*, 115–22

Graham-Watson, Paul, 80

Grimond, Joseph Grimond, Baron, 88

Guinness, Hugo, 221

Haddon, Richard, 234

Hailsham, Quentin Hogg, Baron, *former Lord High Chancellor of Great Britain*, 123–6, 180, 183

Hall, Edward Thomas, 225, 226

Hamilton, Walter, 57, 59

Haslam, Nicky, *interior designer*, 127–31

Headlam, W. G., 164–5

Heathcote Amory, Mark, *literary editor of the Spectator*, 132–7

Hely-Hutchinson, Henry, 225

Herbert, J. S., 148, 156

Hills, J. D., 156

Hogg, Hon. Edward, 125

Home of the Hirsel, Alexander Douglas-Home, Baron, *former Prime Minister*, 138–41

Home, Hon. William Douglas-, *playwright*, 86–9, 165

Hope-Jones, William, 37–42 *passim*

House, Adrian, *publisher*, 142–6

How, Fred, 127

Hudson, Hugh, *film director*, 147–51

Hurd, Douglas, *Home Secretary*, 25, 152–5

Huson, A.C., 163

Inchcape, Kenneth J. W. M., 3rd Earl of, 39–40

Iredale-Smith, Miss, 57

Jacomb, Sir Martin, *banker*, 156–9

James, Montague Rhodes, 165

Johnston, Brian, *cricket commentator*, 87–8, 160–67

Kidston, G., 111, 135

Lane Fox, Robin, *writer*, 168–71

Laurie, Hugh, 221

Lawrence, Peter, 52–3

Leary, David, 233–4

Llewellyn, Martin, *architect*, 172–8

Lloyd, Sir Anthony, 230–31

Londonderry, Alexander Vane-Tempest-Stewart, 9th Marquess of, 116

Longford, Francis Pakenham, 7th Earl of, *crusader*, 179–84

Lycett-Green, Rupert, 34

Lyttelton, George, 22–4

Lyttelton, Humphrey, *jazz musician*, 185–91

MacAndrew, Ronnie, 186

McConnell, James, 208

McCrum, Michael William, 252, 253, 260, 263

MacIndoe, David, 95, 168

Macnee, Patrick, *actor*, 192–6

Malcolm, Derek, *film critic*, 197–206

Marsden, A. J., 280–81

Marsden, H. K., 39, 225, 226, 227, 229

Marten, Henry, 139

Martineau, Richard C., 155, 169, 170, 282

Michell, Charles, 34

Monson, Hon. Nicholas, *journalist*, 207–13

Moorhead, John, *author*, 116, 120, 214–18

Mott-Radclyffe, Sir Charles, 87

Nicholson, Archie, 232, 234

Nicholson, Mary, *advertising executive*, 219–24

Norwich, John Julius Cooper, 2nd Viscount, 156

Oaksey, John Lawrence, 4th Baron Trevethin and 2nd Baron, *racing commentator*, 225–31

Oldham, David, 186

Onyeama, Dilibe, 52, 277

Ormsby-Gore, Julian, 133

Owen, Miss, 86–7

Paine, John, *general medical practitioner*, 232–8

Parr, Mrs R. J. N., 198

Parr, R.J. N., 29, 197, 198, 269

Payne, Raef, 31, 62, 154, 234

Pitt-Miller, Timothy, 33–4

Porritt, Hon. Jonathan, *Director of Friends of the Earth*, 239–48

Prescot, Hitchley K., 100, 132

Ray, Anthony, 174, 263

Ray, Sophie, 263

Ray, Veronica, 263

Riley-Smith, Jonathan, *medieval historian*, 249–53

Roberts, John, 282, 283

Rothschild, Jacob, 130

Routh, C. R. M., 21, 25

Sainsbury, David, 116, 218

St Aubyn, Giles, 73, 76, 77, 251

Sheppard, Oliver, 271–2

Simpson, David, 260

Sladden, C. E., 192

Smith, G. B., 24

Snow, George, 68

Sumsion, Virginia, 219

Swinnerton-Dyer, Sir Peter, 45, 47

Tait, G. A. D., 43–4, 272

Taylor, Benedict, *actor*, 254–8

Taylor, Claude H., 22, 30–31, 281

Thomas, David, *features editor, the Mail on Sunday*, 220, 259–67

Thorpe, Jeremy, 23, 48

Upcott, J. D., 98–100

Van Oss, Oliver, 169–70, 249

Vickers, Hugo, *author*, 273–9

Vivian, Anthony Vivian, 5th Baron, 201

Waldegrave, Hon. William, *politician*, 121, 280–85

Warner, Pelham, 19

Wells, C. M., 86, 179

Wheadon, Richard, 270

Whitworth, A. W., 124, 138

Wilkinson, Dennis, 158

Willinck, Charles, 153